A

PERFECT

VINTAGE

A PERFECT VINTAGE

a novel

CHELSEA FAGAN

ORSAY PRESS
NEW YORK, NY

The views and opinions expressed in this book are solely those of the author and do not reflect the views or opinions of Gatekeeper Press. Gatekeeper Press is not to be held responsible for and expressly disclaims responsibility for the content herein.

A Perfect Vintage

Published by Orsay Press
New York, NY
aperfectvintagebook.com

Cover painting by Elizabeth Lennie https://elizabethlennie.com

Library of Congress Control Number: 2023934345

ISBN (paperback): 9781662938627
eISBN: 9781662938634

*To the incredible women of my life,
the romantics, the ones who feast fully of life
and refill their plates without shame.*

1

Perched over her laptop at the impeccable white marble bar of Branca, Lea Mortimer put the finishing touches on her to-do list. It was three PM, the hour she most enjoyed at her favorite all-day café, where she could linger at the corner of the bar with her cappuccino and her work without bothering anyone. She loved being a spectator of the quiet moments between services: the staff joking with each other while tasting new menu items, checking their phones, and being blissfully unaware of customers like her. In fact, this feeling of anonymity was one she had come to experience over the years as exquisitely indulgent.

There was something intoxicating about the rituals behind her solo outings, especially in how she dressed and made herself up, as Lea relished being put-together when she had no one in particular to see. She felt free to be at her most sensual when she was least at risk of being truly *sensed,* and it turned otherwise-unremarkable occasions into a party only she had received an invitation to. Today, she'd styled her cropped, dark hair into soft waves and wore sleek trousers that widened through the leg to balance out her hips, paired with a silk blouse and heels fitted with custom insoles in which she could run a marathon.

The prep work she was doing for her upcoming summer client was the perfect kind of task for this aloneness. She would be leaving in exactly three weeks for the Loire Valley in central France to work with the Lévesque family, doing what she did best: transforming the neglected country estates and vineyards of defunct French aristocracy into trendy boutique hotels. She had named her business LeMor Consulting, a legitimate portmanteau of her name, but also something easy for her French clientele to pronounce. Her work, and her reputation in the industry, were the rare success stories of a total outsider carving out a niche in the incredibly insular world of French hospitality.

But despite their preconceived notions, Lea was not their wide-eyed American stereotype, as her clients all came to learn one by one. No matter how sold or skeptical a prospective client happened to be about working with her, each of them included a pointed cultural inquiry in their interview process, and Lea always volleyed back in her autodidactic, precise, near-accentless French.

In the case of her latest client, the Lévesque family, the inquisition was led by the eldest son, Gabriel. He had condescendingly run down her CV—interning at the French embassy, working in events for French liquor conglomerate Pernod Ricard, opening the first Jean Bellanger restaurant in the US, becoming the first American employee of notorious interior design bad boy Loïc Grenier—and seemed genuinely disappointed when she didn't miss on a single question about the project.

She was already an expert on their property in the Loire, and what it would require to realize the transformation from dilapidated chateau to boutique hotel and serviceable vineyard. She knew the extent to which the vines would need to be rehabbed, and the porcelain tile she would be using to refinish the grandiose pool, which she would also be converting to saltwater.

She had several sketches detailing the reimagined entry gate already vetted with a local ironworker, a floorplan of the upper levels converted into guest rooms, and schematics for turning what was once a large horse stable into a glamorous beauty spa. She had narrowed down a short list of head chefs to run the hotel restaurant, and curated the welcome basket each guest would receive upon arrival to their room, including a bottle of local sparkling wine (unless the guest indicated they did not drink in their questionnaire, in which case it would be artisanal, nonalcoholic sparkling cider).

The plans for the actual estate were impeccable, as they always were, but Lea knew by now that it wasn't enough to become an expert on the property, or the region, or even the texture of paper the eventual restaurant menus would be printed on. She also needed to become an expert on the family itself, to learn the shifting tectonic plates of their power dynamics. As these families almost universally inherited these properties through no skill or hard work of their own, their specific blend of egos and incompetence were often Lea's greatest obstacle. It was her role to keep the overall vision, and to bring everyone else around to it while making them each feel sufficiently important and listened to. She needed to scour search engine results, perform forensic social media analyses, and gather as many context clues as she could to know this family inside and out before she stepped foot in their unearned manor.

Lea relaxed, leaning back to take a long sip of her now-lukewarm cappuccino. She clicked her pen and flipped to a clean page in her Moleskine to begin her "Lévesque Family" notes and, just as the tip of the pen kissed the fresh sheet of paper, she felt her bag vibrating against her leg with an incoming call for the second time in twenty minutes.

This had better be good.

Getting up and silently signaling to the bartender that she needed to momentarily step out—she knew the place well enough to leave her laptop for a bit—Lea emerged onto the stately side street just off Dupont Circle. It was an unusually cold spring day in DC, and she wished she'd grabbed her jacket before she walked out as soon as she saw STEPHANIE BRYCE lighting up the screen; this call would probably take a while, as calls with Stephanie invariably did.

"Everything okay, Steph?" Lea asked, bypassing the usual formalities.

"It's *over*," Stephanie replied, her tone clear and piercing even with the ambient white noise of a moving car interior around her. She was driving, as she always was whenever she needed a private conversation with Lea.

"What do you mean, *over?*" Lea asked, cautiously sitting herself down on the immaculate staircase of a neighboring Victorian townhouse.

"I mean that I packed my bags and I'm living in an Airbnb in Morristown until I figure out what I'm doing next. I never want to see him again."

Suddenly, Lea found herself a thousand miles from her to-do list in the restaurant. The usual DC noises around her—cyclists, students, men in gingham shirts talking loudly on phones—faded into a kind of tinny hum as she attempted to process the information she was receiving. This was the call Lea had been dreaming of for decades, and it *felt* like a dream, like something that could snap out of existence if she acknowledged it too head-on.

"Are. . . you serious?" Lea finally managed.

"Yes, I'm serious," Stephanie replied, breathless with rage.

"What happened?"

"I honestly don't want to go into any details right now, I'm still too upset. Please just believe me that I had to leave."

The truth was that there could be no particular inciting incident and this would still be the most joyous news of Lea's life. Marcus had already proven himself unworthy of Stephanie a million times over.

"Why didn't you tell me sooner?" Lea asked, unable to resist her admittedly unfortunate habit of making moments like this about herself.

"Because I had to get all of my ducks in a row, and I had to actually pull the trigger in a way I couldn't walk back from." Tears began to color her voice, even through the shaky audio of Bluetooth. "I didn't want to say anything if I was going to chicken out again, especially not to you. You've been there way too many times when I wasn't brave enough to do anything about it."

"Steph, don't say that. . . you know it's never been a burden."

Lea meant it: being Stephanie's closest confidante, best friend, and cousin—and the favorite auntie of her daughter, Maya—was the rare source of emotional confidence in a life otherwise devoid of profound relationships. That Stephanie trusted her above anyone else with the reality behind the perfect image of her marriage was an honor, even if it was also a decades-long frustration.

"Thanks, Lee," Stephanie sniffed, "But you really don't need to say that. It hasn't been fair how much I've put our stuff on you all these years."

"You didn't have anyone else to put it on. Look how much your mom loves him!"

"She'll probably take his side." Stephanie went quiet for a moment, the sound of the road the only thing rolling behind her. Lea heard a turn signal flick on. "As crazy as it probably sounds, though, I actually don't care at this point. Something in me just finally snapped. I spent so many years being terrified of what would happen if I said no to him, if I even wore a dress he didn't like to one of his stupid work events! But I genuinely don't care anymore. He's tried to call me about sixty times since I left, and I don't even *want* to hear what he has to say. I almost feel sorry for him!"

Lea could hear Stephanie thumbing through her phone as she talked, likely to check exactly how many times Marcus had *actually* called her.

"Steph, don't use your phone while you're driving."

"Sorry! Sorry. You're right."

"Anyway, you're a better woman than I am, because I don't feel sorry for him. I don't even know what he did this time and I want to rip his balls off."

"You don't need to do that," Stephanie chuckled, somewhat deliriously.

"Well, let me know what I *can* do for you, besides giving the world's fattest deposition when the time comes," Lea offered, keeping the tone as light as possible. "Do you want me to come up to Jersey?"

"No, it's going to be a mess here for the next few days." Stephanie cleared her throat. "It's a one-bedroom and Maya's coming home on the weekends to stay with me."

"Well, maybe we could do something else? Do you need a place to stay longer-term?" Lea wouldn't say it, but she knew that Marcus used the fact that he worked in finance, while Stephanie was "just a teacher," as convenient rationale for his decades of financial control—and that whatever resources Stephanie had squirreled away would evaporate pretty quickly if she had to fund her Airbnb much longer. "I leave for my project at the beginning of June. You can take my place for the summer if you want!"

"No, no." Her voice was trepidatious, testing. "That's okay." Stephanie was obviously circling the drain of whatever it was she *actually* wanted.

"Anything, seriously." Lea paused, thinking. "How about I spam his entire firm with an email about how atrocious he's been?"

"Hah! Those lizards would probably give him a promotion. But. . . if you really want to know, Lee. . ." Her words hung in the air momentarily.

"Yes, obviously?"

"Well, there *is* actually something that would make my life so much easier right now." She took a deep breath inward, and rushed out the rest of her words. "I would love to tag along for this summer's project. Me and Maya."

The headiness of the past few days' events had clearly led Stephanie to be much bolder and more overtly demanding than she would normally be in a moment like this. After an adult lifetime of putting herself dead last, she was finally asking for exactly what she wanted.

And Lea froze. It was the one ask she hadn't anticipated, if only because it tapped into every one of her worst anxieties. Lea's work—her *projects*—were the cordoned-off part of her life that allowed every other aspect of it to flow relatively without incident. As a single woman, newly thirty-six years old and with a one-bedroom apartment she owned alone, her glamorous business allowed her to largely avoid categorization. She could move freely between continents without expectation, and remain at least partially a creature of mystery rather than an object of pity. Besides Stephanie and Maya, really, it was all she had. Someone from her actual life coming into contact with her work in this way was a load-bearing Jenga piece she simply couldn't pull.

"You want to come with me?" she tentatively asked. "Why?"

"What do you mean, why?' Why would I not? It's going to be a miserable summer here while school is out and Maya's off-campus, and we can't just both move to DC and share your place. I don't want to sit here and twiddle my thumbs until all of this awfulness works itself out and I go back to work in September. I need to get away from my life right now."

Lea knew what she should say—what a kinder version of herself might say in this moment—but the invisible electric fence she had constructed around her work prevented her from accessing the words, and her initial response was much sharper than she'd intended. "I honestly don't know if that's the greatest idea, Steph." There was no response, so she soldiered on, softening as best she could. "I know it probably seems really glamorous, but these are work trips, and it's not exactly easy for me to bring an entourage."

At the continued silence, she was rambling now: "And besides, this is the biggest project I've ever taken on. If this goes well, I might actually get the *Architectural Digest* profile that editor has been dangling over my head for three fucking years."

There was a long pause between the two of them. Lea heard every step of Stephanie flicking her turn signal on again, turning into what was obviously some kind of parking lot, and putting the car into park. She even turned off the engine, so her words came through much more clearly.

"Okay, Lea. You can't understand this, and I'm not *mad* at you for not understanding this," Stephanie said, her voice quietly wavering, "But I have completely forgotten what life is like when I'm not with Marcus. I don't even really know who I am as an individual, and it's terrifying."

There was silence as she composed herself.

"I can't be with him this summer. But. . . I can't be alone, either. I can't be here. I just. . . can't be here."

"Steph," Lea tried to keep her tone as warm as possible, even as she felt the bone-deep fear of having a *force majeure* cross her most precious boundary. She took her last, unfortunate swing at reasoning them both out of this.

"I know what it's like to break up with someone, okay? I know what it's like to be alone again." As soon as the words escaped her, Lea regretted leveraging even the lightest comparison of her own experience, and Stephanie immediately pounced on the misstep.

"No offense, but you cannot compare what happened with David to what I'm going through right now. I am forty-four years old and, quite frankly, not even sure how many years I have left to even *be* a single woman," she stammered, her tears now audibly flowing.

Lea felt awful.

"You're right. I shouldn't compare. David is a good guy. Marcus is. . ."

"A piece of shit."

"A piece of shit! You're right. I just don't know that coming along with me on this work trip is the answer, you know what I mean? I genuinely don't think you and Maya would enjoy it," she lamely protested. "Why don't we meet up for a week somewhere in August, maybe Italy or something?"

Stephanie paused again, a pause that held the weight of the eight years she ultimately had on Lea, no matter how put-together and impressive Lea's professional life might seem. It was the kind of pause that always took Lea back to her childhood, when Stephanie spent night after night babysitting while her mom was off with whatever new man she happened to be in love with that month.

"Lee, I'm being honest with you right now because I love you, and because I don't know how many people in my life I can be honest with about all of this." She drew a weak breath inward, prickles of rain beginning to fall on the roof of her car. "I need you to compartmentalize a little bit less for once, okay? You've brought subcontractors on these trips before—we can be like that! I'm not going to come be some embarrassing American on one of your fancy trips to France. Neither is Maya. We will be quiet and do whatever work you need us to do. You won't even know we're there if you don't want to. But I really need to get out of here, and I don't know where else to go. I don't even know when he's going to cut off the credit cards—" Stephanie began openly sobbing, too anguished to stop herself. "Please don't leave me here, Lee!"

"Hey, hey, hey. Come on. Don't do that." Lea felt an immediate, visceral disgust with herself. *What was wrong with her?*

"I don't know what's wrong with me. You're totally right. I'm so proud of you for finally standing up for yourself, and for Maya. You guys absolutely deserve to have a great summer sitting by the pool at a chateau. It's just a lot to all take in at once, you know?" Lea picked her tone up a little too sharply at the end, aiming for friendliness but arriving at lightly deranged. "I will talk to the owner and let him know I'll be bringing two plus-ones." Her mind was already reeling with how exactly she would phrase this in practice.

"Thank you," Stephanie released, catching her breath. "I love you."

Seated in front of her laptop again, still in a daze from the conversation that had kept her outside long enough to numb her entire body, Lea clicked over to her email inbox. Deliberately minimizing a long and tedious thread in which Gabriel was pushing back on her selected paint colors for the hotel restaurant, she started a fresh email addressing just Alain, the consistently friendly and pliable Lévesque patriarch.

She set to crafting the perfect note explaining that she would be bringing along two guests for the summer, that it was a family emergency and nonnegotiable, but that it would only enhance her ability to realize their shared vision. She marveled at her own ability to spin something that was so deeply terrifying to herself into something straightforward and convincing, so airtight that one now couldn't even imagine the project without the warming presence of these two additional women. Alain was a family man—all the more so after losing his wife four years ago—and Lea knew exactly the buttons to push on his emotional keyboard when it came to getting her way.

She might not have been many other things in life, but she was fucking great at her job.

2

"Can you tell me a little bit about why picking up Stephanie's passport is such a source of anxiety for you?" Dr. Miller asked, sunlight cutting across his face from the oversized bay window in his office.

"Because he's going to make it a goddamn nightmare," Lea blurted out, fiddling with the fringe of a throw pillow on the sofa. She felt the full absurdity of volunteering unprompted to travel to Montclair, New Jersey, for the weekend to get the rest of her best friend's belongings from said friend's soon-to-be ex-husband. "Sorry for cursing."

"You know you can curse in here. We're all grown-ups." He paused until she met his eye. "How is Marcus going to make it a nightmare?"

"Well, he's going to follow me around under the pretense of asking me if I want any coffee or whatever, making snide comments about Stephanie. Then he's going to ask me all kinds of questions about her that I don't want to answer or don't even know *how* to answer, until I finally crack and give him some kind of information that he can use against her later. This time probably in court."

"It sounds to me like you have a pretty detailed map of the situation. Maybe you can create a game plan for *your* behavior on Saturday, so that you're not just responding to the way he behaves."

"I always have a 'game plan' when I go in, but he breaks you down in ways you don't expect."

A pause, as Dr. Miller considered. "Then why are you going?"

"Because he's made it abundantly clear that he's going to basically squat in their house until Steph is forced to go there, and then he can have whatever Hannibal Lecter confrontation she won't let him have over the phone."

"Are you worried about her safety?"

"No. . ." Lea thought about it sincerely, and shook her head again. "No. He's an awful person, but he's not dangerous."

"Then why is this not something Stephanie can do? You're already accommodating her quite a bit by agreeing to bring her and her daughter to your work site for an entire summer."

Lea knew the question was valid, but she felt the familiar flush of irritation at further introspection over things she had already decided. "I just have to do it. Otherwise, he's going to suck her back into his web."

She paused before deciding to put a final point on things. She didn't need him to coax the truth out of her: that if Marcus got Stephanie alone in their house again, Lea feared she would call off the divorce—a completely unacceptable option.

"I just have to do it."

Dr. Miller cleared his throat and shifted in his seat, probably considering a tiny push further before waving the white flag on her stonewalling. "Well, it sounds like you have thought this through."

Keeping a regular appointment with a therapist for the past two years had turned into muscle memory for Lea. There were days she went and had almost nothing to say, but given her overall inability to maintain profound, long-term relationships with anyone other than Stephanie and Maya, she felt that giving up on her relationship with her therapist would only add to the mounting evidence that there was something deeply, fundamentally wrong with her. So she kept seeing Dr. Miller, a forty-something man with impeccable, side-parted gray hair, soothing half-zip sweaters, and questions which were good but rarely too probing.

Today, as was often the case, they were talking about Stephanie. Lea had broken down the entire situation in detail for Dr. Miller: the divorce, the phone call, and the hundreds of text messages they'd exchanged in the weeks since in which Stephanie asked easily Google-able questions about international travel. Predictably, his primary observation had been that this was all probably a good thing for Lea. With her, he often repeated the cloying phrase, "Allowing yourself to really *feel* things," and whatever highs and lows the summer would likely bring, at least she was already *experiencing* the trip more acutely than she usually allowed herself.

As she watched the minutes tick down on the day's session, once again spent talking about Stephanie, Lea had the darkly funny thought that she was sometimes paying for therapy by proxy, talking more about her cousin's problems than her own. As if reading her mind, he pivoted to another topic Lea had no desire to explore.

"How are things going with Nathan?"

She bristled at her own shortsightedness in telling Dr. Miller about him before they'd even been on three real dates.

"They're fine."

"Just fine?"

"Well, we're not seeing each other anymore, if that's the question. But it ended amicably, nothing bad happened."

"How does that feel?"

He met her gaze head-on, and she tightly re-crossed her legs. From everything she had gleaned about Dr. Miller's life through her exhaustive research, he was one of those married people who genuinely loved and felt active passion toward their spouse decades in. She didn't need his pity.

"It feels fine, really. I hadn't even thought about it until you asked."

She actively opted out of describing her last night with Nathan, their dinner at a beloved Peruvian restaurant she'd never brought anyone to before, at which he ended up mostly pushing his food around his plate. She didn't talk about their long walk home during which he made gently mocking comments about her business, punctuated by pulling *Lean In* off her bookshelf when they arrived back at her apartment and asking if she bought it ironically.

And she certainly didn't mention that she slept with him, anyway, because she hadn't had sex in nearly a year and longed for the weighted blanket of a man on top of her, that she'd even faked an orgasm once they'd been at it for a believable amount of time, and that she couldn't even tell for whom she had faked it. She just smiled, in her best approximation of a woman who had nothing else to disclose on the subject.

"Well, I'm glad it was amicable and you're feeling good about it."

She seized on his seeming satisfaction with her response. "Totally. And besides, it wasn't like we would have been able to stay together through the summer anyway, so there was no use drawing it out."

"Lea, we've talked about that."

She winced at the trap she'd walked into.

"I know," she took on his tone of voice, *my work should not be a reason to avoid living my actual life.*

He laughed genuinely. "You're good at this." Looking at her squarely, he added, "And I know it's not always easy for you to talk about your dating life in here, so I appreciate you letting me in a little bit."

It was true, there was nothing harder than talking about her dating life. Not even her work, which she usually avoided discussing out of a marrow-deep belief that she didn't need any advice. But the love stuff, the dating? She felt her inadequacy in that department was in her DNA, with the way her parents had ripped one another apart over the course of ten years, first as an unhappy married couple, then as a perennially separating and reuniting couple, and finally, as a bitterly divorcing couple.

She saw the way her mother, in Lea's YouTube diagnosis, latched onto a series of increasingly wrong men in order to soothe the raging mental illness that led her to join a jam band on the festival circuit for an entire summer, or to stay in bed criticizing the people on TLC shows for an entire winter. She saw the way her father skated along under the banner of being "the stable one," using his money and judgment to belittle and control and undermine his wife and children. And she viscerally remembered the shame he made her feel about herself as she came of age, in a body that increasingly came to resemble the ex-wife he so resented.

Even before typing "best therapist DC" into her search bar two years ago, Lea had long decided that her parents were going to be the answer waiting at the bottom of many personal rabbit holes. And her habit as a child of finding surrogate role models scattered around her life—her friends' parents, Stephanie, even certain French teachers—was one of the first bricks in the current structure of her fiercely independent life. She had her people, few as they were, and she would simply never allow herself to be laden down by the wrong partner, even if it meant being alone.

"Anyway, it would have been a nightmare to have to think about a boyfriend on top of all the Stephanie drama going on," Lea finally continued, maintaining a chipper exterior.

Talking about Stephanie instead of herself: her happy place.

"It feels like a pretty big step for her to have fully moved out," he commented after a brief silence, scribbling something inscrutable on his notepad.

"Yeah," Lea replied. "I guess it is."

"That's a big gift that you're giving to her. And it's lucky that she has the whole summer to figure things out without having to work." He paused, adjusting himself in his seat. "It's interesting that you both have your work lives divided in this way. She doesn't work during the summers, and that's when you start your big projects."

Lea dismissed the parallel he was drawing, eager to finish the session. "A lot of my work needs to take place during the warm months. It's a lot of outdoor stuff."

"Hmm," he intoned. "I can imagine." Another pause.

"Well, in any case, I'm sure she's very grateful that you're helping her through this process of leaving what you have described as an emotionally abusive marriage. And leaving things that aren't right for us can be a powerful thing."

Lea winced at the comment; it reminded her of their earliest sessions together, when they first unpacked the story of her breakup with David. She always felt a brief, hot flush of resentment when Dr. Miller insinuated that her ending their relationship was akin to performing some sort of charitable act.

While Stephanie finally leaving Marcus was a testament to her continued spirit and resilience, that Lea was no longer with David—especially as the years ticked by—was cause for pity and judgment. She could *feel* what everyone thought about the situation, and what some people, like her father, went so far as to actually say: that David was as close to a perfect man as a woman could hope for, and that it was only due to his support on every level that Lea was able to create the flourishing, dynamic business she now owned. He was the good guy, down to his densely curled hair and nubby sweaters, which, next to Lea's angular features and short, dark bob, practically made him look like a teddy bear. He was even kind when she broke his heart, moving back in with his parents while she relocated, allowing Lea to stay on a few of his subscription services, and congratulating her for her professional victories on LinkedIn.

Now, he was married, and Lea was single. He had a beautiful two-year-old boy, and she had an IUD that was proving more superfluous by the year. He was enjoying the kind of success her gratingly normal brother had: simple and perfect and impervious to judgment.

Dr. Miller looked at her with his familiar gaze, the one that told her he knew this was a fraught path that he wouldn't force her to take today, but which he wasn't going to be convinced didn't exist. He looked for a moment as if he might still say something insightful regardless, something that would linger under her skin for weeks to come, but instead he darted his eyes over at the clock on the wall and announced that their time was up for today.

Back at her apartment, Lea appraised the multiple open suitcases and weekend bags assembled in front of her. Her iPad was propped on her bedside table, open to the meticulous packing sheet she'd created the previous week, cells being grayed out as she neatly rolled each article of clothing and added it to its respective container. Between items, she sipped her stemless wine glass full of ice and homemade lemonade, complete with a few fresh sprigs of muddled mint. It was lightly sweet and tart, relaxing without being intoxicating, and perfect for an evening like this one. Just being in her room, amongst these varied artifacts of her competency, soothed her beyond measure, and certainly beyond anything she experienced that afternoon with her therapist. Hers was a more reserved bedroom decor than she usually opted for in her work: tones of beige and camel coming together to create an almost spa-like experience, with custom Roman shades in a rich chocolate tweed that partially blocked out the western-facing evening sun aggressively pouring through her windows.

Scrolling over to the "footwear" column of her spreadsheet, she laughed gently at the sight of so many shoes with at least some degree of heel to them, a life choice that had snuck up on her almost unnoticed. David had never asked, but them both being a solid five-foot-eight had meant six years of wearing ballet flats and kitten heels, even to formal events; of crouching down slightly to make him appear bigger in photos, a reflexive visualization of her desire to seem less powerful. In the years since she left, she had come to relish extending herself fully, sometimes even showing up to dates at nearly six feet tall (a choice that resulted in more than one man angrily insisting she wasn't *actually* the height she claimed, as it would call into question his own dubious description on the dating site).

The week ahead of Lea was daunting, no doubt. On deck was her trip to New Jersey, a briefing with the neighbor who would look after her apartment that summer, and about a thousand last-minute calls with her contractors in France, all punctuated by the actual flight itself. It would test even *her* storied ability to stay three steps ahead of her workload, to be the American woman who arrives with solutions rather than problems, who creates an effortless façade through an enormous amount of daily effort.

But nothing in life alighted her like the feeling of sticking the landing after a particularly complicated move, and having these unusual circumstances compounding her most high-stakes client would give her the chance to shine brighter than she ever had. If she could pull this off, she would forever have her pick of projects; she could even start to chip away at the ultra-competitive Parisian hotel market, edging out the typical French firms whose work she had already been exceeding for years. She would finally have the career she deserved, and the most important people in her life would be there to see her accomplish it: a thrilling possibility she would have never opted for but now felt predestined.

A text message popped up on her iPad, temporarily sliding over the top third of her spreadsheet. Stephanie again, overusing her beloved ellipses, but filling the room with her warmth from four states away.

S: Officially hit my two-week streak on Duolingo!! French is harder than I thought. . .

Lea smiled, picking up her phone from across the room to reply.

L: No way it could be harder than Arabic.

S: It doesn't count if you grow up speaking a language. . . I wasn't using Duolingo when I was three.

L: Are you watching the movie list I sent you?

S: Yes!! They're all so good.

A lot of sex in French movies, though. . . Maya was so embarrassed watching Les Beaux Jours *with me*

L: Hah! It's not a crazy amount, the French just aren't prudes like we are. Sex is part of life!

Lea felt the searing irony of the statement, given how untrue that was for the both of them. And reading her mind as always, Stephanie replied almost instantly:

S: Sex is part of life?? Since when??
L: Lol. I gotta finish packing, congrats on the Duolingo streak! I'm gonna quiz you when I get up there to test your progress. :)
S: See you tomorrow night, love you!! Xx
L: Love you, too.

3

"*To France!*" Lea, Stephanie, and Maya exclaimed over the blindingly lit, white-and-navy bar of the airport lounge, Maya swapping in ginger ale for champagne; she was not allowed to drink for another six months in the States and, around her mother, she studiously maintained the pretense that she never engaged in underage drinking.

"This is just so amazing, Lee. We can't thank you enough, but we'll try!" Stephanie was still holding her champagne aloft, eyes rimmed with tears.

"And we have an entire suitcase of just thank-you gifts for the host family," Maya added.

"That's sweet of you guys, but they're not a host family. They're paying me to be there, and I will be very much putting both of your asses to work this summer."

The two guests laughed happily, if nervously. This was going to be an incredible adventure, yes, and they were both thrilled to be getting away from the situation at home. But it was also deeply scary for them both, for the wife who had spent decades chasing the ever-moving goalposts of her husband, and for the daughter who had spent her whole life with parents who had no business being married. They were tipping their skis out over an incredibly steep incline, and no matter how fun it promised to be, there were also muscles they would need to rely on that they hadn't used for years, if ever.

Maya in particular radiated anxious energy, looking over at her mother and checking her phone compulsively. They were incredibly similar in personality, and they even looked the same, with their long, thin limbs, olive skin, and dense, curly, black hair, Stephanie's flecked with gray-white around her face. Lea sometimes found herself envying them—both their similarity and their bond, neither of which she shared with her own mother—but had over the years carved out her own important niche with Maya, providing a refuge from her toxic household that sometimes put her closer to second mother than favorite aunt.

"Can I look at your notes again?" Maya asked, wanting to reread the details Lea had painstakingly written about each member of the family.

"You can," Lea laughed, reaching into her perfectly organized travel bag hooked under the bar. "But I don't know how much new information you're going to get out of it."

"She's basically memorized it at this point," Stephanie said, smiling over the rim of her glass.

"I have not!"

"Don't worry." Lea handed it over. "I've memorized it, too."

"But have you memorized what they look like?" Stephanie was now openly giggling.

"*Mom!*"

Stephanie grabbed the book from Maya and began reading aloud from the handwritten notes Lea had made on each of the family members in her best imitation of Lea's clipped, serious work voice: "*Théodore, early twenties. Still in engineering school (top three program), but graduated high school five years ago (skipped grades?). Less sporty than Gabriel, but former competitive fencer—*"

"Stop it!" Maya's eyes shot down to the floor, neck and cheeks flushing. "Aunt Lee, make her stop!"

"Yeah, stop reading my notes, please." Lea looked over at her cousin as she reassured Maya, giving her a wide-eyed look of *come on, stop embarrassing her.*

They all fell momentarily silent, sipping from their flutes as Stephanie now quietly leafed through the handwritten notebook, traces of a smirk still on her face.

"Anyway," Maya pivoted, desperate to speak of anything else. "I know Mom is probably going to forget, so can *one of you guys* please bring me back some cookies from first class?"

"It's business class," Lea replied without even thinking, having long ago committed almost everything about work travel and logistics to a kind of reptilian memory.

"Okay, *business class.*"

"And yes, of course I can. I can bring you back whatever you like."

"Thank you." Maya shot her mother a pointed look before pushing further into an unusual moment of petulance. ". . . I still don't understand why I can't be up there with you guys, anyway."

Stephanie set down the notebook and gave Maya an exasperated look. "We went over this on the train. You aren't flying with us because you are twenty years old, and you already have a perfectly comfortable window seat to France paid for by your Aunt Lea's miles, and the last thing you are going to do is complain about the fact that you're not in business class."

Lea put her hand on Maya's delicate shoulder, a little too eager to play the cool aunt. "Sorry. I offered to upgrade you, too, but your mom wouldn't let me."

"*What?!*"

Stephanie glared at Lea before retraining her gaze on her daughter. "You can fly in business class when you have your own money to pay for business class. This subject is closed."

Maya spun off her barstool and stormed off toward the bathrooms, likely grateful to have a more legitimate excuse to leave them than her embarrassment at her preemptive infatuation with Théodore.

"Let her go," Stephanie instructed.

"I wasn't going to follow her to the bathroom."

"Well, I'm just saying, I don't want to indulge this behavior. She has ten times more than I ever had of anything. It's enough already."

It was true: Stephanie and Lea may have shared the bond of deeply dysfunctional parents, but only Stephanie carried the lifelong rules and insecurities of having grown up poor. After Lea's uncle left her mother, a Jordanian immigrant named Rachida with few marketable skills, to start an entirely new family with a woman he met at a bar, the standard of living in Stephanie's childhood home plummeted. Brand-name clothes were swapped out for thrifted ones, two new cars were replaced by a single, heavily used one, and never checking the prices at the grocery store became a humiliating food stamp routine performed for every item.

Stephanie, as the only child, began working to contribute to the household budget as soon as she was old enough to get paid under the table for *anything*, and Lea remembered the dance any time they visited that branch of the family, the shopping they would do the day before to buy toys and clothes for Stephanie. Lea's mother always carried a level of guilt that it was *her* brother who left his family, who hid his money and transferred things to his girlfriend to reduce his liability, who made Rachida beg him just to pay the child support he was court-ordered to provide.

Even the babysitting which happened to suit her mother's dating life was a convenient way to funnel money to the family, wildly overpaying Stephanie and sending her home with huge Tupperwares full of food. To this day, Lea still swung between resentment that her mother's sense of duty didn't extend to her own children, and gratitude that the circumstances led her and Stephanie to form a bond that existed beyond the constraints of title, age, or obligation. They were everything to each other, and by extension, so was Maya.

Even if she wasn't allowed to join them in business class.

As the two women lingered in a moment of slightly anxious silence, so much still ahead of them, MARCUS BRYCE lit up the screen of Stephanie's phone before she could flip it face-down to conceal the name. A brief flash of embarrassment crossed her face as she apologetically slid from her barstool and moved toward the little "phone call" nook near the bathrooms.

Lea suppressed a feeling of righteous indignation, reminding herself of Dr. Miller's important advice to separate out her actual interactions with Stephanie from what she *wished* Stephanie would do with her own time, as long as those things didn't impact her. They were past security, so the likelihood of her turning back now was pretty slim. Whatever thin pretense he was using to *need* to talk to her right now wouldn't be enough to get what he actually wanted, which was to maintain total control over the woman he'd never deserved once in his life. He would bother her a bit, maybe make some cutting comment about her being too old for this kind of trip. And she would humor him, and the credit cards would stay on for now. The bills would keep getting paid, and he would still feel like he could have her back whenever he wanted.

But Lea knew that once she made it to altitude, she would already be gone.

"Which wine do you think is better?" Stephanie stage-whispered to Lea after a diligent ten minutes of browsing the surprisingly elaborate business class menu. Arranged in their center-section, lie-flat seats, they were essentially laid out in twin coffins, with a partition to put up between them if they chose to (which they likely would, as they both accused each other of snoring after a few drinks).

"You can just taste them."

"*What?* You can taste the wine here?"

"Yes, it's not like in coach where they just give you one of those shitty little bottles. I never drink those anymore. I'd wake up looking like The Mummy. Speaking of—" Lea leaned down to rummage around in her purse for her overnight flight skincare kit, containing perfectly portioned amounts of everything she needed to sleep well, and to remove the no-makeup makeup she curated for air travel. She liked to set it aside before her food arrived, when her bag on the floor would be inaccessible under her tray.

"I can't believe you're so prepared. I'm lucky if I make it onto a plane with my actual luggage."

"When you fly a lot, you quickly get to know the difference between a good flight and a bad one, and a lot of that is little stuff like this."

"Your shit is so *together*."

"I don't have kids or a husband. I have a lot of time for shit-gathering."

Lea gave her order to the passing flight attendant, all at once and with a polite request to pace her main course a bit after the cocktail-and-warm-nuts service. She liked taking her pre-dinner drink while doing her last-minute work, and then having her dinner while watching a movie, and never the twain shall meet. Stephanie followed suit, and without realizing the implication of her wine-tasting request, received a sample of every single wine they offered, which looked rather ridiculous arriving on a little tray just for her.

"I look like a crazy person!" she exclaimed, looking down at the six glasses arranged in front of her after delicately tasting each one.

"No, you don't. This is business class. I once saw a guy in a pinstriped suit board with a twelve-inch Jimmy John's sub and immediately order two small bottles of Bombay Sapphire and a glass of ice. The freak flags are *flying* in here."

"My stomach hurts just hearing that." Stephanie indicated her final choice to the attendant with more than a little embarrassment, as he smilingly cleared everything away except her glass of chosen wine, which he filled generously.

"Thank you again so much for taking us with you. You really didn't have to do this."

Lea resisted the urge to point out that given the nature of their conversation outside of Branca, she basically *did* have to do this if she wanted to keep being Stephanie's best friend.

"It's really no trouble at all." She paused, burning with desire to ask for more details about the divorce, but willing herself to keep all conversations light while at cruising altitude. "Maya seems to have a bit of a crush." She smiled coyly from behind the rim of her glass.

"She does," Stephanie agreed, quietly nodding a thank you to the passing hostess placing a delicate little bowl of mixed nuts on her tray.

"She picked well, too, I think," Lea noted. "I've done a deep dive on everyone in this family and I haven't turned up a single red flag on him."

"Didn't he give you all that trouble on the phone interview?"

"No, that was his brother." Lea felt a fresh wave of indignation at that insufferable phone call. "He's going to be trouble, I can tell."

"What do you mean? Didn't they hire you to make the decisions?"

"His father hired me. Gabriel never wanted me to be on the project. He has a more. . . traditional vision of what this hotel should be like." Her attempted softening on the word "traditional" failed, and Stephanie's eyebrows rose at the venom in her tone.

"Oh, wow. Does. . . does he work in hotels?"

Lea chortled at the implication that men like Gabriel needed to have actual expertise on something to insert themselves into it. "No, not at all. He's a management consultant, but he has Rich Boy Disorder. He thinks he can just walk into anything and be amazing at it."

Stephanie looked nervous, peeking under the hood at the complicated engine that drove the class dynamics they would be living with for ten weeks.

"But don't worry," Lea clarified, perking up her tone. "I know how to handle men like him. And the one Maya likes seems great."

"Well," Stephanie started slowly. "It's just good to see her excited about someone."

"Yeah?"

"Well, you know how she is. She's always so cagey about boys she likes with her dad around. Having a crush on someone who's three thousand miles away from him might actually let her feel comfortable for once." Her voice caught slightly on "comfortable."

"Oh, Steph, don't do this to yourself again."

"No, no." She picked up a little square cocktail napkin and dabbed under her eyes, steadying her gaze. "I'm fine. I just hate that she's had to live in this house for so long, with Marcus clipping her wings all the time."

"Please," Lea reached her hand across the median between them, taking Stephanie's soft hand in her own. "My father did nothing but clip my wings until I was out of grad school and look at me now, flying. Literally."

"I know," Stephanie laughed weakly, sipping from her glass of sparkling water and uncomfortably clearing her throat. "I know."

A familiar limitation in understanding had once again silently asserted itself between the cousins. Lea was flying in business class, sure, and taking them on an adventure to a prestigious and aspirational job site. But she was also thirty-six and alone, childless, and in every way embodying some of Stephanie's worst anxieties for Maya's future. The aseptic separations between aspects of Lea's life were something Maya was already beginning to recreate on a much smaller scale, and though Stephanie would never say anything less than supportive, an outcome like this for her own daughter would be regarded as a disappointment.

And though Lea couldn't explain it—because her own reasons for never wanting children were at least somewhat tied up in how they always seemed to anchor the women in her life to horrible men, including Stephanie—she knew in her bones that even *if* Maya were to ultimately choose her path, she could be happy this way. Or satisfied, at least, the way Lea was. She couldn't explain that every time she considered the life she would be living right now, had she stayed with David, she felt like someone who'd been pulled back from a subway platform seconds before the train came barreling through the station. And David was a *good* man, he just represented the same narrowing of horizons that every man eventually did for her.

She could hear Stephanie jumping in to tell her that a child means an eternal *opening* of horizons, a boundless expansion of potential and capacity for love, without her even needing to say it. She could hear the same old back-and-forth play itself out and felt no need to start it again, so she let the moment pass. They couldn't fully understand each other, but they could love each other enough to make up the difference.

"Are you happy with your choice?" Lea gestured to Stephanie's wine glass, eager to change the subject.

"Yes! I can't believe a plane wine is this good."

"That's a nice Chablis," Lea said, opening the menu to the wine page. "I don't know the producer well, but I've been at a few events with them."

"That's amazing! I can't believe you know wine that well."

"Oh, I really don't. I subcontract all the wine stuff out to actual professionals. Horticulture and wine production are different things, first of all, and my clients often need both. And the entire sales part mostly happens through co-ops, at least for the vineyards I work on."

"Co-ops?"

"These properties almost never have enough grapes to be an independent wine producer, so they have to join these cooperatives where their crops get thrown in with a bunch of others and they sell under one label. It's a whole thing."

"Wow. I would love to learn more about the whole wine process. It's so fascinating."

"Well, then, you're in luck, because we have a whole day scheduled with our viticulture guy in a week or so."

"Viticulture guy? He sounds cute."

This was a common occurrence between the two of them: Lea mentioning an even vaguely male-sounding name with a job, and Stephanie conspiratorially suggesting that she date him.

"Why don't you see if *you* can get his number, then?" Lea smiled across at her. "You're single now, too."

Stephanie smiled as best she could, the thought clearly never having occurred to her, and finished the last of her wine in one swift gulp. "Yeah. I guess I am."

4

"I told you," Lea reiterated, quickly eyeing Maya from the rearview mirror before returning her eyes to the winding, tree-lined road. "They're not going to be there when we arrive. It'll just be the staff. The family usually doesn't show up until a few weeks later at least, when most of the hard work is done."

"Oh," Maya sighed, ineffectively hiding her disappointment that Théodore wouldn't be greeting them on arrival, ideally holding a bouquet of flowers. She leaned her head against the window, sadly taking in the lush, early summer landscape of the Loire Valley.

Lea took the momentary silence to open her own window further, inhaling the familiar air that grew heavier in the late afternoon but still lacked the inevitable haze of July and August. This was the first time she'd worked in the Loire Valley, and though much of the French countryside had a similar feel, there was something particularly majestic about this region, with the regality of its world-unique style of chateau, the brilliant blue of the sky, and the slight crispness in the air, even in summer. This was a place for nobility, for heritage, and for history. Even the natural landscapes seemed to command a level of respect.

In light of Maya's sadness, Lea made a point not to show just how much this standard order of events—hardworking staff upon arrival, followed later by family—was ideal for her. Spending a few uninterrupted weeks clearing out accumulated centuries of aristocratic dust with the staff was crucial, especially when dealing with a micromanaging family member like Gabriel. It was important for her to establish as early as possible that they should see her as one of *them*, since they were the invisible machinery that made these projects come to life (on-time and under-budget, of course). Ingratiating herself with them was the crucial leverage she always came to count on. If they viewed her like one of the pampered, capricious family members, she could end up in a summer-long morass of no one getting their way, because no one had rallied enough troops to do so.

"We're heeeere," Lea sing-songed, the gate that usually sat at the edge of the property absent while its replacement was being finished. The trio quietly marveled at the length of the driveway, the endless curving stream of immaculate white gravel that twisted through the magnificent, rolling, green-on-green property.

"Hey!" Maya called from the backseat. "They're all—"

"Oh, Jesus Christ," Lea gasped as she pulled around a final turn and the full chateau came into view.

Not only was the entire Lévesque clan out in front of the entryway in matching hotel polo shirts—patriarch Alain, eldest son Gabriel, second son Théodore, teenage daughter Chloë— all beaming with the perfect white smiles of Alain's recently-sold Parisian dental practice, they were *dancing*. They'd placed a large Bluetooth speaker on the entry steps, blasting the original Italian version of "Gloria" and spinning large white cloth napkins over their heads, in the way French people sometimes did at weddings to welcome the newly married couple into the reception. They'd clearly even rehearsed a little routine, turning in sync at certain intervals.

Stephanie and Maya burst into an excited laughter as they poured out of the car, dancing along to the music while Lea flushed with embarrassment. It wasn't just that she hadn't prepped her guests for this scenario, she'd been totally wrong about everything. This was a family who wanted to be there from minute one—not a staffer in sight—and who, on top of that, were taking the welcome into their own hands with a *surprise,* among Lea's least-favorite things in the world, especially on a job site. She put on her most capable smile as she walked around the car to join them, bopping awkwardly to the music.

"Is this normal?" Stephanie laughed in Lea's ear, pulling her close as they took in the spectacle.

Lea made a mental note to break down the fondness that wealthy French people have for these kinds of *aren't-we-so-crazy* moments, especially when welcoming people from afar or at big celebrations, but settled on a perky *"It happens!"* for now.

Despite herself, Lea felt the twitch of a genuine smile breaking through her composure. The scene was just too infectious: Alain exaggeratedly mouthing along with the lyrics, his tall, thin frame and slicked-back gray hair giving him a perfect "older French actor" appeal, the lines of his face deepening with his generous smile. And Gabriel was everything Lea had expected; his near shoulder-length, wavy brown-blonde hair, paired with his piercing blue eyes and muscular build, made for an exhaustingly perfect vibe, someone she could picture successfully running for President of France in twenty years or so, down to the measured-yet-charming way he spun his napkin.

As the song flooded around them, Théodore bounded over to remove their luggage from the car, smiling at the gathered women as he passed, the broad sincerity of it similar to his father's. He was much taller than Lea had expected, taller even than his father, with gently flushed skin that indicated he spent slightly less time outdoors than the rest of his family. His similarly dirty blonde hair was more tightly curled than his brother's, forming a kind of halo around his long, striking face, and the pair of rimless, rounded glasses sitting atop his Roman nose made him almost reassuring. As he passed them, Lea picked up a subtle but unmistakable scent of good cologne, maybe Hermès or Tom Ford.

"Okay, the song is over!" the daughter, Chloë, called from the top step, unceremoniously turning off the speaker. Dressed in perfectly chic black trousers and leather tennis shoes with her hotel polo shirt half-tucked in, she read as much older and more sophisticated than her sixteen years, with only a telltale adolescent gangliness—and petulance—to give her away.

Alain briefly looked over to her with disappointment before jogging up to the American women for a proper greeting, pulling them each in for a vigorous *bise* across each cheek. "We are *so* glad you're here," he started in a heavy accent, breathless from his animated napkin spinning, "and bringing such lovely guests."

"Alain," Lea replied in her impeccable French, "It's such a pleasure to be here. We're all so looking forward to getting started, and they are incredibly grateful for your hospitality. I'm going to switch to English for everyone's comfort, but this is going to be a wonderful project together." It was important for her to establish with everyone up-front that they weren't going to be able to talk any shit around her under the cover of their own language. "Where should we set our things?" she continued in English.

"No, no, do not worry about this. Théo will set your things in your rooms. You'll see them on the tour. You are just in time to take the apéritif!" He looked like an eager puppy, practically bursting with anticipation.

Of course, the apéritif. Cocktail hour. A touchstone of French culture, that liminal space between late afternoon and dinner where finger foods were arranged and casually picked at over ample conversation, and somewhere between a chaste half-glass of rosé and multiple refills of whatever the host was pouring were consumed, depending on how indulgent the ambiance was. It was something Lea had fallen in love with about the culture early on—how decadently they stretched out moments of gathering and pleasure, how everything had its proper time and energy, and nothing should be rushed—but today, it felt like a sentence to be served before she could crash face-first into her bed.

So never mind that they were all practically hallucinating from a full day of travel and had been stunned on arrival with that welcome, the last thing Lea wanted was to start things off on the wrong foot by denying the apéritif. Instead, she gamely nodded and returned his smile.

From behind her, Théodore grabbed the lone, heavy weekender bag she was still carrying, nodding with a chivalrous insistence that he bring it up to her room, to which she reluctantly agreed. She wrinkled her nose at the crest on his polo shirt, bearing the name Hôtel Château Victoire, the stiflingly traditional name for the hotel that she had pushed back on but ultimately ceded to, given how amenable Alain seemed to his son's instincts on the matter.

And to be fair, though the name Hôtel Château Victoire was miles from what Lea would have chosen, the hotel was indeed the crowning victory of their property. She stepped back a few feet to take it in, a seventeenth-century, eleven-thousand-square-foot chateau which sat atop the highest hill of their sprawling twelve hectares. The structure itself was as grand as it appeared in the photos, all limestone with tall blown-glass windows on every floor and dark turrets that gave it a distinctly storybook quality. The front entrance had already been completely redone to Lea's specifications, the dilapidated old wooden doors replaced by white French doors that echoed the pure white stone bordering every window of the façade. Her heart swelled at the early evidence that her instincts about this place—to make it feel fresh, light, and modern—were correct.

She had barely made it into the lobby when Alain seemed to materialize with a chilled flute of local sparkling wine (not champagne, he would no doubt clarify).

"This is a local crémant, just as good as champagne and very reasonably priced. Maybe soon we will be making some of our own!" He smiled infectiously.

"Well," Lea began to correct him about the type of wine his grapes would be fit for—if they were even able to get them to an acceptable state to join a co-op—but thought better of it. "Maybe you're right." She raised her glass.

"This is such a beautiful property. The pictures don't do it justice," Stephanie gushed, running her free hand along a banister.

"Thank you, I took those pictures," Gabriel responded, smiling cheekily.

"No. . . no, that's not what I meant. They're beautiful pictures, I—"

"Of course. I know what you mean. I'm only kidding." His English was like the rest of him: mannered, studied, a little too good for its own good.

"He's not kidding," Théodore snickered from a plush armchair in the corner.

"Théo, don't start," Alain chided him in French, before turning back to his guests. "Have you two been to France before?" He smiled at Stephanie and Maya, clearly desperate to change the subject.

"I've been here once with my dad on a work trip," Maya responded, "But just to Paris and then Brussels."

"Brussels is in Belgium," Stephanie corrected.

"I know, Mom." Lea could see Maya's cheeks flush from across the room as she nervously fumbled through more commentary. "But anyway, this place is amazing. It's so. . . French."

"This place *is* so French," Chloë snorted, sipping her sparkling water with grenadine. She was the exact sort of ultra-chic, ultra-privileged French girl who found anything overtly Gallic to be tiresome and passé. Lea estimated it would take her many years to truly appreciate her heritage.

"And I haven't been to France before, myself," Stephanie answered, slightly shamefully. "I actually haven't traveled much at all, outside of Jordan."

"Why Jordan?" Théo asked from across the room, genuinely curious.

"That's where my mother is from."

Alain's face lit up. "Jordan? That is so interesting! I've always wanted to spend time in the Middle East. I've only been to the Maghreb, when I was much younger." His interest was a nice departure from the usual responses Stephanie received, which were either vaguely Islamophobic or totally ignorant of what part of the world Jordan was in.

As the two of them broke off into a side conversation on the ins and outs of Jordanian tourism, Lea took a moment to truly process the state of the space. Often, when she arrived at these properties, the family (who had a decisive list of tasks to complete before she arrived, if they were to meet their deadlines) put off as much as possible until they could pass it off to her supervision. But this space was already well into the shifting of its bones required to move from a single-family castle to a center of luxurious hospitality.

The lobby itself was sumptuous: the soaring high ceilings were all white, save for the original beams Lea had ordered stripped to restore an era-specific feel, creating a contrast between the gleaming paint and the dark, textured wood. The sweeping staircase to the right of the entry led to the second floor, where the many bedrooms were well on their way to becoming guest suites, while the hallway wrapped around much of the lobby, allowing guests to lean over the railing and take a peek at who was coming in and out of the chateau at any given moment. Lush, colorful armchairs and sofas dotted the space, offsetting the checkerboard gray-and-white marble floor, and the reclaimed 1950s wooden reception desk with hand-carved façade provided an unexpected moment of almost American-feeling midcentury design.

Without her noticing, Gabriel had approached Lea from his perch at the edge of a desk, loosely holding the stem of his glass as flippantly as a cigarette. "So, are you ready to start?" he opened in a French that was colored by the bourgeois accent of the most tony Parisian suburbs.

"I'm ready to *finish*. We don't have a lot of time for all we want to get done."

"Yes, but it's your timeline, after all. Isn't it?" She couldn't tell whether he was being playful or if he was seriously questioning her. But even if he were joking, it was a strange thing to say, especially for an informal first meeting over an apéritif.

Lea looked around and noticed that Chloë had left to inspect the catered dinner supplies awaiting them in the kitchen, while Théodore seemed to be speaking to Maya with a level of curiosity similar to the one his father was showing Stephanie. She suddenly felt quite cornered.

"Yes," she started cautiously, "it's my timeline. I think it's going to be a really spectacular property." She sipped her drink. "So you work for BCG, I heard? That's very impressive." She had a quick, minor spiral that he might catch on to how deeply she had researched every family member.

"Yeah? I guess it is. I'm actually thinking of taking a year-long sabbatical, maybe travel the world." This was a common thing to hear from young French adults of his heritage, and it never failed to trigger Lea's deeply held sense of injustice.

"That sounds fun. I'd love to spend time anywhere other than France for a change, honestly."

"You should go. What's stopping you?"

A thousand sarcastic responses flickered through Lea's mind before settling on, "You're right. At least during the winter when I'm not working, anyway."

"Do you ski?"

Ah, yes, the banal assumptions in families like this that "*do you ski*" was a normal thing to ask a person, and not a trap door leading to a freefall of socioeconomic differences (even if skiing was more affordable in Europe).

"I didn't until I was older, but I taught myself living here, and now I love it." Without Lea noticing, he had gotten unusually close to her, to the point that her back was nearly against the wall as she edged away.

"You should come to Zermatt this year. If you want."

"Ah, yes, maybe." His eyes were close to hers now, slightly glassy but very intense, and she chose her words carefully. "I haven't been there yet, myself."

"It's not bad, I—"

Théodore clapped his hand on Gabriel's shoulder, startling him enough that he spilled a bit of sparkling wine down his perfectly crisp trousers. "She just got off a plane. You can tell her about Zermatt later." He smiled diplomatically down at Lea, ignoring his brother's frantic napkin triage.

"Shit, these are new." Gabriel immediately turned on his heels and went to rinse himself off before a stain could develop, without a goodbye or excuse me, much to Lea's relief.

"Thanks, I am pretty tired," she managed, looking up at the remaining Lévesque brother with a mix of curiosity and nerves. Théodore's gaze was unreadable, and the late-afternoon light cutting through the ancient windows cast his angular features in a way that made him seem almost imposing. She felt an implacable shiver run up her spine as she muttered something about needing to talk to his father, escaping from that feeling as quickly as possible.

After a few polite "we're so jet-lagged, but we *really* want to enjoy this fabulous meal you've organized before we head to bed, so we'd better get started" back-and-forths with Alain, the group embarked on the mini-tour of the chateau they would need to complete out of a combination of courtesy and genuine research on Lea's part.

Starting in the "family" kitchen, which was in the early process of being converted to host cooking classes through the addition of things like a large marble island for students to work at—the servant's kitchen downstairs was being expanded to facilitate the actual restaurant of the hotel—Alain held court, detailing the history of the space and how it had been passed down through generations of his family after being bequeathed to an ancestor by a former king.

Lea's eyes scanned the details of the kitchen: the beautiful vintage ranges with massive copper hoods, the wall of hand-hammered cookware, the arched doorway that led to a sumptuous (if currently empty) informal dining room overlooking the gardens where breakfast would be served every morning. It was indeed one of the more magnificent spaces she'd had the pleasure of working on, and not just because it was already in such an advanced state. She found herself experiencing her usual mix of gratitude for being able to do a job this aesthetically and creatively challenging, and resentment at the generations of families who let this place fall into disrepair.

"This is like Julia Child's kitchen," Stephanie marveled, unaware that her hosts would likely have no clue who Julia Child was. "I'm sorry to gush over everything. I just really can't get over this place."

"Do not apologize for loving our property, this is what we hope people will feel!" Alain beamed.

"It's so huge I can't believe this was built just for one family." Maya had fallen slightly behind the group, closer to the hall entrance than the dining room, where Théodore was lingering near her, clutching his empty glass.

"Yeah, one family and about a thousand servants," he clarified, softly smiling at her.

"Is this where the restaurant is going to be?" Maya asked, blushing.

"No—" Gabriel and Lea replied simultaneously. "No, go ahead," he gestured toward her.

"Sorry, no, this is the informal dining room—it's going to be where the guest breakfast is served every morning. The formal dining room is being turned into the main restaurant, which will also accommodate people not staying on the premises." She could hear how stilted she sounded, and hated it.

"On the *premises*," Théodore laughed, almost reading her mind. "That's a good word for us to know."

"I knew *premises*," Alain protested.

"We should start looking at the guest rooms upstairs," Gabriel interrupted, "Or we won't be eating until midnight."

Much later that evening, Lea meticulously unpacked her suitcases in the guest suite that would be her new home for the next ten weeks. As she was filling her top dresser with lingerie, she heard a gentle, rapping knock on the door she would recognize in any country.

"Come in, Steph."

"Heyyy," she whispered, sneaking in through the door like a cartoon cat, curls cascading around her face, "How are you?"

"I'm doing great, just exhausted. I feel like I'm hallucinating." The fact that this extreme exhaustion compounded by champagne wasn't enough to prevent her from unpacking nearly all of her belongings felt like a LinkedIn-worthy testament to the power of habit.

Stephanie smiled deliriously. "I'm not even tired! How crazy is that? I feel like I could run a marathon right now."

"Then you're probably hallucinating, too. You need to get some sleep—do you want a Unisom?"

Stephanie waved her offer away, sitting down on the bed. "No, no, that stuff always makes me nauseous."

"Suit yourself." Lea resumed putting her things away, itching for a compliment about what she knew were exquisite guest suites, sprawling and warm with restored picture frame moldings and hand-embroidered curtains surrounding the immense double-door windows. "Do you like your room?"

"Lea, it is *fabulous*. It's so you in the best way. Are ours the fancy ones?"

Lea smiled as she arranged her drawer. "No, no, ours are standard suites. You're thinking of the 'artist suites,' but those are being individually designed by three different artists, so they're not going to be done until July."

"I see." Stephanie sighed from across the room, distracted. "Everything okay?"

Stephanie shifted slightly on the bed. "Yeah. . . it's just, well, you didn't tell me how handsome Alain was." She giggled. *Giggled.*

"These guys all look like that. It's one thousand years of elite genetics."

"Okay, well maybe you're used to it, but I'm not usually around men like that. He's so *polite*, too."

"Well, between you and Maya, this is going to be a season of *Love Island.* She and Théodore basically spent the entire night next to each other." She paused, full of a surprising desire to speculate past what was appropriate. "I'm sure they're already in a committed relationship. He seems like the romantic type, anyway, with the glasses and the hair." *Why did she say that?*

"I didn't even notice . . ."

"Well, you were too busy falling in love with his father."

"Stop it! I just think he's handsome."

"So handsome that you came in here specifically to tell me how handsome you think he is." Lea looked over her shoulder coyly.

"Well, I'm sorry for being excited! Give me a break, okay? It's been a rough few weeks." Her eyes glistened with tears that seemed to take her by surprise.

"Hey, whoa, hey," Lea started, gently, careful to remain at her dresser and at a safe distance to let both parties suss out the sudden shift in mood. "I'm just kidding, all right? I think it's great that you like Alain. I was worried you would find them boring, if anything. And I know that this has been really rough for you, I—"

50

"No, you don't."

"What do you mean?"

Stephanie sat on the bed, a steely seriousness overtaking her nascent tears. "I didn't tell you the whole story."

Lea's heart jumped, but she remained unreadable, waiting out the heavy seconds of silence before Stephanie spoke again.

"Marcus cheated on me."

Lea fucking *knew* it.

"I fucking knew it. With—"

"Yes, with the catering girl."

Lea's mind swirled with the social media deep dives she had done on this woman—Emilia, a preposterous name—when Stephanie had confessed her suspicions, before gaslighting herself into believing she was being paranoid and dropping the subject for the holidays. The mental Rolodex unfurled before her, almost visibly:

- *She has a young son from a previous relationship*
- *She loves a cutout bathing suit that gives her strange tan lines*
- *She has a makeup YouTube channel with 600 subscribers*
- *She pronounces it "Barthelona"*

Lea burned to pry for more information, to give a motivational speech about how women should believe their instincts, or to at least say a few horrible things about the mistress. But she knew that in moments like this, Stephanie was a rare animal in a nature preserve: to be appreciated and observed with respect, but never startled or pressed beyond her comfort zone. So she let her continue at her own pace.

"I know you probably want all the gory details, but I really don't want to talk about it. I'll just say that I saw the proof with my own eyes"—she saw the horrified look spreading across Lea's face—"*on his phone.* On his phone. But I saw everything, and I'm never going back to him."

"I'm so sorry, Steph."

"I know. And I just think Alain is cute. I'm not going to run away with him. For one thing, I would never put your work in jeopardy like that."

"Oh, don't worry. It's not going to affect my work. If anything, having him distracted will make my job easier."

She could feel the air in the room softening as the conversation returned to Alain and the beautiful summer that awaited all three American women, seizing the opportunity to reassure Stephanie slightly beyond what was wise. "Besides, you don't have to worry about some HR violation. The French are all about mixing business and pleasure."

Lea closed her lingerie drawer, gently running her hands along the fine, hand-carved wood. "You'll see."

5

Lea was happy to find only the two key staffers, with whom she'd exchanged about a thousand emails, at the breakfast table when she arrived. Her notebook and iPad were in hand and one of her many "get to work" uniforms was confidently applied. Today it was navy slacks, a tucked-in white linen shirt, white leather sneakers, a few subtle dashes of makeup, and her shoulder-length, dark hair pinned half-up. She felt great.

Breakfast at the chateau was to be an outdoor affair until the informal dining room was painted and its furniture arrived in a week or so. Downstairs from that dining room was a hallway leading past the servant's kitchen and a wine-tasting room, opening to an expansive stone patio bordered by the flower gardens. A large ivory-and-gray awning jutted outward from the chateau siding and provided cover to the patio area, and the space was serviceable for a large, family-style wooden dining table until things were more settled. The tufted patio sofas and other *actual* outdoor items would soon be liberated from their holding spot in the old horse stable, which was currently being used for bulk storage on one side while the transformation to beauty spa took place on the other.

"Good morning, Lea!" Philippe called out, standing up at the sight of her. The fifty-something general contractor was overseeing all construction for the hotel, and his energy in person was exactly like it was in his emails: wiry, friendly, and old-school, down to his '90s-era dad jeans cinched tightly with a black leather belt. "It's so nice to finally meet you!"

Remaining seated next to him was his hospitality director counterpart, Marie, who simply smiled at Lea's entrance. "Are you ready to get to work?" Her French carried a distinct southwestern accent, maybe from Toulouse or Pau, and it was instantly charming in this sea of neutral, proper dialects.

"Yes, of course. But I'll take some breakfast first!" Lea walked to the far side of the table, greeting them both with a *bise* across each cheek.

"Help yourself." Marie passed a basket across the table once she had taken her seat. "I didn't know what you Americans like, so I got a little bit of everything this morning." With red drugstore reading glasses perched on her head and a tucked-in work shirt unbuttoned just enough to reveal a swath of deeply suntanned chest, she was the no-nonsense brand of older French woman with whom Lea had become familiar enough on these projects to feel they were like extended members of her own family.

"Believe it or not, I don't eat bread in the mornings." Lea smiled, loading up her plate with her standard breakfast of two eggs—any way they came was fine—and a scoop of berries.

"No *bread*?" Philippe's eyes went wide at the declaration. "Not even croissants?"

"Don't get me wrong," Lea laughed, "I love them. I just can't have too many carbs in the morning or I'll be too tired to get my work done."

"I can't keep up with these new diets." Marie shook her head, peeking over to see what Lea had pulled up on her iPad, which she happily offered up.

She scrolled through photos of the boldly patterned Schumacher fabric that was scheduled to arrive later that day for the new lobby curtains, which would be assembled by a local artisan. But just as soon as they had settled into their conspiratorial worker's breakfast, it was broken by the arrival of Alain and Gabriel, fresh off a game of tennis and still holding their rackets, sweating slightly through their white polo shirts.

"He got me this time, but it was anyone's game until the last minute!" Alain exclaimed, clapping his hand on his oldest son's shoulder.

"You think so?" Gabriel asked, pouring himself a glass of cold water. "I don't think you were ever in danger of winning."

"I taught you everything you know. I know when I'm winning." Alain wiped his hands on a cloth napkin before grabbing himself a small, toasted piece of bread and slathering it with soft butter. "Lea, I see you're already involving Marie and Philippe in your schemes." He winked.

"They're actually involving me in theirs, if you can believe it. I'm just showing them the fabric for the lobby curtains."

"I didn't think I would like something so bold, but I actually do," Marie offered, the roughness of her compliment feeling surprisingly warm in its honesty.

"When Lea first said a print with zebras on it, I thought it was a joke. But it actually looks sort of minimalist from a distance, and it makes the space feel more modern, which

I know she is going for." Gabriel looked directly at Lea while delivering his commentary, feeling more pointed than flattering.

"I like it, too!" Philippe chimed in, scrolling happily through the iPad photos.

As Lea searched for a conversation topic that wouldn't elicit more bizarre passive-aggression from Gabriel, Théodore came running from around the front of the chateau, slowing to a halt a few feet from the table to lean over with his hands on his knees and catch his breath. He had taken his shirt off at some point during his run—it was an unusually hot mid-June morning—and it looked soaked through, balled up in his hand.

His body was surprisingly well-formed for as slim as he appeared, gently muscled shoulders dotted with freckles and a long, elegant torso lined with the kind of lightly defined ab muscles that only come from being unintentionally in excellent shape, never from trying to develop them proactively. His height felt even more expansive with so little fabric to break it up, and his stomach had become concave in his bent-over position, the exquisite definition of his body sharpening with every inhale. Lea watched as a single drop of sweat followed the small ravine along his center, from the base of his long neck to the belly button just barely met by the line of dirty blonde hair emerging from his cropped running shorts.

"Put a shirt on," Gabriel commanded, snapping Lea out of her observation.

"I'm hot, and my shirt is soaking wet." Théodore turned to the group of non-family members seated at the table, still lightly panting. "I apologize for my informal appearance. I promise I'm usually wearing a shirt. Ah, ugh." He grabbed a napkin and started vigorously cleaning his glasses. "I forgot my contacts in Boulogne and I can't get new ones until next week."

Lea cleared her throat. "It happens to me all the time."

"Can I help with anything today? After a shower, obviously?" He reapplied his glasses and blinked a few times.

Philippe immediately jumped in. "Yes, you can help us with the plaster in the guest rooms—the mantle mirrors are being delivered Wednesday."

"Or you can help me unpack all of the stemware in the tasting room," Marie added, not looking up from her notes for the day.

"We know Chloë won't be helping if her *girlfriend* is in town," Gabriel sneered, lingering on the word "girlfriend."

"Shut up," Théodore snapped from across the table. "Joëlle was pulling weeds all day yesterday, and you know they're just friends now." He turned himself gallantly to face Marie, having dispensed with his brother's mockery. "I sense that my reach would be more useful in the plaster work, even if I would love to hang out with you in the tasting room all afternoon, Marie," he offered, biting into a nectarine.

"I also need you to help me with the invoices at some point," Alain added. "I'm about a week and a half behind on the books."

"I thought Gabriel was overseeing that," Théodore quipped back, with more than a little edge in his voice.

Gabriel opened his mouth to respond and Lea quickly jumped in to clarify, not wanting more of a reason for him to feel hostile. "No, Théodore, actually, I've been working on the books with your father, since he has to approve basically everything, anyway."

"Call me Théo." He smiled, the elegant syllables *Tay-Oh* landing gently on her ears. "And that's fine, I'll help you both later with whatever you need."

At this, Gabriel slipped away from the table, undoubtedly to shower and change into another one of his French-Country-Meets-Ivy-League outfits.

Lea felt the tips of her ears turn red from frustration—Gabriel had a lot of nerve insinuating that his sister wouldn't be helpful when his primary contribution since the beginning of the project had been barging into email threads to shoot down Lea's ideas with the entire chateau unnecessarily copied. During the interview process, he'd been so clear about his ultra-traditional vision for the hotel, frequently invoking his late mother, whose idea it was to restore the property to its former glory in the first place. But when it came time to actually bring things to life, he seemed totally uninterested in the work itself.

As the table resumed the rundown of the day's to-do list and who could help with what, Maya and Stephanie emerged onto the patio, both surprisingly well-styled for breakfast and looking abashed for being the last to arrive (except for Chloë who, being a teenager, didn't count in this regard). Stephanie had pinned her hair back into a low chignon with a few soft curls loose around her face and wore a beige linen maxi dress, cinched at the waist by a thin, black belt that matched her black, leather sandals. Her freshly moisturized deep bronze skin was practically glowing, and a deft swipe of stick blush had been applied to a few key areas of her face.

Like her mother, Maya had gone above and beyond for breakfast, looking ready for an afternoon on a yacht in a navy striped shirt and crisp white shorts that breezed around her long, tan legs. She'd styled her long, dark hair into two French braids and even forewent her normally imperceptible lip balm for a soft, slightly pink gloss that drew attention to her mouth, hanging just barely open as she took in Théo's bare torso.

"How embarrassing," Stephanie opened, "I hate being the last to arrive."

"Nonsense," Alain insisted, switching to an excited English, "It's not even five AM where your mind is. Can I get you something?"

"I'd love some black tea, if you have it."

He immediately began preparing her teacup. "Maya, anything for you? I know I've just done some sport, but I promise my hands are clean." He laughed warmly, holding up his hands as an offering of evidence.

"Umm, I'll make myself a plate, thank you." She had gone from taking in the spectacle of Théo's body to studiously avoiding it, sitting down across from Lea and focusing intently on the beverage options at hand.

Théo seemed to sense the cosmic disturbance his partial nudity was causing at the table. "Well, on that note, I'm going to shower and then I will come find you, Philippe. Have a great day, everyone!" He tossed his nectarine pit into the garden and picked up a croissant, holding it in his mouth as he gathered a stack of dirty dishes to drop off at the kitchen before disappearing into the chateau, his gently muscled back glistening under the diffused light of the awning.

"Actually, I should probably head out, too." Lea started collecting her things. "I have to meet with the upholstery people soon, and then I have to go to the nursery to get the entryway plants. Alain, I'll text you when I'm done and we can coordinate about the books. But it shouldn't take too long. There haven't been many new receipts this week. Most of this stuff is prepaid."

"Okay, let me know if you need anything," Alain offered, pulling up a chair near Stephanie.

A few of them called out a friendly goodbye behind her as she walked into the cavernous downstairs hallway.

She blinked her eyes hard against the sudden shift from glorious morning sunlight to the dark stone of the restaurant kitchen, full of more utilitarian but no less impressive appliances than the one upstairs, stainless steel refracting light like the mirrors they used to illuminate Egyptian tombs.

"Anything to do with the accounting beyond just entering receipts, check with me, okay?" From one of the gleaming double sinks where he was sorting the dirty breakfast dishes, Théo's voice struck Lea where she stood, returning to the deeper tone it had in his native language. "My dad means well, but he's terrible with computers. He used to have his receptionist print out his emails until like five years ago."

Lea laughed awkwardly, his shirtlessness feeling even more pronounced indoors. "Wow, he's more old-school than I realized."

"He's older than he looks. He's turning fifty-eight this fall, but don't tell him I told you that."

Lea took a beat to marvel at the utter resilience of male desirability: Alain was having children from his late twenties through his early forties and now, pushing sixty, could still compel scores of women to line up for him, Stephanie included.

"Okay, sure. No disclosing ages, and all computer stuff goes through you. Got it."

"Good. I'll see you around, Lea." With another wide smile that creased the tiniest dimple into his right cheek, Théo wiped his wet hands on his shorts and dashed off up the stairs.

Lay-Ah.

It was the way all French people tended to pronounce her name, and she'd heard it a thousand times before. But in his mouth it sounded different, more intense, like a hopeful patron voicing the password to a speakeasy for the first time. The shiver she'd experienced the evening before returned, lingering at the base of her stomach and turning into a kind of heaviness, as if she'd swallowed a hot stone.

She could see why Maya liked him.

Later that afternoon, Maya, Stephanie, and Lea found themselves surrounded by piles of dirt, sporting oversized bucket hats to protect their faces from the sun as they carried out the tedious business of planting a half-dozen hydrangea plants around the chateau entryway. It was late in the season for this task. Lea usually liked to have bushes like this in the ground by mid-spring, but the complete rehabilitation of the entry door and staircase precluded her usually perfect timing, something she made sure to underscore with Alain when going over the horticultural plans. If something would have to be nonoptimal, it at least needed to be established that it was out of her control.

"No, Maya, stop!" Lea half-shouted at her niece, grabbing the base of the plant Maya was cradling before she could lower it into the hole she'd dug. "That hole needs to be much wider."

"Oh, sorry." Maya pulled back, looking more than a little deflated. "I've never done this before."

Lea smiled in as reassuring a way as she could manage, tamping down the light frustration that came with two extra sets of hands who were making the job harder. "Of course not. I shouldn't have snapped at you. You're doing a great job."

"Thanks. I'm trying, anyway."

Lea watched her niece fall quiet again, taking a new care in her work.

On her way through the upstairs kitchen to fill her tumbler with water, Lea had found her two plus-ones hanging around, full of the awkward, undirected energy of party guests who had arrived too early. They didn't know what to do, and didn't have the necessary French to get instructions from Marie. And though Alain had taken an obvious interest in Stephanie, even *he* had a full enough calendar to be unavailable for the afternoon. So Lea took them under her wing and, as she'd promised in the airport lounge, put them to unglamorous work.

At least Stephanie was chipper, clearly grateful to have a purpose that didn't leave her turning around in circles all afternoon.

"Breakfast was such a blur! Marie runs a tight ship," she happily observed, patting down the fresh dirt around her plant.

"Well, she has to." Lea smiled with the warm familiarity of game recognizing game. "She's in charge of everything it takes to make this hotel actually work. Have you guys seen her clipboard?"

"No, why?" Stephanie looked up, her deep-set almond eyes even more striking under the shade of her hat.

"There's about a thousand-cell spreadsheet for every day."

"Théo made that," Maya volunteered, eager to share dispatches from the hours she'd spent talking to him after dinner the night before. "He acted like it was no big deal, but Alain told Mom and me at breakfast that it made everything, like, a thousand times easier."

"Oh, really?" Lea kept her eyes trained on the hydrangeas, taking care to seem only casually curious.

"He put it together during spring break. He said his dad was handing Marie, like, a dozen post-it notes a day before he made a system for them."

Lea chuckled. "Well, it's not like he's ever run a hotel before."

"Why did they even decide to do this?" Stephanie asked, picking up a quick facility with her plants. "It's kind of a big undertaking, no?"

"Huge," Lea nodded, lowering her voice slightly. "He sold his dental practice and took out a huge loan to finance the rest, as far as I know."

"Whoa, I thought they were just rich since forever? I mean, they have a literal castle. . ." Maya's eyes grew wide, and it occurred to Lea that this wasn't necessarily the most professional disclosure, but her shorthand with these two overrode any normal discretion.

"You'd be surprised," she clarified, dropping even further into a whisper. "Properties like this are sometimes the only thing these families have, and they can be a big financial burden. *They* have money, don't get me wrong, but it's from Alain's job. His brother just lives a regular life somewhere. He signed his shares of the chateau over to Alain years ago."

"Oh, really? Why?" Stephanie set down her tools, rapt.

"Probably couldn't pay for the upkeep, but I didn't ask." Her eyes darted over to a sudden noise to find a sprinkler turning on. "You don't really ask about that kind of stuff."

"That's so fascinating."

As she moved to stand up, Lea could see the machinery of Stephanie's mind working in real time at this river of new information.

"Hey, I have to go grab a few things from storage. I'll be back in a bit. Don't do anything I wouldn't do while I'm gone."

Lea removed her gardening gloves and began walking across the gravel. As soon as she was out of earshot of her mother, Maya came running up behind her, clearly desperate to ask something she couldn't in front of her. Lea took the hint and walked them around to the far side of the beauty spa, where they could speak freely.

"Everything okay, May?"

"Umm, yeah. It's going okay." Her eyes flicked downward as she said it, and she pushed one of the small, white stones with the tip of her tennis shoe.

Lea softened herself, leaning in slightly toward her. "I know it's probably weird seeing Alain so gushy all over your mom after only one day."

Maya looked briefly confused, shaking her head. "No, no. Mom deserves to be happy for once. I'm not mad at her."

"That's really mature of you. It took me forever to be okay with stuff like that after my parents separated."

The truth was, at least as it pertained to her mother, she *still* really wasn't okay with it.

"Well," Maya looked off toward the line of trees at the edge of the property, diffusing the intensity of the subject. "I just wanted us to get out of there. When Mom put all those printed-out texts on the dinner table, I thought I was going to die."

Lea reeled: Stephanie had told her about printing out the adulterous texts and confronting Marcus, but not that she'd done it *in front of her daughter*. Her instincts that this was deeply inappropriate battled against her knowledge that parenting advice was one of the few places she wasn't allowed to go with Stephanie. "Jeez, that sounds awful."

"It's fine." Maya steadied herself, changing the subject. "But actually, can I ask your honest opinion about something?"

"Of course."

She averted her gaze again. "Did I look crazy at breakfast?"

"What do you mean? Because you came in later than the rest of us?"

"No. . . because I was so dressed up. I just wanted to look nice, and I didn't realize everyone else would be all sweaty or wearing work clothes. Well, I mean, you looked nice. But I felt really dressy." As she talked, Maya got progressively more worked up, until her voice began to tremble.

"Oh, sweetie, no. You looked beautiful." Lea reached out to gently rub her niece's delicate shoulders. "I should have warned you both, French people are *extremely* casual in this kind of environment, especially when they're rich. Like you saw with Théo. Sometimes they can't even be bothered to put on a shirt." She felt Maya tense up slightly at the mention of his name, another shiver of embarrassment running down her spine.

"It's just," she was actively sniffling now, "everyone looks so cool and like they're not even trying. And I know it's silly because it's not even been a day, but I really think Théo is special. . . And now he probably thinks I'm this stupid, try-hard American."

"I can assure you he doesn't think that." She moved them both over to sit on a neighboring stack of wood that would soon become a pool deck.

"When I first came here, I felt so insecure because of how effortless everyone else seemed, and I always thought that no matter what I was wearing or how I acted, I was just the American who stood out like a sore thumb." She brushed a small piece of lint from her pants, reflexively smoothing over the fabric when it was gone. "But over time I realized that this way they all have of being so *cool*, of never wanting to seem too invested, also gave me an advantage. I didn't have to play by their rules, and that's how I was able to build my business. To someone like Théo, I bet your outfit today felt unexpected and beautiful, because a French girl *wouldn't* come to breakfast like that, and that's a great thing. I bet it's what he saw in you last night. I'm *positive*, actually."

It was true and it wasn't. They probably *did* all think she looked a bit silly at breakfast, but the harder thing to explain was that it would be their loss if so. And if Théo were attracted to her—and why wouldn't he be?—then he would find anything she did charming by default.

Maya wiped her eyes, obviously heartened but still unable to consider the situation head-on. "I should stop obsessing about it."

"I think that's probably wise."

"I'm gonna go finish helping Mom with the plants."

They both stood up, eager to not prolong the vulnerability of the conversation, with Lea offering a tiny piece of practical parting advice.

"And Maya—don't try to dress like them. That would *actually* look weird, trust me. I learned that one the hard way."

She laughed, miming a check mark as she headed back to work.

6

"Please use the box cutter to open your boxes *along the seams,*" Lea instructed, gesturing with her own cutter down an imaginary line. "And when you finish, please *fold* the box and put it in one of the large trash bags by Marie."

"Trash bags," she clarified in French toward Marie, who held the box of rolled-up bags next to her for effect.

"I don't have a screwdriver," Chloë complained through her curtain of pin-straight, brown hair, sounding only half-sad that she wouldn't be able to do her job properly.

"You can use mine," Lea handed hers over unceremoniously. "And there's plenty more where that came from. Let's go!"

Sliding her iPad toward her from its perch on one of the many boxes, she checked her screensaver—the hotel insignia with a permanent, ticking countdown clock to the friends-and-family party, precisely fifty-six days away—and quickly clicked the screen off again, a tic that had come to agitate her as much as it soothed.

This morning, the task at hand was unboxing the restaurant furniture that had been languishing in the lobby while the dining room paint—a dusty shade of sage, save for the ornate moldings, which were painted a barely perceptible shade darker—fully dried. The space was perfect, flooded with light

69

cut by the museum-style filtering blinds Lea insisted upon to give total control over the mood during lunch service. Earlier in the year, it had been expanded to integrate the adjoining smoking room, creating enough space for forty-four additional guests. Opposite that was the sitting room, which had been completely revamped to include a stately marble bar with brass railings and vintage leather stools where patrons could grab a drink while waiting for their table. The "dining" wing would not be complete until the magnificent, reclaimed art nouveau doors Lea had snagged from the French equivalent of Craigslist arrived, but it was already alighting every synapse of creative satisfaction in Lea's brain.

Now in her second week on the property, Lea had entered the full bloom of her usual confidence. As she suspected, Alain's boyish affection for Stephanie was making her job easier, inclining him to rubber stamp nearly everything that passed his desk and to find Lea's ideas even more charming and ingenious than usual. (It didn't hurt that Gabriel had returned to Paris for work, taking with him his constant passive-aggressive criticisms punctuated by Lea's name—a tactic Lea assumed was directly lifted from a Harvard Business School Essay Collection for Psychopaths.)

And, if she were being totally honest, the *goodness* of how things were going had also relieved Lea of some of the anxiety she'd experienced the week prior. Immature as it might be, much of her fundamental stability came from the protective bubble of her career being prestigious and successful, even if other things in her life were not. And while she would likely never say something like this out loud, not even to Dr. Miller, an aspect of what made her dynamic with Stephanie work so well was that, while Lea was a single, childless thirty-something, Stephanie was forty-something and in a terrible marriage. This was not what Lea wished for her in the abstract, but it also conveniently insulated her from much of the preemptive defensiveness she experienced around married women. Now, with Stephanie suddenly joyful and desired, Lea had feared her aloneness would feel more humiliating than inspiring—but she was pleasantly surprised to discover that being relentlessly good at her job in front of people she loved gave her a new armor of confidence.

Around her, Maya, Théo, Chloë, and an especially harried Marie worked to unpack and assemble the furniture in as organized a manner as possible. Despite her best efforts, though, her optimal protocol for assembling the furniture was not being universally respected: Chloë had a habit of ripping the boxes apart rather than unsealing and folding them meticulously, while Maya had still not mastered the aligning of the right screws with the right holes underneath the Hollywood Regency-style dining chairs.

Théo, however, worked with an engineer's precision, frequently taking over for his sister mid-assembly with one of the many exasperated, guttural sighs French men are fond of leveraging to express their discontent. Chloë eventually asserted herself with a deeply teenager-y, "If you don't want my help, then do it yourself," before storming upstairs to call the friends she was likely looking for an excuse to call all morning, anyway.

"I think this will happen," Marie chuckled in her rusty English.

"It's better this way. We don't need a chair collapsing under someone during dinner because my sister can't use a wrench."

Théo set to tightening the chairs and tables Chloë had managed to assemble before abandoning the effort entirely.

"You shouldn't say that. She's trying her best." Maya smiled, relishing the opportunity to give the flirtatious reprimand an actual girlfriend might offer.

"That's what she wants you to think." He looked up from his work, pushing his glasses up his nose and winking at her.

Despite her best efforts, Lea couldn't help but flash back to the scene she'd witnessed while repairing some vineyard fencing on a far end of the property earlier that morning.

Maya and Théo had set up two large beach towels near the still-unusable pool to sunbathe before the day got too hot, catching Lea's attention when their voices rose to laugh about something unintelligible. Maya, in a pale blue bikini that contrasted beautifully against her rapidly darkening skin, was leaning over to read something in Théo's book. She was perched in such an uncaring way, so beautiful and young as to be wholly unaware of the details of her body, looking up from behind her gleaming black hair to ask questions. And Théo looked similarly untethered to the world around him, resplendent in his cropped swimming trunks, looking at Maya over the rims of his sunglasses as he sounded out words, twirling a blade of grass in his long fingers.

Lea froze, fencing still in her garden-gloved hand as she watched them, feeling distinctly perverse as she did. Because the truth was, ever since that morning he'd come running around the side of the chateau shirtless, Lea had been keeping an eye on him, on the quietly confident way he moved, a stark contrast to his older brother and, frankly, to most of the men she'd dated. Seeing him engaged in this private moment confirmed every suspicion she had been trying to push out of her mind since seeing his body that morning: he was incredibly sexy, effortless yet intentional with every movement.

She saw the way he leaned into Maya, laughing easily and re-forming those glorious ravines of muscle along the side of his torso, and she couldn't help herself: she wanted to *be* Maya. She wanted to be young and carefree and not have any work to worry about, sure, but specifically she wanted to be her *in that moment,* with that exact man leaning in to better hear her words.

Lea felt her heart race as her grip tightened within her gloves and she forced herself to resume the work at hand. And for the most part, she'd been able to push the scene that morning to the back of her mind. Until she saw him wink.

Back in the lobby, Marie stood up, flipping her last table upright and testing it for wobbliness. "If you finish this, I need to. I need to. . . Shit, I can't do this in English. I need to get ready for the Wine Director, and I want to change my shirt first. Can you explain this, Lea?" She gathered her clipboard and nodded goodbye to the group, hurrying down to the tasting room.

"Of course. Marie has other things to do, so we need to finish this ourselves." Lea turned to Maya, who was looking at her red hands with the distinct expression of someone who was also hoping to be excused. "Oh, come on. Not you, too?"

Théo peeked from behind the table he was working on, running a hand through the now slightly damp curls falling on his forehead. "It's okay, Lea, I can finish this up myself. There isn't much left."

"No, no, that would be exploiting student labor." She laughed.

"Trust me, you wouldn't be the first."

Lea turned back to Maya. "It's fine, you can go and I'll finish your last two. Also, please tell your mom that we're leaving for lunch at 12:30 sharp. I have to be back by 2:30 and she takes forever to pick an entree."

"Tell me about it." Maya unfolded her gazelle legs to stand, setting her screwdriver down and brushing some invisible dust from her cutoff shorts. She bounded off through the lobby, snow-white Keds squeaking on the tile, just barely touching Théo's shoulder as she passed him by.

It only occurred to Lea then that it was just the two of them, and she became suddenly more aware of herself, and especially of the inch of waist peeking out between her high-waisted jeans and the black button-down shirt she'd knotted at the hem for comfort. For a while, there was a distinct silence which Lea feared she was imbuing with heaviness, so she cut it with the first innocuous thing she could think of.

"Speaking of your exploitation, how is your internship going?"

He let out a genuine burst of laughter. "You're the first person to ask me that. It's extremely boring, but thank you."

"What is it again?"

"Teaching boomers who make twenty times my monthly stipend how to use basic office software. That, and data entry."

"You're right, that does sound boring."

"Ah, it's fine." He picked up the assembly instructions for the table he was working on and flipped through them while holding his pencil in his mouth. Finding what he was looking for, he set the papers and pencil down and met her gaze. "This is the last one like this—I have six months left of actual school; then I do my 'serious' internship, which will hopefully turn into a job. It's just frustrating because I should already be in my 'real' job by now."

"Why?"

"I'm twenty-four in two weeks."

"Happy early birthday." Lea set to unpacking the last dining chair, taking pains to hide the rush of excitement at learning he was older than she thought.

"Thank you." He sarcastically mimed party hands. The room momentarily fell silent again before he continued.

"So yeah, it's not what I would have picked, but I needed something remote that would allow me to do this with my downtime. And it's honestly such easy work that I can get it all done in a few hours in the morning, which is great."

"It's really good of you to be helping your dad this much with the chateau."

"It's my family, too. I want this place to be incredible."

"No, of course, I just mean that no one would have faulted you for staying in Paris, just working through the summer and having fun."

"Do I not look like I'm having fun?" He flipped his table over in what felt like record time and moved over to her last remaining chair, which she was struggling to line up on its legs. "Here—" he grabbed the legs and pushed them just enough to allow the screws in the remaining points of contact. "Go ahead, you do the screws while I hold it like this."

Lea could feel his seemingly infinite arms straining beside her as she moved in to place the two remaining screws. Their faces were only inches apart as she willed her hands not to tremble, and to finish the job as quickly as possible. She could feel the heat rising off of him as she turned her wrist, his loosely hanging work shirt brushing her bare arm.

He chuckled. "Sorry if my shirt is gross, I've been assembling furniture all morning."

Her heart raced, thinking back to the scene by the pool, breathing him in deeply and imagining what would happen if she turned her face just slightly enough to meet his mouth with her own.

"You're not gross." She tightened her grip on the screwdriver, concentrating on every micro-movement of her fingers, unable to not notice his scent. "Is that Hermès?" Lea asked in her best attempt at casually interested, the words flung from her chest before she could corral them back in. *Fuck.*

She couldn't look up, even as she felt his eyes turn down toward her as he laughed in response.

"What? Oh, no. I'm flattered, though. My friend works in perfumes in Grasse—I go to that area sometimes for work. I actually created this scent myself."

He created it *himself?*

"Ah, you could have fooled me. There." Lea had barely finished tightening the last leg when she practically tumbled backward away from him, bringing herself to standing and wiping her hands off on her jeans. "I have to rinse off and get ready for lunch, but thanks again for doing this. It would have taken all day without you."

He looked slightly hurt that she recoiled from him so quickly, as if he were a poisonous plant she'd come dangerously close to touching.

"No problem, seriously," he reassured her as he stood up to gather the remaining recycling. "Enjoy your lunch."

"I always do." She was going for jokey, but realized she might have come off as condescending. It was beyond time for her to leave the room.

Stephanie was waiting by the front entrance at 12:29, which made Lea's 12:32 arrival cause for a distinctly older sister-esque smirk as she bounded down the stairs, rummaging through her crossbody bag to double-check she had everything.

"Oh, come on. I'm two minutes late."

"I didn't say anything." Stephanie's smile widened. "Come on, I'll drive."

The drive in question was a little under half an hour, to a nearby town known in the region for its dining and nightlife. Alain had insisted they try this restaurant for lunch, as it was owned by longtime family friend Sofian, along with two other restaurants and Apostrophe, a sprawling indoor/outdoor restaurant-lounge-bar-club combination along the banks of the Loire that drew patrons from a hundred-mile radius for its famous summer parties.

Blessedly for Lea, the ride was mostly absent of conversation after her initial protest that she needed a minute to relax after the morning's exhaustive work. Really, hiding herself behind the curtain of French pop music filling the car was more about unwinding the heightened and complicated energy still vibrating through her from her time alone with Théo. There was something about him, something so casual and comfortable, even with a professional woman twelve years his senior who was working in his home, for his father. The way he mindlessly held objects in his mouth, the way he answered her questions with an unanxious honesty, the way he interjected to give her exactly the help she needed without her having to ask. It all felt. . . *older*. Older, yet somehow foreign to the many full-grown men she had known intimately and otherwise.

Because yes, men like Marcus were confident and proactive. But there was a contempt to it, paired with a reflexive need to control every situation he was in, down to the reactions of others. And then there were men like David, who were unassuming and generous like Théo, but lacked a fundamental kind of conviction that emanated "I'm doing what I'm doing, whether or not you're in the room." David's tendency to ask questions, to seek approval, to make sure everything with Lea was okay often reminded her of the Sims she would create as a teenager, their free will slid all the way to zero, content to set the stove on fire and stand there watching the kitchen burn until Lea entered the room and told them to put it out.

As her mind spun, she realized this was quite a lot to project onto a not-even-twenty-four-year-old who was definitely in the early stages of dating her niece. It flooded her with a visceral shame, knowing that Stephanie was going to spend their meal talking and asking about Alain, an *actual* grown man who had married a woman his own age, raised a family, had a long career as a dentist, and was now investing his substantial wealth into his family legacy. Everything Stephanie was experiencing was *right*, as was the fact that her daughter had a weighty crush on

Théo, who was the exact kind of young man anyone would want their daughter to bring home from college.

Get ahold of yourself, Lea thought so vividly she almost spoke the words. But she couldn't. Her mind was already running free of her control, replaying the moment just before the legs of the chair lined up on their base, when his muscles were at their most tensed, when she could feel his breath on the side of her neck.

She imagined the soft, warmly wet feeling of his tongue making contact with her skin right where that neck met her shoulder, tasting her for the first time as his elegant hands abandoned their task and moved hungrily to her blouse, opening it just enough to slide underneath and fill his palms with her breasts, pulling her into his chest and overtaking her, packing materials and paper instructions scattering noisily underneath them as he turned her to face him and—

"Lea," Stephanie repeated, cutting the music. "We're here."

"Oh, yes, sorry. Sorry." She unbuckled her seatbelt and reached for her bag, feeling the electricity in her extremities begin to cool.

"Are you okay?"

"Yeah, I'm fine. I've just got a million things on my mind right now. The new pool tile is supposed to be fully cured already but they're just finishing it today, and the deck lumber is just sitting under a tarp. The timing is completely wrong. The pool chaises and umbrellas are coming by the end of the week!" She was surprisingly convincing at transmuting her emotional and sexual spiraling into logistical spiraling.

"Alain said it would be fine at breakfast. We're still ahead of schedule, right? I mean, we also don't have to get lunch if it's going to stress you out."

"No, no, I need to eat. And I want to catch up with you! What *else* did Alain say at breakfast?" Lea fluttered her eyelashes mockingly across the center console.

"Okay, enough out of you. Let's go eat."

The restaurant, tucked away on a winding side street of the medium-sized village, was in a converted home of a much smaller scale than the chateau. The women were greeted, barely, by the hostess, a teenage girl just visibly bored enough to suggest she was directly related to the family who owned it. (This was a common dynamic in these types of towns, and in the families who built their small empires in bars and restaurants: surly teens from the family tree staffing them.) Lea gave her name, and the girl began drowsily scanning for it in her oversized planner before settling on their reservation with a barely audible, "Ah." But before she could show them to their small table by a window, a spindly, handsome, older man in a light gray suit came fluttering up to the stand.

"Is this Lea and Stephanie?" he asked in a lilting English much too friendly for a Frenchman.

"Yes! Sofian?" Stephanie stepped forward and he pulled her in for a vigorous *bise*, followed by Lea.

"What a pleasure to have you two dining with us. Alain has said many great things."

"He's said wonderful things about you and your restaurants, too!" Stephanie beamed at the giddy feeling that knowing people in another country after only a few weeks can evoke. "He also told me you and your wife are from Morocco?"

"Yes! From Agadir. Do you know it?"

And Stephanie launched into her Arabic, which Lea knew well enough by now was the Modern Standard version that her mother had insisted she learn alongside the Jordanian dialect she had brought over with her, and which she had taught her tight-knit group of AP students every year since she began teaching. It was genuinely moving to see Stephanie get to be an insider, to be spoken of highly before she entered a room and then dazzle beyond expectation when she arrived. And Lea noticed her usual, pedagogical manner, leaning in closely to understand what Sofian was saying, bridging the gap between their versions of the language.

Sofian was enamored, and opened their conversation up to Lea to say as much.

"Oh, your friend has such elegant Arabic."

Lea secretly loved when people referred to Stephanie as just *her friend*—the victory of loving and being loved beyond their familial obligations.

Sofian continued, shepherding them toward their table. "She could probably teach me many things! I need to work on mine, *and* my English."

Stephanie blushed. "Oh, no, I've always loved Darija. It's probably my favorite dialect."

"And your English is beautiful." Lea offered, smiling.

"Ah," Sofian chided, gesturing for them to sit and bringing over the large chalkboard full of daily specials. "But your French is so beautiful, I hear, which is no small feat for an American. My wife and I have heard great things." He offered the compliment in the literary, mannered French of his Moroccan schooling.

It never failed to strike Lea as unfair how someone like Sofian—a hundred times more impressive than the majority of people you would meet in France—would constantly be downplaying himself, but she knew that this was part of the immigrant dance, even if her version of immigration was infinitely more privileged than his.

"Well, thank you," Lea blushed. "Is she here? Alain told us she makes most of the desserts." She scanned the specials, homing in on her choices.

"Ah, no, she is not here today. She is with our daughter in Paris, helping her move into her new apartment. But she will be at Apostrophe for Disco Night!" Sofian gave a little shimmy.

"Disco Night?" Lea arched her eyebrow at Stephanie, who was clearly familiar with the concept.

"Alain's been talking about it since we arrived," she explained. "It's one of the biggest parties Sofian throws every summer. He's had his outfit picked out since March."

"Alain loves Disco Night! Ladies, I will let you look at the menu. May I offer you a glass of champagne? On the house."

"Why not?" Stephanie replied, a smile creeping across her face. "When in France!"

They were midway through their main courses—a delicate filet of white fish in lemon butter sauce that melted on the tongue for Lea, and a perfectly summery mixed grill of lamb and vegetables over a fluffy bed of rice for Stephanie—when the latter finally broached the topic she'd clearly been dying to discuss.

"So." Stephanie set down her utensils, grabbing her nearly finished glass of champagne (she would refuse another; unlike much of the country of France, she treated driving under the influence with due seriousness). "I should tell you about Alain. I just needed a space away from the chateau to do it, really."

"Spare no detail. I'm a single woman who hasn't been properly laid in about a century."

"*No!*" she practically yelled, before realizing how much her voice had raised and reducing it to a whisper. "We haven't even *kissed*. Not yet, anyway."

"Oh. . . my god? How is that possible? He's practically been glued to you twenty-four seven since our plane landed."

"I know, I know. But I have to be honest, Lea. When I first got here, I thought Alain was just this handsome guy that I might have a summer fling with before getting back to my real life and figuring out the divorce. But I'm starting to really think Alain is someone I could *be* with. Or at least, someone I could actually care about. So I want to take it slow."

Lea could tell Stephanie was hedging and in need of a slight push toward full honesty. "And. . ."

"And. . . well, I don't know that Chloë is the biggest fan of her dad moving on, and I think Alain is sensitive to that. He doesn't want to upset her."

Not a shocking development, but still likely upsetting to Stephanie, whose usual ease with teenagers was literally her career.

"Ah, I get it." Lea's finger traced the rim of her glass, hovering between wanting Stephanie to play her cards right and wanting her to just rip off the band-aid and get laid. "Well, I'm sure she's open to getting to know you. And in the meantime, it's not like you have to make out with her dad in front of her."

"Of course not."

"Have you talked to him about it?"

"Yes."

"And?"

"He thinks I should try to spend a little more time with her one-on-one. I'm taking her to her stable tomorrow for riding practice, and I'll watch her."

Lea's hand hovered mid-air, fork full of flaky fish, as she considered her response. She had a strong feeling that the girl may not love having her dad's new crush foisted on her in this way, but Stephanie was already looking fragile enough that she didn't want to make things worse.

"Well, if it's any consolation, not all of his kids are fans of me, either."

"You mean Gabriel?"

"Yeah. It's relentless. He acts like he has this über-traditional vision for the hotel—you should have *seen* the deck he sent me when I first got hired—but he has no clue what he's doing. I just think he wants to win."

Stephanie pushed her food around her plate, eager to assume the best of the children whose father she was falling for. "Well, Alain doesn't think so. He gets where Gabriel is coming from."

"How? How is that even possible?"

"Lee, don't get so territorial. You know how traumatic it was for all of them when Anne-Claire passed away." Stephanie said her name reverently, as if she were asking for permission to love the same man this woman did for so many years. "He says this is Gabriel's way of keeping her legacy alive, you know?"

The mother had been invoked. There was no arguing against it, even if Lea didn't buy the rationale and felt a flare of bitterness toward Stephanie for attempting to sell it.

"I don't know that she was all that traditional a woman, from what I've heard." Lea gently asserted, refilling her water glass. "But it doesn't matter. Alain trusts my vision. And, I'm sorry, I still didn't get an answer—I know Chloë isn't a fan, but you can't even kiss him?"

"I know it probably wouldn't be a big deal to *you*, but I haven't even kissed a man who wasn't Marcus since I was nineteen. And honestly, it's been a long time since even Marcus and I have kissed, beyond a peck goodbye or for a photo or something."

As heavy as the admission was, it was interesting to hear Stephanie refer to her ex with such detached matter-of-factness. She really *was* moving on.

"Really?"

"Yes. I probably haven't had a tongue kiss in at least two or three years."

"A *tongue kiss?*" Lea stifled a laugh at the profound middle-school energy of her confession.

"This is all very embarrassing, please don't make me repeat this stuff. Let's just say that I'm nervous about not being up to Alain's hot French standards when it comes time to actually. . . you know."

"Don't be embarrassed. I may have 'tongue kissed' more than you in recent years but, if we're trading war stories,

I haven't had an orgasm with a man present since David. And even then, he was mostly just a hype man to my vibrator."

Stephanie snorted into her glass. "Dear lord."

"Yeah."

"God, I can't even *imagine* using a vibrator with a man. Marcus would have been so judgmental."

"Well, this is one of the many reasons we're divorcing him, isn't it?"

"Yes, one of the many reasons we will. Eventually."

"Steph, come on. You still haven't started the paperwork yet?"

"I don't want to go down this road again, Lea. We agreed to handle the legal stuff when we get back, once Maya and I are both able to properly move out. He didn't want to ruin my summer with lawyers and paperwork, and I didn't want to make an enemy of him while he's still paying the credit cards. He knows he messed up, and this is a nice way to not make things worse on his part."

Lea found she sounded suspiciously like the Stephanie who had eventually gone back to him every time over the years.

"Well, I'm not going to tell you what to do, but—"

Before Lea could indeed tell Stephanie what to do, Sofian was at their tableside with a dessert menu and an offer of orange blossom tea that sounded too delicious to refuse.

7

After hours spent bent over and tending to vines, the midday summer sun created a specific exhaustion that never failed to take Lea by surprise. It was a struggle to maintain the chipper, professional tone she needed for this outdoor Wine Education Day she'd scheduled months in advance, for which the extended chateau crew was assembled to finally learn about their grapes. Her eyes scanned the day's checklist on her phone, which she'd snuck out of her pocket while the others were talking amongst themselves:

- *Review local wine landscape*
- *Breakdown of Lévesque grapes/timeline [CONSERVA-TIVE]*
- *Quiz on best horticulture practices*
- *NOTE: Downplay co-op stuff re: Gabriel*

As she executed her agenda, her eyes frequently darted to Théo, who, standing amongst the estate's vineyards with the rest of his family, emanated a kind of natural, confident humility. While the other men—even Gabriel, who'd made the trip from Paris for the lesson—were in high-end outdoor gear to protect them from the elements, Théo was in a Hôtel

Château Victoire polo shirt, with an oversized bucket hat loosely tied below his chin, giving him a distinctly Steve Irwin quality. He looked goofy and wonderfully handsome, the papercut-fine angles of his face moving in and out of the light as he posed surprisingly thoughtful questions about grape cultivation.

Today, they were being instructed by the local viticulturist, Rémy, who had come well-recommended to Lea for years, and with whom she'd been dying to work once she arrived in the Loire. The two of them had been effortlessly tag-teaming all morning to give the Lévesques a sufficiently inspiring but realistic vision of what their estate could look like as a functioning wine producer. Lea felt at her most competent and practiced, and the fact that Rémy was handsome—dark hair with high cheekbones, deep-set eyes, and a five o'clock shadow you wanted to rub yourself against like a cat—only helped matters. Lea could see Stephanie's smug look from a mile away, knowing she would later get a mini speech about how she definitely *should* get his number.

"Sauvignon blanc has a fairly blah reputation in the States," Lea elaborated to the assembled group, Rémy looking on approvingly. "It's sort of known as the go-to wine if you want a neutral white or want to avoid a butterball chardonnay, but—"

"What is *butterball?*" Alain asked, a sweetly confused look on his face. Beside him, Stephanie clicked a button on her phone from inside her pocket, undoubtedly rejecting another call from Marcus—she'd gotten much better about not letting him interrupt the flow of whatever she happened to be doing at that moment.

"Oh, sorry," Lea laughed. "A lot of chardonnays in the US undergo a specific process that makes them extremely rich and buttery, too oaky and heavy, sometimes even syrupy. And 'Butterball' is a brand in the States."

"Ah. *Butterball*." His delicate accent emphasized the "uhh" in *butter*.

"Anyway, obviously those with sharper palates know these grapes can be complex, and beautiful, and versatile, but we have to make sure that our positioning is really fighting against that reputation as we start to bring the vineyard into maturity."

Gabriel piped up from slightly behind the group, mindlessly playing with a leaf as he talked. "Why does it matter what Americans think of our wine?" The distaste for the word *Americans* was palpable.

Rémy quickly interjected, "Because Americans account for fifty percent of all French wine purchased. They are our most important market. More important even than French."

"Huh." Gabriel could barely manage a grunt of acknowledgment.

As if reading her thoughts, Théo jumped in to move the conversation back to Lea's comfort zone. "Are we going to be tasting some with our dinner tonight?"

"Excellent question!" Lea turned to face him and immediately regretted doing so, as the combination of his physical attractiveness and his direct attention made her blush, and she now had to fight her body's autonomous responses in addition to sounding competent. She soldiered on: "So, we're going to be tasting a few different local wines—including some excellent sauvignon blanc—but we'll be adding a bit of a mystery element to it. There'll be two options paired with each course, and we want each of you to try both and choose which one you prefer. Once you've picked, you'll learn what you preferred and why. This will help you all get a sense of the art behind wine pairing."

"Will you be doing that, Rémy?" Maya asked, thrilled to be of age to participate in a wine tasting with the grown-ups.

"No," he laughed. "I help you grow your grapes, but I don't put them with food. That's for your Wine Director Daniel, who is a good friend. I trust his taste."

Lea leaned over and joked with him in French under her breath—he and Daniel had a bit of a reputation for being the life of the party at some of the region's wine events—and they laughed together before continuing to explain the grapes their vineyard would be capable of bringing to fruition in the near term. And though she knew it was somewhat inappropriate to be so familiar with another contractor on such a big day, she couldn't help herself. Being seen as competent *and* desirable in front of Théo felt painfully necessary to her, embarrassing as it was to admit.

So the two of them carried on teaching, passing the torch back and forth with explanation and context, until the inevitable Tiring of the Teenager began—as was customary whenever they spent too long on any chateau-related project.

"Sorry, Rémy." Alain turned around to chide his daughter, who was laughing at something on her phone. "Shh. Put that thing away and pay attention."

"I don't know why we have to do this in English," Chloë protested in French—a convenient alternative to directly protesting Stephanie's presence.

Théo jumped in to put a stop to her complaints, always more resonant in his native language. "Because not all of our guests speak French, and Mr. Meunier is gracious enough to explain this to us in a language everyone can understand. Why don't you try being gracious, too?"

Lea swooned a little at the simple righteousness of his correction. He turned back to Rémy and gestured apologetically for him to resume.

"Oh, it is really time for questions, if we have them. I have talked enough today!" He laughed good-naturedly as he looked around the group.

"Can we eat the grapes?" Maya asked, close to doing so before even hearing the answer.

"Yes, you can, but you probably don't want to," Rémy explained. "They're not like table grapes, and these are in weak condition. But they will make good wine someday!"

A ripple of curiosity moved through the group, who were all clearly now considering popping an under-formed fruit in their own mouths.

"I have a question, actually," Stephanie started, nervously raising her hand.

"Yes!"

"I know this wine is going to a co-op, and not its own label, but I don't really understand what that means. Could you explain that? Unless it's too much of a basic question, which is very possible." She looked over at Lea, silently trying to signal that she'd been paying attention to the details of her work.

There was no way Stephanie could have known the landmine she'd stepped on. Lea hadn't briefed her on the extended proxy arguments she'd had with Gabriel through his father about the importance of starting off with a co-op before moving to their own house label, offsetting any possible risk of launching with terrible wines and undermining the reputation of their vineyards before they even had a chance to establish themselves. It wasn't glamorous, it wasn't particularly lucrative, and it wasn't all about their estate, but it was the best choice for the family to establish itself and its property, and Lea had rarely experienced such strong resistance to her expertise on the matter.

She couldn't explain the winemaking process, and she deferred to her trusted experts on when, where, and how each group of grapes would meet its bottle, but she was among the best in the world when it came to reviving faded French properties—and the positioning of their wine production, when applicable, was a big part of the puzzle only she could see in full. Eventually, after much back and forth and backing up her suggestions with all the data and anecdotal evidence she could find, she had won Alain over to her vision.

But now, Stephanie's innocent question was enough to shift the tectonic plates of Gabriel's ego.

"Not all of us wanted to sell to a co-op, but Lea thought this is what we should do. So this is what we're doing." He directed his comment to Stephanie's face, but his intended target was clear.

"Well, I cannot say where you should sell your grapes, but—" Rémy started, before Alain attempted to cool the temperature.

"I think Stephanie just wanted to know what a co-op is, really."

Gabriel snorted a small, derisive laugh. "It's where you give your grapes to a big company that blends them all together and sells bottles for three euro on the bottom shelf at Lidl."

There was a brief silence, punctured by a valiant attempt from Rémy to clarify.

"Well, this is not always the case. There are some which sell low-cost wines, but many sell wines at all prices and qualities. It is not a shameful thing to be part of a cooperative."

"No, but it is also not why we're spending millions of euros to reestablish our heritage and resume our winemaking tradition." He openly looked over at Lea now, working himself up to the full bloom of his condescension. "To be in some label-less table wine that college students drink to get drunk."

"Gabriel, don't start. For once, just don't start." Théo's soft French plea was quiet and full of restrained anger, even as he looked downward, rubbing his forehead to avoid a more full-throated confrontation.

"Oh, yeah?" Gabriel shot his eyes over at his brother, challenging him.

Alain stepped forward, putting himself in the line of sight of both of his sons, who glanced in his direction before retraining their eyes on each other. "I have looked at the plan and the projections, and starting our first several years in a co-op is the best option right now. That doesn't mean it will never be our own label." He spoke slowly and firmly, while Stephanie and Maya looked at each other with great anxiety over what he might be saying.

The pin-drop silence in the group felt overpowering. Lea's eyes were trained on the hills in front of her, blurring with nerves, holding her breath until it became clear that Gabriel would not be carrying on further. Rémy timidly resumed his lesson in a falsely chipper voice while Lea tried her best to seem unbothered, even naïve to the implications of the exchange.

Behind her, Lea could hear Gabriel petulantly continuing his protestations to his father under his breath. She could make out a few remarks about the quality of their grapes, and how one of his business school connections would put them in touch with an amazing bottler if he wanted a meeting. And through the din of the group talking and rustling around in the grapevines, she managed to make out the most cutting of his whispered words, "She doesn't understand the importance of legacy like this. She doesn't even have children."

Lea felt every drop of blood in her body rush to her face, burning the tips of her ears and filling her mind with the slight, tinny ring of humiliation. She had always imagined the kind of comments these families must make behind her back, about the single woman so content to abandon her life in the States for months at a time, ingratiating herself into happy families that would continue on for generations without her. In a country as obsessed with children and lineage as France—with a persistently strong population growth in a declining Europe to show for it—her life choices must put her somewhere between object of pity and zoo exhibit. But to hear it out loud, to hear that her unfamiliarity with the concept of wanting to pass on a legacy to an heir was considered a weakness in her professional competency, felt like finding a leak in her lifeboat after she had already rowed out to sea.

If her job couldn't protect her from this, if it couldn't be a place of pure confidence based on her own skills and not her tax filing status, where could she go? Where could she hide?

Later that afternoon, Lea and Marie found themselves in their now-familiar comfort zone of quiet, repetitive work, this time arranging the sitting room bookshelves to look both credibly lived-in and thoughtfully designed. Marie had been floored the first time Lea told her there are entire services to buy books specifically for the purpose of interior design, and her pragmatic nature simply wouldn't allow it. So she insisted on going to local thrift shops and estate sales to find old books, even bringing a few titles from her home library to flesh out the collection. Lea, meanwhile, had brought a familiar roster of knickknacks from her storage unit in Paris: vintage watering cans, pillar candles under glass cloches, hand-thrown ceramic vases.

Their rhythm together was nearly musical: Marie arranged and Lea adjusted, Marie unpacked and Lea neatly folded the packing materials for recycling. They could go hours like this, often not speaking, basking in the gentle hum of their own efficiency.

Today, though, Lea found herself unable to resist the temptation to dress her wounds from Gabriel's comments. She had gathered by now that Marie was equally exasperated with him—with his presumptuousness and his insistence on meddling where he had nothing to offer—even if she knew better than to voice it. And she also knew that Marie was everything Gabriel couldn't judge—French, understated, a married mother of two grown children—so his undermining of her work made his dynamic with Lea feel at least slightly less personal.

Although she knew it wasn't particularly mature of her, she cracked open the door to a good, old-fashioned bitching session.

"The wine lesson was a bit of a disaster today," Lea opened.

"Ah?" Marie looked up over her reading glasses—blue, this time—from her position on the floor, sorting through books.

"Well, Stephanie asked why we're selling to a co-op."

"Ah." A gentle chuckle. "And not everyone was happy?"

Lea dropped her voice, even though the door was firmly closed behind them. "Exactly. Gabriel made all of these horrible comments about the family wine being sold to drunk college students. It was *so* uncomfortable."

Marie snorted, shaking her head. "He's a child."

A shiver of emboldening relief passed down Lea's spine. This was a safe space.

"Well, speaking of being a child. . . I overheard him telling his father that I didn't understand the issue because I don't have children."

"*What*? What does that have to do with selling wine?"

"Well, because it's about their family legacy, and I'm not respecting it. Like, I don't understand because I don't have a legacy to carry on."

"That's disgusting."

"Well, I mean, I—"

"No, Lea. That's not an acceptable thing for anyone to say about you, you have every right to be furious. Are you going to say anything?"

"No, no. I'm not going to make a scene about this. I wasn't even supposed to hear it."

Marie rolled her eyes, setting down her work to look directly at Lea. "Oh, give me a break. Of course you were."

"Well, maybe." She fiddled with the ceramic platter in her hand, turning it around slowly as she spoke. "But I know it's probably a sensitive subject for the family. Moms, I mean."

Marie raised a single eyebrow as she considered the implication. "You mean, because of Anne-Claire?"

"Well, yeah. That must have been devastating."

"I knew Anne-Claire very well. It *was* devastating. But she has nothing to do with what you're talking about."

"I don't know if that's true." Lea set down the platter, baffled as to why she was now playing defense for Gabriel, but unable to stop herself. "She's the reason he wants this place to be so traditional—to honor her, you know?"

"That's what he tells his father, anyway."

"What?"

"He knows that it's a rationale his father responds to, so he uses it." Marie resumed her work as she spoke, totally matter-of-fact. "Anne-Claire was the one who started this whole project before she got sick, but she never had a super-traditional vision. She was a progressive woman."

"Did he work on it with her at all? Maybe she told him something."

"Gabriel was never here. His brother was the one who was taking care of everything. Can you hand me the step stool?"

Lea wordlessly walked it over, more desperate than ever for intel. "What do you mean?"

"Théo dropped out of school to take care of his mother for two years."

Lea reeled at this information, feeling almost physically overwhelmed by it.

"Oh, wow. I had no idea."

"He doesn't talk about it. Please don't tell him that I told you, Lea."

"Of course not, I would never."

That was why he was older than the rest of his classmates. *That* was why he was still in his shitty internship, when he should really be in the early stages of his career. Despite his being much younger than her, Lea couldn't help but think that even now, she probably wouldn't be able to do something like that. She was far too attached to the meticulous level of control she had acquired over her life, not to mention others' perception of her.

And if she ever *did* make that kind of sacrifice, she would feel the need to print it on a tee shirt and wear it everywhere so people would understand that the delay in her professional development was because of an altruistic personal choice, not her own incompetence. That Théo took pains to hide those realities made her feel vaguely embarrassed of herself, and envious of him—and whatever it was in his DNA or upbringing that allowed him to move through life that way.

"Anyway, are you going to say something or not?" Marie asked, impatient. "About what Gabriel said?"

"I don't think I should."

There was a silence between them, Marie reading into Lea's face for an unusually long time before shaking her head and getting back to unpacking her box.

Lea knew that this was a disappointment, that Marie didn't just want her to say something to defend her own dignity but Marie's as well. Unlike her, Lea wouldn't have to maintain a copacetic relationship with every member of the family indefinitely. Standing up to Gabriel, pushing back on his terrible ideas, would be a service to everyone working there—especially those who were in it for the long haul.

But she couldn't. She just wanted a closed circuit of reassurance from Marie that this was, indeed, complete bullshit. The truth was, she didn't know how much pushing back would jeopardize her standing with the rest of the family, and she knew that to engage in any kind of back-and-forth would only lend credence to the unfair portrait Gabriel was attempting to paint of her: the brittle, controlling American woman come to impose her will on an innocent family.

"Marie, look, I know you think I'm chickening out here."

She looked over at Lea above her glasses again, unreadable. "I didn't say that."

"I just need to play my cards close to the chest for a few more weeks, until we're a little further along in the process."

"It's your issue. You should say whatever you want. Or not. I just think if you don't push back against Gabriel now, you're only causing more problems for yourself down the road. You think he didn't try this stuff with me?"

"I mean, no? I have a hard time picturing anyone intimidating you, honestly."

Marie laughed, a hearty warmth arising from her chest. "Oh, honey. Plenty of things intimidate me. Just not that boy."

"Hah, you're probably right." Lea slotted a final book into a neat little cluster next to a vintage lamp, before turning back to this woman whose moments of approval she was coming to bask in. "But I'm going to need you to teach me your tricks."

8

As brutal as the afternoon in the vineyards had been, the tasting dinner was shaping up to be a symphony of Lea's competence. Caroline Saidi, Sofian's favorite niece and the chef Lea had hand-selected to launch the still-unnamed Hôtel Château Victoire restaurant, was the perfect co-pilot for the evening. Alain had been instrumental in helping poach her from one of Sofian's restaurants with the promise that this would be a massive opportunity for her career, even if losing her was a loss to his restaurant group.

And for the hotel, it was a win for its press opportunities as much as for its culinary strength: in a country as old-school about cuisine as France, hiring a relatively unknown, young, female, Moroccan head chef would automatically differentiate them from nearly every other hotel in the region. Caroline could bring early attention to their property, leading even the crustiest dinosaur foodies to visit out of morbid curiosity. But she would have to be a paragon of both gastronomy and professionalism in order to overcome the inevitable—and unfair—additional scrutiny she would be under, no matter how newly feminist Alain's affection for Stephanie was likely making him these days.

But Caroline was just that paragon. The tasting dinner Lea had organized for the family and core chateau staff (including plus-ones) was one of the marquee moments she always included in her rollout, the kind of experience that not only reassured the family of her excellent taste and judgment, but also provided a firsthand look at just how fabulous this hospitality experience was going to be for their inevitable guests.

Lea and Caroline had pored over the night's menu for hours, every detail solidified to properly blow the Lévesques away. While Caroline's ultimate vision for the hotel restaurant was much bolder, they wanted this initial gastronomic greeting to demonstrate her skill while still feeling familiar enough to the Frenchies to earn their trust.

And after the vineyard incident, Lea worked overtime to turn the temporarily expanded wooden dining table on the garden patio into something truly magical. Large, glowing string lights crisscrossed their way under the awning, giving an ethereal quality to the space. The elongated table for sixteen was perfectly set, with elegant-yet-casual place settings and a flowing centerpiece of local wildflowers and short, tapered candles that spanned its entire length. There were hand-written name cards and small favors for every guest, along with a few disposable cameras dotting the table to capture the evening, demonstrating the vision of this hotel which could easily be host to weddings and private events at all levels of opulence.

Lea had also leaned into the formal seating aspect of the evening because, if she were being honest, the ability to control who sat where and with whom she would be in the direct line of sight was very important. She had placed herself with Stephanie and Alain of course, but kept Théo intentionally difficult for her to see—next to Maya, who sat two seats down from Lea on the same side. Gabriel—attending with his latest "girlfriend," an aspiring fashion influencer with bee-stung lips—was similarly removed, next to Philippe and catty-corner from his father, where he could not possibly take issue with the perceived importance of his placement but also could not easily hear what Lea was saying, and therefore couldn't criticize it.

Even Chloë's position had to be considered, as her plus-one for the evening was Joëlle, who was once again back in town and whose relationship status had returned to "blurry." Joëlle was two years older, which at their age implied a host of intricate power dynamics, and they all had to be accounted for. They looked like a matching set, in their chic, understated outfits—even the twin tréma accents in their names felt coordinated—but there was enough of a possibility that they were just friends that Lea took a moment to make sure Chloë wanted to be seated next to her, or if she would prefer the comfortable distance of being across the table.

So far, though, even the cocktail hour of passed appetizers, fizzy glasses of champagne, and herbaceous apéritifs was running smoothly, despite the lack of curation on guests' proximity to one another. Lea was in one of her favorite "power" outfits: a billowy, cream, silk blouse, unbuttoned just enough to show a lacy, fitted camisole, and perfectly pressed, wide, navy trousers that nearly brushed the ground when she wore her highest heeled sandals. Her dark hair was in gentle, face-framing waves, and her rapidly tanning skin was offset by the delicate gold jewelry she'd placed around her neck. She'd even tried a more elaborate foundation routine for the evening's makeup to soften her face, which she at times worried could be dominated by her relatively aquiline nose. She felt genuinely lovely, and the effortless confidence it gave her was translating seamlessly through her behavior, a kind of self-fulfilling prophecy of being taken seriously.

"This is exquisite," Marie whispered to Lea, clinking her negroni to Lea's champagne. "Good job."

"Thank you, but I barely did anything—this is all Caroline," Lea demurred.

"We both know that's not true. You should embrace your accomplishments."

"Maybe you're right." Lea popped a savory petit four in her mouth from a passing tray. "But I also don't like to celebrate until I've stuck the landing."

"You're sticking the landing." Marie briefly rubbed Lea's shoulder in an almost maternal way before heading off to rescue her husband from Daniel's speech on local sparkling.

Lea wiped a tiny, rogue tear from the corner of her eye as she surveyed the evening. It was the magic hour and, between the fading sunset and the glowing string lights, everyone looked truly beautiful. Against her better judgment, she allowed her gaze to wander over to Théo and Maya, who were in a small semi-circle with a few others, laughing about something Lea couldn't quite hear. They did look *good* together: the regal longness of all Maya's extremities—accentuated by her lavender cap-sleeved mini dress that brushed her mid-thighs— were suddenly in perfect proportion to Théo's grand, angular form. And with Théo in freshly ironed khakis and a navy, linen blazer, his lush, curly hair more tamed than usual and radiantly golden in the warm light, one could imagine that this was a party celebrating the two of them. Together, they looked like two Egyptian statues, the kind with elongated limbs who guarded palace entries.

It wasn't just envy that Lea felt looking at them, though there was definitely some of that as well. There was a kind of nostalgia, for a time when she herself might have had an innocent summer romance with a young man who made perfect sense, if only she had allowed herself the experience.

She knew that, despite the very real turmoil of her life at home, the fundamental goodness and stability of Stephanie would forever gift Maya a confidence in relationships that Lea had never known. None of the relationships modeled for Lea prepared her to love and be loved in a way that flowed easily and fulfillingly. So her twenties were defined by relationships that could not work, with men who either did not love her or men who loved her too much. And her thirties, so far, were defined by mostly avoiding men altogether, cutting things off well before they had a chance to confirm her bleak predictions. She both envied and admired Maya at this moment in her life, and only partially because she was alongside someone like Théo.

One of the evening's waiters approached her with a bottle elegantly supported in his right hand, wrapped by a large cloth napkin, offering a refill of champagne. *Just a bit,* she signaled. She needed her wits about her to ensure the evening went exactly as she needed it to, and also to prevent her from slipping into another bout of maudlin self-pity.

Alain cleared his throat, tapping a fork gently on his glass as he rose from his seat at the table. The first course had just been served, and before everyone was to dive in, he wanted to say something.

"I would just like to say thank you to Lea and Caroline for arranging this incredible evening. Seeing my family home made into such a special place, having the people I care about most gathered in this way, it is a very great feeling. I will remember this summer for the rest of my life." He raised his glass, making meaningful eye contact with Stephanie.

"Gross, dad," Chloë deadpanned, she and Joëlle reluctantly holding up the splashes of champagne they were given for the toast. It occurred to Lea that Stephanie had never followed up about how the trip to the stables with Chloë went, and it was seeming increasingly clear that the answer was "not well."

"It is *romantic,*" Alain corrected.

"Here, here! We need more romance in life!" Lea immediately regretted saying something so cloying—clearly her pre-dinner glass and a half of champagne were too much. Alain smiled and gently tapped his glass to hers, and from the corner of her eye, she distinctly caught Théo looking at her, an unreadable look on his face. A tiny shiver rippled through her body.

Before Alain could fully sit back down, Gabriel was tinking his fork further down the table. Lea braced herself and felt the ringing in her ears return as he came to standing; he looked just like the evil prince she often visualized him as, with his feather-light cashmere sweater and flowing, pristine hair. He kept one hand on the delicate shoulder of his incredibly bored-looking girlfriend, who limply raised her own glass.

"I would also like to say something." He paused, all eyes on him. Théo was a few seats behind Lea's turned back, but she could almost feel him holding his breath in anticipation of what his brother might say in such an important moment. "Lea," he turned to her and held her gaze in his typically intense way, filling her with nerves. "Your work here has been very important, and our family estate is making a transformation we did not think was possible. We did not have the vision without you." He paused again, never averting his gaze. "I have not always given your expertise its credit, and I apologize for this. I am a supporter of your work, and of evenings like this. Bravo!"

He raised his glass forcefully as the table echoed his *bravo*, and immediately moved toward Lea to offer her a conciliatory *bise* across her cheeks. She imagined that this strange apology-toast was at least partially encouraged by Alain, and she could feel Gabriel's girlfriend narrowing her eyes across the table, but she wasn't going to make things stranger for the several attendees who had no idea what was going on by refusing his apology.

"Let's dig in!" Stephanie exclaimed, clearly feeling a bit relieved by the display of contrition.

"Yes, let's," Gabriel echoed, passing the basket of bread down his side of the table.

From behind Lea, a waiter seemed to materialize with that same bottle of champagne perched in the crook of his arm like a painter's palette. "May I?"

"No, thank you." She watched as others tipped their glasses in abandon, but she knew herself well enough to know that any indulgence could only happen once the meal was being successfully enjoyed.

And to her delight, it was.

Dinner consisted of small tartlets of all kinds of local vegetables, a creative, creamy take on gazpacho, "French-style" paella with clams and mussels, lacquered duck with citrus roast potatoes, and a blind test of wine for pairing with each course, led by an increasingly tipsy Daniel. Small sounds of gastronomic pleasure rose from the table, along with easy laughter facilitated by the romantic, universally flattering candlelit atmosphere.

From further down the table, Théo was holding court with some of the chateau staff about a family of deer he'd seen on the outskirts of the property that morning while gallantly making sure everyone was served before he filled his own plate with each course. And when he did finally eat, she noticed, it was with a kind of joyous abandon, closing his eyes to savor flavors and remarking loudly on what he loved and heaping his plate high with the things he loved the most. It was like the rest of him: unapologetic, full of life, and not at all how Lea herself lived.

She also noticed Stephanie and Alain growing increasingly close as the evening went on, touching each other in subtle ways—leaning into each other to hear better, brushing fingers as they passed a family-style plate, bumping shoulders when one of them made a particularly clever joke—but it was clear they were becoming much more overt with their affection. If this wasn't their coming-out party, it was pretty damn close, and Lea found that in the rosy energy of the evening, she couldn't have been happier for them, even if Chloë wasn't.

By the time the cheese course arrived, Lea decided it was safe to slip away from the table and properly congratulate the chef. She found Caroline in the kitchen, alone. Her sous chef for the evening had been her teenage cousin, and it was far past his curfew. The dessert course, slices of a delicate lemon mousse cake from a local pastry chef, was sitting on the counter, already perfectly portioned-out on sixteen little plates and ready to serve. Caroline had the look of someone who had just run a marathon, down to the thick, black curls of hair that were finally starting to break free from their extra-tight clip and surround her exhausted face.

"Everything has been incredible. Alain *cannot* stop talking about the duck," Lea gushed.

"The duck *is* quite good. It's one of my show-stoppers." Caroline smiled knowingly, wiping her hands on her apron.

"After this, he's just going to rubber stamp whatever menu you put in front of him. Consider your judgment officially trusted."

"That is such a relief to hear. Thank you."

"No," Lea replied, grabbing Caroline by the shoulders and gently mock-shaking her. "Thank *you*. You have made me look *so* good tonight."

Caroline laughed. "Well, you can repay me by watching the kitchen while I run to the bathroom and change my shirt. My cousin spilled broth on it before the service and I have felt disgusting all night."

"Of course! Go! De-broth. I've got it under control here."

Caroline dashed out of the kitchen, heading up the stairs. Lea immediately set herself to being useful, loading a few plates into one of the dishwashers and wiping down a counter. She felt the easy, generous relaxation that can only come from everything going exactly to plan, and knowing she didn't have anything left to prove. (And the wine pairings she'd finally indulged in didn't hurt, either.)

"Hey, I can do that." A deep, gentle voice came from behind her, just inside the kitchen doorway. Théo.

"Oh, hi." Lea set the platter she was rinsing down and gave her best attempt at a casual smile. "It's really no problem. But honestly, neither of us needs to be doing this. We paid the catering team to clean up for the evening, and whatever isn't finished Marie and I will handle in the morning."

He walked the pitcher he had brought in with him over to the large double sink where Lea was standing, turning the faucet toward himself and filling it with cold water. Given that this was something the waiters were already doing at regular intervals, it seemed like a bit of a pretense—a thought she banished as soon as it involuntarily arose in her mind.

"You don't have to do that, either. This evening is properly staffed!" She laughed nervously.

He looked at her over the top of his rimless, rounded glasses, bent over slightly as he required to comfortably use the sink, a single curl moving into his line of sight. "I like to be useful. I feel like we've been over this."

"Well, I do, too. That's why I'm holding down the kitchen while Caroline takes care of something." *Why did she clarify that Caroline wasn't coming back right away?*

"That's nice of you." He paused, standing up to lean against the counter, where his towering height felt slightly less intimidating. "I actually have been wanting to tell you something, while we're here."

Lea braced herself, feeling her pulse quicken and her stomach drop slightly. She had no idea what he wanted to say, and it filled her with a nervous, fluttering energy.

"You did a really good job yesterday."

The compliment, in this context, felt so intense that Lea could only swerve out of its way. "Oh, yeah, Rémy can make anyone look good."

He raised an elegant hand to his mouth and pursed his lips closed with a single finger, appraising her, remaining silent until she spoke again.

"Well, *and* I had been preparing for a while. It's one of my tentpole activities."

Seemingly satisfied with her acknowledgment of his kindness, he moved on. "And the way you have been handling my brother, especially yesterday, has been really admirable. I know better than anyone how difficult he can be, and it takes a lot of strength to not let him get into your head or stoop to his level."

He kept her gaze in a way that felt distinctly related to Gabriel—they were both from a noble family who inherited confidence like they inherited tennis skills, after all—but his stare felt more respectful, pleading almost.

"Oh," she near whispered, struggling to find her footing. "I deal with opinionated people on these jobs all the time. I get it."

He looked at her curiously, before gently shaking his head. "Not like my brother. I know how wrong what he says to you is."

Lea looked down at her hands, turning her bracelet around as she brought herself to respond. "Well. . . it wouldn't be professional for me to confirm or deny that. But thank you." She re-met his gaze, smiling gently and feeling her confidence.

"You're welcome." He returned her smile. "Honestly, we didn't even think he was going to be here this summer."

"Really?" Lea's heart nearly stopped at the possibility of real, useful Gabriel gossip.

"Yeah. He's had a rough couple of years since Mom died. He hasn't been himself." The euphemistic phrase was paired with the kind of expression that indicated real trouble.

"I see. . ." Lea strove to say as little of substance as possible. "Well, that can happen."

"He's not a bad person. He just can't get out of his own way."

"I know some people like that." She could have been referring to any number of family members, but on some level, she meant herself.

"But you don't deserve to get the brunt of his bullshit just because you're great at this job and he isn't."

Lea felt a warm expanse of joy move through her chest at his kind words and found herself leaning further into him, their arms close as they both leaned them against the counter, her with her back firmly to the sink and him cheating in toward her slightly, almost enveloping her with his stature.

"Thank you," she barely managed to reply. "Did you like the food?"

"I loved it. Especially that paella." He laughed quietly, glancing down at his own hand, now inches from hers on the counter. "But I felt like an animal scraping rice off the bottom of the pan."

"That's what you're supposed to do. If you don't look at least somewhat deranged when eating a paella, that means it wasn't good."

"Did I look deranged?"

"You looked hungry," she offered sincerely, feeling herself pulse with attraction at just how hungry he looked at that very moment.

"That sounds like a nice word for deranged." His eyes were close enough now that she could see every band of color, even in the dimmed light: the blues, the greens, the lavender-grays. He continued, his voice dropping to a lower, more conspiratorial tone. "You know—"

As he spoke, Caroline ran back into the kitchen, shouting a moment-shattering, "I'm baack" in a sing-song voice. Turning the corner to their line of sight, she stopped herself short as her face fell into a light expression of embarrassment.

"I'm sorry, am I interrupting?"

"No!" Lea clarified, a little too sharply. "We're just going over something from the other day. Should we help you bring the desserts out?"

"Oh, no, don't worry," Caroline assured, gesturing for them to return to the table. "You've done more than enough."

Before they could make their exit, though, a notably tipsy Alain bounded into the kitchen from the patio, winding up one of the disposable cameras for another photo.

"Let's go!" he chirped, raising the camera to his eye. "Photo time, the three of you!"

Caroline moved over to the two of them by the counter, and Lea opened a wide space for her to stand between them, so that she would not be pressed against Théo. Caroline settled in and Lea and Théo placed their hands behind her, closing in around her and saying *"Hôtel Château Victoire"* on Alain's command as he took the photo.

Lea felt the air vanish from her lungs as the tiny camera clicked and the little flash bulb popped. Théo's long fingers had migrated to an unmistakable resting place on the small of her back, bearing down with the gentlest pressure as if to be exploring the topography of her body. Lea instinctually leaned back into it, pressing her spine further into his palm, offering up more of the region to canvas. Alain implored them to stay put for another photo, winding up the little camera before they could protest. They smiled again, Lea willing herself to seem casual when every nerve in her body felt electrified from within.

The room seemed to move in slow motion around her, Caroline bounding forward to take the camera from Alain and Théo following immediately after as Lea remained frozen in place, skin burning through her blouse at the exact spot where his hand had been.

9

Days later, Lea was still unable to get the moment with Théo in the kitchen out of her head. In a somewhat pitiful attempt to distract herself, she'd opted to go over her morning to-dos on the sidelines of the tennis court, where Alain was teaching Stephanie some basic moves, something he did regularly these days. Sitting there made her feel a little like the third wheel on a high school date, but it was preferable to the breakfast table, where Théo would undoubtedly stop by to effortlessly butter a piece of bread, bringing it to his full lips while making innocent conversation in Lea's general direction, as if he wasn't tormenting her simply by existing.

She ran over their conversation again and again, reconsidering what she'd said and nervously imagining what Caroline saw when she came back to the kitchen. She thought about his hand on her back, the expanse of it feeling both powerful and gentle, the near-painful eroticism of making such intimate contact behind the literal back of a blissfully unaware third party. She felt almost guilty, as though Caroline was a pawn in a deeply inappropriate game.

"I have to head back in," she managed to call over to Stephanie, doing her best to sound as if she was going to do any real work and not just continue to spiral in the privacy of her room.

"Are you sure?" Stephanie turned around, holding her racket in a surprisingly expert way. "It's not even nine!"

"Yeah, I have a big day ahead of me."

"Don't work too hard!" Alain smiled in her direction as he gestured for Stephanie to prepare for his next serve. *Easy for him to say.*

Lea gathered her things and walked back to the chateau and up to her room, skirting the pool area for fear of seeing a reclining Théo on one of the cream-colored chaises, wearing nothing but the cropped bathing trunks he favored and reading some dense nonfiction book while beads of sweat formed on his smooth, freckled chest.

She also feared that she would find Maya reclining with him, full of girlish sincerity, in one of her colorful two-pieces and reading a summery romcom she probably borrowed from Lea's suitcase. Seeing Théo would be incredibly fraught, but seeing the two of them together would be nothing short of a cosmic punishment for Lea, who could no longer plausibly deny that she was fully, intensely lusting after the same man as her niece.

Whatever had happened between the two of them in those early days, and whatever Théo's reasoning was in pursuing two branches of the same family tree within a span of weeks, it was Lea's job to be the adult in the room. Maya had pulled Lea aside countless times since their arrival to ask for advice, to recount all of the wonderfully smart and funny things Théo had told her, or to get outfit approvals before group meals so as to never look overdone again. While Stephanie was generally aware of her daughter's head-over-heels crush, Lea had always been the person to whom Maya ran with this sort of thing, even well before they were living in the same chateau.

Lea knew that Stephanie's fear—that Maya never allowed herself to get close to boys because of her father's menacing presence—was only half-true. Maya actually tended to be a bit of a romantic, falling in love with the idea of certain boys as much as their practical selves. It was true that she didn't often bring them home, but Lea had been party to many frantic phone calls obsessing over exactly what a vague text message from a boy in "one of the smart frats, not one of the evil ones" *really* meant. Lea had never been like that, not even when she herself frequented frat parties at Georgetown and drank jungle juice in a pastel Lacoste polo shirt with an upturned collar. She always looked at those boys with vague suspicion or disdain, feeling herself go bored underneath them as they jackhammered away at her in their smelly shared bedrooms.

Maya was different. She loved like her mother, open and vulnerable to the raw experience of life. And in Théo, she had found everything a girl like her would want out of a summer in France. He didn't need to be amplified or justified in her retelling of him. He really *was* that amazing, and she was more smitten than she'd ever been. For her aunt to take that away from her in any capacity was simply unacceptable, no matter how much she might want to.

As if hearing her internal monologue, Lea's current round of unproductive obsessing was interrupted by Maya's unmistakable rapping at the door.

"Come on in," she offered from her beloved perch on the blue tufted stool at her vanity.

"Hey, Aunt Lea." Maya slipped into the room and sat herself on the edge of the bed nearest the vanity, smoothing the seat of her rather short sundress as she placed herself down.

Something was wrong.

"Everything okay? You're not hungry?"

"I don't really feel like going to breakfast this morning. There's always so many people there."

"Hah, yes. Breakfast at these big French country homes is always kind of a train station. Sometimes I need to avoid it, too." Lea smiled, holding up the cappuccino she'd secreted away from the upstairs kitchen earlier that morning.

"I should have done that when I woke up. There's even people in the kitchen by now." Maya looked down at her lap, playing with the hem of her dress in her fingers.

"Do you want me to go get you something? No one will bother me in the kitchen if I have my iPad with me. I can be there and back in two minutes."

"No, no. I'm fine." Her lip began to quiver. "Can I actually hang out with you today, though?"

"Oh, Maya, sweetie! What's wrong?" Lea hustled over to the edge of the bed and knelt in front of her niece, holding both of her hands in her own.

"I don't know. Nothing. I just don't feel like myself." She valiantly held back her tears, pausing to gather herself. "And tonight is Théo's birthday, and I feel like he's avoiding me."

Lea reeled at this disclosure, flooded with a mix of relief, sadness, and desire for more detail. She chose her next words carefully.

"I'm sure that's not true. It's been a really busy week around here, and I know that he's doing a lot. I wouldn't read too much into it."

Maya was unconvinced. "I don't think it's that. I can tell it's me."

In some ways, it was exactly what Lea wanted to hear: that Théo was distancing himself from Maya, maybe in an explicit attempt to get closer to Lea without hurting either party (an impossibility men tended to be naïve about in this kind of situation). There was a part of Lea that wanted to gently shepherd her niece in exactly that direction, to help her get over this failed romance and maybe even put her in proximity of one of the several attractive young local men who were often coming in and out of the chateau.

But almost against her will, the protective auntie who'd spent years cultivating this precious relationship, who needed Maya to look at her a certain way and to trust her above everyone in the world except her mother, just couldn't allow herself to see her hurt. Stoking Maya's suspicions that he was no longer interested would be devastating. And worse still, if Maya's hopes were completely dashed, she may insist on leaving the property, taking her mother with her and throwing off the perfect equilibrium that had been established. Alain would be devastated, Lea's work would suffer, and the kismet of this project would evaporate in her hands. So Lea pushed forward with her usual encouragement, only feeling slightly disgusted with herself in doing so.

"That's not true. You are beautiful and smart, and everything a guy like him could want. I'm sure he's just busy right now. He's got a lot going on, on top of all the work around here. Don't read too much into it."

"He basically hasn't paid attention to me since the big dinner."

When he had touched Lea in the kitchen. She burned with the memory of it.

"I'm so sorry, Maya. That has to be tough." She struggled to find words that felt both sincere and comforting, and a betrayal to neither of them. "But please don't take this so personally, at least not until you've talked to him. Have you tried?"

"No way."

"Why not?"

"I honestly don't want to mess this up any more than it already is. Especially since Mom is basically planning her second wedding at this point." She looked up at the ceiling to hold in the fresh tears straining to break free.

"Oh?"

"He's all she talks about. She probably doesn't want to talk to you about it too much because you work for him. But I think she loves him."

"*Loves* him?"

"Yeah. It's basically all she ever talks about with me anymore."

Lea didn't know how to respond without selling Stephanie out, but she also flushed with the increasingly familiar feeling that this was beyond inappropriate. Maya was tall and mature for her age, but she was still so young. To have her this entwined in the specifics of her parents' divorce and her mother's new romance simply wasn't fair.

"I'm sure that's a little awkward."

"Yeah, and it's like. . . I'm not mad at her for it. I get why she would love Alain. He's a really good guy. But I just don't know if *I* want another dad right away. . . I kind of want my mom to just be by herself, at least for a little while. She doesn't even have her own place, you know? And what is she going to do? Quit her job? Live in France? She doesn't even speak French!" Maya was whisper-shouting as the tears freely streamed down her cheeks. "And now her new son hates me!"

"Hey, hey, shhh." Lea wiped her thumbs across Maya's sweet, delicate face, her large brown eyes brilliant and quivering with raw emotion. "You're not getting a new dad. Your mom is not going to quit her job or move to France. Théo doesn't hate you. This is all going to be fine."

"I know, I know. I'm just being stupid." She sniffled hard, composing herself.

"No, you're not. And I'm sorry you're having to deal with all of this."

This was serious. Lea had to do something to help, something better than just repeating that this was all in Maya's head, mostly because it wasn't.

"Listen, we're clearing out the rest of the wine cellar today, just me and Marie. We're gonna set up a little tasting nook down there, too."

Maya seemed interested, if skeptical, so Lea pushed into overselling it.

"It's nice and cool and dark. It's a good place for being sad." She smiled up hopefully at her niece, who didn't deserve any of this. "You help me out today, and then I'll treat you to a beautiful new dress for the birthday dinner tonight, okay?

There's a really nice boutique in town I've been dying to check out, anyway."

Maya threw her arms around her favorite aunt, who wasn't even *technically* an aunt, burying her still-wet face into her hair. "*Thank you.*"

The wine cellar was indeed a great place for being sad, or, in Lea's case, stewing in a toxic blend of guilt and piercing curiosity. Théo was pulling away from Maya, that much was undeniable. And while Maya's initial, overwhelming crush meant Lea could never openly pursue him, perhaps the fact that it ended before it began meant she could at least enjoy him in secret. Maybe they could meet in the vineyards at night, backs against the soft earth, her pulling his weight down on top of herself until she was flattened out of every worry or excuse.

In fact, she allowed herself to imagine while meticulously unwrapping her various decorative baubles that it might even be *helpful* to Maya, since the last thing she needed was an ill-fated love story with some guy she could never keep seeing when she went back to school. Better that it end now, before real investments were made and hearts were broken. Because unlike her naïve, endlessly well-intentioned niece, Lea was experienced enough to know that this kind of fling was only good when it leaned into its brevity.

The corner of the wine cellar was the perfect architectural expression of Lea's desire to be alone with her shame-filled thoughts. It felt, in her heady state, like Gollum's cave: An arch-ceilinged nook carved straight into the dark stone walls, it was only about twelve feet across and lined on all sides with a chiseled stone shelf about counter high and two feet deep. Arranging the display bottles and wine books along the shelf—along with the occasional decorative lamp and the tasting glasses—she felt as if she were appointing the cold, damp interior of her own psyche. And the four wine barrels clustered in the center to form a makeshift tasting table felt as rough and stripped-down as she did, devoid of pretense or elegance.

Because no matter how she tried, she could not help her thoughts from returning to a base, strategic obsession with her own fulfillment. As much as her higher brain looked forward to cheering Maya up with a new dress that afternoon, she had also spent the past hour meticulously reviewing her *own* outfit plans for the evening, which conveniently involved a stop at the boutique she'd suggested. A semi-formal birthday dinner at a nearby restaurant was the perfect excuse to wear something attractive and noticeable without appearing to be catering to the birthday boy.

He had technically turned twenty-four a few days ago, but this Friday night celebration would be the first time they were in the same room for an extended period since that moment in the kitchen. Now that she'd had official confirmation that he'd retreated from other romantic entanglements, she felt comfortable approaching him again after days of avoidance. She wouldn't be direct, of course, but she knew well enough how to brush against him with plausible deniability, or to laugh at his jokes in a way that implied, *"You can have me later if you want me."*

She looked over at Maya, dancing slightly to the pop music emanating from a corner speaker as she carried cases of wine from the entryway to their storage area in the main cellar, and felt flooded with relief that she seemed happier and would be going to the dinner with an unsullied disposition.

"I'm glad to see you're feeling better," Lea offered from the tasting nook, smiling.

"Yeah! I was just in a weird mood this morning."

"Are you excited for dinner?"

"I'm excited for shopping!" She shimmied a little, causing the bottles in the case of wine she was holding to clink against each other. "And the dinner, yes." Her mother didn't raise her to be anything less than well-mannered.

"It's going to be fun, I think."

In her finest English, Marie yelled from across the cellar. "This restaurant is good. I know it since many years!"

"What kind of food is it again?" Maya called back.

"It is French food, but different. From Peru. Lea, tell her it's inspired by Peruvian cuisine. The chef is half-Peruvian."

Lea turned to Maya. "It's a kind of French-Peruvian fusion. I'm picturing ceviche bourguignon."

Maya chuckled. "Sounds delicious, Marie!"

"I know the owner, too. He was my little friend!" She gave one of the gravelly laughs she typically reserved for her own commentary.

"Boyfriend, Marie," Lea corrected.

"Yes, boyfriend. Like Théo." Marie popped out from behind a towering stack of barrels and winked at Maya, who smiled in a way that made Lea's stomach pang with fresh guilt.

It would be a long afternoon.

"Well, the spa is almost done, finally. After a week of Raphaël and his team coming late and leaving early almost every single day," Philippe complained hours later, picking up an olive from the Peruvian-inspired charcuterie tray the restaurant had placed for their arrival. The ample private room their group occupied for the evening was perfect for the pre-meal milling and conversation French people were religious about having before diving into the main event.

"Yeah?" Lea did her best to seem interested, but could barely manage a grunt of agreement as her mind spiraled.

"It's a calamity, honestly, the amount they charge for as little work as they do."

"Tell me about it." She looked over her shoulder briefly, scanning the room for the only person in it who mattered.

She had done everything right: the perfect look; the perfect, casual "hello" on arrival; the perfect positioning of herself within easy conversation distance, and yet Théo was mostly keeping to the far corner of the room, where he was frequently leaning over to translate for a hovering Maya. Their dynamic was as seemingly well-matched as it had been at the tasting dinner several days prior, before he had unmistakably touched Lea and stopped showing interest in her niece.

It had seemed like such a clear gesture to follow him, and here she was, following. Maybe a few days late, but she had gotten the message! How could he not know all of this effort was for him? How could he not find another pretense to come near her, to touch her hand or whisper something innocent-seeming into her ear? What had she done wrong?

"You look amazing," Stephanie whispered in Lea's ear, wrapping a long arm around her waist and pulling her in conspiratorially. She was happy, tipsy, and falling in love.

"Hey, Steph," Lea mustered, clinking her flute with her cousin's in her best approximation of festiveness. She felt sick to her stomach, from Théo ignoring her *and* from the fact that she could never share even one bit of what was happening. This was the first secret she had ever really kept from Stephanie, and doing so weighed on her soul.

"Isn't this just perfect?" Stephanie's head bobbed to the music in their little corner of the room, looking all of twenty-five years old, curls bouncing everywhere.

"Yeah, it's pretty great."

Lea recognized Stephanie's long sundress, deep crimson and bursting with summer flowers. It was the dress she bought for her anniversary trip with Marcus last summer, the dress she never ended up wearing because of the horrible fight they'd gotten into at the airport, the fight which canceled the entire trip. It was satisfying—poetic, even—to see it flowing and settling around her beautiful body as she fell for a man who actually deserved it.

Stephanie adjusted the long golden pendant necklace on her chest, steadying herself.

"Alain says we might go to one of Sofian's bars after dinner, depending on how everyone is feeling."

"Oh, yeah? That sounds fun."

"Do you want to go?" There was no response, so she pressed on, sounding every bit the young girl in love. "Oh, come on, Lea, tell me you'll come with me. I don't want to go alone."

"I probably will! But I think you'll be fine if I'm a little tired." Lea dropped her voice, temporarily forgetting her sadness in elation for her friend. "I guess this means you guys have finally *tongue kissed?*"

"Shh," Stephanie chided, playfully slapping Lea with her cocktail napkin and looking around to make sure no one could hear them. "But, yes, I have. We actually kissed so long last night my lips went numb."

"*And?*"

"And. . . that's that, for now." She paused, sipping her champagne. "Well, a little more."

"A *little more?* Did he, euhh, grab-uh your boobeh?" Lea chuckled, slipping into a comical imitation of a French accent.

"Stop it!" Stephanie whipped her again with her cocktail napkin, laughing openly, too infatuated to take offense.

"I'll take that as a yes."

Before she could confirm, Stephanie was whisked away by her handsome prince hooking his arm through hers and bringing her across the room to meet one of the friends he'd invited. He was polite enough to ask Lea to join them, but she knew it was one of those obligatory couple invitations that wouldn't be appropriate to act on. He wanted to introduce his new love to his friends, and Lea was best staying in her corner, nibbling on a piece of cheese and commiserating about the state of the construction work with the other staffers.

It was moments like this when she found herself returning most masochistically to David and the alternate universe in which she had married him. She could be standing in this same room with a supportive plus-one, just like Stephanie was. But there had been one last, brutal fight about having children—the fact that she didn't want them filled him with a bitter sadness, despite his early insistence that he accepted it—after which she took to sleeping on the couch, as much to avoid any further sex as to initiate a breakup. By that time, it had been months of his touch feeling increasingly like the irritating pawing of a clingy child, months of her growing resentment at how good and sweet he insisted on being despite her coldness, and *years* of contorting herself into the kind of watered-down partner who would be happy with his benign sameness.

But only once in her life had a man truly, unconditionally loved her, and turning her back on that feeling long enough to walk away for good had driven her into a kind of emotional permafrost, unable to receive any man's warmth. And then a very tall college student with high cheekbones and curly hair paid attention to her for a few minutes in a kitchen, and the true depths of her emptiness were laid bare: She was barreling toward forty and totally alone. Her ex had a wife and a child and a Cape Cod-style home, and she had a vanity in a guest suite full of expensive skin creams she'd flown over in a travel bag with ice packs to keep them cool. David was probably at home, curled up with his family watching a movie, while she had spent an hour styling her hair just to get ignored by the cute guy her age-appropriate niece had been flirting with just a week prior.

It all made her want to break down and cry, and she turned to do just that, in the privacy of one of the individual bathrooms. On her way, she ran head-on into Chloë, who had apparently been having a bathroom cry herself, for totally different reasons.

"Is my dad still with *her?*" she asked, seeming every bit her sixteen years despite her preternaturally chic outfit.

Lea had no idea how to navigate that particular minefield, and no patience for softening herself to teenage fragility. "You mean Stephanie?"

Chloë winced at the clarification, or maybe just the name itself. "Yes," she affirmed, looking down.

"Yes, I think they're talking. Is everything okay?"

"It's fine."

As different as their situations were, Lea felt unusually empathetic to Chloë's. "I know that has to be tough."

There was a world in which this was throwing Stephanie under the bus, but she couldn't find it within her to care in her own current state of self-pity.

"It's not even like it's terrible, I just don't want to have to come along for their stupid dates."

"I get it."

Obviously not expecting such a warm reception from a grown-up, Chloë pressed on. "I really don't care what my dad does, honestly. I don't even want to be here. Joëlle's mom said I could stay with them in Switzerland for the summer, but Dad won't let me."

Lea scanned Chloë's incongruities: her highly grown-up Gerard Darel blazer; her tasteful, minimalist makeup; her stature, all contrasted against her undeniable childishness. She was many things, but above all she was a girl who missed her mother, and at a time when she likely needed her most, a feeling Lea recognized and gravitated toward, almost involuntarily.

"Hey, I'm feeling pretty tired. Do you want to head out of here? We can go home and watch a movie or something." It was at least one benefit of adulthood: being able to get the hell out of a place when you wanted to leave.

Chloë looked suspicious, but interested. "Really? We can do that?" It was a move that always dazzled teenagers.

"Yeah, leave it to me to do the talking. I'll get us out of here. You can go wait for me in the car."

"Are you sure?"

Lea smiled, feeling the way she did when she was at the height of her auntie competency with Maya. She looked around at the assembled party and saw Stephanie so absorbed in Alain that her absence would surely go unnoticed, a fact that provided both relief and a twinge of sadness. And a bit further across the room, she caught Théo's eye for just a moment, that familiar shudder coursing through her body as she looked away.

If he was trying to get her attention, it was too late. She turned back to Chloë, determined to salvage the night on her own terms.

"Of course. But you have to show me how to use that crazy stove upstairs. I want to make popcorn."

10

"He *fucking served me*!! That piece of shit *served me*!!"
Stephanie's piercing voice burst through the suite
door, startling Lea awake from her deep afternoon nap after a
long morning of unpacking and washing hundreds of variously
sized towels for the beauty spa.

"Wh-what? What?"

"Marcus. My piece of shit, cheating husband had the
audacity to serve me with divorce papers at the lunch table,
in front of everyone. He found a fucking process server in
the Loire Valley, and he's alleging infidelity *on my part!* He's
accusing *me* of cheating on *him!! That catering whore is living
in my house and he's serving me with divorce papers!!* I can't
breathe. I can't breathe."

Stephanie was pacing maniacally around the room, waving
her iPad as she yelled, tears streaming down her face.

Lea felt the haze of her REM sleep fade into a sinking
recognition of the situation playing out in front of her and sat
upright, gesturing for Stephanie to sit down on the other side
of the bed. "Come here, Stephanie, you have to calm down."

"I can't sit right now. I'm going to kill him. I'm going to
fly back to Newark and I'm going to fucking strangle him with
my bare hands."

"No," Lea calmly asserted, walking over to take Stephanie's shoulders in her hands and steady her. "You're not going to do any of that. You're going to take a few deep breaths, then you're going to tell me what happened *exactly*, then we're going to get a lawyer on the phone."

The two of them breathed together in a slow, steady rhythm at Lea's instruction, hands still firmly on her best friend's shoulders.

"Do you feel better?"

"A little," she flatly replied, still death-gripping her iPad.

"Okay. I'm going to sit down on the bed and you're going to sit wherever you feel comfortable to talk, and you'll explain it to me."

"Okay." Stephanie moved to the plush armchair in the corner by the full-length mirror, in a position across from Lea not unlike what one might see in a therapist's office. "I'm sitting."

"So what the hell happened?"

Stephanie steadied herself, taking another deep breath inward. "So, like I told you, I agreed to not move forward on the actual, legal part of the divorce yet, at his request. It was a favor to him, and in exchange he was not giving me hell about this trip, and he was keeping the cards on for Maya and me. He was making it easy on us." Lea opened her mouth to specify that the cheating, emotionally abusive bastard was not doing her any favors. "I don't want to hear it, Lee."

"Sorry."

"I knew I had the upper hand, and that I would do okay in the divorce when it actually went through." She inhaled hard, steadying her shoulders. "But I also knew it was going to be a huge nightmare and time-suck, and he could do a lot to mess with me financially before a judge actually made him give me a settlement or spousal support or whatever. I'm a public school teacher. I have no savings. I can't afford my life without him, and he can do a lot to railroad me in the meantime. These lawyer fees are nothing to him."

"I understand."

"No, you don't," she gravely corrected, darting her eyes up to meet Lea's. "Your money is yours. My money is *his*, and he controls it. He's cut the cards off on me before over smaller things."

"He's *what?*"

"Lea, come on, I don't want to get into that right now."

"Well, when are we going to get into it then? He can't just keep dangling your financial security on a string like this."

"You think I don't know that? You don't think I've thought about it?"

"I didn't say you didn't."

They'd been through this argument before, a long and tedious road to nowhere. Stephanie gave a final, withering look before restating her initial point. "Just believe me when I say that playing nice with him was my only option to not have a disaster of a summer, or to not come on this trip, which has changed my life." Her chin quivered. "It has *changed my life.*"

It was impossible to be angry at Stephanie when she was so. . . Stephanie.

"So what happened between then and now?" Lea asked tenderly.

"Well, I don't know the full details yet, but I'm guessing that he must have talked to Maya, or saw something online, or maybe he's spying on my phone again. But he must have found out somehow that Alain and I are happy together, that *I* am happy without him, and not planning to come home and get back together with him after my little French vacation." She reclined back in the plush chair, brushing her hair away from her delicate face. "And so he's serving me with divorce papers, alleging infidelity *on my part*. He's trying to ruin my life from three thousand miles away, and I was stupid enough to believe he wasn't going to do this."

Lea's mind was reeling. "But. . . I don't understand. How can this work? He's been cheating on you for months that we know of at *minimum*, way before you separated. You have all kinds of proof."

"Alain thinks this will eventually work out in my favor, but it's going to be a lot harder now."

"Alain. . . Alain thinks that?" Lea's brow furrowed, uncomfortable with how much faith Stephanie was putting in Alain's dubious expertise on the matter.

"Yes, he talked to his lawyer friend, who said it's not going to be as cut-and-dry as it was supposed to be, especially because New Jersey is a state where adultery actually matters."

"Catholics."

"I know. I might have to leave early. . . I might have to go back home." Her voice caught on the word "home," sending her into an open-throated sob as she buried her face in her hands, crumpling in on herself.

"Steph, no, no. Stop. It's going to be okay." Lea moved toward her, but was quickly rebuffed by an outstretched hand.

"I can't do a hug right now. I'm too upset." Stephanie wept uncontrollably.

Lea set herself back on the edge of the bed, defeated. It was true that this was a world she knew nothing about, and her single-gal platitudes probably rang hollow to a woman going through a brutal separation from a vindictive man, with a still-growing daughter to protect. And for as much as Lea had been party to decades of confidences and complaints about Marcus, there was still an ocean of truth she didn't know, and tools at his disposal that someone with her fiercely independent lifestyle couldn't fathom.

She had never felt less helpful, or more removed from the often-intoxicating day-to-day minutiae of life at the chateau. All of her silly little fabric swatches and marketing presentations felt pathetic in the face of such life-or-death issues, and she simply didn't have the experience to offer something meaningful beyond her outstretched arms.

"Do you have a tissue?" Stephanie looked up, her face a Rorschach test of mascara.

"Sure, of course." She walked over to the vanity to grab a box and gently handed them over.

"Thanks." A loud nose-blowing. "I probably look insane." Another.

"You look beautiful, and besides, who cares? We have bigger fish to fry. Why don't we get a lawyer on the phone?"

"I have a call scheduled with one in New York at eight PM our time. It's the earliest he could talk."

"Well, that's good! That's progress right there!"

Stephanie looked up with a flat, unimpressed expression. "Is it?"

"It's better than spinning your wheels with little information." Lea wished she had more default words of encouragement that didn't sound so hopelessly business-like.

"Right."

A light, rapid series of knocks hit the door, causing Lea to jump slightly.

"Come in, Alain," Stephanie sniffled, recognizing his knock. Lea felt a brief flush of *you-go-girl* before returning to the seriousness of the moment.

"Hi, ladies." His face was stricken. "May I come in?" They both nodded.

Clearly he had already been briefed on the situation— before Lea, even, which had implications she wouldn't fully unpack until she had the time—and was coming back to offer more moral support. "I am sorry to bother, but I am so worried. Stephanie, my beautiful, how are you?"

Lea moved aside as he slipped across the room, kneeling before Stephanie and taking her face in his hands. The deep intimacy of the gesture, the history it implied, left Lea with a distinct feeling that she should leave the room, even though it was hers.

"I'm better than an hour ago," she looked up slightly to meet his eyes, eking out a tiny smile.

"This will be alright. I told you. We will take care of this together. You will not have to leave."

Together?

"I know. You're so good to me." She laughed softly, closing her eyes and nuzzling her cheek into his hand.

"Lea, thank you for giving her such good advice as always." He looked up at her earnestly.

"Oh, I really didn't do much. This isn't my area of expertise." She chuckled awkwardly.

"Just listening helps, Lee. You know that." Stephanie met her gaze and managed another tiny smile of encouragement.

Alain jumped on the minor change in tone to keep the train moving in the right direction. "Should we eat something small before this call with the lawyer? You need your strength."

"I have no appetite," Stephanie answered, eyes closing again. He sighed heavily before kissing both of her eyelids with an impossible tenderness. "I need to lie down I think," she whispered.

"Come here, let us lie down together." He slowly brought her to standing. "Is this alright, Lea? I do not mean to interrupt your conversation. But perhaps it is time to sleep." Lea shook her head no, knowing that Stephanie likely wanted nothing more than to lie in the arms of this handsome, kind man she had come to adore over the past month, and she deserved to do just that. He held on to one of Stephanie's hands and led her slowly out of the room, touching Lea's shoulder as they walked by her.

And that was it.

Lea had been consulted, as she normally would when something terrible was happening in Stephanie's life, but only after she had relayed everything to *Alain*. More than that, they barely had a chance to talk about it before Alain swept back in to reclaim her, taking her to his expansive suite to care for her, to kiss her pain away, to make her feel needed and loved.

Lea knew enough about him and his family to know that he was no Marcus, that his desire to protect Stephanie stemmed from his deep wellspring of goodness, likely heightened by the untimely death of his wife. But the end result was, in some ways, superficially the same: a painfully familiar dynamic in which the limitations of Lea's perpetual singleness and the counsel it could provide left her without something compelling to say to her best friend. In that way, she probably didn't have much more wisdom to offer than Maya on the subject.

She moved over to her bedside table to check her phone—her screensaver dousing her with cold reality as always of *forty-one days* until the friends-and-family opening—and saw that it was 5:32 in the afternoon. She hadn't eaten since breakfast, and the ravenous hunger that usually followed afternoon naps, heightened by the chaos she'd awoken to, overtook her with a violent force. And at this hour, the downstairs kitchen would be totally empty, post-lunch cleanup done and pre-dinner prep not starting for another two hours. She fantasized about the hulking blocks of cheese and fresh fruit and crusty bread that awaited her, the large ceramic bowl full of freshly made chocolate mousse the pastry chef had dropped off for tasting that morning, the bottles of ice-cold sparkling water she would greedily drink down while barely scratching the surface of her thirst. In the absence of a long, satisfying conversation with her cousin, she would take it.

Still in her loungewear, Lea padded downstairs unthinkingly. As she turned the corner in the stone basement kitchen, the vision in front of her stopped her in her tracks: Théo, sitting at the counter with a book and a small mug of chocolate mousse, clad in a college sweater and heather gray running pants that made him appear every inch the "rowing team star" fantasy Lea had imagined a thousand times before. One of his long legs stuck out to his side from behind the edge of the island, half-supporting him as he leaned forward on his barstool, messy hair falling *almost* into his eyes and glasses shining with the reflection of the sole countertop light he'd flicked on for the occasion, having kept the garden door closed behind him. She thought of turning back, but it was too late.

"Lea, hi." He looked up at her, setting his book down cautiously. "I didn't expect anyone to be down here."

"Neither did I." Lea crossed her arms over her chest, suddenly aware that her lightly knit sweater, when worn braless in a cold basement kitchen, likely left extremely little of her breasts to the imagination.

"Are. . . are you okay?" He pulled in his leg to sit more upright on his stool, giving her his full attention. "I heard there might have been some bad news today."

"I'm fine. Thank you for asking." If it hadn't been for his brutally unpleasant birthday dinner, and the fresh humiliation of being passed over for a man by the woman who had always put her first, she might have been polite. But in this moment, most of what Lea could feel was exhaustion and a vague desire for retribution.

"Is *Stephanie* okay?" His eyes implored hers, seeming both genuinely curious and vaguely apologetic.

Good lord, even *he* knew about it before she did.

She flushed with frustration, but allowed herself to take in the full experience of him, the slightly ratty sweater with the college insignia, the wildly curly brownish-blonde hair, the full, pink lips that hung just the tiniest bit open as he awaited her answer.

"She will be."

"Do you want to sit down?" He gestured to the barstool next to him, bathed in the small, warm light, a small oasis of connection in the cavernous stone space.

"No, thank you." She didn't feel he deserved such a thing, or that she did, for that matter.

"Well, my father has a lawyer friend who specializes in this kind of thing. He should be able to give some advice."

"Your father has a friend who specializes in American divorces?"

Lea felt a strange kind of contempt for all the privileged, well-meaning men in this family swooping in with such effortless solutions that mostly boiled down to throwing money at a problem.

"No, complicated ones." He held her gaze, uncowed by her intentional hostility.

"I'm pretty sure divorce law is different in the US"

"Of course it is." He stretched slightly as he talked, pulling his arms up in a defiant display of relaxation. "She's very lucky to have you with her, in any case."

"You don't know us."

"You're right. But I know what good friendship is. You really care for her."

"I'm sure that's what it looks like."

He looked across the kitchen at her, almost curiously. A tiny smile flickered across his face. He could tell she was being petulant.

"Yes, that *is* what it looks like." He took a sip from his glass of water. "And it looks like her soon-to-be ex-husband is a bit of a nightmare."

Despite herself, she couldn't resist the desire to bitch— especially since she couldn't do so with Stephanie. "That's an understatement. He's a monster."

"You know him very well, I assume?"

"I've known him since I was about twelve. But back then, he was still putting on this front for Stephanie, trying to seem like the perfect guy. After Maya was born, though, he just got worse and worse." She paused, overcome with a bizarre desire to overshare. "He controlled everything Stephanie did. He told her what to eat, what to wear. He even kept track of what she was reading."

"*Jesus.*"

"Yeah. But he still keeps the perfect-guy front for basically everyone but Stephanie and me. Her mom still thinks he's Prince Charming."

"Why doesn't he keep up the front with you?"

"Because he knows Stephanie tells me everything. He hates me." She took a deep breath, letting the memories of his hatred wash over her. "He used to do everything he could to keep us apart, but it didn't work. Obviously."

Théo smiled. "Obviously." He cleared his throat, looking slightly uncertain for the first time since their conversation began. "And, if you don't mind me asking, who is David?"

"Oh, gosh." Lea felt herself flush. "I'm going to kill her."

"No, no," Théo laughed. "Stephanie just mentioned that name here and there. It's not like it was a frequent topic. But he's someone that you dated? Or, that you're dating?"

The words hung in the air. He was nervous to ask, Lea could tell.

"He's someone I dated, but we broke up almost six years ago. Stephanie still keeps in touch with him. The two of them always got along."

Théo's follow-up question was buoyed with obvious relief. "Is that weird for you?"

"No, no. He's a genuinely good person. I have nothing bad to say about him. And we *really* weren't meant to be together."

"Well, that's his loss. Obviously."

She couldn't bring herself to thank him for his kind, sincere words, or to even internalize them. It felt strangely too intense, too close to the core of what she wanted. But she *did* want to thank him. Lea paused for a moment before moving across the room to the refrigerator, letting her arms fall fully to her sides and revealing the vivid outline of her chest. She grabbed a basket of strawberries from the refrigerator, letting the ice-cold air waft onto her and further firm the details of her breasts before leaping up to sit on an opposing counter directly in his line of sight, setting the small container down next to her and bringing one to her mouth. His eyes never left her, following her smallest gestures.

"Those are excellent," he finally managed.

"The strawberries?"

"Yes."

He swallowed hard, and she allowed her fundamental, relentless lust for him to overcome her mental exhaustion. She transmuted her temporarily limited cognitive ability into reckless honesty.

"Why did you ignore me at your party last night?" She could barely conceal the hurt in her question.

He pulled back as if shaken from a trance, pushing his sweater sleeves up along his forearms and laughing in gentle disbelief. "Why did I ignore *you?* Why did you not come within three meters of me for four days straight after your tasting dinner?"

"You noticed that?"

"Of course I did. I felt like some kind of monster. I figured you wanted nothing to do with me."

"No." There was a pounding silence in the kitchen, almost physical in quality. It seemed to bear down on Lea's chest, forcing the truth out of her. "Everything about that dinner was wonderful."

"Everything? You mean, like the paella?"

"You know what I mean."

His gaze bore into her like a welding tool, so unashamed of the intensity of the experience. "You mean when I touched you while we were having our picture taken."

He wanted her and he had no problem making it known, no problem demonstrating the desire Lea felt the need to subvert and hide.

"Yes," she responded, admitting defeat.

He smiled, a small flick up at the corners. "You should have told me that."

The explicitness of what they were saying, what they were admitting to, filled Lea with a desperate exhilaration. She feared her pounding heart might be visible through her top, along with the rest of her. "I couldn't."

"Why not?"

"You wouldn't understand."

"Why do you insist on talking to me like I'm a little boy?"

"Because you *are* a little boy." She could barely maintain the faux-condescending façade in the face of his profoundly masculine, full-grown beauty, his broad shoulders straining slightly under his sweater as he leaned forward on his elbows.

He steadied his stance across from her, asserting himself. "And you are a grown woman who can't even tell me why she was avoiding me for days on end. Why can't you just be honest?"

"You know why not." She let a strawberry hover inches from her mouth, waiting for him.

"No, I don't." He relaxed his face into a foxlike half-smile, taking his time cleaning off his glasses on the edge of his sweater before setting them back on to enjoy another long, gratuitous look at her. "I want you to tell me."

And suddenly, though she knew he was daring her to say something about how turned on she was, Lea realized that the truth of why she couldn't come near him after the dinner was so complicated, so wrapped up in the niece she could never bear to mention in this context, that the very thought of responding honestly torpedoed the suggestiveness of the moment.

She wanted nothing more than to jump down from that counter and approach him, to let his vast, perfect body wrap itself around her, to feel the sheer weight of him take her under and away from every problem currently filling her overworked mind. But she knew that she did not have this luxury, that the time in her life to follow her desires and make mistakes had passed nearly without incident, and that she was in the phase of things where best friends burst into your room talking about being served with divorce papers before running off with grown men who are better equipped to help her than you are. She had entertained a brief fantasy about this, about him, but the reality of it so close on the heels of such a heavy day reminded her only of how impossibly far apart the two of them were.

As if a light had been shut off inside her, Lea lowered herself from the counter and replaced the strawberries in the refrigerator, re-crossing her arms in front of her chest. She took in the hurt-puppy confusion on Théo's beautiful, Roman statue face and fought an active desire to take it in her hands and tell him that it wasn't his fault, to tell him that she wanted him as badly as he wanted her, and that she would probably spend the rest of her life fantasizing about a few tiny, fleeting moments in a kitchen with him, even though nothing *technically* happened.

But instead, she moved deliberately through the kitchen and back toward the stairwell, turning only once, briefly, to remind him to turn off the light when he was done.

By the time the next morning came, Lea felt as disoriented and uncomfortable as if she'd run a marathon the night before. Her body ached with fatigue, with worry for Stephanie, and with the overwhelming force of the pounding desire she felt in the kitchen with nothing to do but recycle back into her. Now that the unspoken had become spoken, even if she knew it was not in her best interest to pursue him, the most basic motions of getting through her day would be nearly impossible. And as Marie's texts started to compile in her notifications—the software rep was arriving in an hour to walk them through the computer system to manage reservations and set up their online portal, a project Théo was overseeing, no less—she buried her face in her pillow, willing the reality of work to magically disappear.

Given that Stephanie's whereabouts were unknown to her, and likely to be compromised, Lea decided that the best way to solicit an update would be via text message, as ridiculous as that felt coming from a few feet away.

L: Everything okay?

Lea sent the question off to the immediate appearance of "responding" ellipses—Stephanie was already on her phone.

S: I'm good! I'm just getting ready, I'll be helping Philippe with the patio furniture in 30 minutes, don't worry!

L: I don't care about the patio furniture lol. Did you talk to the lawyer? What's going on??

S: I have a call with him at 3 this afternoon, but Alain and I went over everything last night and this morning. He's going to help me if I need it with the lawyers' fees etc but his friend has already been very helpful by email. I'm feeling good.

Much better than yesterday. . .

L: Is divorce law the same in France?

S: No.

I mean, I don't think so. . . But he knew enough to help. Don't worry about me!

I'm not giving into Marcus' bullshit. I will not give him what he wants, which is to ruin my summer and get between me and Alain. . .

I'm going to enjoy my time here while I have it. It's Disco Night!!!

Good lord, it *was* Disco Night. Lea had completely forgotten.

L: You are suspiciously chipper, given everything that happened yesterday. Did you get laid?

Lea looked at her text window with one eye closed, staving off her pre-coffee headache.

S: Getting laid is what teenagers do in the back of cars. I MADE LOVE!!!

L: Congratulations!

And?? Did the BDE deliver on its promise??

S: What is BDE

Lea laughed quietly to herself as she waited, picturing her cousin innocently googling the acronym in a separate window.

S: Oh, come on!! I'm not talking about that!!

But. . . I will say that I came three times

In three different positions

Ok I can't believe I wrote that. . .

But it's true.

L: I'm extremely happy for you and your magical mystery tour of the French orgasm. Now if you'll excuse me, I have to go get ready so I can learn about a reservation management system for three hours.

S: Don't be jealous :P

L: You have no idea.

11

"DISCO NIIIIIIGHT," Alain called from the doorway of the bar space just off the hotel restaurant. The extended group had gathered there in their '70s best to do a little pregaming, but were mostly just scrolling through their phones in silence. He carried a magnum of actual champagne in one hand—not local sparkling this time, but old habits die hard—and as many glasses as he could weave through his fingers in the other.

"What are you all doing?! It's Disco Night!" His outfit of flared white polyester pants with matching vest and wide-open, silky, blue button-down, revealing a large gold pendant nestled in his mostly-gray chest hair, indeed underscored the theme. He set down the stemware and gestured Gabriel over to start serving everyone before fishing for his iPhone and connecting to the freshly installed restaurant speakers, blasting Patrick Hernandez's "Born To Be Alive" as loud as the group would tolerate. It was a delirious, everything-is-amazing party energy that only a freshly laid man could bring to an event. And despite it all, Lea was genuinely happy for him getting to live his Disco Night best life. He *had* been looking forward to this for so long, after all.

Lea, on the other hand, was not thrilled to be spending a loud, humid evening at Sofian's famous Apostrophe, even if under other circumstances it might have been the highlight of her summer given its extensive hype. It had been a brutally long day, Marie unrelenting in the face of her clear lack of sleep. And the software rep had also cut no corners, presenting a fifty-slide deck that explained the ins and outs of both acquiring and managing optimal reservations for the hotel, which had to be finalized before their official social media rollout the following evening.

Making matters worse was the presence of Théo for the afternoon's adventures in IT. Just a week ago, he might have made Lea feel as giddily charged as a high schooler finding out their crush was seated next to them in biology class, but today he only made her uncomfortably hyperaware of herself. He was hurt by her abrupt departure from the kitchen the night before, and did everything in his limited ability while surrounded by unsuspecting others to convey to her that he forgave her, and to tell him what was wrong, and the many other sweet, well-meaning things a twenty-four-year-old would attempt in that moment.

Combined with the flourishing relationship between Alain and Stephanie, unimpeachable in the face of Marcus' cruelty and padded by wealth, it all felt crushingly unfair. She and Stephanie had spent an afternoon coffee going over the details of her divorce plan—which sounded reasonable, but also heavily reliant on Alain's help, financial and otherwise. It was nice to see her feeling better, but it was also another way in which a woman's life was supported by the invisible infrastructure of a man. This was something Lea hadn't experienced in the six years since she left David, and something she always found herself resenting, even from Stephanie. These women couldn't understand what it was like to be her, alone against the world, freedom meaning having to be the grown-up in the room at every possible turn.

It was all enough to resign Lea to a kind of defiant, reckless vow to let herself go tonight. She would show a little too much skin, she would say yes to every glass offered, she would smoke a cigarette or two, she would let herself drown in a sea of bodies on the dance floor. And she wouldn't give a shit what anyone thought about it, because all of this burdensome freedom had to count for something.

Meanwhile, a newfound freedom of its own was coursing through Alain. He strode across the room to his new love, half-dancing to the music and holding his freshly poured champagne aloft. "Ah, Stephanie, magnificent!" He opened his arms to her, insisting she stand up and let him take in the full impact of her look. It was admittedly excellent, with her dark green palazzo pants, boldly patterned silk blouse, platform heels, and deep black curls. She'd banished her grays a few days ago in her bathroom sink, and had brushed out her curls to an almost-frizzy disco queen perfection.

Lea had gone the opposite but equally era-specific route, in a pale blue, mid-length halter dress that tied at the nape of her neck and around her waist before pleating and flaring out around her knees, leaving her back completely open in a very Halston way. (Marie would think it too bold, but Alain would find it charming and that was permission enough.) Her strappy brown leather heels and matching clutch weren't what she would have picked for a full-on costume party, but she still wanted to look reasonably chic. And given that her shoulder-brushing dark hair wouldn't hold the kind of curls Stephanie had going in this humidity, she opted for a low chignon accented by a spray of Baby's Breath.

In fact, the whole family was surprisingly on-theme, even Gabriel's childhood friend Amaury, who was in town and roped in for the evening's festivities. The two of them looked like twin drug dealers, more *Miami Vice* than pure '70s, with light beige suits and pastel shirts pulled out over the lapels. (Lea was surprised that Gabriel's plus-one wasn't one of his usual rotation of semi-professional models, but was relieved to not have to attempt to make conversation with yet another woman limply pushing a salad around her plate.)

Chloë, meanwhile, had claimed an upset stomach and was holed up in her room on FaceTime with Joëlle, but Lea had the distinct feeling that her absence had little to do with illness, and everything to do with seeing her father in a state of festive bliss with the American interloper. She could tell that this was weighing on Stephanie, and was likely part of the reason she'd gone so far to make herself look as exquisite as she did. If she couldn't have the approval of all of this man's children, she'd at least make him triple down on his own infatuation.

And Théo, true to his enthusiastic-but-not-ostentatious approach to most things, had quietly finagled a pair of flared corduroys at some point. He paired them with what was certainly the largest-buckled belt he could find, and a skintight, tucked-in, cream polo shirt with brown and orange piping on the trim that screamed basement rec room. Lea hated that she found this hot. It distinctly made her feel like Matthew McConaughey's character in *Dazed and Confused,* leaned up against the high school way too long after graduation to admire the goods.

"You have to give me confidence for my performance tonight!" Alain called from his perch on the arm of the plush chair in which Stephanie was seated.

"I can't believe you talked me into this," Gabriel chuckled from his seat at the bar. "I thought that era of suffering was over."

"What performance?" Lea asked cautiously.

"You don't know?" Théo chimed in from near the doorway.

"No?" she replied, barely making eye contact. This was supremely annoying, as knowing everything that was happening to and around the chateau—including during leisure hours— was her most powerful locus of control. Making things more unpleasant, from a seat a bit further down the marble bar from Gabriel, Maya spun slightly on her stool, looking about ten feet tall in her bell-bottomed, yellow jumpsuit. Having her directly in her line of sight with Théo made the dance floor feel like a minefield.

"Every year at Disco Night, Sofian has a few of his old friends do a lip-sync performance on stage, and this time Gabriel is doing it with Dad. It's our bourgeois equivalent of a coming-of-age ceremony, I guess." Théo seemed undeterred by Maya's presence between them, keeping his eyes trained on Lea as he explained.

Amaury jumped in, mid-top off on Stephanie's champagne, having politely taken over for Gabriel. "I've been dying to see one of these performances in the flesh."

"Well, you're lucky," Gabriel clarified, "He hasn't done this in a couple of years. I thought he might have entered retirement."

The mental math quickly worked itself out in Lea's mind. He hadn't done this since his wife died. No wonder Chloë was holed up in her room.

"Well, I'm very excited to see this!" Lea offered, raising her glass in his direction for a distant cheers.

Before she could even take a sip, though, a new song poured through the speakers. Stephanie's face flashed with recognition as a familiar kick drum and piano chords rattled through the space. She closed her eyes and shout-sang the anticipated opening lines, *"Oh, what a night!"*

Only, the lyrics were in French and said nothing about a teenage hookup. Her face immediately crumpled into a mix of disappointment, confusion, and embarrassment. Alain burst into laughter, pulling her toward him and kissing her forehead. "No, my dear, this is not the American version of the song. This is the French version!"

"Yes—it's like the American version, but worse!" Théo chided him.

"How dare you! This is your heritage." Alain tipped his glass to let Amaury refill him. He would never allow a guest to serve him, not even a lifelong friend of the family, but the man was utterly *besotted*, too steeped in his ravenous new love to care about formalities. It made Lea smile despite herself.

Carefully pouring, Amaury clarified, "Claude François is not French heritage."

"I thought we banned this song," Gabriel deadpanned.

"I thought we banned Claude François!" Théo added. It was strange, but sort of sweet, to see them share a little brotherly banter. It was like a peek through a tiny window into their childhood, long before whatever had since transpired between them.

Alain rose from the armchair, setting down his glass and taking Stephanie's hands to dance with her. "You cannot ban anything from my home, especially not on Disco Night. And these comments have secured another Claude François song next."

"Is it crazy that I don't know who that is?" Maya asked innocently.

"No," Théo reassured her. "He's a corny French popstar from the '60s and '70s. I would be very worried if you knew who he was."

She laughed gently, causing Lea to flush with a humiliating jealousy. She did not want Théo to speak to Maya, she did not want her to laugh at his jokes, and she above all did not want to be feeling such childish feelings toward her niece. She watched as Amaury joined the brothers and Maya in their cluster by the bar, which only further highlighted that they were the *kids,* while the dancing Stephanie and Alain were the *grown-ups,* and Lea was some third, other thing, once again finding herself in a kind of purgatorial middle ground.

In an effort to suppress the unpleasant blend of emotions rising in her, she walked over to a far wall and leaned back against it, taking a deep sip of her champagne and pulling out her phone to pretend to read an email. It was the only protection she had.

But just as soon as she'd repositioned herself in an area that felt safe and not-pitiful, the music switched—as Alain had threatened, another Claude François song—and Gabriel got up to dance in spite of himself. This one was a much more upbeat number, full of explicit lyrics that blended a love for Alexandria, Egypt, with a love for an entrancing woman named Alexandra. Lea hadn't heard the song in years but found herself humming along and nodding her head involuntarily, eventually slipping her phone back into the hidden pocket of her dress.

Théo, who had taken over champagne service from Amaury, dance-walked over to Lea, mouthing the lyrics with an exaggerated, faux-seductive look on his face. She reluctantly tipped her glass, suppressing a smile at the utter cheesiness heightened by his '70s outfit. As he poured, he looked up from the glass at her, pointedly mouthing a lyric about how the singer *would eat her raw if she didn't stop him*. She loosened her grip on the glass for a microsecond, and it clinked hard against the mouth of the bottle as she re-steadied it. He gave her a brief, smug smirk of victory before moving over to check everyone else's glasses, leaving Lea to quietly fume at her slip-up while gratuitously replaying his lips mouthing those words to her in her mind. *Why did French pop lyrics have to be so. . . French?*

"Everyone, finish your glasses," Gabriel called from the makeshift dance floor. "We have to leave in five minutes if we don't want to be late!"

A full thirty minutes late, their group filtered into their long picnic-style table, reserved adjacent to the dance floor, where Marie, Philippe, their spouses, and several other locals friendly with Alain were already seated. They were in an overlapping chorus of apologies and explanations about how their designated drivers, Amaury and Maya, didn't know the area well and got lost. The truth was that it took about three times longer than planned to pull Stephanie and Alain out of their trance, even with all the reminders that they would have plenty of time to disco at Apostrophe.

And indeed, as soon as she arrived, Lea felt the impeccable energy of the space overwhelm any previous doubts about the night she was going to have. A sprawling indoor/outdoor establishment pouring from a converted carriage house and running right up to the banks of the Loire, Apostrophe was bursting with string lights and mismatched vintage decorations, dozens of heavy wooden tables for dining, several bars, and a massive outdoor dance floor with an elevated stage on its river side, which currently housed a lone DJ turning a curated list of disco classics.

It was the kind of place where people booked a nine PM dinner reservation and stuffed themselves with the unpretentious small plates that arrived in seemingly-endless waves, flagged down servers to replace the upturned, empty bottles of rosé in their ice buckets, and then danced off all the calories into the wee hours of the morning. In short, it was meticulously designed to let French people of all ages come together and make proper fools of themselves, especially on one of Sofian's themed nights, and that was exactly what everyone clearly planned to do.

Philippe shooed away the apologies for lateness by clarifying that all they'd missed were the complimentary welcome cocktails Sofian had sent around. Alain clapped his hand on

Philippe's shoulder while moving in next to him, assuring him that he'd had plenty of time to attack the champagne before arriving (an expression French men of his age were particularly fond of using when describing an indulgence of any kind. . . they *attacked* it).

Nearly everyone in the establishment—and certainly everyone at their table—had gone all out for the theme. Lea was so fixated on appreciating the mosaic of '70s regalia on display—Marie smoking in bell sleeves was nothing short of a revelation!—that she didn't notice as Théo slid next to her on the bench, helping himself to an oyster from one of the trays already ordered by their group. She felt herself tense up at both him craftily arranging himself next to her in the arrival order without her realizing, and the bombastic casualness of him, squeezing a lemon onto his oyster and gulping it down as though it were completely normal to be sitting next to her. He swallowed it audibly and smiled in her direction.

"What are you doing?" Lea whispered through gritted teeth, turning her head away from the table and taking advantage of the overwhelmingly loud ABBA song enveloping them.

"I'm not letting you say I ignored you again," he whispered back, his face barely turned toward her. "Not in *that* dress."

She turned back around to read her menu, willing herself to contain the smile she desperately wanted to let spread across her face. They would not be able to touch, or to really even acknowledge each other, if they were to keep their seating arrangement innocent-seeming to the high-stakes group gathered around them. But knowing that he had chosen to sit with her and exactly why, feeling the heat rise off of him as he gently moved to the music, had her nerves more alight than if they had been tearing off each other's clothes.

Dinner came in the overwhelming rounds of shared small plates she had been told to expect, everyone helping themselves to mussels with chorizo in a broth she wanted to pour in a glass and shoot, blistered shishito peppers, skewers of buttery grilled monkfish, seared lamb chops in a fresh gremolata, patatas bravas blanketed in homemade mayo, and about a dozen other things she greedily heaped onto her plate. She was ravenous—as was Théo, who was sopping up the blend of sauces on his plate with crusty bread between every serving. There was something so intense about seeing him eat like this, the bottomless hunger and hummingbird metabolism of his youth and its inevitable connection to the broad reality of his body, constantly teeming with energy. It was a testament to the incredible food that she was even able to taste it with him next to her, and she was grateful for its distracting deliciousness. And there was of course the rosé, coming to the table in bottle after bottle, keeping them all *just* lubricated enough to outpace the ample dishes filling their stomachs.

Alain must have given ten toasts before the platters of mini desserts arrived, along with espressos and digestives to transition them to the dance floor: toasts to Lea, to Stephanie, to Hotel Château Victoire, to Sofian, to the music, to life itself. She had never seen him—or really, she thought, any man—so beautifully happy and fulfilled. Even Gabriel's usually removed, judgmental stance seemed warmed by the sight of it. He, Amaury, and Philippe's youngest son, Jules, had also blessedly taken Maya into a small cohort toward the end of the table, explaining all kinds of idiosyncrasies about French culture while she smiled on, curious and endlessly charming to explain to, with her long, beautiful, black hair in twin braids cascading down her chest in a very Cher-esque way.

It was a relief made all the more glorious when Amaury announced that he would be heading back with Maya before the dancing started. They were both tired, and he had a seven AM train to catch the next day. (Gabriel put up a small protest, but relented when a cluster of local girls he seemed to know waved at him as they walked by the table.) Lea briefly wondered why *Maya* would want to leave the party early, but she allowed herself the uncomplicated answer that she was indeed tired, or tired of seeing her mother all over Alain, or really anything that didn't have to do with Théo barely saying a word to her since they'd arrived. Whatever the reason, Lea was leaning into the disappearance of her niece, as it meant a blessed reprieve from the guilt she felt for being so achingly turned on by Théo in such close proximity to said niece, who also adored him.

As they waved their goodbyes, Sofian bounded up to the table with a conspiratorial look, grabbing Alain from behind by his shoulders and announcing that it was time for Gabriel and Alain to start getting ready for their performance. Stephanie, giddy from love and ample rosé, asked if she could join to help with his costume, indicating that she knew much more about this performance than Lea herself had been made privy to. Philippe leaned over to his wife, explaining the coming spectacle, and Marie cracked a joke about Alain's apparently infamous performance five years prior.

Sofian gathered the three of them (including Stephanie) to head "backstage," and turned to Théo with the familiar look of a restaurateur about to give a clear order.

"Théo, you must get mojitos for everyone at this table. Tell Johann it is my gift, and tell him to make one extra strong for Marie!" He pointed at her and she laughed, shaking her head in faux protest.

"I guess you're going to fetch mojitos," Lea quietly said to him as the remaining group resumed their raucous conversation and "Staying Alive" by The Bee Gees blasted around them. "Apparently Sofian agrees with me that you make an excellent errand boy." She couldn't quite explain why, but she *relished* demeaning him in this low-stakes way. She loved leveraging her relative authority against this perfect, towering statue of privilege crowned by his halo of golden-brown curls.

"You talk like this to a man who is about to be armed with a secret, extra-strong mojito? I could give it to *you*, you know."

"You would never betray me." She smiled a wide, Cheshire cat-grin, her every extremity buzzing with anticipation.

"I don't know." He smiled back, pulling himself out of the bench and away from the table. "You kind of seem like a woman who could use it."

12

The wait for Théo to return to the table felt impossibly long, and was surely related to the teeming post-dinner crowds approaching each bar and spilling onto the already-packed dance floor. Lea sipped her remaining rosé and did her best impression of a woman invested in Marie's conversation, but every cell in her body was straining toward Théo, who was visible through even the immense crowds thanks to his rowing-team tallness. She could see him nearing the bar to order and even a few girls his age starting to cluster near him, drawn to form a circle around him like flowers around a maypole. Lea banished a brief, derisive thought about *those girls* as the opening beats of "I Feel Love" by Donna Summer started to pulse through the floor beneath her, her all-time favorite disco song whose siren call to the dance floor was impossible to resist anytime, but especially in her current state.

"Excuse me," she shouted to the table over the music, before slipping out to a corner of the dance floor—close enough to the bar where Théo was ordering, but far enough to be out of view from the rest of their party. She did not need Marie seeing her with her eyes closed, hands raised above her head, and back fully exposed, glistening with light sweat as she moved to the music in the crowd. She lost herself in the throbbing rhythm of the song—gloriously, the DJ had opted for the extended mix—and felt a delectable pleasure about her own life that she rarely allowed herself to succumb to.

She was here in this beautiful country, on this incredible job, completely free and independent, dancing to one of her favorite songs in a dress she would have been too shy to wear at twenty-five, feeling more alive and empowered in her body than she'd ever imagined possible. No woman got to live this way in her late thirties, not any of the soccer moms from high school on Facebook, and certainly not the women of her family, most of whom were saddled with multiple kids and a failing marriage by her age. The possibility of it all felt nothing short of intoxicating.

"There you are," Théo yelled down to her, holding two mojitos slightly aloft to avoid the moving crowds. "I thought you would be at the table."

Seeing him caught her off-guard, especially while in this heightened state of rare self-love. "I was! I just had to dance to this song!"

"Well, here is your errand boy with your drink." His words blended in and out of Donna Summer's velvety, ecstatic voice, practically mid-orgasm as she cooed about feeling love. Lea grabbed her glass and tinked it to his in a gentle "cheers" before taking a long, indulgent sip that went straight to her head.

"Is this the strong one?" she asked, stirring the sugarcane in her drink before taking a small bite from its end.

"Unfortunately for both of us, they're *all* extremely strong."

"Good." Between the drinks, the song, and this glowing object of so many younger women's desire wanting *her*, she felt invincible. "Dance with me," she said. "But not too close—they could easily come over here." She moved to the music while gesturing with her bobbing head toward the table.

He looked across the teeming crowd at the group in question and chuckled softly, before bending himself down to lean into her ear. "But what if I have to say something to you, and the music is so loud that you can't hear me unless I'm very close?"

She smiled, eyes closing to the music and the hum of Théo in her ear. "Then I guess you would have to be speaking very close to me."

"And what if," he continued, his lips brushing her earlobe with every word, "one of your little flowers fell out of your hair and onto your back, and I have to grab it to fix it?"

"Then I guess you would have to grab it."

He placed his hand at the nape of her neck, gently touching the knotted fabric holding the top half of her dress, and a full-body chill electrified her spine. "And what if I told you that I could take this dress off with one pull?" He paused, lingering, letting the music fill the silence. "Come with me, or I'll pull it."

Her lips hung open in a slack, breathless intensity. She barely managed a soft cry of acknowledgment before raising her hand, wordlessly, to meet his own, and he pulled himself back from her to smile in that infuriatingly casual way. He led her toward a far corner off the edge of the dance floor stacked high with shipments of extra supplies, just slightly out of view of the crowds. And in her current state—mind altered as much from the drinks as from the blinding elation of being with Théo—she didn't even register how close they actually were to the thick of things, or the revelers walking around them as they sought the extra bathrooms on the far end of the property. Once there, he set both of their glasses down on a lower stack of crates.

Her back was against the wall, and he faced her, towering, a single arm extended to prop him back just enough to take her in fully. The glowing string lights above them seemed to filter him with a kind of cinematographic sheen, lighting reserved for the A-list star they were finally able to convince to join the movie. She willed herself to stay present despite the chaos, to fully acknowledge the experience even as she struggled to believe it was really happening. As if reading her mind, the DJ shifted to "You Make Me Feel" by Sylvester, the loud, pulsing music weaving around them like a kind of protective blanket. Without thinking, Lea threw back her head in laughter, and Théo's gaze moved to her exposed neck for an instant before darting back up.

"What's funny?"

"This song." She smiled. "This whole playlist. It's like the DJ knows about us."

"I think you're just reading into it. I bet anything would make you think of us right now."

"Excuse you." She gently pushed him, willing herself to seem imperious even when her body and mind felt like jelly. "I'm not thinking of us. It just happens that—"

Before she could finish, his mouth was upon hers, his fingers finding their way through the damp hair at the base of her neck to bring her up closer to him. His lips were perfectly soft—softer than she'd even expected—and everything about his kiss seemed designed in a lab to meet her needs. The way he applied pressure, the way he directed her with a gentle assurance, the way he seemed to ask an unspoken permission a microsecond before each new movement or exploration: it was just like the rest of him, exactly what she had hoped for without even knowing it existed.

In turn, she wrapped her arms around his neck and pulled him further into her, ravenous and just inebriated enough to show it with no restraint or embarrassment. With her new eagerness, he became more uninhibited, his hands moving down to her seat to pull her legs up around his hips, pinning her against the wall. His breathing recycled into her own, relentless, devouring her even as he preserved and admired her. And she couldn't get enough, not nearly enough, no matter how much she tried.

"Get a room!" The male half of a dance-disheveled couple shouted as they walked by, his girlfriend promptly elbowing him in the stomach. "Hey!" He laughed, wrapping his arm around her shoulder and turning back to face them as they walked away. "I'm just saying, this is how mistakes happen! Let me know if you need a condom, buddy!"

"Simon! You're disgusting!" His girlfriend suppressed a laugh, herself turning back to offer a half-hearted apology. "Ignore him, have a good night!"

Oh, no.

Théo broke into a hearty laugh, totally unfazed by the danger, and Lea ripped herself away immediately. She shot him a cutting look before blindly walking back toward the dance floor, flushed with a humiliation and regret she hadn't experienced in years. *Fuck, fuck, fuck.* Only in emerging from her stupor did she realize just how dangerous that was: her dress had been pushed up nearly to her waist, feet away from the dance floor that contained the entire chateau, and surrounded by wandering locals who all likely knew the Lévesques by one or two degrees of separation.

Did that couple know them? Would this get back to Alain, or, god forbid, Gabriel? *How could she have been so reckless?*

She shut her eyes to the crowds swirling around her, leaning against the corner of one of the bars to steady herself, willing the panic to subside. When she opened them, clear as if she had been standing in front of her, Lea saw her mother, dressed in one of her "going out" outfits. It was just as Lea remembered, skirt barely brushing her toned thighs, on her way to see a man who wouldn't stick around long enough to get a last name, telling Stephanie that there was money on the counter for pizza and to double-check that Lea had brushed her teeth before bed.

The distance Lea had so meticulously kept between her own life and the life of that woman—chasing after men to the detriment of everything that mattered—suddenly felt erased to nothing. *She* was the one with her dress half-off in the middle of the dance floor. *She* was the woman who didn't realize how old she was, that the party should have been over years ago, that it was time to cover up and have a little dignity. *She* was the one who everyone would be whispering about in the morning.

She folded forward and took a deep breath, willing herself not to be sick.

"Whoa, there you are." Théo appeared behind her, grabbing her shoulder amidst the crowd of drink-seekers. "What are you doing?"

"Stop that," she shook his hand loose, infuriated that he could be so reckless. "Don't touch me here."

"That guy was just being an asshole. Don't let him bother you."

"I'm not worried about *him*! I'm worried about—oh, Jesus Christ, no."

"Oh, my god," Théo laughed, turning to the stage, still somehow totally unbothered by what they'd just done. "I totally forgot about this!"

All at once, the music faded around them as Sofian took the stage and the floor lights raised on the crowd, casting everyone in an unflattering sharpness. The dance floor suddenly felt much too vivid, and their table, still full of familiar faces, was much closer than she had remembered. She felt as exposed as a trapped animal, but couldn't afford to behave strangely, so she took a large step back from Théo and pretended to be very interested in what was happening on the stage.

And to be fair, what was happening on the stage *was* interesting. Sofian was standing in the center of a group of six older French men plus Gabriel, all dressed in a very haphazard kind of drag, holding sparkling microphones to lip sync to an iconic French pop song by Michel Sardou, all about how hard and wonderful it is to be a (then)-modern woman. The original music video *also* featured a gaggle of middle-aged men in drag, and the searing political incorrectness an American would feel watching it clearly still did not translate to a French crowd, even all these years later. Frenchies of all ages cheered and screamed as the assembled group performed, ironically pulling up their skirts to show flashes of thigh as they moved around the stage, valiantly lip-syncing lyrics about the contradictions and pressures of being a woman that still resonated as strangely feminist.

It was too much for her to not comment to Théo, even if it meant leaning back toward him in view of the table.

"I can't believe your father is doing this," she yelled up to him over the music.

"I can. He lives for stuff like this." Perhaps feeling emboldened by her new acknowledgment of him, he let a deeply earnest smile spread across his face and leaned further down to whisper in her ear again. "Actually, when I heard they were doing *this* song, the first thing I thought was that it reminded me of you."

Lea smiled through her internal cringing, mind racing with exactly how she was going to undo this evening and never acknowledge it again. Because although the idea of a beautiful twenty-four-year-old who could have anyone he wanted choosing her was immensely flattering, associating her with a working-woman, vintage female empowerment anthem was exactly the kind of thing a twenty-four-year-old would do. And that he would see her as aspirational, when she was pathetic enough to do what she just did with him, only underscored how much he didn't understand. He lived in a completely different universe than the one she inhabited, and she felt like a lecherous old woman for even attempting to bridge the gap.

But none of this was expressible on the dance floor, so she kept swaying to the music, as if everything were just fine, resolving to act as normal as possible when the group gathered back together after the performance. As long as her eyes were glued to the stage, she could pretend that tomorrow wouldn't come, and that she wouldn't be responsible for bringing *both* of them back down to reality.

13

The bluish-white glow of her iPad in Alain's cavernous office was making Lea so nauseous she could only bear to look at it in brief glances, reading only the absolute minimum before moving her eyes back up to Alain, whose relative composure and energy only made her brutal hangover feel that much worse. She had taken enough ibuprofen that any more would probably present a substantive risk to her liver, but at this point she was considering the risk worth it if it provided her even a fraction more relief. The fact that she allowed herself to drink as much as she did the night before—ending with multiple sugary mojitos no less, which Alain had pushed on the group while still in drag after his performance, and which she was too embarrassed to refuse—felt like a betrayal of her most essential convictions. She was a grown woman, she was on a work site, she was supposed to take herself seriously in order to *be* taken seriously—not move through what was a working Sunday afternoon with the creakiness of someone who had been hit by a car.

And there may not have been a car, but she *had* cheated death last night, avoiding being caught in the most compromised position in which she'd ever put herself. Every time she thought about the chain of events, she felt such a deep pang of regret that her face braced into a grimace, eyes squeezing shut. In harboring such a ridiculous crush on a college student, she allowed herself to behave like one, making out behind the dance floor so aggressively that a drunk twenty-something had the high ground to make fun of them. That his mouth had felt so wonderful on hers, that she could still feel the pressure of his body, his slender, muscled hips between her legs, was only more cause for shame. She knew that she had an awful conversation ahead of her when she could get Théo alone—it was a bolded and underlined bullet on her to-do list—but knowing that she had a plan for letting him down gently but firmly was providing her enough mental clarity to make it through the day's work.

"Can you print this out?" Alain finally asked, struggling to navigate the spreadsheets Lea had emailed him to pull up on his own computer rather than leaning over to see her screen, something that was only compounding her headache.

"Um," she started, not wanting to be difficult. "I *technically* could, but it would have to print out across, like, a dozen pages."

"You can't just make the sheet smaller or something?"

"Let me see what I can do. Hold on."

Today was launch day for a few of the hotel's big social media pushes, as Lea herself had insisted that Sunday evenings were the best times for engagement in this industry. So in every respect, at least in terms of the biblical hangover she was fighting off, she did this to herself. Spending several hours blearily checking URLs, SEO terms, and link connectivity while her head throbbed and her stomach churned with the conversation that awaited her was just going to be what she had to do to ensure *her own plan* rolled out on schedule.

As Alain plucked each reformatted spreadsheet sliding out of the printer, back in his analog comfort zone, his voice turned slightly impish. "It was fun last night, yes?"

She smiled at him conspiratorially, as if nothing were wrong at all. "A little *too* fun, with those last mojitos."

"Ah, it's good to have fun from time to time. You can let loose, you know." The delirious after-effects of the hangover, and of spending so much time in an office that could easily pass for a therapist's, had clearly put Alain in a state of unusual candor.

"I think I let plenty loose last night." She smiled, tucking a falling piece of hair behind her ear as she typed away.

"It was good for you to see my son not so serious, as well."

She felt her heart stop, spinning through the various dance floor escapades he could have witnessed as he was walking from the restaurant interior to the stage. *God, did he know that couple?*

He continued, interrupting her spiral. "I know Gabriel can be difficult, but he really does respect you." She felt herself collapse internally in relief.

"I don't doubt he does," she said, capitalizing on her narrowly missed disaster with extra diplomacy. "And I respect him, too." *Vomit.*

"He has many very good ideas. He always has."

She searched for a sincere compliment to offer, eventually landing on, "He went to an excellent school."

A smile of pride flashed across Alain's face, before looking at her more seriously. "Gabriel and Théo were both always very serious about their studies, but their mother's illness impacted them differently. You must know this."

It was the last thing Lea wanted to talk about, but she had no choice but to play along.

"Oh?"

"Yes. Gabriel did not know how to process it. It was his last year of business school, he was doing his internships, he was under so much pressure. He had always been an intense boy, but he began to do everything with extreme intensity. Too much school, too many parties, too many hours at work. He was barely sleeping."

Despite herself, she was becoming interested to hear more. And she could feel the unspoken supporting character of drugs in Alain's story, but knew better than to pry. "Well, it looks like it's worked out for him now, right?" she offered hopefully. "He's got an excellent job."

"Yes." Alain paused, weighing the appropriateness of divulging further with his obvious need to talk about it. "He does. But this is not the job he wanted. He was supposed to be doing my job."

"*Your* job? Dentistry?"

"No," he laughed. "I'm retired. My job running this estate."

Lea felt the jolt of sudden recognition: she was doing everything Gabriel was supposed to be, if he hadn't messed up in whatever unmentionable way he obviously had. No wonder he seemed to resent her every move.

Alain continued. "One day, he will take over for me here. He is just not quite ready yet. But I sometimes worry that he would already be doing so if his studies had not been disrupted so badly."

The fact that Gabriel would indeed inherit everything, despite Théo's obvious merit and aptitude, filled her with an aching tenderness. She may not be able to pursue him romantically, but she could acknowledge how good and deserving a person he was, and advocate on his behalf in ways he would never have to know about.

"And Théo? He came home, right?"

"He did, yes. He left his studies completely, and took care of his sister for a while. It was too much for me." He sighed, recalibrating his honesty before charging ahead again. "Gabriel needed my help in Lille."

Help? What did that mean, exactly? Lea found the only response that felt genuine to her not-negligible amount of judgment. "I'm sorry, that must have been very hard."

His expression quickly changed to a kind of pained insistence. He did not want her sympathy for his eldest son. "Yes, but Gabriel is *much* better now. He is himself again. He just has so many ideas, and he doesn't know which ones are the ones to fight for."

In spite of herself, she felt a brief pang of recognition in that statement.

"Well, all of your children are very impressive people." After a beat, she tentatively brought the conversation back around to Théo. "And it was really special what Théo did to take care of you all." *Why couldn't she stop talking about him this way?*

"Yes. He probably delayed his career in doing this, because the first years out of school are very competitive in his field, and there aren't many excellent jobs."

There was silence, and much clicking from both of them, before he allowed himself to continue. "I sometimes think this is why he can be so angry with Gabriel, because Gabriel needed so much of my time after his mother passed away."

"Sometimes brothers butt heads," she offered unhelpfully.

"I know, I know. I fought with my brother for years about everything. We've gotten into fistfights over tennis matches." A barely perceptible smile flashed across his face—it was odd seeing someone so sweetly nostalgic over fistfights. "But with their mother gone, the family needs to be a healthy unit. We need to take care of each other." Another pause, another door opened to things that Alain clearly needed to unburden himself of. "And my daughter, you know she does not approve of my story with Stephanie."

"Really? I hadn't noticed, honestly," Lea lied.

"Yes. She is very afraid, I think. That the family will be devastated again. That it's safer for everyone if I am alone."

"And that it would be impossible for anyone to replace her mother, I'm sure."

"No one could ever replace Anne-Claire." He looked at her with a deadly, devastating seriousness. "Chloë knows this."

It was not the first time in her career that a family member had confided in her. And especially after one of those work-hard-play-hard evenings the French were so fond of, there was always an easy shorthand of camaraderie that developed and typically made her job easier, if anything. But being party to these specific confessions from Alain only felt like a *distraction* from their work.

Alain was a very good man, but she was realizing that she saw in him the same lack of boundaries that had kept Stephanie in a kind of purgatory for the past twenty years. Stephanie's endless excuses for Marcus, her softness and predictability when it came to forgiving him, it had created a prison for her that only the possibility of another man could ever *really* free her from. And Gabriel's obvious lack of respect, his childish sexism, his petulance, all of it would inevitably be profoundly limiting to the family once Lea was no longer imposing her will and Alain was increasingly handing over the reins. It was a car crash she could see happening in slow motion and could do nothing to stop.

Perhaps her final act at the chateau could be suggesting that Théo be the one to take over its stewardship, if that were even something he wanted.

As if reading her mind, an unmistakable baritone cut through the dreary business at hand. "Dad?" Théo asked, leaning forward in the doorway, holding himself up with his two arms stretched out on either side of the doorframe above his head, like an Olympic swimmer mid-stroke. He was barefoot, clad in sweatpants and an old fencing tee shirt that rose up to reveal a sizable swath of his lower stomach as he stretched forward. Lea suddenly forgot all about the pounding hum in her head.

"Ah, he rises from the dead!" Alain joked, looking over the small, square glasses positioned at the end of his nose toward his overgrown son.

"I can't believe the two of you are working." He looked over to Lea, not a hint of irony or even humor in his gaze. He looked deadly serious, desperate.

"Someone has to work," Lea replied, grateful she had opted for what was a relatively sexy workday outfit of a sundress and heeled sandals.

"Not on Sunday. This is France." He kept her gaze a moment longer than he should have before returning it to Alain. "Anyway, Dad, Uncle Nico called because he can't reach you. He can't figure out how to open the tickets you sent him."

Alain released an extended sigh of exasperation before checking his personal phone, which had indeed been silenced to many calls. "Nico lives in Brazil," Alain explained across his desk to Lea, apologetically. "He can barely use a computer. You must forgive me."

He hustled out of the office with his phone, leaving Théo just inside the doorway, about ten feet from where Lea sat in the guest chair of the expansive mahogany desk. She immediately drew her gaze back down to her iPad and tapped around busily, afraid to meet his eyes, which she knew would be trained upon her. She could feel him assessing her, challenging her to say something or to even look in his direction. And the fact that she could also sense his coolness, the extent to which last night was just great fun for him, and the start of something even more so, was deeply disorienting. It was Lea who had to hold the weight of what they were doing, the gravity and the danger, and the thousand complications it presented. His ease, totally unpunctured by reality (or perhaps, the experience of age) was a permanent, unflattering mirror to her own anxiety. *Why couldn't she just enjoy this?*

"You're not going to look at me?" he finally spoke, walking into the room and closing the door behind him.

"I'm working," she answered with faux friendliness, eyes down. "And your father is going to be back any minute."

"No, he won't. His calls with Nico always go an hour at least." He dropped his volume to just above a whisper. "And I know you're working. But it doesn't mean you have to pretend last night didn't happen."

"I didn't say it didn't happen," she chastely clarified, re-crossing her legs.

"Do you need help? With the social media stuff?"

"I'm fine. Thank you." She glanced over to the closed door, feeling her stomach begin to flutter with nerves, and took a sip from her ice water, cooling herself. "Seriously."

"At least let me do *something*." He sounded painfully earnest, and enviably unafraid of the potential consequences as he moved across the room toward her.

God damnit. They were going to have to have this conversation *right now*.

She wanted to snap the both of them out of this recklessness, and could think of only one genuinely effective way to do it. Setting down her iPad and standing to face him head-on, she dropped her voice to an icy whisper. "If you wanted to be helpful, you could have started by not pinning me against the wall in front of everyone last night. Do you know how much this could hurt Maya if it got back to her?" She winced at her own verbalization of Maya's name, and her pathetic invocation of this concern when it hadn't stopped her from anything she did the night before. It was not at all how she wanted this conversation to go, but it was the sharpest tool she had against what they were doing.

He looked as if someone had thrown a glass of water in his face. *"What?"* he managed. "I 'pinned' you against the wall? You were practically swallowing my tongue! And since when does Maya have anything to do with this?"

"*Shh*," she hissed at him, blood rushing to her face, as embarrassed by his lack of shame at the possibility that someone might hear. "Keep your voice down! You know very well that she likes you. You were the one that led her on in the first place."

"You have got to be kidding me. I didn't *lead her on,*" he cut back, never breaking his gaze. His whisper had become barely audible through his gritted teeth. "If your niece has a crush on me, that is not my fault. I was nice to her when you guys first arrived because my sister was completely ignoring her, if you didn't notice."

She would never admit it, but she *hadn't* noticed. She'd just assumed that since they were vaguely similar in age, they would hit it off in at least some small way. The million-mile chasm that existed between a sincere college student and an ultra-cool high schooler simply never registered.

Théo continued, unrelenting. "And you never *once* mentioned her, by the way, so don't try to use her against me now because you're embarrassed about what you did last night."

Lea had never seen him like this and found it shockingly sexy, mostly because he was right.

"Listen," she kept her tone as flat as possible, bringing herself to heel. "I am not going to fight with you about this. I have work to focus on."

"Ahh," he chuckled, "so now we're going to make this about work again?"

"It *is* about work for me."

And it was also about how she couldn't have him.

"You can make this about whatever you want, Lea, but I'm not going to pretend last night didn't happen." He took a step toward her. "I'm not going to pretend with you about anything anymore."

"Neither am I." She stepped back in equal measure, clearing her throat and meeting his eyes as intensely as she could manage. "Théo, I'm not doing this to play hard-to-get.

I'm being serious: I *cannot* do this with you. It's not just about Maya. It's also about the fact that this is a job for me, and one that I could actually lose. This is my work, this is my *entire life*. I can't have anything with you, and it's not because I don't want to. It's because the stakes are much higher for me than they are for you." She could barely catch her breath, could feel her voice starting to shake. "If we had gotten caught last night, it would have been fucking catastrophic for me."

"I understand," he whispered back, his breath shallow.

"No, Théo, you actually don't."

The determination in his gaze broke briefly, flashing with the bone-deep pain of something he knew he couldn't argue against. "If this is about how much I don't understand, why didn't you say any of this yesterday? Or in the kitchen?"

She didn't want to hurt him, and she could tell she was. His beautiful blue eyes, bearing down on her from behind those rimless glasses, felt like lakes of youthful possibility she could never allow herself to swim. She attempted to soften, to meet him in his sincerity.

"Because. . ." She paused, thinking of how to properly phrase something she couldn't even admit to herself. "Because I couldn't stop myself." The honesty burned her lungs. "But you should be with someone your own age, not wasting your time with me." She put her hand on his shoulder in as kind a way as she could manage without being intimate.

He looked at her hand with confusion, maybe even a little disgust. "Don't patronize me." He shook her hand loose, eyes unwavering. "I don't want someone my age. I want you."

"But you can't have me. And that's not a challenge." She could feel a heavy ball of sadness welling in her throat, threatening to break into tears. "It's a favor. Please just leave me alone and let me do my job. Please."

"I would never compromise your job." His eyes had become pleading.

"But you *are*. And I wish you weren't." She was barely audible. "But you are. And I'm begging you to stop. Please just leave me alone."

His entire body seemed to be straining toward her with earnestness, with desire, with desperation. "Lea, I don't need—"

"Fine, then I'll leave," she clipped, gathering her belongings blindly, humiliating tears stinging her eyes as she turned away from him and back toward the lobby.

She held her tablet and her folder of Very Important Documents so tightly it hurt, trying to draw power from their authority at a moment where she felt none herself. Even saying goodbye was not an option, as she couldn't bring herself to acknowledge that her actions went against every screaming cell in her body. If she could pretend to be powerful and decisive, she didn't have to admit that she was terrified, scared beyond belief at feeling *anything* this intensely.

Tears now flowing freely with her back turned to him, she could no longer see the intricate wooden door in the dark office, and as if by some cosmic joke, smacked her face directly into one of the four-hundred-year-old door jambs. *"God damnit!!"*

She instinctively brought her hands to her face, slick with tears and now with blood, flowing lightly from her nose as bright sparks illuminated her blackened vision.

"Jesus," Théo called over, instinctively grabbing tissues from his father's desk and filling them with ice roughly grabbed from Lea's glass. "Sit down and tilt your head back, I'll be there in a second."

She stumbled backward onto the first chair she could find, still barely able to see, the panic of the initial injury giving way to a throbbing pain in her sinuses. As promised, Théo returned almost immediately, standing over her and pressing the impromptu ice pack to her face, where he held it for a few quiet moments, lifting it occasionally to see if the bleeding had subsided. She wiped under her eyes to clear away the worst of the smeared mascara, and in doing so briefly looked up at him, his face furrowed in seriousness. It was as if the previous conversation hadn't happened, as if there was only a problem to be solved and his uncanny, selfless ability to solve it.

"It's not broken," he finally observed dryly.

"How do you know?" she asked, muffled under the rag, hurting to move.

"My family plays sports. I've seen a lot of broken noses in my lifetime."

"That's good." The sharpest pain was already beginning to ebb, and with it, her resolve to be harsh in her responses to him.

"Here," he said, handing her another tissue, this one dry. "You keep that pressed to your nose. I'm going to clean your face off a little bit." She did as she was told, and he began delicately wiping, cradling her jaw in one hand as he brushed her skin with the other. "You split your lip pretty good, though."

"I did?"

"Yes, shh, stop talking."

He removed a single piece of ice from the pack and brought it to her lip, which stung enough for her to recoil. Steadying her with his hand still cupped beneath her chin, he whispered again for her to *shh* as he slowly, delicately opened her mouth wider, running the ice along the very inside of her lower lip where the split continued. The cold felt immaculate against her skin, hot from fresh injury and increasing humiliation. She could feel his fingers brushing the edges of her mouth, and instinctively she parted her lips wider, until the ice cube slipped completely from his hand, clattering on the floor by her chair.

The pretense was gone now, evaporated as his fingers slipped more deliberately inside her mouth, her tongue running gently along them, closing her eyes and welcoming the lush, overwhelming feeling. His other hand had migrated to her shoulder where he steadied himself, so heavy with desire that he could barely stand upright, eyes closed and breathing in rhythm with the near-imperceptible movements of his wrist. A gentle, almost mournful moan escaped from him, settling on her ears like honey, warming her from within.

From outside the door, a familiar sound of delivery men dropping off something tedious and important filled the room, boxes sliding along the parquet floor, causing Théo to jump several steps back from her. The trance was broken, and she was freshly horrified at her own behavior.

He looked around in a brief panic to confirm that no one was coming in, and by the time he had re-trained his eyes on Lea, she had already stood back up and was removing the last traces of blood, tears, and melted ice water from her swollen face. She was back to herself.

"I have to go unpack that," she said, entering the professional autopilot mode that was her only defense.

"Okay," he managed, tentative. "Do you want to talk afterward?"

"No," she organized the papers in her folder, avoiding eye contact, determined to return to reality. "I think we said everything."

"You want me to leave you alone." His words were sad but matter-of-fact, the usual boyish need to fight her on every point abated by the exhaustion and whiplash of the past twenty minutes.

"I do."

She didn't, she didn't, *god,* how she didn't want him to leave her alone.

He looked at her for a while, longer than she probably should have allowed, a dozen emotions and protestations passing behind his intense, blue eyes before finally settling on, "Fine. I'll see you around, Lea."

With him safely gone, she threw herself back down into the chair, tissue once again pressed to her nose, feeling deeply pathetic. If she were truly the grown-up in the room she was constantly cosplaying as, she would be able to shut this entire thing down without wavering, she wouldn't be so overcome with desire for him that she let him slip his hand into her mouth just seconds after telling him to leave her alone. There was none of the usual satisfaction that accompanied moments when Lea did something difficult but ultimately right. She knew that ending this now, before she got too invested, was the move she needed to make for both of them. But she only felt awful now that it was done.

Alain returned, almost to the minute that Théo predicted he would, chatting mindlessly about how much of a hassle it was to get Nico to France these days, but that it was very important he attend the end-of-summer party opening the hotel to friends and family, now thirty-nine days away, her screensaver reminded her. She performed her best version of politely interested, nodding and smiling where appropriate, but she could still feel Théo's lingering presence. She could still hear his voice vibrating through her, so deeply embedded as to feel like her own internal monologue.

Hours later—because she couldn't get away from dinner, couldn't say no to dessert, couldn't cut any of the giddy conversations short that had been raised by the official launch of Hôtel Château Victoire's social media presence and the coordinated influencer campaign blowing up everyone's Google Alerts—and Lea was finally dragging her stone-heavy body up the stairs. The launch was a success, at least, even if every bit of the usual joy she experienced from this part of the process was drained by her conversation with Théo, who didn't look at her once during dinner, making only an errant compliment here and there about the rollout, especially when Gabriel said something casually dismissive of the influencers she'd chosen to help promote the launch.

It was as exhausted as she'd ever felt, and her sadness, combined with the last dregs of her hangover headache, left her feeling delirious, ready to sleep for twelve straight hours, and unsure if she could find the arm strength to wash her face.

"Lee, hi," Stephanie said, catching her on the landing of the guest room floor, already in her drapey, caftan-like nightdress with her hair pulled up into a neat, terry cloth turban. "Do you have a minute?"

Lea couldn't even form a coherent "of course," settling instead for a gentle nod.

Stephanie led her into her guest suite, a less common meeting ground for the two of them, but still a familiar one. Despite being its mirror image from a decor standpoint, her room felt nothing like Lea's. Stephanie had dedicated space in her luggage for some of her favorite framed photos and knickknacks, smiling pictures of Maya and Lea and Rachida, her teacher friends, and a beach vacation in which she looked particularly gorgeous. (Lea always wrinkled her nose at the last photo: it was from a double-date trip she and David had taken to the Turks and Caicos with Stephanie and Marcus, a silent reminder of the era in her life where she was actually capable of a long-term relationship.)

Little, hand-carved wooden animals Stephanie had brought back from her first solo trip to Jordan dotted the nightstands, seeming to welcome Lea into the room, and there were also a few too many empty water glasses, which Lea immediately cataloged. The bed hadn't been made that morning, but it all felt like Stephanie, warm and loving and full of history. The two of them sat down across from each other at the vanity and armchair, instantly at home.

"I want you to do me a favor," Stephanie started, unusually frank. "Whoa—is your lip okay? I didn't notice at dinner."

She'd totally forgotten about her split lip, and the sound of yet more tasks to add to her never-ending to-do list was like fresh hell, but Lea was too tired to protest. "It's fine. I hit my face earlier by accident. What's up?"

"I need you to talk to Chloë."

"What? Did something happen?"

"No." Stephanie paused, grabbing yet another half-empty glass of water from the vanity. "Well, nothing that hasn't been happening since we got here. She still hates me."

Lea couldn't help but notice how similar this interpretation of other people's perceptions was to her daughter's. Anything less than an open embrace was *hatred*. "I don't think she hates you."

"Yes, she does."

"Steph, come on. She's a sixteen-year-old girl."

"She's Alain's only daughter. And she won't even look me in the eyes."

"Have you tried talking to her?"

"Yes, about a dozen times. And it only makes things worse."

"Okay, well stop doing that then." Lea chuckled quietly, to Stephanie's horror.

"This isn't funny, Lee!"

"I know. I'm sorry. I'm fucking delirious right now. Please give me a break; I've been working all day."

She couldn't hide the slight edge in her voice, the resentment that she was, indeed, shouldering an enormous responsibility *and* having to turn down the only man she'd truly been interested in for years, while Stephanie's greatest problem was whether or not a high school girl would let her sit at her table.

"You're right. I'm sorry. I just don't know what else to do, and neither does Alain."

"So I'm your best option?"

The fact that this was an HR nightmare—Lea's boss asking her, via her best friend, to convince his daughter to approve of his relationship—simply never occurred to Stephanie, and Lea was too tired to explain it. At the end of the day, keeping Alain happy was key to her success here, and since she was no longer speaking to Théo, she might as well focus on getting that *Architectural Digest* profile by any means necessary.

"Listen, I can try to say something. No promises, but I'll do my best."

"Thank you so much." Her deep, brown eyes rimmed with tears. "Just please tell her that I'm not a bad person."

"She knows you're not a bad person. She's just a sixteen-year-old girl and her mom is gone. She wouldn't like anyone in your position."

"I know, I know."

"Listen, I have to go to bed." Lea brought herself to standing, smoothing out her dress around her thighs. "But I'll try to get a minute alone with her."

In a strange way, the immaturity of Stephanie's request was comforting to Lea. It made the irresponsibility of her own behavior the night before feel slightly less abnormal, a quiet reminder that everyone was fighting their own battle against their worst impulses.

"And seriously, don't worry about it—she's just a kid. She's not trying to be mean." She kissed Stephanie softly on the cheek on her way out of the room, unsure of what exactly she'd be able to do aside from making this poor teenager feel even more awkward and besieged by the adults around her.

Before arriving at her room, Lea stopped at one of the grand, blown-glass windows in the hallway, taller than her and made of many little squares that distorted and framed the scene outside. It was dark, finally, and the stars formed a curtain of pinpricks behind the gently waving trees. Nearer to the chateau, she could see shadows on the illuminated patio stone, a few people lingering long after dinner with their small coffees, talking about something she couldn't make out.

Suddenly, she could feel the hot sting of tears welling at the corners of her eyes, the familiar lump forming in her throat. She would help Stephanie, she would do a fantastic job on this hotel, she would live up to every promise she had ever made to these people. But she couldn't help but feel a twinge of pity for herself, for having to just go through the motions of living in this beautiful castle while everyone else—even the very grounds themselves—got to be *alive*.

14

"No, a little higher. A little higher. A little higher, whoa, not that high!" Lea threw her arms up to stop the two men it was taking to hoist the eighteenth-century chandelier to the proper level above the upstairs kitchen.

They lowered it again slightly, deadpan expressions on their faces.

"I didn't think I would like this light here," Marie observed, looking up at the glorious crystal refracting the light throughout the open, airy space. "But I actually do."

This was Marie for "*it's fucking fabulous.*"

"Thank you, Marie." Lea smiled. "I think it really adds some visual interest vertically, and we're going to need all the lighting we can get for the cooking classes."

"And it was just collecting dust in the attic otherwise," Marie scoffed, always ready with an observation when something was going to waste.

"Is this good, ladies?" One of the men looked over his shoulder, straining to hold the chandelier in place as the women discussed.

"Yes, that's perfect, Renaud." Lea turned back to Marie, gesturing her over to the tidy little group of bistro tables overlooking gardens, away from the noise of the work. "If the lighting stuff is sorted, do you need me to come with you to pick up the wallpaper?"

Marie raised an eyebrow.

"No, Philippe and I are going. It's not a three-person job."

"Okay, well, I just thought I'd offer."

"Well. . . thank you."

With a glance down at her clipboard, Marie was off again, likely more than a little confused as to why Lea was offering to help with such a menial task. She had no way of knowing that it had been exactly three days *(and one hour, and twenty minutes, but who was counting?)* since her last conversation with Théo, and that her only way of maintaining sanity was to avoid him completely. Lea came up with clever reasons to dodge group meals, and added new items to her to-do list as soon as one was crossed off so that her brain never had time to settle into actual awareness. Even now, remaining in the upstairs kitchen was not an option, as it was exposed on multiple sides by large, arched doorways that remained almost permanently open.

She headed upstairs to the comfort of her room, large pitcher of water in hand to prevent needing to leave again until absolutely necessary for the afternoon's menu tasting. Lea's moves now required the militaristic precision of a general protecting his troops from an advancing army. She needed private spaces with only one entry point, doors she could lock, and resting points far away enough from the rest of the chateau inhabitants that no one could cross her path by chance. As long as she didn't have to see Théo, and as long as she had deleted every one of her internet deep-dive screenshots, she didn't have to ache with the thought of him. She could pretend he didn't exist, and just get on with her job.

By reflex, she pulled up the day's to-do list, passing by her dreaded screensaver—thirty-six days until the party—and ran her stylus pen through the most recent finished task:

- *Morning yoga [DEEP BREATHWORK]*
- *Print menus for tasting*
- *Finalize upstairs kitchen lighting*
- *Tasting lunch [CHECK GUEST LIST?]*
- *PR conf. call*
- *Research NJ divorce law*

The tasting menus were sitting on her desk, printed in a deep green ink on a lightly textured, cream-colored paper. She had been looking forward to Caroline presenting her first proposed menu for weeks, but in light of recent events, it mostly just meant a long meal with Théo that Lea couldn't avoid. Her hands smoothed over the paper as she mentally walked herself through how she would behave, what she would say. It was exhausting even to think about.

At least, she thought, looking at her calendar, she'd had the foresight to take the day off tomorrow. It wasn't much, but it was enough to provide her a small light at the end of the tunnel after what would certainly be a day of unwanted emotion.

Under the folder of menus, her phone began to buzz with an unlisted number.

"This is Lea Mortimer." She cradled her phone between her shoulder and her ear, looking out the window at Philippe pruning some flowers.

"Hi, Lea, how are you?"

A chill of recognition shivered through her, slowly setting down the stack of menus. *Of course.* Marcus. He had tried contacting Lea approximately twenty-five times since leaving DC, and she'd thus far managed to avoid him—both his outreach and the leaden thought of him—every single time.

"Marcus. . . hi." Lea set down the menus for the afternoon tasting and felt her breath become shallow with anxiety. "I'm fine. How are you?"

"I'm okay. Thank you for asking." His tone was at its most imperceptible, and he let his words hang in the air for a prolonged period, something he was prone to doing in tense conversations.

"Well," she started, undeterred, "how can I help you?"

"I've been trying to reach you for a while now." *No kidding.*

"Sorry about that. I've been busy."

"I'm sure you have." He cleared his throat, taking his time. "How is it going over there?"

"It's going really well, actually. Thank you for asking." It was almost comical how stilted their interactions were, twenty-plus years into each other's lives. "Did you want something?"

"Yes," he took a deep breath inward, "I'm actually trying to reach my wife."

His wife. Unbe-fucking-lievable.

"Stephanie isn't at the chateau right now, but I also feel like the best way to get her is probably just to call or text her, right?"

"Stephanie isn't *at the chateau?* Is she at *la bibliothèque?*" Lea didn't laugh, so he continued. "Normally, yes, but I've been trying that for the past few weeks now and she hasn't answered me. So I'm trying you."

"I can definitely pass it along that you called. Is that it?"

"No, it's not. I would also love to speak to my daughter, if she's *at the chateau.*"

"Sorry, but she's not here either."

"Fine, Lea. I'll talk to you, then." She braced herself. "I don't know what Stephanie has been telling you, but I'm trying to do this without lawyers, especially since now some of them are French, apparently. *And* I know she's basically re-married at this point, from what I've been hearing."

Lea's heart was racing in the familiar way of her conversations with Marcus. But this time, now that Stephanie was fully released from his influence, he no longer had any leverage against her.

"Right. According to whom?"

"Let's just say that not all of *Alan's* children"—he insisted on a drearily American pronunciation of the name—"are fans of this impromptu love affair."

Chloë. Of course. She probably found Marcus on Facebook, or vice versa.

"I don't know what you're talking about," she feigned.

"I'm sure you don't," he simpered. "But I know what's happening, and I would still like a sliver of a chance to do this the right way."

Her recklessness rose within her. "The *right way?* Weren't you the one who had all those naked photos from the catering girl?"

For a moment, he was stunned. But he regrouped quickly, pushing forward in his narcissistic way. "I'm sure that's the version of things you heard."

Marcus paused for a while, challenging her to take it back, or to apologize. And when he realized she was going to be silent, he assumed his favorite position when a woman became emotionally charged in any kind of argument: belittling condescension. She could hear his infuriating smile through the phone.

"Lea, I'm not going to explain marriage to you." Another long pause. "But I love Stephanie and Maya more than you could ever understand. I want us all to come out of this okay."

She could feel her heart nearly bursting through her hotel polo shirt. "Then maybe you shouldn't have cheated on her. I have to go."

Lea hung up the phone, setting it down on the delicately veined marble countertop and struggling to catch her breath. To be caught off guard in this way felt disorienting and invasive, but it also gave her a not-insignificant flash of resentment toward Stephanie, who was fully tiptoeing through the tulips with Alain at this point, currently at a farmer's market with him, filling their cloying wicker baskets with fresh produce and good cheese for a dinner Maya was going to cook that night.

It wasn't just that she had found another rich man to facilitate her departure from the last one, it was also that this new relationship was one she got to follow to its logical end and enjoy publicly, even if Alain's only daughter didn't approve. Meanwhile, on top of being the hired help whom Stephanie's perfect new boyfriend was paying—even if her rate was a very good one—the most wonderful and exciting attraction Lea had experienced in years was something about which she had to feel unequivocally guilty and ashamed, something she had to completely deny herself out of consideration for others.

It simply wasn't fucking fair.

L: Marcus just called me,

Lea texted Stephanie, wanting more than a little to shock her out of her morning's pleasantness.

S: What?

Stephanie replied almost immediately, shocked.

L: It's fine, I didn't tell him anything. But he's pissed about Alain. Apparently one of the kids has been telling him things. My guess is Chloë.

It was important information, but Lea was still twisting the knife a bit.

S: Are you serious? Did he say what?

L: No. I didn't stay on the phone long, I had to get back to work.

Twist, twist.

L: Do you have a few minutes to talk, actually?

S: Of course. Give me a minute.

The texts proved to not be satisfying enough for Lea's sense of cosmic justice, and she found herself wanting to carry this on via phone, where she could truly lean into her resentment while the moral high ground was on her side. The truth was that so much of what was infuriating her at the moment was inexpressible, and the normal outlet of being able to call Stephanie to complain about her love life was out for obvious reasons. Beyond that, Dr. Miller couldn't see her for another week, and any of the many people in her address book that a normal person might call—family, other friends, even acquaintances—were either people she generally avoided, or people who would never understand.

"Hi." Lea swiped on her phone to answer Stephanie, intentionally keeping her affect as flat as possible.

"Lee, hi. . . I'm *so* sorry he's dragging you into this. I'm absolutely mortified."

Lea had to admit that hearing her voice like this, the tenderness and optimism that made Stephanie the person she clung to even as a child, made it hard to stay angry. But Lea was doing her absolute best to power through and release some of this awful tension.

"Yeah, he's been trying to get me for weeks, and I was doing a really good job of avoiding him. But he called me from an unlisted number today, and I wasn't thinking."

"That's one of his go-tos. I should have warned you. You need to treat Marcus like you're dodging a debt collector."

"I'm understanding that now." Lea gave no acknowledgment to what was obviously an attempt at levity. "Anyway, I really don't appreciate having to deal with this in the middle of a very busy work week. I thought he wasn't even supposed to be talking to you, now that the lawyers are working."

"He. . . he isn't. I'm so sorry."

"It's fine, Steph. We don't have to get into it. But I feel like I need to remind you here that this isn't just some fun summer vacation for me, I'm actually doing a job. And having so many extra personal problems on top of what I have to get done is making my life a lot harder." Lea never spoke this way to Stephanie, and her eyes were squeezed closed as she pushed on, forcing herself to finish each thought.

"I totally understand." Stephanie sounded extremely chastened. "I would never want to make your job harder. Do you want me to leave? Do you want us both to leave?"

Even in her anger, Lea couldn't let herself do something so catastrophically petty. "Of course not. I just want everyone to figure this out so it's not interrupting my workday, okay?"

"You're right, this won't happen again. This isn't your problem."

"Thank you. I have to run."

Lea set down the phone again, swirling with a blend of emotions that was impossible to parse. The resolve she was trying so desperately to sustain in avoiding Théo only worked if everything else was going well. If she had to take unexpected calls from Marcus during her workday, if she had to play camp counselor for everyone else's problems, then she really didn't know if she could make it another six weeks in this house.

At the strike of 1:30 exactly, Lea walked into the hotel restaurant to find that the rest of the group—the family, Stephanie and Maya, Sofian, Marie, and Philippe—were already gathered around the table, eagerly chatting amongst themselves. Stephanie was unsurprisingly seated to Alain's right, and automatically mouthed an "I'm sorry" to Lea across the room as she entered. Her stomach flipped a bit at being the last to arrive, and she made a mental note to double-check her emails when she was done. *Had she accidentally written 1:15?* But being off her game was not an option, so she immediately transmuted her anxiety into productivity, plastering on her most convincing smile and handing out the menus to the assembled group.

As she reached Théo, she was struck by his beauty—it was as if she'd never *fully* registered it before, even in her immense attraction to him. The lighting she had created here was partially responsible for everyone looking so lovely, yes, but Théo seemed to have become more tan in the past few days—maybe working outside with Philippe?—his skin taking on a creamy golden tone that seemed to emit light rather than simply reflect it. His eyes settled on her as she handed him his menu copy, and she felt herself shake slightly as his finger brushed along hers while taking it.

"Thank you," he said simply, bringing his eyes down to the paper. She watched his lips move as he spoke, the soft pinkness of them, their textural contrast with the high, dignified angles of his face.

"Lea, this is magical!" Alain held up the all-day menu from further down the table. "Even the paper looks perfect with this amazing space!"

He was right, and she was grateful that he noticed the coordination. The restaurant truly *had* become a flawless oasis of dusty, understated greens, hand-restored moldings, and unexpectedly modern yet refined furniture.

"Are you going to join us?" Sofian gestured at the open seat next to him.

"Of course," she said, passing out the glasses stacked in the middle of the table to each guest and filling them with water—it chafed at her that she hadn't thought to set the table before everyone entered the room. "I hope everyone is hungry!"

The time had come to finalize the all-day menu, including things like the welcome petit fours for guests. The dinner service would take longer to agree on, but after much back-and-forth with Caroline, the family had acquiesced to her general vision. (They had *still* not decided on the name of the restaurant—something that had become a frequent source of frustration for Lea—but that would be decided in the coming weeks, one way or the other.)

Caroline was insistent that going regionally traditional would be a mistake in such an established wine country, and more importantly, she was eager to embrace the modern, dynamic take on Maghrebi cuisine that her uncle eschewed in his own restaurants. She'd explained to Lea the nuances: he was from a different generation, and his primary concern in building his empire had been to defy preconceived notions and not just have "the little tagine and couscous place on the corner," a perception about which he was very sensitive. But Caroline was not bound by the same concerns— *"I'm already named Caroline, I don't have to prove my Frenchness to anyone"*—and longed to show her family's recipes the respect they deserved, especially in a region to which they had so heavily contributed. So they were going to have a nouveau Moroccan small plates menu, influenced by local flavors.

"Is Caroline joining us, too?" Théo asked.

Meeting his eyes to answer him sent Lea's heart directly into her throat.

"Yes, of course." She coughed slightly, adjusting herself. "She'll be running in and out, but she has a little walkthrough to give us with our meal."

She noticed the way he was holding his menu, gently running his thumb along the paper, as if he were touching her by touching something she had created.

"This harissa eggplant is something I must steal," Sofian laughed, pointing at a line on his copy.

"Does that mean you will put harissa on your menus now?" Caroline chided, pushing the swinging doors open with her backside as she carried a tray of hot hand towels toward the group.

Sofian muttered something sweet-sounding in Darija to her, and Stephanie's face lit up with her teacherly curiosity.

"Can I pre-order extra couscous croquettes?" Philippe looked up at Caroline, warm and paternal as always.

"Don't worry, I made extra of everything." She noticed a confused look on Alain's face as he studied the menu, and set to reassuring him. "They're kind of like polenta fries. They're very good."

"That's what *I* said!" Maya smiled, nudging Théo with her elbow. A hot flash of envy ripped through Lea. *She* wanted to be able to do that.

"I tried them last week when she was testing recipes," Gabriel offered. "They're actually good."

"It all looks *very* good," Marie qualified, unexpectedly returning the conversation to French, "but we need to see the weekly ingredient budget to approve any of this."

"Oh, I actually already sent—" Lea started.

"Lea and I went over this last week," Alain joined in, giving her a millisecond-long look of reassurance. "It comes in under our projections."

"You went over this?" Marie looked up from her menu incredulously.

"Yes, sorry. I thought you'd received it." Lea had completely forgotten to loop Marie in on the estimates, and had offhandedly told Caroline everyone had seen the numbers. An awkward silence fell over the table.

"No, I didn't see anything." Marie returned her eyes to her menu, looking more than a little dressed down at having not been considered.

Down the table, Gabriel let out a barely perceptible snort of contempt, and Théo immediately piped in to cover the sound: "Actually, Marie, that's my fault. I told her that I sent it along with a bunch of other documents from last week and I completely forgot. We're switching over to that Smart Document system, you know, so I'm trying to filter everything through it."

Lea was speechless. This was objectively untrue, they were only using it for legal documents as of now, but she couldn't recall a time in her professional life that she'd ever been saved that way. The idea of someone having her back, of someone helping make *her* look good instead of the other way around, was so foreign as to be incomprehensible.

"Yes, thank you," Lea managed, re-crossing her legs underneath her. "Marie, I should have double-checked on that, but I'd been told you had it."

"I told you that program is a bad idea," Alain chided, shaking his head and returning to English for the benefit of his beloved.

"You're right," Théo laughed. "We should all be handling the hotel records by carving them into rocks."

Lea fought a smile, looking down at her menu to hide her pleasure.

"Well, that is great news that this is approved!" Sofian offered, lightening the mood. "Because this menu is perfect."

"We still have to actually taste it all!" Lea reminded, leaning into the brief reprieve she had been offered.

"Well, on that note, before I bring out the first dishes, I wanted to ask everyone to close their eyes." Caroline positioned herself at the head of the table, standing over them like a master of ceremonies. "I want you to picture yourselves as a visitor coming to this hotel for the first time, maybe coming to this country for the first time. You have read many books about French wine country, you're ready to taste some sauvignon blanc, you've probably watched *Amélie* at least twice to prepare yourself for France."

A quiet laugh rippled through the group.

"And France is already turning out to be better than you'd hoped. The food is delicious, the history is rich, and the countryside is beautiful. And if you were to stop at just the tour guide version, the Eiffel Tower and the macarons and the old-school Loire Valley vineyards, that would be fine. But you're a sophisticated traveler, and you want to learn more about what this country is, who makes it, and who lays a claim to its story. So you come to this hotel, designed by the chic, world-famous LeMor Consulting," Caroline bumped her hip to Lea's shoulder, "and you find so much more than the roast chicken and the upside-down apple tarts. You learn about what France is *today*, the history and color and beauty brought by people like my uncle, and you see just how beautifully our cuisines can come together, how perfectly a white fish with chermoula pairs with a crisp Sancerre. You will return home to your countries with a version of France that few tourists get to see: the real version."

Caroline clapped her hands. "I wish you all bon appétit. I'll bring out the first dishes!"

Lea hadn't realized, with her eyes closed, that she had been facing Théo down the table from her. She opened them and found him staring directly back at her, unmoving in the seriousness of his gaze. The others immediately busied themselves with unrolling napkins and chattering about the menu, but she couldn't force herself to break her eyes from his, no matter how unusual it might have seemed if anyone were to notice.

With the tiniest adjustments of her expression, she tried her best to convey everything: that she was sorry for pushing him away, that she was so grateful for his protection of her, and that she was sick of having to be so reasonable when everyone else got to have fun. Could he forgive her? Could they try this again? Across the table, a tiny smile flickered across his face, and he looked down at the delicate salad that had been set in front of him.

"Bon appétit, everyone," he said, his voice more confident than she'd ever heard it.

Hours later, Lea opened the grand, hand-carved door to her suite. She heard the distinct sound of paper slipping along underneath it as it moved across the parquet floor, and she closed the door behind her urgently, bending down to grab what was an envelope taken from the concierge desk. It was sealed, a simple letter L dashed on its face.

She slipped her fingernail under the seal of the envelope and tore along the joined sides, her heart racing, ravenously pulling out the folded sheet of hotel paper before she even finished opening it. On the page, in a thin, minimalist all-caps handwriting, her eyes devoured the words:

You said you want me to leave you alone, but I don't believe you. And I don't think you do, either.
Tomorrow, wear the black shirt you wore when we were assembling the restaurant furniture, and don't wear anything underneath it.
T.

Breathless, Lea fell back against the door, the glorious relief of permission flooding her body. She didn't have to humiliate herself in apologizing to him, or backtrack, or beg him to touch her again the way he had on the dance floor, all of which she would have done if it had come to that. But she didn't need to say anything at all. She just needed to wear a certain shirt and she would communicate everything. Without even realizing it, her free hand was already moving along her stomach, fluttering with the potential tomorrow held, mind racing as to where that shirt actually was, and if it was clean.

Her hand was moving of its own will, drawing power from the note, which she read over and over until the words were committed to memory. Her fingers slipped beneath the waistband of her slacks and she closed her eyes, feeling possessed by him in a way she never had by a man. She thought back to the scene at the table, to the intoxicating feeling of him anticipating her needs and supporting her when she least expected it. She could hear his voice in her ear, and she opened her eyes to see herself across the room in her full-length mirror.

To her surprise, there wasn't even a flash of shame or desire for modesty as she took in the image of what she was doing.

In this moment, holding that note, she saw herself as he saw her: powerful, desirable, and in total control of her experience. She smiled at herself from across the room, the paper crinkling in her hand as she writhed with pleasure. It was as if she could hear him encouraging her, telling her that she *deserved* to feel wonderful, to enjoy this one beautiful body while she had it, that she had nothing to be ashamed of. Her breath quickened, chest rising, as she murmured his name over and over, shivering at the prospect of seeing him in the morning.

15

Lea had never experienced a breakfast at the chateau quite like this one. Normally, she was so overwhelmed with things to finish and lists to check that she didn't even notice who was having full-blown conversations within two feet of her and who was just passing by to grab a bite. On a normal Monday, someone could set off a bomb during breakfast and Lea would be none the wiser, head firmly buried in her iPad as everyone went flying in ten directions.

But today, everything was in Technicolor and the volume was turned up to eleven. Not only was she unarmed with her typical list of Very Important Things to do, which allowed her perfect control over what she did and did not engage with, she was also wearing the black button-down shirt as requested, bare-chested underneath and feeling more than a little exposed. (She had never in her life worn a shirt like this with no bra underneath it, but there was an invisible thread between Théo's words and her actions that left her helpless to deny him.) And though only *she* would ever know that she didn't even have this shirt clean, that she hand-washed it in the sink before bed last night and gently hung it in front of an open French-door window in her suite to have it ready by morning, she relished the feeling of having dedicated such energy to please him.

She also found herself unable to stick to an eggs-and-berries routine, loading her small plate with several tempting mini pastries, washed down with a whole milk latte. She needed to laden herself with as many carbs and calories as she could manage, so as to prevent her body from floating away with its own electric anticipation. Every person who passed through the doorway to the garden table felt like a potential predator: she needed to be perfectly aware of Théo's entrance without looking like she noticed him at all.

"I didn't know you liked those," Chloë nervously started, pointing to the mini almond croissant on Lea's plate. "I'm usually the only one who eats almond stuff here."

Lea felt as though someone had splashed her overeager face with a bucket of cold water. "Oh, right, yeah. I remember your dad hates almonds. No, I actually love it. Marzipan was my favorite candy as a kid."

"I love marzipan!" She smiled, her long, brown hair framing her effortlessly clear, tanned skin.

"It's really good, right? It's underrated." Lea realized then that she'd never actually considered that there might be foods Chloë liked and disliked. She'd always perceived her as this incredibly cool, untouchable young French girl who was making her cousin's life needlessly difficult. It probably wasn't very fair, looking back.

Chloë reached across the table, emboldened, and grabbed a spoonful of berries. "Are you off today?"

"I am! It feels strange."

"What are you going to do?"

"I actually have no idea," Lea responded with an almost giddy honesty, so rarely able to say such a thing and mean it.

"Hi everyone!" Stephanie and Alain came through the door together, not holding hands but unmistakably joined by their kinetic new-couple energy. They both looked deliriously happy and relaxed, clearly having slept together last night if not this morning.

"You are looking lovely," Alain remarked to Lea, taking note of the extreme care with which she'd styled her half-up, wavy hair and glowing, soft makeup.

Without a word, Chloë left the table, leaving her plate full of freshly scooped berries to head over toward the vineyards, phone in hand.

Trying not to notice but obviously wounded by the actions of this sixteen-year-old girl, Stephanie kept her voice at a newly-in-love lilt. "Everything looks so great. Did you do the pastry run this morning, Lee?"

"No," Lea clarified. "I'm once again just benefitting from Marie's hard work."

Marie waved her hand in a dismissal of the thank you, head buried in her clipboard while the other hand scooped bites of scrambled eggs into her distracted mouth.

"Well thank you, Marie." Stephanie loaded her plate with a few items and filled up her coffee mug, eyes flitting over toward where Chloë had walked away.

"It's really such a beautiful day," Alain added, keeping the morale high. "Not too hot at all."

And it was true: for nearly mid-July, the morning was still relatively temperate, perfect for another breakfast in the garden. Even though the informal dining room on the main floor was set up and ready to accommodate guests, and the proper patio furniture was waiting to be assembled in the increasingly manicured garden, they had kept the big, family-style table. There was just something so convivial about coming to and from this long wooden table, with its picnic-style benches and frequently changing tablecloths. Everyone felt so much more comfortable and casual stopping by to grab a pastry or piece of fruit, and could drop their dishes in the restaurant-grade sinks in the servant kitchen downstairs as they came inside. The daily ritual of walking through the dark stone lower floor into this beautiful, intimate, sunny little garden felt like a mini rebirth every single day.

"Hi." Théo stood at that very precipice, back in the shadow of the lower floor and beautiful, angular face blinking against the sun, even under the awning. He was surprisingly well-dressed for breakfast, in a fresh Oxford shirt tucked into vintage jeans and worn, brown, leather loafers. He took up nearly the entire doorway, having to duck his head slightly to remain within it if he stood on the frame.

"Hi," Marie responded, still not looking up.

Lea couldn't break her gaze from him, no matter how she tried. "There are almond croissants this morning." She gestured the basket toward him, struggling to think of anything else to do with her hands.

"Ah, I don't love almonds." He smiled coyly at her, clearly recognizing her nerves, before stepping onto the patio and walking toward the table. "I'd love some brioche, though."

He walked around to the far side of the table and stood next to her, taking his time as he leaned over the table and grabbed a thick slice of brioche, generously coating it with fresh marmalade. He set it down on a small plate and grabbed the French press, pouring himself a little cup of coffee, all while towering behind her. She knew that he was using every opportunity to sneak a look down her shirt while his father and her best friend were rapt in conversation, and she leaned forward slightly, increasing the gap between her thin black blouse and her bare chest. It was an attempt, with her total acquiescence, to say *"Thank you for giving me what I was too scared to ask for."*

It was a profoundly thrilling dance, but it would be suspicious if she kept showing such an unusual level of interest in him when her default state at breakfast was ignoring everything around her. So as soon as he sat next to her, she excused herself and picked up the rare novel she was allowing herself to enjoy on her day off to move over toward the pool. There, she could linger under a parasol, tantalizingly out of the reach of Théo and any plausible reason for him to come near her.

She wasn't expecting to see Chloë planted there, out of view from the patio, in one of the two cabanas at the far end of the pool. She had holed up with her phone, a towel, a water bottle, and a few other survival items that implied her intent to spend a good while under this secure tent of privacy. Lea signaled a question to her, pointing to ask if she could sit in one of the chaise lounges a little further along the pool. Chloë smiled shyly and nodded, less the intimidating, perfect teen and more the uncertain child, going through what were undoubtedly a million life changes over the past few years and still trying to make sense of them, all while watching the only parent she had left fall in love.

Considering it further, Lea decided that if she were going to try and help Stephanie as she'd promised, this was likely the most natural time. And beyond that, the beautiful heat of Théo's eyes on her at the table was making her feel unusually generous. She didn't just want to do what she'd agreed to, she actually wanted to solve this problem so that everyone would be happy with her, and she could feel better going after what she wanted, herself.

"Is it actually okay if I join you for a minute?" Lea asked, gently.

"Yeah, that's fine."

"You left the table so fast."

"I didn't want to stay." Chloë's eyes stayed trained on the pool.

"Because of your dad?"

She nodded, small and delicate.

"Well, I just wanted to say that I know how you feel, and I would probably feel the same if I were you."

"About what?" She wasn't very good at playing naïve, but Lea played along.

"Well, about him and Stephanie. It's gotta be really hard dealing with all this change at once, especially since you're not even home with all your friends."

"I have friends here, too."

"Oh, I know, but it's still a weird environment—and until you can drive, it's kinda hard to get away." Lea recalled the agonizing dependency she felt before she got her driver's license in Virginia, hoping to create more common ground.

"I guess that's true."

"And if it isn't weird to say, I felt the exact same way about my dad when I was your age."

"What do you mean?" Chloë was looking at her now, still guarded but intrigued.

"My parents are both still here, but they separated when I was twelve and it was awful. They were always bringing new people into my life. I actually got a stepmom, too." She took pains not to mention that they, too, were divorced after a few years, not wanting to cast the figure of a stepmom in anything less than flattering light.

"Did you like her?"

"Well," Lea considered it, genuinely. "I thought she was okay. I mostly just wanted everything to go back to normal, even though normal wasn't good before her, either."

"Mhmm."

"But I realized after a while that being really scared of change wasn't going to keep things the same. It was just going to make the changes harder when they did happen, you know?"

"Yeah," Chloë answered, playing with the hem of her shorts, working up the courage to say the grown-up thing. "I know it's normal for Dad to date again. It just really makes me miss my mom."

"I can imagine. . . but Stephanie will never replace her. And she knows that."

"I know."

"And she makes your dad really, really happy. I promise you that she's a good person, and she won't hurt your dad or you. She won't ever try to replace anyone."

"Yeah, you're probably right." There were tears in her eyes, but Lea knew better than to get closer, or to even acknowledge them. Better to let her regroup on her own terms and regain her confidence. After a few moments of silence, she finally continued. "I shouldn't be so hard on them."

"I think that's really mature of you."

"I guess so."

"I'll let you get back to your day, okay?"

"Yeah, I'll see you around."

It wasn't a perfect conversation, or a guarantee that she would be different going forward, but it was something. And now that Lea was allowing herself to have what she wanted—what she knew, unfortunately, her niece also wanted—she felt an expanded generosity toward everyone else, wanting to make them feel as good as she did. She settled into her chaise to read her book, feeling like she'd balanced her accounts, at least for the time being.

Around her, the chateau seemed as vibrant as she could ever remember it, the rolling greenery extending in every direction gently waved in the breeze; the crystalline blue of the pool refracted a thousand golden threads of sunlight; even the warm red clay of the tennis court seemed to glow in the summer warmth. She never took time to notice these things, always so busy considering how they could be improved or worrying about what remained on her to-do list before the sun began to fall behind the trees. She ran her hand along the cream cushion of the chaise and noticed its contrast with the blue and green flowers of her skirt settling gently around her knees. From behind her, she could hear the distant sound of Théo talking to Stephanie and Marie, the warm depth of his voice seeming to wrap itself around her from behind.

Later, after a snacky lunch standing in front of one of the restaurant refrigerators, letting the cool air blow on her the way it had that night with Théo, Lea sat on the counter, overwhelmed with the possibility of an entire afternoon in front of her and nothing to do. She thought about going to the next town over—where she had taken Maya on their little shopping excursion—and decided that, no, she probably didn't need to buy more things.

"Am I bothering you?" Gabriel turned the corner from the stairs, navy blazer perfectly offsetting his crisp white linen pants.

"Oh, no," Lea scrambled, setting down the large chocolate bar she was nibbling on as she scrolled through her phone. "I'm just reading."

She was suddenly aware that she'd taken off her shoes and was sitting on the counter with her legs dangling, barefoot, her shirt widely open with nothing underneath it. She straightened her posture to minimize exposure.

"I was just at lunch with my father and Sofian. He was asking after you."

"Sofian?" She swallowed the last of her chocolate.

"Yes."

"Just. . . saying hello?" She felt so profoundly off-kilter in exchanges with Gabriel, even more so when they were alone together. Every question was a spring-loaded trip, and every answer was wrong.

"Just asking if you were okay." He walked over to her and swung open the refrigerator door, grabbing a sweet petit four the pastry chef had dropped off that morning.

She slid herself a little further down the counter, further away from him. "I'm fine. Tell him thanks."

He looked down at her new position on the counter and his face dropped for a barely perceptible second. "You don't have his number?"

"What do you mean?"

"You seem to have a good handle on the men around here."

Her heart immediately started racing. "I'm sorry?"

"Don't be so sensitive! I mean you have long talks with my dad, you and Philippe are always working together, Rémy agrees with you about what we should do with the wine. You are getting your way!" He smiled with the perfectly condescending, let's-not-make-this-a-big-deal look French men like him were so fond of.

She felt the same rising discomfort, the same clamminess as when she was left alone in a room with Marcus. It was as if they could smell her nerves, the fundamental disadvantage of her sex and her aloneness. And it was one thing to be pitied by a rich forty-something father, quite another to receive the same degradation from a twenty-something, pretty boy who'd had everything handed to him.

"I don't know what you mean," she started, gathering her courage. "I work with these people because this is my project. You seem to have had a problem with me since I got here, but I am not your enemy. I'm trying to make this place the best it can be."

"Why do you keep calling this 'your project?' You're talking about my family home."

She slipped herself down from the counter and looked him in the eye, willing her entire body not to tremble. "This is *your father's* family home. And he hired me to work on it."

"Or he hired you to bring your friend."

She recoiled. "Excuse me?"

"I'm sure it's just a coincidence that your friend is now *taking care* of him, and he's agreeing to everything you're proposing, including that spa addition that's costing an extra forty thousand euros."

"That addition," she struggled to catch her breath, "is necessary for the water filtration systems."

"But that wasn't in your plan."

It's true that it wasn't in her initial budget, but the contractor she had sent to assess the materials for the spa hadn't sent her the best report. She spiraled at what else Gabriel could be whispering in his father's ear, the ways in which he was painting her as incompetent. Perhaps she *was* still only here because of Stephanie.

"I didn't know until I came to the grounds myself. I didn't—"

She saw Théo turn the corner from the stairs where Gabriel had entered, and the idea of defending her work in front of the one person whose approval she wanted above all else was too much to bear. She grabbed her shoes from the floor and gathered her belongings off the counter, dashing across the room before his presence could even be acknowledged. She slipped down the stairs off the hallway to the wine cellar, where things were dark and cool and she didn't have to engage with any of this.

Standing behind the closed cellar door and composing herself, she leaned against the stone wall and listened to the slightly muffled male voices in the kitchen. She could make out Théo's words, vibrating with a stifled anger.

"What the hell was that?"

"I don't know. She went downstairs." Gabriel sounded chastened despite himself. He probably didn't intend for it to reach quite that level, or to be seen by anyone else.

A pause.

"Can we go one day without your bullshit? Can we pay you to stay in Paris at this point?"

"You'd like that, I'm sure."

"Dad hired her for a reason. She is very good at what she does. Can you please stop torturing her for doing her job?"

"She didn't even know the spa was going to need an addition for a water filtration system. That 'very good' decision is costing Dad forty thousand euros. I know money doesn't mean anything to you, but—"

"Gabriel, shut up. Money doesn't mean anything to *you*. How much did Dad have to pay when you hit that girl with your car? Was that more expensive than the new water system?"

Lea reeled at this revelation: he hit a girl *with a car?*

"She was jaywalking in the dark. And she's *fucking fine!*"

Another long, agonizing silence.

"I don't care. Just stop taking your shit out on Lea." Hearing Théo say her name in this context nearly made her heart leap out of her chest as she stood in the dark stairwell, ear now pressed to the door.

"You still don't believe me, do you?"

"It doesn't matter what happened that night. I honestly don't care anymore. I just want you to stop treating Lea like it's her fault Dad isn't letting you run this hotel. That is *your* fault."

"I'm glad you're able to assess the situation so accurately." Gabriel sounded close to tears. "I'm sure that will really help you in life when someone tries to screw *you* over."

Lea heard Gabriel's Italian leather shoes clicking out of the kitchen and back up the stairs, followed by yet another silence. She silently padded her bare feet down to the wine cellar, unable to breathe, fully aware of exactly what would be following her.

16

A band of clear sunlight from the upper floor flooded the cellar stairs and disappeared in an instant as Théo closed the door behind him. Silence again, before he began descending the stairs slowly, each ancient wooden plank creaking slightly underneath him. He knew that she was waiting for him and, despite her self-preservationist instincts, she was okay with affirming that. She appeared around the corner, standing at the bottom of the stairs on the cold, stone floor, still barefoot. His gaze on her—so earnest, so devoid of judgment, so eager for her to give in to him—nearly broke her heart.

"I'm sorry," she managed. "I'm sorry you had to see any of that." More words burned at the back of her throat: about the scene upstairs, about his gallant defense of her, about how she knew she didn't deserve it.

"It's okay." He descended the remaining stairs and joined her. With her barefoot and him in loafers, on the uneven stone floor, he stood nearly a full foot taller than her. He wrapped his long arms around her to pull her close to him, and she pulled away.

"I'm okay." She cleared her throat, steadying herself. "I'm fine."

"It's okay if you're not, Lea."

"I'm not, but I will be." She darted her eyes up at him, overwhelmed by his presence.

He looked back at her, smiling gently. "Am I too tall?"

"You *are* extremely overwhelming."

"You know what," he offered, looking around him, "let's try this." He took her by the hand and led her just up the stairs until she was several steps off the ground, making them almost perfectly eye-to-eye. "How is that?"

"I *do* feel more powerful." She laughed, still holding his hand.

"You are *too* powerful. I'm almost reluctant to give you more of that feeling."

"No, I'm not. I just have a job. I can get fired by your father at any moment, and your brother is doing everything he can to make that happen."

"My brother is a pillhead idiot."

Hearing Théo say something so harsh—so unloving—was difficult, despite how much Lea wanted to reinforce her own dislike of Gabriel.

"Don't say that," she whispered, leaning her forehead against his.

"You're right," he whispered back, glancing downward. "But I also should—"

"Théo, stop. You don't need to defend me against him; it's not your responsibility, and honestly—"

"Lea—"

"No, please, let me finish. His behavior isn't acceptable, but it's also not something you have to ride in on your white horse and—"

"Lea, seriously, you—"

"I know what you're going to say."

"No, you don't."

"Yes." She smiled, feeling a tenderness toward his youth she rarely experienced. He *could* be a little naïve sometimes, but she was grateful to walk him through those occasional moments of imperfection. "I know exactly what you're going to say. You're going to say that he's had an extremely rough couple of years, and that he's not himself."

"Actually, I wasn't going to say that at all." An impish smile began turning his mouth up at the corners.

"Oh?"

"I don't know how to say this, but I know you would want me to point it out if we're going to have a serious conversation. Your. . . your whole boob is out."

Lea's eyes darted down to her chest, indeed exposed as if she were intentionally flashing him, and she burst into laughter.

Her laughter grew so great, so abandoned, that she practically tumbled forward into him, supporting herself against his chest as he broke into laughter with her, effortlessly lifting her down the stairs to meet him.

"I'm sorry," she pleaded through her laughter, head buried in his chest, too caught off guard to be ashamed. "I've never just walked around without a bra on before. I don't really know the logistics."

"I'm very flattered, Lea." He gently rearranged the collar of her shirt to better preserve her modesty. "But you don't have to find a pretext to show me your breasts. I'm happy to take a look at them whenever you want." He raised an eyebrow, smiling.

"Hey, you asshole," she playfully shoved him, "I did this for you. Don't start pushing your luck."

"Well, you know this was just practice for when I'm going to require you to come to the family tennis match naked."

She laughed again, and rose to her tiptoes to plant a soft kiss on his lips, as happy and un-self-conscious as she'd ever been.

He pulled back to look at her and his smile grew wider, his voice dropping into a quiet joy. "I love this."

"What?"

He paused, biting his lower lip slightly as he considered his words. "Making you laugh."

"Oh." She blushed, not having considered the possibility. "I laugh all the time."

"You actually don't, Lea. You have everything so under control, always. It's like you don't want to let yourself have fun."

"I have fun," she offered lamely.

"You know what I mean." He took her by the hand and led her to the tasting nook, where they sat on the floor, leaning against the carved stone ledge in the wall. "It's like any time you're enjoying yourself too much, you have to torture yourself about it until you're serious again. Sometimes things can just be good, you know?"

She smoothed out her skirt as she listened, taking it in. It was true, and something it had taken her about a dozen sessions with Dr. Miller to even identify herself.

"You're right. I should let go more often."

"I know it's hard, trust me."

"How do you know?"

There was no prickliness in her question: she wanted to learn about him.

"Well," he removed his glasses, cleaning them on the end of his shirt. "There were a couple of years where things weren't really very fun around here, either."

"Because of your mother."

She feared the comment might be too forward, but he seemed to immediately relax in it.

"Yes," he offered. "Losing her was very hard. On everybody."

"Would you tell me about her?" Without realizing it, they had both turned to face forward, taking solace in the heightened verbal intimacy allowed by not making eye contact.

"Of course." He paused, breathing in slowly. "She was beautiful, very tall, and blonde. People always thought she was Nordic, but she was one hundred percent French."

"I saw pictures. She *did* look Nordic, like a Swedish model or something."

"Hah! Exactly. And she was so brilliant. She was actually a physics professor, before she got sick."

"I didn't know that! That's really impressive."

He nodded, making a gentle sound of agreement. "And when she *did* get sick, no one really knew how to deal with it. My brother was getting into a lot of trouble, and I think sometimes that my dad kind of focused on that because it was something he felt like he could fix, and we knew we couldn't fix my mother."

"You were taking care of her then, right?"

"And my sister. My mom wasn't capable of taking care of anything, and my dad was gone every weekend with my brother. Chloë was only twelve."

"It must have been so hard taking care of your mother."

"Ahh." He ran a finger across his lip, taking his time. "I actually liked a lot of it. It kind of felt like getting to repay the favor from when I was a baby. You know, feeding her, brushing her hair."

Lea imagined the scene and couldn't help but nestle her head further into the crook of his neck. "I know your dad must really appreciate everything you did."

"He does." Théo shifted slightly, cleared his throat. "Of course he does. He just isn't always the best at dealing with difficult stuff head-on, you know?"

Lea's mind immediately went to Stephanie, to her ongoing vulnerability in refusing to deal with her own problems. "I know what you mean."

"And there's a lot he doesn't even know other people are doing behind the scenes to make everything work so smoothly. Including you, by the way." He bumped her with his shoulder.

"Thank you. It's really important to me to do a good job here."

"I know. And you're doing an *amazing* job." He turned to face her, moving a lock of hair that had fallen in her eyes. "I promise I would tell you if you weren't."

She darted her eyes away again, unable to not forge ahead into another taboo subject. "I'm sorry to bring up your brother again, but you called him. . . a pillhead?"

"Oh." He coughed, looking abashed at his former harshness. "Yeah, I mean, I shouldn't have said that. I don't know what he's actually doing now, and he claims to be done with that stuff. But yeah, Adderall, Vyvanse, whatever uppers he could get his hands on. He was fully addicted to them in college."

"After your mother died?"

"Please." He looked over at her, eager to put a finer point on his assessment. "That's what Dad tells himself, but he was doing all kinds of shit even before that. He used to deal coke in prep school."

"Wow." The elite French liminal space of preparatory school, somewhere between high school and college and perpetually outside of American understanding, still felt like a bad place to be dealing cocaine.

"They used to bring girls to their rugby parties and take their shirts at the door as an 'entry fee.' He hit a girl with his car when he was wasted. My dad has spent a lot of time and money making sure Gabriel gets to live the life he was supposed to, no matter what terrible shit he does." Another heavy pause. "No matter how much he doesn't deserve it."

"I don't know what to say. Is she okay, at least?"

"She's okay, thank god. And you don't have to say anything. Just be careful around him."

"You think he would do something to me?"

"No," Théo clarified, a deep reassurance in his voice. "Of course not. But he doesn't think the rules apply to him, and to be fair, they never have."

"I'm sorry you had to deal with that." She was quiet, chastened. "If it's any consolation, he sounds kind of like my mother."

"Did she deal coke in prep school, too?"

Lea laughed. "No, but the rules never applied to her, either. She was always off doing exactly what she wanted, with whoever she wanted, and it got to a point where I was happier when she was gone. Even though my father was no picnic."

"What did he do when she was gone?"

"He hated her, just like he hated her when she was around. I don't think I ever heard him say one genuinely nice thing about her."

"That's terrible." He put his hand on hers, swallowing it whole with the expanse of his palm. "But let me tell you from experience: I don't think it would have helped much if he was making excuses for her bullshit."

A charged silence bloomed between them, a lingering vibration of all the things they had admitted, some of them for the first time. For a few minutes, there was nothing but the sound of their breathing.

"I'm sorry I've been kind of avoiding you these past few days," Lea finally said.

"*Kind of?*" A slow, knowing smile moved across his face. "It's alright. I'm used to it by now."

She fought a similar smile. "You just have to understand how difficult this is for me. You're—" She caught herself, feeling full of nausea and anxiety at broaching the subject head-on, but plunging ahead out of sheer necessity. "You're my boss' son. My niece adores you." She deliberately did not say the thing that terrified her the most: the fact that he was twelve years her junior.

"We've been through all of this before. If you don't want me, you can just leave me alone. It's not complicated."

"Of course it is."

"You're making it more complicated than it needs to be, and I'm honestly a little tired of this back-and-forth."

She felt taken aback by his frustration. "Well, I'm sorry. I'm not trying to be difficult here. I just don't really have a playbook for this."

"You think I do?"

When she didn't answer, he continued.

"We need to really talk about what we're doing here."

Knowing what was happening, Lea couldn't face him. She stared directly ahead, counting the small imperfections in the stone. "Fine, let's talk."

"You can't even look at me. And *I'm* the immature one?"

"I never said you were immature."

"Every time you get scared, you talk about how much I don't understand. You act like I'm just so young and naïve, like I can't possibly know what I'm doing."

"But you *are* young."

"I'm younger than you, yes."

"A *lot* younger." She hated herself for saying it.

"Look at me."

She reluctantly turned her head to take him in, stunned anew by his beauty. "I'm looking."

He took her hand and looked into her eyes with as much sincerity as she'd ever experienced. "I'm younger than you. I know that. And you and I have lived very different lives, and there are things about you that I can't understand. But there are also things about me that *you* can't understand. And not all of that is about age."

"A lot of it is." She chuckled, averting her gaze again. He brought his hand under her chin and gently faced her back toward him.

"Maybe. But I also think you are incredibly sexy, and incredibly interesting, and your age is part of that. And there is nothing about it that makes me doubt myself. I'm young, but I'm not stupid."

"No, you're not." She felt hypnotized by him now, unable to break eye contact, hanging onto his every word.

"And I want to actually try this, for real."

He leaned and met his lips to hers, a much softer and less urgent kiss than they had shared on the dance floor. His hand again found its way up the nape of her neck and into her hair, pulling her closer. His tenderness was almost too much to bear.

"And I know that you do, too. Even if you won't say it," he breathed, pulling himself just slightly back from her face but still meeting his forehead to hers, eyes closed, lips hanging open.

"I know," she whispered back, and they fell into another, brief silence. The important things had been said, finally.

All at once, he drew back from her, his face suddenly changed. He had broken into a subtle, devious smile. "Undo my belt."

"What?"

"We're going to have sex, but I'm not going to start it. I'm not going to let you keep pretending that this is all me. I want you to do everything, so that you *know* it's you, and you can never lie to yourself again." He pulled back from her completely, and she let the hand that had been gripping his shoulder fall with a near-silent thud, mouth suddenly dry.

"*Here?* But everyone is upstairs right now."

"I bolted the door."

His eyes stayed trained on her, fearless, waiting for her to move. And after a long silence in which it was clear he wasn't explaining himself further, she finally leaned forward, dutifully unbuckling his belt, hands once again possessed as they had been the night before.

Before she even understood what was happening, she was devouring him, one hand plunged into his opened zipper, marveling at the impressive dimensions of him that she'd imagined approximately a thousand times before. His youth proved itself in moments like this, straining against the front of his pants, full of concentrated energy, so ready as to surely be almost painful. And her mouth was glued to his, panting, taking his kiss in as deeply as she could, pulling him toward her by his thick, golden curls. She couldn't get enough of him, of his glorious body, of the brain-flooding confidence she experienced when his broad, curious hands were finally enjoying the bare chest under her shirt.

Suddenly, it mattered not at all that they were in the chateau, that they were on a dusty stone floor, that this went against every professional and personal rule she'd ever had. All that mattered now was getting more of him, experiencing him as fully as possible. She ravenously freed what she needed from his jeans as he tore open the little square of foil he'd been carrying in his pocket with his perfect, white teeth. She couldn't even feel her fingers as she moved herself on top of him, knees digging into the stone beneath her but unable to feel pain, too in need of him to even bother removing her underwear, settling for pulling them to the side as quickly as possible before bringing herself down upon him.

He felt *so* good.

This felt *so good.*

There was something animal about her, moving deftly atop him while pulling him upward to kiss her deeply again, chests together, unthinking beyond their ragged breathing and moaning of each other's names. She had never been this abandoned, this overtaken by lust. But there was also something so beautiful about him, and it was as if she needed to absorb as much of it as she could *while* she could, to stock and catalog it for the years to come in which she undoubtedly wouldn't be getting laid in quite so excellent a fashion as she was now.

He could feel her intensity cresting, the unmistakable internal shuddering of her pleasure, and his breath quickened beneath her. She felt him increase his pace, his lips against her ear whispering that he was close, too, that he wouldn't be able to wait much longer. She took his face in her hands and turned him toward her, putting her forehead against his for a second time, insisting that he look in her eyes as he lost himself entirely within her. It all felt predestined, their bodies uncontrollable in the face of the intensity, of her direction, of the accumulated, pounding need between them.

"I like your shirt," Lea mused, minutes later.

His button-down was nearly soaked through with sweat and covered in dust, but still almost completely buttoned, and Lea mindlessly played with the collar as they lay on the floor, catching their breath. "That was incredible."

"Yes, it was."

He pulled her up toward him slightly to kiss her again, full of tenderness and gratitude. He let a long pause go between them before breaking the heady silence.

"I guess this is a bad time to tell you I was a virgin."

Lea caught her breath and felt her eyes go wide and heart race with terror. "Théo, I had no idea, I didn't—" She pulled herself up from him slowly as she fumbled through a panicked apology.

He burst out laughing as he brought her back against his chest. "Of course I wasn't. But you should have seen your face." He kissed her forehead as she relaxed into a laugh.

"You scared the shit out of me."

"I could see that."

She looked up at the arched ceiling, avoiding his eyes as she continued on. "And honestly, you've probably had a lot more sex than me over the past few years." She resisted the urge to ask exactly *how* much, which, as someone twelve years his senior, she had no business getting petty about.

"I don't believe that."

"Why not? I'm a thirty-six-year-old, single, type-A workaholic. Men aren't exactly banging down the doors."

"Don't speak that way about yourself. You're the most vibrant woman I've ever met. Every man wants you."

She buried her head in his chest, embarrassed by the intensity of his attraction for her. "I don't think that's true."

"I *know* that's true," he whispered down toward her. "I wanted you from the moment I saw you. I just didn't think I'd ever get to have you. I assumed you must have someone."

"I haven't had a serious relationship in six years, since that one I told you about." The bluntness of it, the weight of it, felt terrifying to admit at once. Lea realized she had never said that to a man before, and certainly not in such a vulnerable position.

"Why not?"

The innocence and total lack of judgment in his question made her smile, and she dotted his neck and clavicle with light kisses as she answered. "Well. . . I don't think there's any one reason. But I'm focused on work, and it just wasn't a priority for me. A lot of men my age come with baggage, and I don't like baggage."

It was true.

"I mean, Lea, I have some baggage. And that doesn't seem to bother you." His hands started to move down her still-damp body and pull her up toward him. "Well, not right now, at least. You could always clam up on me again for the fifth time."

"Okay," she laughed, resting her head on his neck and considering the statement. "First of all, I'm not going to 'clam up' on you again. And second of all, I guess that's true, but you just seem to handle it so well. And honestly, your baggage, I don't really mind."

"It's chic, Hermès baggage." He kissed the top of her head.

"I don't know about that," she laughed. "But it doesn't scare me."

He looked at her, serious and full of meaning. "Nothing about this scares me."

She felt so weak from lust and emotion that if she weren't already laying down, she might have fallen right over. "Good."

17

The next week was a blur of excellent sex, of endless conversation, of Lea tipping headfirst off the cliff into exactly what she wanted without compromise or apology. It was already Friday again, and twenty-nine days until the party, but she barely even checked her countdown anymore, as the workdays only felt like inconveniences to the stolen moments she grabbed at every opportunity, regardless of hour. She and Théo were foregoing sleep to slip into each other's rooms, sneaking off into the vineyards, and reconvening in the wine cellar that had become its own aphrodisiac through memory alone. They had ravaged each other in the office, in the kitchen, in the pool cabana, and in every other location they could manage.

She was perpetually physically exhausted, yet so teeming with adrenaline and serotonin that it didn't even register. All she could think about was the next time he would pin her against a wall or bend her over a desk, so immense in his height and his broad shoulders that she felt weightless in his arms. He was so *good* to her, so caring and attentive without ever seeming pitiful the way David often had. And even at his most lustful and greedy, he never made her feel used the way she sometimes did with her dating app men, the divorcés and overgrown man-children who had long ago blunted themselves on porn and only knew how to operate her body as means to an orgasm.

Théo was attuned to her needs and desires, and derived his greatest pleasure from giving her exactly what she wanted, but he also kept a firm sense of self and wasn't waiting for her every call. If she was late, he was already gone—especially if she didn't give him a heads up. But if she arrived on time, he rewarded her with lavish attention, telling her how beautiful and magnetic she was, whispering her name with his face between her thighs, offering up his silken blonde-brown curls to be pulled and guided as she desired. She had never felt this sexy, or alive, or desperate for another person.

It felt fucking fantastic.

Her work, meanwhile, had become more than an afterthought. She justified to herself that she was pretty far ahead of schedule—and it was true—but she was no longer behaving like her usual, overachieving self. Her work today was one of the things she typically looked forward to most: re-potting and arranging the myriad of indoor plants for the lobby and dining wing, which she'd hand-selected at the nursery a few weeks back. Normally she relished the process of bringing life into the space, and given that it was mid-July, she also had the satisfaction of doing so earlier than planned, giving the plants a bit more time to adjust before the brutal August heat.

But none of it was enough to keep her attention. The lobby's airy, light-filled atmosphere, all bright whites and creams with fresh pops of color and flecks of gold on the more decorative moldings, suddenly felt all wrong. Lea was looking forward to the dark, compact, discreet moments, the places she could sneak away and hide with Théo; being in such an exposed, central space made her feel like she was in a Victorian operating theater, much too visible to curious passersby. Even worse, the annual family tennis match—which she was essentially contractually obligated to attend—was this afternoon: a further distraction from work *without* the ability to do to Théo what she wanted. All in all, it was shaping up to be a very long day.

She went through the motions of delicately removing the parlor palms and birds of paradise from their containers, painstakingly filling the vintage ceramic planters she'd found at a flea market in Paris the previous year and kept in her storage unit for the right space. Already, the lobby was feeling more lush and inviting, as if the tall, elegant greenery were themselves guests. She had also curated herself perfectly for when Théo would casually pass through on his way somewhere else, as if completely by chance. She wore a fresh, white tee shirt tucked into high-waisted, cropped jeans, paired with delicate, white tennis shoes. Her hair was tied back into a low chignon with some face-framing pieces falling out, and she was wearing one of the heather gray hotel aprons along with her navy gardening gloves. She looked like a young, dark-haired, sexy Martha Stewart.

Théo would want her to keep the apron on later.

"Hi, Lea," came a familiar voice from behind her. Similar enough to Théo's to make her heart briefly jump, but clearly belonging to Gabriel.

"Oh, hi." She turned around and stood up, taking off her gloves. He was already dressed for tennis, in his familiar white polo shirt and shorts, his long, layered hair tied back in a neat knot.

He gestured toward the scattered dirt surrounding her pots, keeping his tone light. "This is looking good already."

He'd been friendlier to her since their incident in the kitchen, but his version of "friendly" felt like a poison apple, shiny and dangerous.

"Oh, I'm not finished, don't worry—"

"I'm joking, Lea. Don't be so serious all the time."

"Ah, yeah, sorry."

A distinctly Marcus-esque pause filled the ample space.

"Théo was telling me you're going to pick up some things from Sofian today—are you not coming to the match?"

"Of course, no, of course. I'll be back in time."

The teeth-itchingly unpleasant prospect of having to watch Gabriel play tennis later that day was offset by the fact that it was the family's annual doubles match: Gabriel and Chloë against Théo and Alain. *My children have youth, but I have experience!* Alain had declared more than a few times in the past several days.

"Good! This match is a classic. We have a few friends coming."

"I'll be there! I'll even put on a clean shirt for it."

Ignoring her clear attempt to pivot back toward her work, Gabriel plunged on with the conversation, even leaning himself against the midcentury reception desk. "Théo told me you'd be getting the new office printer tomorrow."

"Oh yeah?" Lea tried to sound casual in the face of his pointed tone.

"He's got his nose in your agenda these days."

"Well, I share my Google calendar with the whole chateau, so anyone who bothers to look can see what I'm up to."

"Hmm." He smiled in a slow, satisfied way. "I'll have to check it out."

Lea started putting her gloves back on, signaling her eagerness to return to her work more explicitly. "Can't wait for the match!"

"Fourteen o'clock sharp. Don't be late." He winked as he turned to leave, and she thought briefly of stabbing him in the face.

As soon as he was safely around the corner, she removed her gloves and fumbled for her phone, pulling up the ultra-encrypted, impossible-to-find message thread she had going with Théo. No notifications, no names, no visibility on the home screen: he had truly walked her through the tech nerd's protocol for having a torrid affair.

L: Why is your brother cornering me about you knowing everything I'm doing?

His reply came six painfully long minutes later.

T: What?

L: Gabriel. He cornered me about going to the tennis match as a pretense to tell me how well you know my agenda. He knows.

T: Lea, he doesn't know anything. Notably, he doesn't know that your calendar is visible to the whole chateau, because he doesn't give a shit about the work happening around him.

This answer didn't satisfy her.

L: You need to be discreet with him.

T: Yes ma'am. What else do I need to do?
L: Don't make this a sex thing.
T: I regret to inform you that this is already a sex thing.
She didn't respond, so he continued.
T: What are you wearing?
L: A white tee shirt. Jeans. An apron. I'm potting plants.
Even in her anxiety, she was powerless to stop herself
from pleasing him.
T: Plants?
That reminds me, I haven't had you in the garden yet.
We'll have to find a time after the match.
L: I have to get back to work.
T: Of course you do. See you later.

The clay tennis courts at the chateau were one of the last
to-dos on Lea's list, and looking around at the unoptimized
space nearly gave her hives. The weedy greenery surrounding
it, the ugly fencing in need of an upgrade, the rusty old benches
that would soon be replaced with the elegant green aluminum
ones Lea had purchased a few weeks ago: it was all wrong, and
gave her the distinct feeling of needing to defend her work and
taste to every attendee. Every cell in her body longed to shout:
"This doesn't represent me!" But the small group of onlookers
seemed happily distracted, arranged on the grass outside the
court on benches with a few extra patio chairs pulled up for
the spillover. Aside from their usual group, it was mostly a few
family friends of the different generations she'd seen knocking

around the grounds over the past month—certainly not the Roland Garros operation Alain had been hyping up.

Stephanie was seated next to Lea in a surprisingly girlish blue linen dress, while Lea had decided to change entirely into a red floral sundress which would maximize convenient access when she met with Théo later. Stephanie was in charge of managing the old scoreboard with the flip-card numbers, the replacement for which Lea had already ordered. (She would have the original one framed for Alain's office as a surprise.)

In addition to scorekeeping, Stephanie had also taken charge of serving cold lemonade, rosé, and beer to their guests, insisting that Lea just relax for an afternoon. It was sweet how quickly Stephanie had moved into a kind of matriarchal role, and how much she loved doing what Alain loved. As Lea tipped her festively striped paper cup for some rosé, she felt a pang in her chest thinking of all the years her cousin hadn't gotten to be this person, how much Marcus had robbed them both by never being the partner she deserved. He could have had *all this*.

Maya, meanwhile, was on the far end of the group with a few of the younger plus-ones: Joëlle, Gabriel's latest conquest—this one had short hair!—plus Philippe's son and a few local friends, including a handsome Greek grad student that Gabriel had met at a rugby club, and who had seemed to take a distinct liking to Maya in her cutoff denim shorts. She was explaining chateau dynamics to him as they sipped their lemonades, the sunlight bouncing off their dark sunglasses and giving them a distinctly cool appeal. It was a massive relief for Lea to see her this way, allowing her to relax into the experience in a way she hadn't expected. She took a hearty sip of her rosé as the father and three Lévesque children poured onto the court in their tennis whites, to whooping cheers from the small crowd. Alain was holding his beloved Bluetooth speaker like a boombox, blasting "Hello" by Dragonette and dancing in such a silly way as to make Lea genuinely burst into laughter.

"Okay, okay, that's enough fanfare!" He jokingly called as his kids dispersed to their respective positions. "Most of you know the rules by now: best of three sets wins family honor and bragging rights for the year. Losers are in charge of maintaining the court for the rest of the season."

"I already basically do it anyway," Théo joked, stretching his arms across his chest.

"Then you should be even more eager to win!"

The group cheered for the start of the match, playing up the faux "rivalry" of the divided family members. And while Lea had to hide her partiality to him, it was genuinely thrilling to see Théo in this capacity, displaying his nimble athleticism in a way she'd only pieced together from old web photos of his fencing tournaments. He was careful not to catch her eye much—especially after her warning texts about Gabriel—but to know that he was playing at the top of his game to impress her was intoxicating.

"They're all so good," Stephanie whispered to Lea, topping up her own rosé.

"I told you, Steph." Lea tipped her cup forward in request, feeling perfectly loose in the hot sun as the sounds of the game surrounded her. "All of these families are good at tennis."

"Yeah, but they're *really* good." Stephanie's eyes followed Alain from behind her sunglasses.

Lea laughed. "No, we're just really bad."

Stephanie warmly nudged Lea's shoulder with her own and tinked their paper cups together in a cheers. It felt good to be happy with Stephanie again, which Lea could freely be now that she, too, was getting exactly what she wanted.

"Is everything okay, by the way?" Lea asked, hesitating between riding their mutual high and being practical. "Did you hear from the lawyers?"

"Oh, yeah, no, it's fine. I'm not playing his games."

"The discovery stuff, you mean?" Lea didn't want to admit that she'd pored over New Jersey divorce law in the past few days, more than a little worried about Stephanie's precarious situation. Not answering the invasive list of questions he'd sent was, legally speaking, not an option.

"Yeah," Stephanie looked around the court, searching as much for her man as a reason to change the subject. "I'm not answering that stuff. How dare he ask me about Alain, you know? After everything he's done?"

Lea avoided probing further, not wanting to disrupt the perfection of the afternoon.

"Can we have some rosé, Mom?" Maya called over from the youthful side of the crowd.

"I don't trust you guys to serve yourselves." She smiled, standing up to bring over a bottle and dole it out.

Alain called over from the court as he prepared to serve. "My dear, it is a very important day. You must make an exception."

"Fine," she rolled her eyes, leaving them the bottle and heading back to her seat. "But you better win." She smiled over at Alain as he air-kissed toward her and hit a powerful serve at Chloë, who volleyed it back expertly, hiding her smile as she heard Joëlle cheering her on.

The match was much more engaging than Lea had expected, an excellent and balanced game where she got to enjoy the family dynamics without complication. In this context, Gabriel was just Alain's son, not an existential threat to her work. Théo was just the cute guy on the team she'd noticed from the stands. And the gathered group cheering them on were all just happy fans enjoying a summer Friday afternoon, watching the big game with a few cold drinks. Gabriel's date was unsurprisingly scrolling through her phone for most of the game, looking up occasionally to take short video clips for the benefit of social media, which in Lea's current state of optimism only felt sweetly amusing. Everything—even her work, even the hotel social stats she'd been compulsively refreshing since they went live—became unimportant background noise to the body high she was currently experiencing.

She even allowed herself to shout a hearty "*bravo!*" when Théo scored a particularly difficult point, making a mental note to do the same for Gabriel or Chloë at some point so as to not draw suspicion.

After her slightly daring encouragement, Théo began playing like a man possessed. He missed no volley, covering an inhuman amount of space on the court and anticipating his father's directions before he called them out. And though they were all starting to accumulate the thin, reddish-brown film that a vigorous game on the clay court almost always produced, after one spectacular dive, Théo found his shirt and upper body practically covered. Almost instinctively, he set down his racket and pulled his shirt off, using it to wipe his face and body as dry as he could before returning to the match, glistening ravines of sweat forming along the borders of his muscles.

Lea vividly imagined walking across the court to lick him clean.

Lea and Théo had dutifully made their rounds at the after party, making sure to leave in a staggered enough manner so as not to arouse suspicion, and allowing him enough time for a proper victory lap (Alain and Théo won, 6–4, 6–7, 6–4). It was always maddeningly, deliciously charged when they were in the same room, putting on their best "I'm so happy to be here" fronts while counting down the minutes until they could successfully slip away.

The clawfoot bathtub in Lea's en-suite was big enough for the two of them. The party was ramping up a few notches downstairs, and things were loud enough that they could talk without risk of anyone hearing. Lea had taken the time between excusing herself to bed and him making much noticeable conversation before discretely following to light candles, fill the tub (bubbles and all), and set up a perfect spa evening for two.

It was a gorgeous bathroom, even without the additional setup: high ceilings flecked with gold leaf on some of the molding details to keep an authentic feel to the era, but with adjustable recessed lighting, an oversized brass mirror over the sink, and unexpectedly dark green tiling to make it feel fresh and modern. The en-suite bathrooms were actually one of the first things Lea had convinced Alain about, well over a year ago now. She'd sent him the inspiration boards for the guest rooms along with a few handmade sketches of this exact bathroom model and she still remembered the phrasing of his reply. *"Your taste is impeccable. Don't let me get in your way."*

Now to see Alain's regal son in this very bathroom, arms running along the high sides of the vintage-inspired tub and perfect chest emerging from the silken bubbles, she felt dizzy with satisfaction. It was as if she had created this entire experience—maybe even her entire career—to be sharing such a decadent moment with such a beautiful man.

"Are you admiring your own craftsmanship?" His words interrupted her musing, always perfectly deft at picking up on exactly what she was thinking about.

"If you must know, yes. I'm really happy with these bathrooms. Especially with you in the tub."

"They *are* gorgeous, but I feel the need to complain that this one is much nicer than mine. I don't have a bathtub."

"You're in one of the junior suites. I didn't choose it— Alain put all the kids in junior suites."

He splashed her gently from across the tub as she smiled coyly, putting her hands up to protect her face. "Every time you refer to me as one of 'the kids,' I'm going to call you an old lady."

"You have no power here." She picked up a bottle of cold sparkling water she'd placed on a tub-side table and filled her glass, taking a sip. "My age doesn't bother me."

"And it shouldn't."

They loved teasing each other this way, subverting the very real barriers their age and role gaps entailed by playfully confronting them.

"I loved watching you tonight." He grabbed her water from her hand and held the cold glass against his neck to cool himself down. "You're so good at this."

"Thank you." In only a matter of days, she had become more able to meet his affection head-on, without the compulsion to disown it. "Present company aside, I feel very special about this project. I think it really is some of my best work."

He smiled gently at her. "It is."

"How would you know?"

"Lea," he set the glass down on the table, "you must know that I've looked into every hotel you've ever done at this point."

She blushed. "Oh, god, there are some real ugly ducklings in that group. But I wasn't the lead on all of them."

"I've already adjusted my assessment for the projects where you were working for Loïc Design."

"Ah!" She buried her face in her palms with embarrassment. "Wow, Loïc Design. I haven't thought about that firm in forever. Their spaces are so *tacky*. But that was the only company that would take an American with no experience in this market."

"I bet. They redid a hotel in Paris recently."

"Oh yeah? Your Googling is as unhinged as mine."

"About you, yes." He smiled at her. "And it *is* incredibly tacky. The double doors to the hotel club are a pair of breasts."

"*No.*"

"I wouldn't lie about something as serious as this."

She threw back her head in laughter, giddy at the prospect of being able to talk shop with someone who cared enough to learn about what she did. "What else did you find in your extensive Googling?"

"If you must know, I found a lot of pictures of you and David."

"Oh yeah?"

Since their conversation in the cellar, Lea had found herself shockingly uninhibited with Théo when it came to talking about other men—it was as if their connection and passion were so self-evident and deep that anything else could only be a funny anecdote or a value-neutral piece of context, nothing threatening.

"Yeah. He seems nice."

"He is. He's a very good man."

"Why didn't you stay with him then?" Théo looked at her with such an open, nonjudgmental curiosity that she had to move over to answer him properly, sliding on top of him under the water until their noses were nearly touching.

"Because I didn't feel about him the way I do about you."

Her response took her by surprise, and she felt herself gasp slightly at the honesty and the implication, and at the surprising tenderness she was offering to her former self about her reasons for leaving.

He smiled, meeting her lips with a gentle kiss, wet hands moving up to her shoulders as he pulled back to look her in the eyes. "I know what you mean."

Her heart was racing, trembling with the intensity of the moment. "Yeah, I mean, there were a lot of other problems, too." She slid back away from him, returning to her side of the tub for a long drink of water.

The predictable harshness of this last disclosure filled her with frustration. It was as if there were a tripwire inside of her that ensured she'd never truly give or receive a certain level of intimacy without panicking and ruining it.

"What kind of problems?" He looked steadily at her, undeterred by her sudden movement.

"You don't want to hear about all that stuff."

"Why would I have asked if I didn't want to hear about it?"

She could feel a flicker of annoyance rising toward him, when she wanted to shut him down and he wouldn't allow her. "Well, fine." Her eyes involuntarily wandered to the corner of the ceiling, avoiding Théo's as the words fell out of her. "I was always very career-oriented, and it was a time in my career when I basically had to work non-stop, which was obviously bad for a relationship. And we didn't have the same sense of humor at all. He always thought I was too mean." She gripped the sides of the bathtub, torn between her usual desire to obfuscate the truth of what happened and her inexplicable pull to be honest with Théo. "Also, he wanted children, and that's never been something I wanted."

There it was. The million-mile-high roadblock that would always stand between them, even if somehow everything else worked itself out. She'd never met a Frenchman who didn't want a family, and even if she miraculously changed her mind, the one thing she didn't have was time to wait around for an existential breakthrough over a twenty-four-year-old.

"Well, then, you did the right thing." His hand was on top of hers, looking at her with the gentle, relaxed expression he assumed when he could tell she was at her most anxious. He allowed the silence to linger between them for a moment, reassuring her that her honesty had been enough, that he wasn't going to press her further. When he spoke again, it was soft, quiet. "I wish I could have done this downstairs."

"Done what?"

"Hold your hand." He slipped his fingers between hers, warm and wet.

"Me, too."

His eyes darted down to their hands, suddenly nervous himself. "You know, I know that you don't want us to do anything public while you're still working here, but I don't think we need to wait the whole summer. We'd have to be smart about it, but I don't think it would be the end of the world."

"I could never do that to—"

"Please don't make this about Maya again. I never even *kissed* her. I know that she likes me but that's not your fault. You have to stop tormenting yourself about this."

"I don't have a choice."

"Yes, you do. And by hiding this from everyone, we're just making it worse. Rip the band-aid off already."

He was right. And beyond just hiding it, Lea had only been compounding the confusion by insisting that Théo keep being especially nice to Maya. But that wasn't something she was comfortable reconsidering, so she pivoted again, dodging him.

"Your father could also fire me."

"He wouldn't fire you. Also, I don't think he even could with French labor law."

"I don't operate on French labor law. My contract is much more favorable to my clients here, and part of that is most of my fee being tied up in the hotel launching 'to client satisfaction,' which means basically anything."

"You think he would withhold your fee?"

"Maybe not, but I also know it would be a mess if I suddenly outed myself as dating you, and I wouldn't be able to finish the job the way I need to. I wouldn't even be able to ask for it." Her tone had become harsh and clipped again, and she hated how it sounded.

He sighed, taking another sip of water. "I don't think that's true, but you know better than I do, I guess."

He held her gaze, so earnestly it hurt to look at. She took a deep breath, knowing that this was not a battle he would win, as the truth of the matter was so much harder to admit, even to herself. He was right that this wasn't just about Maya or jeopardizing her job, though both of those things were true. The truth was that she had begun to want him so badly, not just in her bed, but in every part of her life.

She wanted to walk into rooms on his arm, to decorate an apartment with him, to bring him to her brother's house and laugh about how exhausting his wife was, with her matching J.Crew pajamas everyone had to wear for group photos. She wanted to have everything with him she could never have with David, a life of adventure and travel and mind-blowing sex. She wanted all of this and she knew that it could never really be, could never make sense. He was twenty-four and she was thirty-six, and many of the things he would inevitably want she could never give him. As long as her reasons for remaining at arm's length emotionally were less scary, less vulnerable, less about her own failings, they couldn't hurt her quite as much. And given that she didn't know how to answer him, she took the only surefire route to end the conversation.

"I think you're still a little dirty from tennis." She smiled, grabbing a washcloth from the side table and once again sliding toward him. "Let me help."

He laughed quietly, every valid concern of their prior conversation temporarily melting from him, leaning his head back and closing his eyes as she lavished him with attention. If she couldn't have him in the way she truly wanted to, at least she could have him like this. And that would have to be enough.

18

"This system is going to last you for decades. It's worth its weight in gold." The water filtration representative was walking Lea and Philippe through the expensive new spa addition that Gabriel had berated her about, tapping things knowingly as he went.

"It better be," Philippe muttered, checking a meter.

"Is Alain here?" the rep asked.

"No, but I'm authorized to approve it on his behalf," Philippe clarified. He understood the classicism inherent to his work on jobs like this, and had long learned to head it off at the pass.

From her pocket, Lea's phone vibrated and she smiled instinctively. It had to be Théo, who had taken to sending her commas every now and then. It was his way of saying that he was thinking of her, and that he'd finish the thought later, when they were together.

"Lea," Philippe turned to her, "You don't have to join us for this part. I have it under control. I just have a few questions about those green upgrades." He said "green" with a distinctly derisive tone—he was an old-schooler who was blissfully unconcerned with the environmental implications of nearly anything, but trained like a hawk to sniff out a scam which, in his defense, these things often were.

"Alain made it very clear that these green certifications were very important to him. A beauty spa can waste a lot of water." The rep was undeterred.

"For what it's worth," Lea reassured, "I basically always recommend these upgrades to my clients now. It doesn't cost much more and it really does save on water enough to recoup the difference in the long term."

"Exactly," the rep added.

Lea continued on, confident, "It's the same thing with the solar panels."

Philippe's expression changed, harshly. "Solar panels?"

Lea's heart dropped. She was *sure* she had sent over the proposal for the solar panels and that they'd all seen it — and that Alain had approved of it. "Yes, the solar panels, I told you about them, Philippe." She flipped open the cover on her tablet—her countdown showing *twenty-three more days* hitting her like a slap to the face—and started searching for the email.

He looked at her with that familiar, fatherly expression, tinged this time with disappointment. "Hmm, I must have forgotten."

Her heart sank as she scrolled through her sent messages and found that she hadn't sent over the proposals for what was nearly six thousand euro worth of solar upgrades, scheduled to begin installation in a week.

"Do you need me to re-send the budget for the water system?" The rep looked over at her.

"No, no, I have it. Thank you, though."

They all stood in awkward silence as Lea scrolled further and further back into her emails.

Philippe started again, heading off further damage. "Well, we will need to talk with Alain before we do anything with those panels; why don't you stick around until he comes back?" he asked, not looking up from the chateau calendar he had pulled up on his phone. "It should be about a half hour."

"Oh, actually, I have to leave in a few minutes," Lea clarified. "I have. . . a personal call."

It was her long-awaited appointment with Dr. Miller, something she would have sooner died than put on her public calendar.

"I see." Philippe cleared his throat. "I can meet with Alain myself. Can you please forward me the proposal now, so that I can go over it with him?"

"Of course," Lea fumbled, swiping through her thousands of attachments.

"When are these scheduled for installation?"

"Next Wednesday," she replied, a little too quickly. "Or Thursday at the latest."

The rep began whistling quietly to himself.

"Listen, I'll handle this, Lea." Philippe placed a hand on her shoulder. "You go take your call."

The rep avoided eye contact as she headed back into the main spa area, too embarrassed to protest. She hated that Philippe was going to be the one to break the news, and hated leaving while the rep was still there, like a spring-loaded trap of other ways she'd potentially messed up. Even the space itself brought no comfort, despite its beauty. What was once a large, dilapidated horse stable was now a sumptuous, whitewashed, Nordic-style beauty spa, complete with massage rooms, saunas, hot baths, and a nail salon. The high stable ceilings felt almost cathedral-like in the redesign, and the skylights that had been opened up strategically made the entire place feel feather-light, weighed down only by the gray stone floors Lea had hand-selected. But each click of her loafers against them felt like an echoing reminder: *"You're losing it, girl. Get a grip."*

It was true that she'd been letting things slip through the cracks with all that had been going on with Théo: there was the addition, and now these panels, and not sending the menus to Marie, *and* rolls of wallpaper were still sitting on the floor of the upstairs kitchen. But it was hard to process even basic thoughts, let alone manage the spinning plates of launching this hotel on time, with so much emotion churning inside of her. She walked confidently along the white gravel of the entryway, waving to a contractor as she passed, doing her best to seem as if nothing was amiss.

She would allow herself this release valve of a phone call, then she would regain her much-needed sense of equilibrium.

The sun poured into her room in an almost accusatory way as Lea primped in the Zoom reflection, waiting for Dr. Miller to join the call. She had changed into one of her more "serious woman" outfits—a black mock-turtleneck with short sleeves and gray linen pants—as she needed all the confidence she could summon for the conversation at hand. Her second cappuccino of the day sat on her suite desk in its neat little saucer, going slightly cold now. It was all she could do not to scream with the anticipation of things. After all, this would be the first time she was verbalizing any of what she'd been experiencing the past several weeks to another human being. As soon as she said everything, it would be real.

The messiness of this morning was also robbing her of the usual professional confidence she brought to these sessions, a confidence which always managed to compensate for her nonexistent personal life. But her desperation to speak to someone overrode everything else, and she knew well enough that no amount of making things about work would give cover to her actual problems. Outside her open window, she could hear the gentle sounds of summer wildlife, a soft breeze lightly blowing the long ivory curtains around her. In this specific moment, they made her think of wedding dresses on a first dance, a thought she banished as Dr. Miller's name popped up in the digital waiting room.

"Good morning, Lea." He appeared on her screen in one of his typical, soothing looks: a navy-blue polo shirt with thin cream piping along the collar and sleeves, his short hair perfectly parted as always. "It's nice to see you again."

"Good afternoon, Dr. Miller. . . I know, it's been a minute."

"We usually don't talk when you're in France."

"I know, I know."

One of his classic pauses filled the space.

She pushed onward. "Thank you for taking this session. I just really needed to talk to someone about what's been happening to me here."

"Happening to you?" He always made her rephrase things she deliberately said in the passive voice.

"Things I've been doing. Things I've been. . . *feeling.* "

"What have you been doing?" He removed his glasses to clean them with a small microfiber cloth out of frame. "Or feeling?"

"Well—" She lowered her voice further, despite everyone of consequence being out of the chateau for the afternoon. "I've been having a kind of affair."

"I see." He was painfully unreactive, as she knew he would be. "With someone who's married?"

"No! Oh, god, no. I just meant affair as in like, 'a brief affair.' I'm having a flirtation, I guess you could say."

"You're dating someone."

"Well. . . yeah, I guess so."

Another long pause.

He continued. "Are you going to tell me anything else about the situation?"

"Yes, I'm sorry. It's just weird because I haven't spoken to anyone about this, and I literally can't, because well, basically because he's one of the sons of the owner of the chateau. And for the first few weeks we were here, he was flirting a bit with Maya, Stephanie's daughter, but they didn't have any kind of relationship. She just had a really big crush on him, maybe still does. But he and I have been seeing each other secretly, and we obviously can't tell anyone because I could get fired, and Stephanie would probably never forgive me for betraying Maya."

"Maya is your niece, yes?"

"Technically, not really. Stephanie is my cousin, so I don't know what that makes her."

He latched onto her hedging. "But you've always viewed her as a niece, and she's always viewed you as an aunt?"

"Yes."

"A very close aunt, even?"

"Yes."

"I can see why that would be complicated."

"Right. So I can't tell anyone." In her desperation to finally speak honestly about the subject with someone, *anyone*, she plunged forward to the heart of the matter. "And it couldn't work anyway."

"Why?"

"Because he's twelve years younger than me."

He continued to pierce through her computer screen with his unreadable gaze. "That *is* a significant gap."

"Too much, right?"

"I don't think there's a rule for those kinds of things. There are laws, obviously, but it doesn't sound like you're breaking laws."

"No, of course not."

Another brutal silence, which she finally filled with more of her circling.

"So, it's a really complicated situation, and I just don't know what to do."

"About what?"

"Well, I mean, I can't keep seeing him. . . right?"

"Lea, you know I can't tell you what you can and can't do. But is that what you want? To stop seeing him?"

She felt her eyes start to sting with tears at the relief and terror of verbalizing all of this for the first time, even to herself. "No, I don't want to stop."

"What's making you cry?"

"I don't know. . ." The tears were flowing more freely now. "I really don't know. I'm just feeling so many things right now, and there's no one I can talk to about any of it."

"We're talking about it right now. What do you want to say?"

Her voice fell to a whisper, quiet enough that she leaned into her laptop's microphone to be heard. "I don't even want to say it, because I can hear my mom in my head talking like this about every new guy she met—"

"I remember that. She was always bringing new men into your life."

"Yes. But. . . I think I'm falling in love with him. I think I might love him already, honestly. And I think it's going to ruin my life, and that I'm not going to be able to be with him in the end, anyway."

"Because he's younger than you?"

"Yes. Because he's going to move on and find some girl his own age, and have kids, and I'm going to go back to the life I had before, alone. And even Stephanie has already found someone again—we won't even get to be single together. Everyone is going to move on, and I'm just going to be alone forever. And now heartbroken, on top of it." She was weeping now.

He paused as she composed herself before continuing in his most reassuring tone. "It sounds to me like you're projecting quite a bit onto this situation, and I'm not sure that it warrants all of this catastrophizing from what you've described. Why not see if there is a way to integrate this relationship into the rest of your life before deciding it's going to end tragically?"

"I can't."

"Why not?"

The truth was that she didn't have a good answer for why not, because the tangle of her reasoning was impossible to parse. It all felt so messy, so intense, the implications reaching everywhere from her work to her childfree status to the few familial relationships she actually felt good about. She only knew that the idea of this relationship being real made her feel brutally exposed, vulnerable to humiliation and rejection in a way she'd never allowed herself to be. And if she were that person, how could Théo ever love her, when what had attracted him to her was the total opposite?

"I just don't think I could."

"I see."

"It's hard to explain but. . . at the very least, we can't do anything publicly until I'm off this job site. It's just too messy otherwise."

"Then why not enjoy it the way it is for now, and then reassess when that time comes?"

It was a good question, and another she couldn't really answer. "I don't know."

He could tell this particular tactic wasn't going to lead anywhere productive with her, so he gently redirected. "You said you think you love him. That's a big word. I don't think I've ever heard you use it before about someone you're dating."

"I know." She looked up at the corner of the ceiling so as not to cry again.

"Can you tell me a little about that?"

She breathed in deeply. "I know it sounds crazy because he's only twenty-four, but he makes me feel differently than any man I've ever known in my life. He doesn't *feel* younger than me. He feels like an equal—I respect him and learn so much from him. He's so smart, and handsome, and he accepts me completely but he's not a pushover about anything. I feel so alive when I'm with him."

"That sounds wonderful."

"It is." The tears were streaming down her face again.

"It's wonderful to be in love."

"I know."

"Do you think you're going to tell him how you feel?"

"Maybe, if it comes up." By that, she meant: *"If he tells me first and removes all risk of humiliation."*

There was another pause, and Lea used it to strategically dab her face and preserve what little remained of her makeup, reclaiming a bit of her dignity.

"I imagine it's difficult for you not to be able to speak with Stephanie about all of this," Dr. Miller continued. "You said she found someone again—how does that feel for you? I know you were concerned about her reconciling with Marcus."

It was the first time she'd made it this far in a therapy session without speaking about Stephanie, a realization that made her chuckle to herself.

"Well, that's not going to happen. Clearly."

Dr. Miller's eyebrow rose; he could sense her somewhat acidic tone.

"Isn't that good news?"

"I mean, yes, it's better that she ends up with this new man than Marcus." She intentionally did not specify that this *new man* was indeed the father of the man she herself had fallen in love with—the messiness of what she was already revealing was simply too much to compound in one session. "But it's a lot of the same old patterns, you know?"

"How so?"

"Well, he's financing her legal fees right now since Marcus cut off her credit cards—something he's not allowed to do—and she's blowing off pretty much everything he sent her, including this fifty-question discovery sheet, which *she's* not allowed to do."

"Hmm, that does seem irresponsible."

"But apparently it's all fine because her boyfriend's lawyer friend is helping her out pro bono. And I guess so am I, since I sometimes have to play translator for the two of them."

"Is divorce law the same in France?"

Lea let out a chirp of laughter that took her by surprise, relieved to hear someone else independently acknowledge the recklessness of the situation in the exact same words she had.

"You know, I wondered the same thing, and I still don't have a very good answer."

Her eyes darted up to the corner of her screen to check the remaining time. She had twenty minutes left, and for once, she *didn't* want to spend them avoiding talking about herself. Now that the seal was broken and the terrifying things had been expressed, she gently turned the conversation back around to Théo and herself, to share all the wonderful things she had experienced in the past few weeks, excited to finally relive them.

And for the first time since she had started seeing him, Dr. Miller was content to smile and listen, nodding along and encouraging her to say more with a relaxed energy she'd never experienced in previous sessions. Her whole body warmed with her descriptions of Théo, and Dr. Miller seemed to glow in her reflected presence from his side of the screen, so wrapped up in her storytelling that he didn't even notice when their time together had ended.

Stephanie and Maya had offered to help Lea and Marie with the late-afternoon work of clearing out the remaining items from the spa storage unit, and it turned out to be much needed. The four of them had spent the past hour going through boxes that had arrived even before summer had started, accumulated pieces of furniture and other random items that people couldn't find a home for and tossed here for lack of an alternative. It was one of the more mindless, repetitive tasks that Lea could fully lean into in moments like this, when she was feeling heady and conflicted—though, frankly, there were few moments that *didn't* feel like that lately. She tried not to check her watch too often, not wanting to arouse suspicion around the pre-dinner hour, where she had planned to meet Théo in a far corner of the wine cellar while the others were safely distracted by the apéritif.

Setting aside her conversation with Dr. Miller earlier that day, and the things she had admitted out loud for the first time, there was the growing tension of Maya's discontent clouding nearly every interaction, especially now, her every action punctuated by an audible sigh. Stephanie was trying to keep spirits high, as she would not allow Maya to return home alone and would therefore have to stick it out for three more weeks. Maya leaving would mean living with Marcus in the house now occupied full-time by The Mistress, as Stephanie found herself unable to accompany her, both because she couldn't bear to return to her actual life, and because her relationship with Alain had become too serious to abandon.

So they were in a purgatory, a despondent Maya held hostage by her mother's love life, unmoored now that her own love interest was out of the picture and seeking guidance from the aunt who was at least in part the reason for her dashed hopes: it felt like the worst of all possible outcomes for her, and Lea couldn't help but feel a pull of guilt every time she thought about it.

At least the spa was feeling as brought to life as the rest of the chateau, despite the minor hiccups. A regional newspaper reporter would be visiting tomorrow with his photographer to talk about the renovation and the upcoming public opening of the hotel, so knowing that even the auxiliary facilities were in spectacular shape was a familiar source of confidence. Even this storage room—essentially never to be seen by guests and soon to be filled with extra towels, cosmetic products, and machinery— was beautifully whitewashed and appointed with clean, airy light fixtures to illuminate the space. Lea had once read that the most elegant people took the time to wallpaper the inside of their closets, or line their drawers, and she'd never forgotten it. Even the spaces which might never get credit for it must be considered, so as to underscore the thoroughness of her vision.

"Do we still need to install these?" Stephanie held up one of the delicate reading sconces to be mounted on either side of each guest bed.

"Yes. We are not finish." Marie looked over the top of her purple-framed reading glasses and gestured to put the fixture back where it came from.

"There are a few more suites that need some finishing touches, Steph." Lea stacked the last extra patio chair cushion onto a small tower of them before moving over to help gently rearrange the sconces in their box and seal them up. "There are those 'artist' suites that don't have the same finishes as the other ones, remember?"

Stephanie looked up at her from her seated position on the floor. "I thought those were supposed to be done last week."

Lea froze with genuine concern at the implication. "Umm, yeah." She slowly began moving again. "We're just a little delayed on that." She looked across the room to see Marie and Maya watching them with inscrutable expressions.

"I'm sure it happens!" Stephanie corrected herself, moving over to organize a large Tupperware of extra kitchen tools. "I was just curious."

"I didn't know you were looking at the guest suites spreadsheet." Lea tried not to sound concerned as she kept her hands busy, avoiding Marie's gaze.

"I wasn't." A moment of imposing silence hung in the air before Stephanie continued on. "Alain just mentioned it the other day, I think he assumed the suites would be done before the reporter came. I don't think it matters."

Lea could feel her cheeks flushing, her entire body tingling with embarrassment, particularly in front of Marie, whose judgment she could feel searing into her skin from across the room. The three of them continued on in their work, but the once-pleasant quiet now felt incredibly laden. Alain had been talking to Stephanie about Lea's work—a transgression in and of itself—and now there were expectations she was not meeting. There were deadlines she wasn't hitting. And this conversation between the lovers was surely only the tip of a pillow talk iceberg.

Lea's incandescent resentment returned, burning the tips of her ears. Stephanie's only job was to prance around the chateau grounds in her sensible linen dresses and have sex with the widowed rich man who was bankrolling her fabulous, Diane Lane-movie divorce. She had no responsibilities, no stakes, no real work to do. She was a fucking houseguest, someone Lea brought here to tan by the pool and maybe eat some good French cheese, and now she was getting a front-row seat to whatever criticisms of Lea's job performance the boss man might have in between lovemaking sessions. This reporter was about to show up for the hotel's first real piece of press, and Lea's entire professional reputation would be on the line again—while, for the rest of them, it was just another fun afternoon of placing bets on whether she would or wouldn't screw this up.

"Can I speak to you in private for a moment?" Lea finished sealing up her box of extra tapered candles and stood before Stephanie, a physical indication that this wasn't really a question.

"Sure, of course," Stephanie quietly replied, looking nervous.

Walking outside, white gravel crunching beneath their feet, Lea launched into her admonishment. "Please do not question my work in front of Marie."

"Lea, I didn't mean to."

"Okay, well, you did. And it's fine. I'm not mad about it, I just have a lot to do and it doesn't help when you're passing on complaints Alain made in front of Marie."

"He wasn't complaining. He was just mentioning it offhand."

This dynamic—that only Stephanie knew the true nature of their conversation while Lea was hearing her recap of it—went against everything she needed to feel confident at these jobs. If she wasn't in charge of everything, who was she?

"Fine, then whatever he was doing. Just please don't talk about any of this in front of the staff."

"Why are you getting so angry about this?"

"I'm not," Lea lied. "I'm under a lot of pressure. If you want to be helpful, why don't you take Maya to go do something fun?"

"What? Why?"

"She's having a really hard time. Why don't you take her to that new film festival or something, get her out of the chateau for a day?"

"I know how my daughter is doing. And Alain and I are actually taking her—"

"Oh, right, I forgot: Only Alain is in charge of the camp activities calendar."

"Excuse me?"

"Whatever, Stephanie. I have to go."

She pulled out her phone and turned sharply, walking around the far side of the chateau, toward the garden patio with its darkened hallway leading to the wine cellar. She knew she was leaving Stephanie to feel deeply awkward in the remaining static from the exchange, but couldn't care less about whatever stilted conversation she would need to have with Marie to explain it. *Good luck,* she thought. *Marie barely speaks English. I'm done being the friendly fucking interpreter.*

L: What are you doing?

She messaged Théo, who she wasn't scheduled to meet for over an hour. A few minutes later, his answer came:

T: I'm finishing some work in my room. Are you okay?

L: Yes, I'm okay. But if you could meet me a little sooner, I would love that.

T: I was going to send a few more emails. 30 minutes?

L: That's fine. I'll be downstairs.

Downstairs meant the cellar. *Their* cellar.

After a few moments of pacing, Lea broke the dam of her pride and admitted that she needed him sooner, needed him desperately, so much so that even thirty minutes felt impossible. There was simply too much churning emotion within her to carry alone: the admissions to Dr. Miller, the humiliation in front of Marie, the biting exchange with Stephanie. She needed the beautiful, deafening silence of the mind that came from being in his arms.

L: Actually, I'm really not okay. Can you come now?

His response arrived almost immediately, hitting her in the chest and spreading a reassuring warmth through every extremity of her body: *Of course, darling. I'll be right there.*

19

"These doors were actually reclaimed from a nearby home that had to be condemned after a fire. It's a small way for us to pay homage to the resilience of the region." Lea pushed in one of the whitewashed entry doors and held it open as the group of journalists filed in behind her, the photographer snapping photos as they went.

"We actually know the family well," Gabriel interjected, taking over what was a planned moment for Lea in the tour. "A few of their children have been working with us on the vineyards. Not too hard, though." *Of course he was able to turn on the charm for moments like this.*

The team from the regional paper was just that: a *team.* Lea had expected a wiry old reporter who had never heard of Instagram, along with a fledgling photographer, no doubt the son of one of the publishers looking to build his portfolio before moving to Paris. These regional papers almost never tested her media training, and often treated her with the same level of borderline-fatherly affection and deference that Philippe had embraced with her. But this was an actual team: two reporters, a professional photographer, and a social media manager, all equipped with dozens of questions and opinions that Lea wasn't fully prepared for. Beyond that, Lea had been undermined at the breakfast table that morning, where Alain had offhandedly mentioned that Gabriel would be joining him to speak on behalf of the family, *"Because Gabriel is so much savvier at handling the press."*

Generally, she always did media and walkthroughs with just the owner or director of the property, and took it upon herself to do all of the technical talking while the owner lent color, family history, and some indisputable local gravitas to the conversation. It was a symphony she knew how to conduct perfectly, positioning herself as the unexpected American tastemaker bringing her signature touch to this sleepy, forgotten corner of the region.

She had even sent Alain her meticulous outline of the planned walkthrough a few days prior: the order of the spaces they would visit, who would take the lead in each room, some key points they should hit or features they should draw the photographer's attention to. He had read it thoroughly, and they'd discussed it the day she sent it, but she saw Gabriel lazily swiping through it on his phone as he sipped his espresso that morning, when it was announced he would be representing the family on the tour. He looked at her from across the table as she finished her usual eggs and berries, remarking on how thorough it was in a way that suggested she was trying too hard, an unforgivable sin in French culture.

Théo had given her a pep talk when he'd snuck into her suite for what had become a beloved morning ritual of sex and conversation at dawn. Lying resplendent on her bed like a baroque nude, he'd approved her neatly hung outfit as she steamed it and prepped her for the inevitable idiosyncrasies of his father in moments of pressure. But when she got the news that Gabriel would accompany them, she couldn't so much as glance down the table at Théo, who was busy pretending to butter his bread, likely fuming inside at his father's endless enabling while Gabriel, once again, got to swoop in and do nothing, no doubt feeling great about himself in the process.

But she didn't have the luxury of being angry. She had to do her job, and now play defense on top of it.

One of the reporters looked up from his notes. "Speaking of the vineyards, I know we're visiting them later but can you tell me a bit about the wine you're going to be producing here?"

Lea's heart jumped to her throat, and she opened her mouth to respond a half-second before Gabriel got the chance—*thank god.*

She explained, willing herself to keep calm. "So, the grapes are still very much in the process of rehabilitation, and we're looking forward to bringing them back to their full glory with a chateau winery—but for now, we've joined a few excellent regional co-ops with what we do have. The Lévesques are very proud to be dipping their toes into the strong regional tradition of wine production. We actually have a brief tasting scheduled for later in the tour." She gave a coy smile that hid her terror at what Gabriel might say about such a sensitive subject.

"If we can convince you to drink on the clock!" Alain added, his usual buoyancy providing a bit of relief.

And to her surprise, Gabriel had nothing to say on the matter. The group laughed and offered a few jokes about making an exception for journalistic research, and for now, she was spared.

The next stop on the tour was the hotel restaurant, one of the most indisputably impressive parts of the property.

As much as the lobby took their breath away—Lea took particular pleasure in explaining her process for choosing the whimsical Schumacher fabric, and how she contrasted it with the gold leaf on the original moldings—it was the restaurant that would make it a destination for travelers and locals alike. The sumptuous green-on-green of the dining room, now lively with exotic plants, felt like an alternate universe to the generally staid, relentlessly old-school hotels of the region.

She sat them down along the bar and walked them through the all-day menu, a few bites of which they'd be tasting along with the wine later. Caroline had been right: the seamless blend of Maghrebi and regional cuisine was the exact gastronomic spark the restaurant needed to attract attention while feeling sufficiently familiar.

"This is gorgeous—can I post it?" the social media manager asked, taking a short video of herself walking from the bar room back into the main restaurant.

"Of course," Lea answered, smiling. "Just don't forget to tag us!"

By the time the newspaper team left, and it was just Alain, Gabriel, and Lea in Alain's office, the full force of exhaustion fell on Lea's shoulders. It wasn't just that it was a long day creating a seamless show for the press. It was also that she'd spent the entire time in a state of high alert, waiting for Gabriel to undermine or correct her, even though he never actually did. In fact, he'd seemed surprisingly amenable to her vision and unconcerned with asserting himself.

If she had been less on edge, she might have seen this coming.

"That went very well," Alain started, moving around a few papers on his desk. *Oh no, he was nervous.*

"Yes, I think so. I can't wait to read the article."

"Hm, yeah," Gabriel added mindlessly, standing by the window and looking out onto the gardens.

Suddenly, Lea felt trapped. "Should we start getting dinner ready?"

"Actually, Lea," Alain started, eyes darting over toward his son, who still had his back turned to the two of them. "I didn't want to raise anything before the interview today, because we know how important a moment it was and I didn't want you to be more anxious. But I do need to speak to you about a few issues."

Her mouth was completely dry. "Issues?" She only realized after she said the word that she'd involuntarily switched to English in her terror.

"Well, yes." Gabriel turned to face them and returned the conversation to French, a subtle assertion of power. Pulling up what must have been the Notes app on his phone, where he had listed the *issues* he'd undoubtedly already reviewed with his father. "We have the extreme expenses in the spa from the unplanned addition and water system, these surprise solar panels, the artist suites not being ready in time to show the press, the upstairs kitchen far from finished, and we have still not confirmed the instructor for the cooking classes."

"I sent you along—" she started, but he raised a single finger. *A single fucking finger.*

"I know we have candidates to review, but I don't want us engaging an instructor until we have an actual finish date on the kitchen. A *real* date. The way things are going, we won't even make the friends-and-family opening"

Lea's throat was burning with humiliation. She'd never been called out this way before, but she'd also never been as sloppy as she'd been in the past few weeks. Normally, she was light years ahead of whatever problems inevitably arose, providing solutions before anyone was even aware of an issue. She would have had to be doubly on her game with Gabriel sniffing around behind her every move, but she'd been too distracted. She'd been falling in love.

"Alain." She turned to the patriarch, who was too full of secondhand embarrassment to even properly look at her. Lea felt overwhelmed with a contempt for the niceness that Théo had warned her could mutate into cowardliness, especially as it pertained to his eldest son. "I know a few things haven't gone perfectly to plan, but overall we are still ahead of schedule and on target with our budget. I have no doubts about our rollout going as planned, *including* the launch party, and I'm happy to prepare interim solutions for all of the concerns Gabriel has presented."

"Yes, I think that would be right." Alain nodded, still looking down at his papers.

"I'm also happy," she continued, now turning to Gabriel, "to reassess my fee, in light of any unexpected expenses that may put our budget at risk. I will take full responsibility for those, of course."

Both men spoke in tandem, with a near-identical voice. "Thank you."

"I would like a little time to gather my thoughts, and I will have a plan to present to you both tomorrow over breakfast.

Gabriel, could you please email me your notes? I want to make sure to get everything."

"Yes, of course."

She picked herself up from her chair and hurried out, back to her room, which she vowed to not leave until the following morning. In fact, being in her room was the only thing that could possibly calm her at this moment.

It was still perfect, still full of her impeccable organization and crisply made bed and thoughtful touches. And it was still gorgeous *as a room*, with its whitewashed ceiling-high windows, the colorful, Japanese folding screen from which she hung her silk robe, and those ornate wall sconces, turned down to a warm and flattering temperature. Even in such a state of anxiety, it was still her perfectly appointed cocoon, free of judgment or consequence. Here, she could regroup and transform back into her most together self. She could assemble the perfect outfit for presenting her little dossier to Alain and Gabriel the next morning, when she would reclaim her dignity and control.

She settled in at her desk, turning on the midcentury lamp she'd hand-selected for the guest rooms nearly a year ago, and opened her laptop, wiping away a frustrated tear.

Around what should have been dinnertime, Lea was interrupted by Stephanie's gentle and familiar knocking. She called for her to come in but remained at her desk, where she was busy drafting up a comprehensive document that would thoroughly address everything that had been brought to her that afternoon. She felt Stephanie slip into the room behind her and sit on the bed, still wordless. It was unlikely that Alain had given her a complete rundown of what had transpired, but her timidness indicated that Stephanie knew more than Lea was comfortable with.

She spun around in her chair to look at Stephanie, an act that almost always calmed her down, as it anchored her in their decades of history, a history full of love, support, and mutual understanding. She could almost always trust the mere vision of Stephanie's kind, elegant face to reassure her. But in this moment, the sight of Stephanie—in yet another flowy dress that Alain probably bought her on one of their afternoon excursions—elicited nothing but bitter anger.

"What, Stephanie?" she managed.

"I wanted. . ." her voice was small. "I wanted to know if you were coming down to dinner."

"No, I'm not. I have work to finish."

"Do you want me to bring something up for you to eat?"

Lea wordlessly grabbed the protein bar on her desk and waved it in the air.

Stephanie continued. "Are you. . . okay?" She started to get up and walk over toward Lea, who threw up a hand to stop her.

"I'm fine."

"Lee, you don't seem fine."

Although she knew it wasn't totally fair to unburden herself of every frustration and outrage on her unsuspecting cousin, she simply could not help herself. She felt the venom tumbling from her mouth like an open wound. "You're right, Stephanie. I'm *not* fine. I'm not fine at all, in fact."

"What happened?"

"You mean your boyfriend isn't giving you the play-by-play of how I'm screwing up on the job? He seemed to be pretty forthcoming about the guest suites not being ready in time."

"No—well, I. . . no. He hasn't been telling me much. He respects your privacy."

"I don't think there's any privacy in this house. And honestly, it doesn't even matter. If he fires me, it won't really matter what he did or didn't tell you along the way."

"He's not going to fire you." Stephanie looked down as she said it, instantly understanding the implication of the statement.

"Oh, so now he's telling you about my employment status? Or did you ask him to keep me as a favor to you?"

"That's not what I meant." Her eyes turned glossy with apologetic tears. "I just meant he loves your work, and he knows projects always have hiccups."

"Or he doesn't want me to leave because he thinks I'll take you with me."

Stephanie paused, breathing in deeply to calm herself before continuing. "He knows I'm not leaving."

"What does that mean?"

"It means that I have to go back to work out visa details, but I'm coming back to be with Alain. We're in love."

A vicious, oily rage exploded in Lea at this revelation. The envy, the unfairness, it was all inexpressible, so Lea channeled it as best she could into something that didn't have anything to do with how she wanted to do the exact same thing with Théo.

"You don't think you might actually want to get divorced first before you hitch your wagon to another rich man?"

"What does that mean?"

"It means exactly what I said. You have one rich man at home who served you with divorce papers, so maybe clean that up before you throw yourself into the arms of *another* rich man who will have the power dynamic one hundred percent in his favor."

"I'm not—" Stephanie stuttered, struggling to form a more comprehensive response.

Lea seized on the moment. "And I'm sure this isn't at all traumatizing for Maya, who doesn't even get a second to breathe before a brand-new father figure enters her life."

"Maya loves Alain. . ."

"Does she? Maybe Maya feels like Chloë, sick of having front-row seats to your irresponsible romcom."

"Irresponsible?"

"Yes, irresponsible. Whose credit card have you been using since Marcus cut yours off, hm?" Lea cocked her head in faux curiosity. "Did you know he can't legally do that, by the way? He can't cut you off once he filed, and you could file to have them turned back on. But I guess it's easier to just let Alain take over the bills, right?"

"I—"

"Do you even know what his lawyer friend is saying before he translates it for you? Can you even speak to him yourself?"

There was truth to it, to the precariousness of Stephanie's naïveté, but the cruelty—the invocation of Chloë and Maya in particular—was purely gratuitous. It felt good, and awful.

"Lea, I don't know why you're talking to me this way, but I didn't do anything." Stephanie looked at her with her huge, hurt brown eyes, but Lea felt nothing past her blinding anger.

"You're right, you didn't do *anything*. I've been doing a job here for the past six weeks, under enormous pressure, and you've been skipping around eating cheese and drinking wine and having a grand old time."

"Isn't that what you wanted me to do? *Isn't that why I'm here in the first place?*"

"I thought I was helping you get a little independence from Marcus"—the repeated, cutting mention of his name caused Stephanie to flinch from across the room—"not immediately helping you get involved with another man who will dictate the entire trajectory of your life."

At that, Stephanie stood up and looked Lea dead in the eyes, showing every bit the eight years of authority and life experience she had on her.

"All you have ever said is that you wanted me to get away from Marcus and actually be happy for once. Now I *am* happy, and you suddenly want to throw it in my face? You want to make me feel like a bad mother? You're lucky that I'm not going to throw any of your stuff back at you, but trust me—I could say a lot right now."

"Oh, yeah?"

"I'm not going to stoop to your level, but I will say that it's pretty damn mind-blowing that you're judging me for 'getting with another rich man' when no one ever brings up the rich man that allowed *you* to become this perfect, independent career woman. I know your dad is awful, but he also financed your life until you were able to earn a living. I still have to send my mother a check every month, which, unless you forgot, Marcus makes me take out of *my* salary."

A hostile silence expanded between them before Stephanie cut it again with more righteous fury. "And you have a lot of nerve throwing how I handle Maya in my face, or how Alain handles Chloë. It must be so easy sitting there judging everyone's parenting when you've never had to do it. You just get to swoop in and be the cool girlfriend and commiserate about how annoying Mom is."

"I never commiserate with Maya."

"Oh, yes, you do, Lea. And I'm fine with it because sometimes kids do that with their aunts and uncles. Kids complain. But it's one thing to throw me under the bus for not letting her fly in business class, it's another to imply that I'm a bad parent for finding happiness with a man whose wife *fucking died.*"

The comment seemed to take even Stephanie by surprise, her eyes brimming with tears. Lea wanted to run across the room to hug her but felt glued to her chair in humiliation.

"Now I'm going to dinner, and I hope that when I see you tomorrow, you're a different person."

Lea felt herself sink into her chair as Stephanie crossed the room and slammed the door closed behind her, ashamed and small. She couldn't even bring herself to text Théo; she felt too unworthy of the kindness he would undoubtedly show her. Everything about the way she was carrying herself this summer was indeed not like her, for better and worse, and she couldn't bear the thought of allowing the things that were going right to derail everything else into such profound wrongness.

She walked into the bathroom to splash some cold water on her face, confronting her drawn, exhausted, and now wet reflection in the mirror. She'd never felt like more of an overgrown child. So, as was her most reliable outlet when she was feeling her lowest, she sat on the cushioned stool next to her bathtub and pulled out her iPad, starting a fresh to-do list for the evening.

- *Write apology text to Stephanie [SEND LATER]*
- *Finish spreadsheet with new budget inc. adjusted fees*
- *Email contractors re: upstairs kitchen*
- *Do calming yoga video [15 MINS]*
- *Steam outfit for tomorrow breakfast*

Maybe, after she completed all of it, she might be able to go to sleep.

20

Seven days later, Rémy held up a glass of wine to the midafternoon sunlight in the tasting barn—a whole goddamn tasting *barn*—of a nearby vineyard, as their Wine Director walked the assembled group through a fourth consecutive varietal of drier, more astringent whites. Lea was diligently taking notes, making sure to engage in plenty of friendly banter with Alain whenever the chance presented itself. Alain remarked that wine tasting had become a lot less novel over the past several weeks, and Lea nudged his shoulder while reminding him that this is why people end up spitting the wine after tasting: *"There's a reason they have those buckets."*

Their small group had come to engage in another mini-seminar about the region's wine landscape, this time with the much more established chateau down the road, whose owners were both heartened and mildly threatened by the increasing buzz generating around Hôtel Château Victoire.

While Lea's meeting with Alain and Gabriel at that nerve-wracking breakfast had gone as well as she could have possibly hoped—not to mention her updated rate, a discount so generous even Gabriel couldn't argue with her revised proposal—she didn't want to linger in the tenuous state of being *forgiven*. She wanted to get back to *excelling*. And that meant showing up early to help set up Wine Education Day, as well as volunteering to do some of the more tedious manual labor in their own vineyards later that afternoon, which would normally fall under Philippe's purview.

The light in the barn felt so warm and cradling—Lea made a note to look into repurposing structures on future properties for this purpose—that it nearly made her forget her lingering tension with Stephanie. Although her apology text had been well-received, and Maya seemed to be in better spirits, there was a clear undercurrent of emotional distance Stephanie was keeping from her—something she had never before experienced. Lea knew that she deserved it, that it was natural to take more than a few days for the sting to wear off, but it still left her feeling unmoored. (A similar note to herself from earlier in the day read, *Acknowledge emotional support that Stephanie provides more often.*)

As the Wine Director droned on about the nuances of the chenin blanc they'd been swirling in their glasses, Alain whispered something mildly conspiratorial in her ear about how their grapes would be better. She clinked her glass to his and they each took a sip, both opting out of spitting into the bucket this time. Perhaps he felt just as relieved as she did, that their relationship was returning to its convivial and productive baseline. It was also immensely helpful that Gabriel was leaving for Paris again in a few days, taking with him the constant slow drip of criticisms filtering into his father's ear.

"Thank you for making time for this," Alain said quietly, as the others were busy chatting.

"Of course," Lea laughed. "It's literally my job."

"Sure, of course, but I know you've been going above and beyond lately. And I really appreciate it."

"Well," she chose her words carefully, "I wasn't showing my best work there for a minute, and I want to make sure I over-deliver for my clients, always."

"I know." He swirled the stem of his glass on the table, aerating the remaining sips of his wine. "We're very lucky to have you working with us."

"Hey, thank you." She flushed slightly.

"You know. . ." His words were taking on the familiar tone of their day in the office together after Disco Night, the slightly embarrassed openness of needing to talk. "Stephanie is planning to come back here once she arranges her paperwork."

"I know. I'm happy for the two of you." While she was also envious, and humiliated at her initial response to the news, it was true. She really *was* happy for them.

"It would be nice to see how we could work together on a more ongoing basis, especially with Stephanie here. I know you are in very high demand, but there's a lot we could still collaborate on after opening."

Her heart fluttered. It wasn't the first time a client had asked her about continuing her work in some way, but it was the first time she was really, truly thrilled to consider the possibility. "That is very flattering, Alain. I would love to talk about it more."

The vineyard work Lea had so readily volunteered for proved to be more involved than she'd anticipated. But this was no time to complain or back out, even with a light wine headache from the tasting. Besides, she wasn't alone: helping her repair the wooden stakes that guided the more dilapidated vines was Théo—and conveniently out of view from the chateau, no less. The two of them in their lightest shoulder-covering linens were hard at work and determined to finish ahead of schedule, leaving them enough time to accomplish at least one more task before dinner.

She hadn't told him about the dressing down in the office, or about the horrible conversation she'd had with Stephanie (she was frankly too embarrassed on both fronts, for different reasons), but he was perceptive enough to suss out that what she needed was breezy conversation with a side of manual labor. They had spent the past hour and a half talking about their favorite movies, finding that they had more common ground than expected. They were both huge fans of Wong Kar-wai, and preferred *Goodfellas* to *The Godfather*. She loved French cinema much more than he did—that was no surprise—but they agreed on a few classics, as well as on the fact that Jean Dujardin was baffling as the big breakout star in the States from his generation. *"I don't trust his eyebrows,"* Théo had commented.

The day felt strangely normal given the circumstances, and Lea even allowed herself to touch him a few times—in broad daylight, on the property—much to his delight. She was still refusing his desire to go public, as it still felt like too much of a transgression. The thought of finishing a day of work and heading off to bed with one of her boss' sons felt unbearably vulnerable to judgment and shame. She had, however, become more open to the idea that they might continue seeing each other after her work was done and, once timelines were blurry enough to obscure the order of events, she could even start to reveal it to key parties if things really were that serious.

But only she knew just how much she had been intentionally deceiving everyone and how atrociously it had made her behave, the neat little prison she'd spent most of the summer in.

"Can you help me with this?" Lea was having trouble getting a stake out of the ground to move it.

"Sure, here," Théo came over behind her and wrapped his hands around the stake alongside hers, his entire body enveloping her in support.

She laughed quietly.

"What?" he asked, pausing to look at her, centimeters from her face.

"This is like when you helped me screw in those chair legs, remember?"

"Of course I remember." He kissed her neck discreetly before returning to pulling, freeing the wooden stake from the dirt and setting it down. "You asked me about my internship."

She stepped back, wiping her gloved hands together to remove the excess dirt. "Yeah, I didn't know what else to say. I was kind of overwhelmed being alone with you." It was thrilling, being able to speak openly about what was such a fraught, taboo moment.

"I liked that you were interested in my work—no one else is."

"I'm sure that's not true." She moved to the next set of vines to restart the tedious process, and he did the same.

"It's fine. I don't mind. Boring work with good employment opportunities is not the worst problem to have." He paused, and she could feel him look over at her. "I can pretty much find work wherever I want."

She knew what he meant. He meant looking in the States, possibly even in DC. Maybe he'd already begun. It filled her with a simultaneous chill of delight and terror, which she quickly headed off with her response: "Well, anywhere that allows you to help out at the hotel on the weekends. Paris is close enough. That's lucky."

He sensed her avoidance of the implications and pivoted to a lighter subject. In her mind it was one of his greatest assets, that he knew when to not press her on a particular topic and wouldn't force her into conversations where she felt trapped. Théo was content to let her know what he was thinking, but then leave it in the ether for her to interact with on her own terms. And as a result, she often found herself coming back around to him independently, like a cat who only wanted to be pet once her human was ignoring her.

She walked over to him and grabbed him by the buckle of the belt holding up his khaki shorts. The boldness of doing something like that *here* flooded her with excitement.

"Hey," she opened.

"Hi." He looked down at her and smiled, still holding a fist full of weeds.

"If you take a job in Paris, I will be around a lot." She wanted to say more, maybe even mention her conversation with his father, but felt the usual terror rising in the back of her throat in the face of real, consequential intimacy.

"I have a while to figure it out, anyway. I still have some school left." He pressed himself up against her, running his finger under the bathing suit strap emerging from her top, and she felt him shudder at the full contact with her body.

"I want to be part of your plans," she said, avoiding his eyes, closing hers tightly as she pushed her face into his chest.

"I want you to be part of *everything,*" he whispered. "Do you feel how much I want you?"

"Yes," she breathed. "I do."

"Jesus Christ," he pulled himself back from her, dropping the weeds on the dirt below him. "We can't do this or I'll have to have you right here, and that's too risky—even for me."

She laughed, elated.

"Come here."

He took her hand in his and walked her to the edge of the vineyard, letting go exactly as she would have insisted once they got within view of the chateau. He walked over toward the pool and pulled his shirt off mid-step, balling it up in his hand and throwing it down on the first chaise longue he encountered on the deck. He kicked off his shoes and removed his shorts before jumping into the deep end of the pool, obscuring the substantial strain his swimming trunks were under. She walked over to the deck as he lingered under the water, calming himself down.

He looked like a cologne ad when he emerged, his curly hair slicked back and his glistening chest muscles making her feel like she might faint on the spot. There was no one else in sight, and it wasn't totally irrational for them to be having a swim after hours of work in the sun (everyone took a dip at one point or another most days), but she knew how difficult it would be to keep her hands off of him if she joined him.

"I'm not coming in." She smiled down at him from behind her sunglasses.

"The hell you're not," he replied, splashing her legs.

"I hate to disappoint," she could feel her pulse radiating down her body, every extremity tingling, "but I am at work right now. So I'm going to go finish cleaning up the vineyards, but thank you for that little show."

"Oh, come on. You can stay at the other end of the pool. You're just hot after a long afternoon of work."

She smiled at his boyish persistence, eager to reward it. "How about this: you get out of the pool, and while you're drying off, you can watch me get in. But in exchange, you have to go clean up the stakes."

"Will you meet me after?" The blue of his eyes seemed in competition with the blue of the water, both so saturated and enticing. "Please."

"*Shh*," she chided, smiling.

"'Shh' is not an answer."

"Yes," she whispered, eyes darting over to the chateau.

"Okay, deal."

He lifted himself out of the pool, tanned shoulders straining, water cascading from his body. He walked over to the cabana and grabbed one of the rolled-up white towels Marie set out in a neat little pyramid each morning. As he dried off his hair, he smiled over at her, gesturing for her to get in.

She stepped out of her tennis shoes, careful not to seem too intentional or to look over at him as she did. Chloë, Joëlle, and Maya were now out on the patio—engrossed in a board game, but still—so not attracting attention was of the utmost importance. She turned around to give him a full view of her backside as she dropped her denim shorts before bending over to fold them and place them on a deck chair. She unbuttoned her short-sleeve work shirt and again took the time to fold it properly, searing with the feeling of his eyes on her from twenty feet away. Adjusting the straps of her backless one-piece swimsuit, she walked over to the stairs and stepped into the water.

It felt so good against her skin, as astringent and refreshing as the whites they tasted earlier. There were a million things to worry about but, as she sank down to the bottom of the pool and opened her eyes to the watery blue skies above her, not a single one mattered.

"You have to be quiet," Lea pleaded as quietly as *she* could manage. Théo had her pinned against a wall on the far side of the spa, his mouth on her neck and his hand rapidly finding its way down her torso.

"I know it's early," he said, lips brushing against her as he spoke, "but I couldn't wait. Not after that scene at the pool."

"I couldn't. . . I couldn't wait either." She squeezed her eyes shut, stifling the cries of joy and pleasure she wished she could yell out.

It was true, it *was* early. There were still people milling around the chateau, lights were on. And as if suddenly coming to his senses about the unusual recklessness of the situation, he stopped, coming to face her and tenderly moving a piece of hair from her eyes.

"I need to tell you something," he said.

Her heart stopped.

"Is everything okay?" she nervously asked, not because she feared a problem, but because she feared hearing exactly what she wanted him to say.

"I could tell you were freaked out when I was talking about getting a job. You think I'm going to follow you back to DC."

"No, I—"

He stopped her with a gentle palm over her mouth. "Shh, let me finish." She nodded silently. "I'm not going to just *follow* you anywhere, but I have added it to my list, and it's something I want us to talk about."

She nodded again, and he continued.

"I love my family, and they need my help, and I want to be here for them." He paused. "But I can't live for them forever. I want to have my own life."

She could tell he was emotional, and she leaned in to give him a deep kiss. "Théo, of course," she whispered when she finally pulled back.

He looked in her eyes, the chirping crickets filling the cool evening air around them.

"And I can't picture my life without you," he said, quietly. "Because I love you."

She felt as if someone had sucked the air out of her lungs, so full of nerves, of joy and fear. Almost in spite of herself, more a reflex than a thought, she felt herself speak the words "I love you, too" in return.

He brought his lips to hers and they did not break for what felt like hours, their faces wet with the warm, humid evening and maybe a few tears. There was nothing more to say— not tonight, anyway. With more words would come more questions, and all they wanted tonight was to be suspended in time, where everything was beautifully possible.

21

"**A**re you *sure* you don't want any?" Stephanie teasingly waved the basket of pastries under Lea's nose. In an unusual change of pace, they were the first ones at the breakfast table, the garden around them in a full, almost delirious late-summer bloom.

"Oh, come on, you know carbs—"

"Carbs make me so tired," Stephanie cut in with a surprisingly accurate approximation of Lea's voice.

"You know what," Lea grabbed a slice of brioche from the basket. "Fine." She slathered it with butter, smiling across the table.

I'll burn this off later, anyway, she thought.

It had been weeks since she and Théo had finally admitted their love to each other, and the effortless confidence their relationship gave her was manifesting in essentially everything she touched. Lea was uncritically happy for Stephanie and Alain. Her work was so far ahead of schedule—in no small part thanks to Théo's frequent, discreet help—that they'd decided to expand the media guest list for the friends-and-family opening party that weekend. She had been meticulously combing through her press contacts, reaching out to everyone personally and feeling a not-subtle jolt of pride at every confirmed RSVP she could flaunt in front of Gabriel.

"What are you wearing to the party, by the way?" Stephanie asked, refilling her coffee.

"I've narrowed it down to two options."

Stephanie drum-rolled her fingers on the wooden table.

"Either this floor-length lavender silk thing I bought last week, or the green one I wore to your birthday the year before last."

Lea smiled, knowing Théo would undoubtedly cast his vote for lavender. It was backless, and therefore allowed him to gently skim his fingers along her skin while walking by without raising suspicion.

"Oh, I *love* that green one."

"I know, me too, but I'm kind of superstitious about wearing new dresses to my launch parties. They always give me that little boost, you know?"

"Well, mine is definitely going to be new. Nothing I brought is nice enough."

"You should treat yourself! We can go to that boutique I told you about later. There were *so* many cute things."

Lea could feel herself relaxing back into the person she'd always been with Stephanie: supportive, loving, open-minded. She still winced at the memory of how she'd spoken to her in her suite that night, as well as the unfortunate, ongoing deception her romance required of her, but overall they both seemed relieved to have each other in a way that felt familiar and natural. Like it or not, their time was winding down at the chateau. And though that meant gathering distance from the more complicated elements of the situation—enough so that Lea and Théo could come out as a couple on their own terms—it also meant saying goodbye to this perfect, almost otherworldly moment in time.

Alain arrived at breakfast with Gabriel, both of them fresh off of a morning tennis match, a scene that had played out at least a dozen times since their arrival yet remained charming in light of Lea's good humor. The two of them lingered at the end of the table—it would be rude to sit down after a long, sweaty game on the clay court—talking with Stephanie about the details of the game. Marie and Philippe came walking around from the front of the building, where they'd been speaking with the contractors arriving to finish the upstairs kitchen and design suite bathrooms with the hand-painted wallpapers Lea had sourced nearly a year prior. *"They finally showed up,"* Marie called over to Lea, who mimed an exaggerated wiping of her brow.

Before Lea knew it, nearly everyone was outside, the table bustling with the train station energy she had come to love more than any other start to her day, Théo stealing glances from down the table and looking like a '50s heartthrob in his clean, white tee shirt tucked into a pair of higher-waisted, belted khakis. She felt herself swoon, the distinct thought of *Look at my man* running through her head even as it made her feel a little silly.

"Ah, Théo," Alain called over to him from across the patio. "You must take Chloë into town after breakfast. She has a list of things to buy for riding camp."

Joëlle replied in French from behind Théo, pushing past him to get to the sole remaining pain au chocolat before anyone else could grab it, which she split with Maya, "She's still sleeping, but she told me to tell you that she also needs a new tiara and ball gown."

Lea stifled a laugh—it was true, the idea of sending your daughter to a week-long sleepaway equestrian camp felt too privileged, even for this family.

Théo answered while pouring himself a coffee. "That's fine, just give me a list because otherwise she's just going to make me buy her a bunch of extra clothes."

"I. . . I can take her," Stephanie offered, looking up at Alain. "I don't have much going on today."

There was a brief pause amongst the group, but Alain quickly diffused any tension with a kiss to Stephanie's forehead and a vigorous *"Excellent idea!"*

He looked back over at Théo. "But that means you're helping in the kitchen today."

"I can help, too!" Maya offered, in significantly brighter spirits since the two ultra-cool teenage girls had taken her under their wing. Even her outfits had taken a chic turn, with more billowy cuts and anchoring, dark pieces.

"Thank you, Maya." Théo smiled generously at her. "But, Dad, you know, I do have an actual job to do. And I don't even know what is happening with that kitchen."

Lea felt herself involuntarily raise her iPad, trying to sound casual as she said, "I can go over how both of you can help me, actually!" He smiled in her direction and nodded silently, stirring a cube of sugar into his coffee.

Marie looked over the top of her red glasses at Lea with one of her signature unreadable expressions, and Gabriel walked away from the table, racket in hand. Lea immediately regretted seeming so enthusiastic and stood up at her seat, tucking her iPad under her arm and gathering her plate and cup. "Well, on that note," she said, still struggling to sound casual. "I should probably get back to work."

Not looking up, she walked back into the chateau, dropping her dishes in the sink and walking up to the main floor to meet the workers in the kitchen. On the way, she pulled up her pre-lunch to-do list and laughed at the updates she'd made from her bathtub last night:

- *Check on wallpaper in upstairs kitchen*
- *Message Théo about meetup [DIRTY]*
- *Finalize contract for cooking instructor*
- *Meet with Théo [OUTSIDE LOCATION? CHECK IF STEPH USING CAR]*
- *Move wallpaper guys to design suite bathrooms*

She was in the home stretch and knew that continuing to exceed expectations was key to keeping things on good terms. Alain and Lea's talks had progressed all the way to an offer of an ownership stake in exchange for ongoing consulting work. It was a great offer, and one Théo obviously supported, but it wasn't a straightforward choice. It was an undeniable recognition of Lea's competence, but it also posed an existential threat to Gabriel, whose authority was being diminished with every passing day. What was once a self-evident birthright for the eldest son was now at risk of becoming an actual meritocracy—and worse than that, one under the creative direction of *a single, childless, American woman.*

Gabriel had become increasingly scarce as Lea's influence grew, and though that was satisfying, it was also his acrimony that made her unsure as to how entrenched she wanted to be in the long term. No matter what was outlined on paper, he would always be the heir apparent and a substantial shareholder, at minimum. Having her very existence be a source of tension for him was not something she wanted to sign on for.

And besides, there had been no formal offer yet. She could take her time, lingering in the unspoiled fantasies as she did so.

Lea rolled over onto her stomach, turning her eyes away from a ray of sunlight that had fallen directly on her face. She and Théo were spending an hour at the remote pond they'd discovered weeks ago and had been returning to ever since. (They once spent thirty minutes debating which impressionist painter this spot most reminded them of, and Théo had won the argument: it was perfectly Renoir.) They loved to lay a blanket in the tall grass, letting the shade of a tree dapple the sunlight against the skin they left exposed after making love.

"Do you think you're going to take any time off before you start your career?"

"Why?" Théo asked, running a finger down the shallow aqueduct of her spine. "Do you want me to?"

"I'm a neutral third party! I was just curious."

"I think you're technically a second party. And, no, I'm already starting my career way too late. I need to get this show on the road."

"You should cut yourself more slack. You work too hard— your internship, the chateau, taking care of your family. What about just some time for yourself?"

"I'm sorry," He leaned back, resting his head in his hands and closing his eyes, a glorious expanse of skin in the summer light. "Have I not been having the time of my fucking life this summer?"

"I meant besides just having sex with me, Théo. Like, traveling or something."

"Well, first of all, I've traveled a fair amount." He squinted one eye open against the sun, smiling at her. "And second, why is it one or the other? What about traveling together?"

She had never been so relaxed or so open to every possible outcome. She twirled a dandelion between her fingers, struggling to remember the version of herself who was afraid of loving him. "You're right, you're right. We can do both."

"There are so many places I want to go together."

"Like where?" She seamlessly moved herself on top of him, her chest pressed against his, his eyes closed but his smile growing as she kissed his neck.

"I want to take you to South America," he intoned, the words melting on his tongue.

"Oh, yeah? Have you been?"

"Of course. I spent several summers in Brazil with Uncle Nico."

"I feel strange talking about Uncle Nico when we're naked," she laughed. "Do you speak Portuguese?" she asked mindlessly, dotting his chest with feather-light kisses.

"No." He opened his eyes to her, suddenly deadly serious, letting the word linger in the air. "That's Portuguese for 'no.'"

They both burst into laughter, and she couldn't help but move up to kiss him properly, feeling him smile as she pressed her lips to his.

"But seriously," she continued, "Wouldn't I really be taking *you* to South America, anyway? Only one of us has a job."

"Okay, sure, if you have to be so boring about everything. But I would want to take you for Nico's sixty-fifth birthday party, and I'll be working by then."

"Why his sixty-fifth?"

"He always said he would throw an insane party for that birthday, because that's the year their dad retired and stopped living, according to Nico. He keeps calling it his 'rebirth year.'"

Suddenly, her mood shifted, and she pulled back slightly. "How old is he now?"

"About to turn sixty."

"Then that's a really long time from now."

"Um, is it? On the timescale of the universe, I feel like it's not a crazy amount." His usual attempt at levity fell slightly flat.

"I mean, Théo. I'm going to be forty-two by then."

"Yes, and I will be thirty. Are we going to do more math?"

"Well, no. But—" She inhaled sharply, pulling herself back as she prepared to be honest about the unsexy practicality of her thinking, "—it seems kind of naïve to assume we'll still be together then. You really want to be thirty, lugging around a forty-two-year-old?"

"Umm," he started, sitting up on his elbows. "That feels like a loaded question. I would like to be with you, and I don't have a projected expiration date, if that's what you'd like to know."

"Sure, it's all fun now—"

"It is."

"But I mean, I don't know how many super-sexy years I have left. And you're just starting out your adult life. I would

just feel bad holding you back from so many other possibilities."
She looked down, acutely aware of how unappealing this all
must be, especially as she said it naked.

"This is really interesting to me," he said after a moment.

"How so?"

"Well, you seem so convinced that you're the one who is
somehow obligating me, when I'm the one who mentioned
the idea of us being together five years from now."

"I just want to be realistic."

"Is the thought of us being happy together really that
unrealistic?"

"Well, I mean. It feels weird bringing your forty-two-year-
old girlfriend everywhere, no?" *What was wrong with her?*

"I can assure you," he took her hand, pulling her back
toward him. "If we're together five years from now, you're not
just going to be my girlfriend."

Her heart stopped. "What. . . what do you mean?"

"You know what I mean." He smiled. "I'm a good Catholic
boy. I don't live in sin."

The idea was dizzying, thrilling, and terrifying all at once.
It sounded so enticing, and so impossible. All she could do
was pivot back to her comfort zone, the bodily high of the
present. "You're not a good Catholic boy," she purred, running
her hand down his torso.

"Oh, yeah?" He leaned back again, returning his hands
behind his head and presenting himself to her for consumption.
"Then I guess we might as well sin some more."

She plunged upon him, aching with desire to oblige.

22

"Uncle Nico!" Chloë called, running down the front entry stairs of the chateau to the car pulling up, with Alain at the wheel and his brother in the passenger seat. Lea was arranging the lanterns along the driveway, perfectly positioned to watch the family reunion that felt pleasingly reminiscent of the day her own car pulled up for the first time.

"Chloë, my best girl, come here!" Nico called back, unfolding himself from the car. He looked like a slightly disheveled and very tan Alain, but even taller and wearing a very "artist living abroad" look: a dark, breezy shirt, unbuttoned well down his chest and tucked into a fairly wrinkled pair of linen pants. (*Linen on a Transatlantic flight?* Lea thought. *He really* doesn't *fly much.*)

"How was the flight?" Théo asked, emerging onto the driveway with Gabriel. "I saw you got delayed a few times."

Alain jumped in, already assuming a new seriousness in the presence of his older brother. "It's strike season. Everyone is on strike, and the ones who aren't are striking being on strike."

"The flight was perfect." Nico smiled, hugging his nephews one at a time.

"Did you bring us anything?" Chloë asked, seeming delightfully like the curious, sweet girl she was, rather than the too-cool teen she was often playing.

"More than you'll know what to do with," Nico reassured her, gently touching her shoulder. "And who is this?" He turned to Lea, who was still on her knees installing a delicate paper lantern to illuminate the driveway for their guests that night.

"Oh, hi." She stood up, brushing off her hands on her jeans. "I'm Lea, I'm working on—"

"I know what you do," Nico interjected, bringing her in for a friendly *bise*. "I have heard so many excellent things."

"Alain is very kind." Lea smiled. "But you'll get to judge for yourself this evening—we've put together a pretty spectacular party, I think."

Gabriel jumped in, his expression predictably flat in the face of compliments about Lea. "We're even inviting some media tonight, to see how well things are going."

"Hi, everyone," a small voice called from the doorway. Stephanie was standing there in one of her most beautiful sundresses, hair and makeup more polished than usual, looking as nervously hopeful as a girl about to be asked to prom.

"And this," Alain beamed, walking up to escort Stephanie down the stairs and properly present her to his brother, "is my love, Stephanie."

Nico brought her hand to his lips and offered a dashing kiss. "You say she is beautiful, but—how do you say?—you did not prepare."

Stephanie blushed. "You're too kind, Nico. Alain speaks so highly of you."

"Now, this, I do not believe." He elbowed Alain, looking at him conspiratorially.

"I'll bring your things up to your room," Théo offered, walking over to the car and popping the trunk. Lea's heart swooned slightly at his consistent, understated gallantry. "You probably want a shower, no?"

Nico switched back to French, exhausted beyond measure. "I want a shower, and a change of clothes, and a coffee, and a cigarette, and a nap. In whatever order I can get them."

"Come," Chloë grabbed her uncle's hand. "I'll show you to your suite."

"Excuse me, ladies," Nico said, bowing his head slightly to Lea and Stephanie, who was fully wrapped in Alain's proud arms.

After everyone had headed back in, Lea sat on the steps of the entry and pulled up her copious notes-to-self about the evening. There were the caterers being led by Caroline, the printed fact sheets for the media guests, working with Marie to place a million tapered candles on the tables arranged outside, coordinating with the jazz trio, who had been explicitly instructed to play covers of Alain's favorite songs, unboxing the dozens of champagne flutes, bringing out the—

Before she knew what was happening, Théo had pulled the iPad out of her hands from his position behind her. Laughing, Lea stood up to face him, barely coming up to his chest from a few steps down.

"Hey, that's mine!"

"Really? Because I don't think I would have known that, aside from you holding it, and looking at it every ten seconds, and the fact that the leather case has your initials embossed in gold on the front." He held the iPad up, out of her reach.

"I'm very busy, come on." She strained to grab it from him.

"I know that. That's why I came out here. Tell me what you need me to do."

They had created a beautiful routine over the past few weeks, where she sent him items from her daily list that he could help with, leaving her with much more free time (to spend with him, usually). In the chaos of preparing for the party, though, she'd forgotten to delegate that morning, so she quickly explained the things he could easily take over, leaving her with ample time to get ready. "I want you to be gorgeous," he said as he walked away, typing his tasks on his phone.

And she would be, for him.

Everyone came out for the party. The family and the chateau crew, of course, but all of the local friends, Sofian *plus* his wife and kids, nearly every single influencer and journalist Lea had personally reached out to, friends of the family from Paris—including several of Théo's friends, which Lea felt strangely surprised by, their dynamic so insular that she'd forgotten he must have friends back home. Even some of Lea's old clients and industry connections came, as well as all of the regional wine scene's key players.

Lea had popped the tags on the dress that Théo had indeed ended up voting for: a floor-length lavender silk number with barely-there straps and a cut that skimmed her body and revealed most of her back. She had pinned her hair into a low, messy chignon, and wore delicate gold sandals that would make walking on the grass easier. Most importantly, she'd worn the long pendant necklace with a stunning blue stone that Théo had bought for her on a recent work trip to Provence. It was her favorite new piece, and he loved when she wore it. To both of them, it felt like saying "I love you"—even in a crowded room full of people who couldn't know.

She caught his eye from across the patio as she was speaking to an old client and, somehow, everything was effortlessly communicated: she would find a time to slip away and head upstairs, ostensibly to grab something from her room, and he would follow her a few minutes later. He would have five minutes to lavish her with his most ardent attention; then she would smooth her dress and return to work before anyone became aware of their absence.

In the meantime, though, there was a party to tend to.

"Rémy," Lea gestured over to him. "You absolutely have to meet Romain. He's the owner of the Hotel Carla I was telling you about." (She stealthily omitted that he'd named the hotel after his much-younger girlfriend at the time, who later left him for a guitarist from Madrid.)

"We're thinking of rebranding, actually," Romain clarified, shaking Rémy's hand. "Lea, I might have to engage you again for a little consulting."

"You know what I'm going to say, Romain." She smiled at him.

"That the brand equity we have now is going to take years to rebuild?"

"You see? You've already benefited from my counsel without even having to pay me."

As the two men launched into a conversation about the wine facilities at the Hotel Carla —which were now in full fruition, after a few years of mostly selling to co-ops, she might add—Lea headed over to the happy, little cluster of Alain, Stephanie, Marie, Philippe, and a few media guests. They were effusive about the space, as Lea knew they would be, and it was nice to see Marie and Philippe, usually too humble to accept a modicum of praise, take proper credit for its exceptional state.

"I've seen the restaurant menu. It looks incredible," prompted the social media manager of a popular food-and-wine blog, tipping her champagne to be refilled by a passing waiter. "Does it have a name yet?"

Lea jumped in, wanting to spin the frustrating reality that there was *still* no name for the restaurant. "Well, actually—"

"Yes, it does," Alain offered, his voice catching on his words. Clearing his throat, he continued, "The restaurant will be called Anne-Claire. For my late wife."

Lea's heart stopped. She looked over at Stephanie, whose eyes were full of tears. Marie, too, looked rather emotional, apparently not having expected it herself. It was beautiful, and elegant, and Lea would never have thought of it herself—her favorite kind of good idea.

"That's lovely," another reporter chimed in. "And your son will be taking this over, I understand? That's a powerful family legacy."

"Gabriel has been working very closely with me, and he will have a serious role to play in the future of Hôtel Château Victoire," Alain replied, conspicuously avoiding any language about actual inheritance, much to Lea's delight. They still weren't sure that her becoming a partner was the right decision, but the fact that he was backing off from the aristocratic defaulting to first-born as all-powerful king was a step in the right direction.

Hearing his name, Gabriel bounded up to the group, his negroni sloshing slightly as he came to a stop. He threw his arm around his father's shoulder and jumped into the conversation, overflowing with a kind of unsettling confidence and failing to introduce the gorgeous dark-haired woman who was his date for the evening.

He must have gotten some good news, or had one too many glasses of champagne during the toasts. Lea felt the hairs on the back of her neck stand up, concerned about what he might say in front of such important guests and attempting to subdue the nagging, familiar feeling of wishing Alain would rein him in.

About an hour later, Lea was adjusting her hair and makeup in her bathroom mirror as Théo stood behind her, gently kissing her neck and shoulders and begging her to stay just a few minutes longer.

"You know I can't," she whispered, turning to meet his lips for a single, long kiss before breaking away and smoothing her dress one last time. "Tonight is too important. You're lucky I came up here at all."

"Please." He smiled, following her as she walked back into her room. "You were so turned on, I thought you might ruin your dress."

"Me being attracted to you has nothing to do with my job," she quietly responded, smiling as she placed her phone and lipstick in her small handbag. "I'll see you downstairs, okay? Come a few minutes after me, and take the long way. I don't want us walking out through the same door."

"Yes, ma'am." He gently squeezed her backside as she walked past him, out into the hallway.

As soon as she neared the landing of the stairs, she knew something was terribly wrong. Wafting up from the lobby was a voice Lea would recognize anywhere: a somber, exacting voice she'd heard a thousand times—and one that had no business at the chateau.

Marcus.

Lea's blood ran cold as she hid herself just out of sight to listen to what was happening.

"Dad, what are you doing here?" She heard Maya say, voice sounding small and nervous.

"I'm attending the friends-and-family opening. I'm family, right?"

From her hiding spot along the hallway walls, Lea could see their shadows moving, Marcus moving toward her while Maya stepped back, closer to the staircase.

"Does Mom know you're here?"

"Well, she might, if either of you would answer my calls or emails. I've probably heard your voicemail about a thousand times—it's nice to see the roaming charges I've been paying are actually working." It was unbelievable how, even in such an extraordinary moment of violating others, Marcus still managed to make himself the victim.

There was a short, anxious pause, and then Maya's trembling voice. "I have to find Mom. . . I don't think you should be here right now," she finally said, close to tears.

Not wanting to leave her niece in that state, Lea shook herself out of her spying and walked down the stairs to join them in the lobby.

"Hello, Lea," Marcus called over to her in fake diplomacy, totally in control. He looked like the most pitch-perfect version of himself: dark hair slicked back, gray suit, black shoes. A parody of a finance monster.

He had no reason to be there other than to ruin Stephanie's night, and Alain's along with it, but it was always up to the rest of them to go along with the farce that Marcus was doing anything but being a narcissistic nightmare.

"Marcus," she replied, keeping her expression as stern as possible, "why are you here?"

"I'm actually looking to congratulate the happy couple on their big night, and to finally see this place for myself." His face broke into a familiar, condescending smile. "And to speak to my wife."

"You are not on the guest list," Lea clarified, standing beside Maya, who was shaking slightly. "I curated it myself." Speaking from a position of professional authority gave her the boost of confidence she desperately needed.

"Actually, I was invited personally."

As if on cue, Gabriel entered the lobby from the kitchen, walking right up to Marcus for a bizarrely familiar hug.

"I've let my father know you're here," Gabriel told Marcus, before turning briefly to Lea to smile at her. Her blood ran cold.

Lea could barely form words. "Is this some kind of joke, Gabriel? What is this?"

"I'm glad you asked," Gabriel beamed, his eyes glassy and wild. "Marcus and I have been in contact for some time now, and he's just as concerned for his family as I am for mine. It turns out we have a lot in common."

"Fine." Lea hissed, her anxiety turning to an incandescent rage in the face of Gabriel's machinations. She could feel herself growing more forceful, and Maya relaxing slightly under her protection. "I honestly don't care what either of you is trying to pull right now, but it's *my* responsibility to ensure that this night goes well, so I'm not going to give you the scene you're both so clearly—"

Stephanie hadn't even fully entered the foyer when she yelled over to the group assembled by the door: "Marcus, *what the fuck are you doing here?* You have explicitly been told to go through the lawyers for all communication."

"Hi, Stephanie. It's good to see you." Marcus smiled, becoming even calmer in the face of her fury.

Lea felt herself cringe inside with the loudness of it all, the scene unfolding at such an inopportune moment. But then she reminded herself that this was Marcus' playbook to a tee, pushing someone to the brink of madness and then using that madness to humiliate and cow them.

The group stood silent for a moment, Stephanie shaking with anger, until Alain ran up behind her, breathless. "This is extremely inappropriate," he started, "We should not be doing this here."

"Alain, it's nice to finally meet you. I've heard many great things." Marcus was unwavering in his quiet, threatening confidence. "I'm not planning to stay long, but she and I need to speak, and I'm sick of emailing her stonewalling lawyers. . . some of whom seem to be French? I'm interested to see if our divorce will be litigated in international waters. . ."

Gabriel chuckled.

"I have nothing to say to you," Stephanie said, her voice low but determined.

Marcus absentmindedly checked his phone before continuing, another one of his exhausting power moves. "Well, there's actually a lot that you'll need to say, one way or the other."

Alain stepped slightly in front of Stephanie. "Is this a threat?"

"No, it's actually not. It's me trying to help her, since she blew off a court summons and put herself at risk of arrest—if she ever decides to go back to her actual life, that is."

"*Arrest?*" Alain looked at her, doing his best to stay gallant and righteous in the face of this new information.

"I'm not going to be arrested," Stephanie clarified to Alain, her eyes still trained on Marcus. "It's called an '*order to show cause.*' I'll explain it to you later."

"Steph, you knew about this?" Lea asked, torn between her desire to form a united front against Marcus and a familiar frustration with the unseriousness Stephanie had been exhibiting ever since she was served.

Marcus continued. "We can do this the easy way or the hard way. But you've been running away from your life long enough, and some of us are trying to be the grown-ups in the room and deal with the mess we're in. Unless you've forgotten, you're still my wife."

"That's enough," Alain stepped forward. "I'm not going to let you do this here."

"Marcus is right," Gabriel coldly interjected, glaring at his father and switching to French to dress him down with a full range of vocabulary. "Both of you have been running from reality. She's playing house and you're giving over the future of our property to an American consultant who has no connection to our heritage," he directed his words at Lea, all pretense of diplomacy evaporated, "and who wants to sell our products to the lowest bidder while going way over budget. And *now* you have a girlfriend you want on your arm for every hotel function, who it turns out is on the run from the law or whatever she is."

Gabriel continued after a dramatic pause. "I am sick of being the only person who cares about protecting and preserving our legacy."

"How dare you," Lea snapped, too angry to speak in anything but English. "I have given everything to this project. All of that press you're currently trying to humiliate us in front of are here because of *my* work."

"Oh, yes, a bunch of second-rate influencers drinking free champagne, who will sell our wine to broke college students and get sluts with travel Instagrams to take pictures of the zebra curtains in exchange for free rooms."

Alain raised his hand toward his son in an attempt to bring him to heel. "Gabriel, that's—"

"You're fucking high again," Théo spat from the top of the stairs. "Go outside and cool off. You're going to regret this tomorrow." He started moving down the stairs in a determined rage, stopping mid-step at the sight of his uncle.

"*No, no, absolutely not,*" Nico and his French swept into the lobby with the full force of his patriarchal status, only two years older than Alain but carrying the familial role of eldest son like a heavy crown to which everyone deferred. "Take this into the office, all of you, *right now.*"

He wordlessly shepherded the group, confused and disoriented as they were, into the darkened office before turning on a large desk lamp and continuing. "There are about a hundred guests out there who will determine the future of this hotel and you are causing a scene in the front entry hall? Alain, pull your family together." Alain looked deeply embarrassed as Stephanie, unsure of exactly what was said, put a timid hand on his shoulder.

The last to arrive, and shutting the door behind him, Théo's voice was so angry he was nearly yelling. "*You have got to be kidding me, Dad.* Gabriel creates this chaos on the night of your big party and the problem is our location?"

"I didn't bring us in this room," Alain responded lamely, failing to address the meaning of his words.

"Actually," Marcus clarified, "Gabriel didn't tell me to come tonight. He told me I had a standing invitation to come if I needed to, and I decided to come when the court summonses were piling up at my front door and this one—" he gestured derisively toward Stephanie "—wasn't answering any of my emails."

"Oh, right, it had nothing to do with wanting to ruin the most important evening of my summer," Stephanie hissed back at him.

Marcus didn't even look at her as he replied. "It had to do with knowing you were going to be here tonight, and not off doing. . . whatever it is you do with your time these days."

Théo jumped in again, almost laughing with rage. "I am hallucinating. We're just not going to address Gabriel being out of his mind? Or maybe all the demeaning and sexist shit he just said to Lea?"

Gabriel narrowed his eyes, and took on an eerily calm tone. "Of course. The lover comes to save his queen."

Lea's heart jumped into her throat.

"Oh, right, you probably don't know—" he turned to Stephanie and Maya, who were both in a stunned, slack silence. "Lea and Théo have been having an affair for months." His eyes gleamed with a reckless intensity.

There was a brutal silence in the group, save Marcus, who gave an infuriating chuckle under his breath and shook his head.

Maya turned to look at Lea, whose frantic explanation only made things worse. "No—that's not true. I mean, yes, I don't know—"

"Aunt Lea," Maya cut her off, looking deeply pained. "What is he talking about?"

"I don't think we should be talking about this here. I—"

"When did you start—" she caught on the word "—dating him?"

"I don't know, I. . . I really don't think we should talk about this right now."

Maya's eyes started filling with tears. Lea moved to comfort her, but Stephanie stepped forward to stop her, putting them toe-to-toe.

"That had better be a fucking joke. I *knew* something was off."

"Steph, I didn't—"

"After how you dragged me through the mud week after week for moving on too soon—how it wasn't fair to Maya, how I needed to think about her more? You were watching her cry and pretending to give her helpful auntie advice? The whole time, you were sleeping with *Théo*?"

"Mom, please—" Maya tried to cut between them, humiliated by these revelations.

"This is priceless," Marcus laughed, watching the scene unfold.

Stephanie's eyes were wild with anger. "You made me feel like a terrible mother, night after night."

"You're not a terrible mother, Steph." Lea's panicked words spilled from her, senseless. "You're the best mother. You know I think that."

Alain came up behind Stephanie and gently pulled her shoulders back, calming her. He gave Lea a single harsh, disapproving look before turning toward his son to give him the same.

Lea made another lame attempt at defending herself. "This was never my intention, I swear. I love you both so much and I would never—"

"Stephanie," Théo interjected, walking over to Lea, who spontaneously recoiled. "I know the timing wasn't ideal, but Lea never meant to hurt anyone. She did her best to navigate a very complicated situation."

Stephanie gave him a poisonous glare before returning her focus to Lea, but he plunged forward. "You should be angry with me, not her. But I won't be ashamed. Lea and I are in love."

The room fell into a dumbfounded silence as Théo moved to wrap a comforting arm around Lea—a mirror of his father's righteous stance with Stephanie—and she pulled away. Her entire body tensed as she imagined what they were thinking, viscerally resenting this naïve twenty-four-year-old boy for thinking he'd made anything but the worst possible move.

She braced herself for the river of judgment she knew was imminent as Gabriel broke the silence with more vicious commentary: "Jesus, Théo, get a hold of yourself. I didn't know you missed Mom *that* badly."

Despite the many unfortunate things that had been said over the past twenty minutes, this was the first to draw an audible gasp from the group. Lea steadied herself to respond in kind but, before she could, Théo was charging toward his brother, meeting his face with a clenched fist so hard that it made a sharp *smack* sound and sent him careening backward.

As Gabriel was reeling to stand back up, Théo began frantically ripping at his brother's jacket, spewing verbal hatred and madly asking where the pills were. Nico, closer to the brothers than Alain, managed to grab Théo around his waist, pulling him back just as he wrapped his hands around Gabriel's throat. Theo's face was red and veiny with fury as he shook his brother's neck, blood beginning to trickle from his nose. Alain joined the melee, working in tandem with Nico to tear his sons apart. By the time Théo was fully removed, Stephanie and Maya were screaming for it to stop while Lea was yelling for them to *shh, so* as to not call more attention to the scene.

"You fucking broke my nose!" Gabriel yelled animalistically, covering his face with both hands, his eyes wide in total panic. "You piece of shit, I'm going to kill you!"

"Your nose is not broken, Gabriel." Nico sternly walked toward him and pulled out a handkerchief to press to his face while Alain held Théo's arms behind his back. "I'm going to give you one chance to tell me that you're using again. The next conversation is going to be with the police."

"Uncle Nico, I—"

"*Who do you think you're talking to?*" Nico gestured to the tattoo of twenty lines on his forearm, a visual reminder of his years sober.

A heavy pause, before Gabriel burst out again.

"I'm the only one who actually cares about the future of this hotel, and I have a full-time consulting job on top of all this!" He looked over at his father and brother, tears flowing freely, a perfect equilibrium of anger and pain. "I get five hours' sleep on a good night!"

Nico shot a somber glance at Alain before returning his eyes to Gabriel, more tenderly. "We're going outside to have a smoke and calm down, okay? *Okay?*"

Gabriel's bloodshot eyes were still fixed on Théo as he slipped an "Okay" through his clenched teeth.

Nico grabbed his nephew to walk him outside, turning to Alain on the way out. "You take Théo upstairs to calm down, and then you get back out to that party and you pretend like everything is wonderful for your guests. We will deal with all this tomorrow."

Alain nodded, moving to take a breathless Théo back into the main hall, but not before icily informing Marcus that if he did not remove himself in the next thirty seconds, the police would.

23

With the men gone, Lea turned to Stephanie, who was now holding her daughter protectively in her arms.

"Maya, please——" Lea moved toward them, but Stephanie looked up at her with pure, terrifying rage.

"You stay away from her."

Maya slipped from her mother's grasp and ran from the room, her face buried in her hands, too embarrassed to look at anyone who might be in the lobby.

Lea willed her heart rate to slow, breathing in a gentle rhythm. "Steph, listen, I know it's been a crazy night. We don't have to talk about any of this now. But you know how much I love you both—you were never meant to find out like this."

Stephanie's rage had drained into a terrifying coolness. "I need to go take care of my daughter. I don't have time to deal with your feelings about what *you* did."

Lea's voice broke with small, nervous tears. "Please, Steph, don't do this. I made a mistake."

"I have made a lot of mistakes in my life, Lea. But what you did, I would never have done to someone. Maya trusted you."

Lea flushed with humiliation. "I just didn't. . . I didn't want to break her heart. What was I supposed to do?"

"How about trying to be an actual grown-up?" Stephanie grew more imposing with each word, seeming to unfold vertically before her cowed best friend.

"I did the best I could," Lea offered, limply.

"He's half your age."

"Come on, no he's not. Don't say that."

"Fine, he's Maya's age. And you're her aunt, not her fucking sorority sister." Stephanie took a moment to compose herself, and the din of the party rose in the brief silence. "She looks up to you like nobody else, and you know how much trouble she's had with boys."

"No, she hasn't."

"Excuse me?"

"She doesn't like bringing guys home, but she falls for them all the time. . . I just thought her infatuation would fade, like it always does."

Stephanie narrowed her eyes, growing furious at the insinuation that Lea knew her own daughter better than she did. "So you lied to her."

"I didn't—I swear I didn't. I just didn't say anything for too long, and then I was backed into a corner. I felt so trapped."

"So you took it out on me, right?"

"No—"

"Yeah." She looked down, freshly disappointed. "That's exactly what happened. You made me feel ashamed for loving Alain, for daring to be happy after living in hell for twenty years."

"Okay." Lea felt herself rise with a burgeoning righteousness of her own. "That isn't fair, Steph. I didn't think you shouldn't love him. But knowing what Marcus is capable of, I was worried that you weren't taking this divorce seriously. . . like you were content to just sit back while Alain swooped in to save the day."

For the first time that evening, Stephanie looked slightly abashed, but powered through with more anger. "You have no idea what you're talking about."

"Yes, I do. You didn't answer those discovery questions, Steph, and I told you from day one that you can't do that. I wasn't trying—"

"You '*told me from day one*' I couldn't do that? How do you not hear yourself, Lea? Why is it always somehow your place to tell me what to do?"

"I don't, Stephanie, it's just—"

Stephanie cut her off again, furious. "Oh, give me a break. I can literally quote every last thing your therapist has ever said about me, because apparently all you ever do in there is bitch about my marriage. And now, I guess, my divorce, too!"

"Okay, I need you to back off," Lea said, reclaiming herself. "I try to be *helpful* because you were in an abusive marriage and I wanted to get you out of it. And I was on you about those discovery questions because I didn't want you to end up exactly where you are right now, getting dragged to court and giving him all the leverage he needs to ruin your life."

Stephanie kept an aggressive stance, but her power had ebbed slightly. "I don't need your help. And don't act like you had everyone's best interest at heart this summer—look at what you were doing to Maya behind her back!"

"Oh, my god, Stephanie, what about what you were doing *to her face?*"

The dam was broken. Lea's defensive position had completely dissolved, and the grievances were flooding out of her. "How was it okay to just trauma dump on your twenty-year-old daughter for months on end and then confide in her nonstop about a man you fell in love with after two weeks? How do you think *that* feels?"

She burned with the memories of her own mother doing the same.

"*Trauma dumping?* Is that another one of Dr. Miller's brilliant terms?"

"No, it's an actual term, and I don't think it's an exaggeration. Like when you confronted Marcus with all those printed-out texts literally in front of her, you don't think that was trau—"

"I'm done with this conversation. I'm not going to sit here and listen to you try to make *me* the bad guy."

"You're not the bad guy. I'm just being honest."

"And I'm being honest, too." Stephanie's eyes bore into Lea, full of sadness and fury. "Pursuing Théo was absolutely *pathetic*. And if you cared about anyone besides yourself and your perfect little business, maybe you'd see that." She paused, weighing how cruel she wanted to be, before plowing forward. "But you don't. Because you're not capable of really caring about anyone but yourself."

Lea had nothing with which to counter, nothing she could offer in the face of such brutal admonishment. Stephanie moved toward the door, smoothing her hair back down as she readied herself to resume the party.

Before leaving, she turned to look at Lea, mournful and resigned. "I'm going to find my daughter. Do *not* follow me."

The door closing behind Stephanie felt like a vacuum, sucking the air out of the room and out of Lea's lungs. There was nothing more to say, only the stark confirmation that every awful thing Lea had ever thought about herself or about this foolish relationship with Théo was absolutely true, and then some. He was embarrassingly young, this was all totally ridiculous, and Lea had constructed a life that appeared glamorous from the outside as a shiny distraction that she was empty and directionless within.

The bass-heavy music of the party rattled the office through the heavy wooden doors, providing just enough cover for Lea to weep as loudly as she needed to.

Théo was sitting on the edge of his bed when Lea slipped in, partygoers outside still enjoying their evening, undisturbed. She walked over and knelt down across from him on the floor, face streaked with mascara from the sobbing she'd done in the office after Stephanie's departure, and then in her room.

"I'm so sorry," Théo quietly offered. "I should have known Gabriel would pull something."

"It's not your fault," Lea reassured, having nearly forgotten about Gabriel after her conversation with Stephanie.

"Why are you speaking to me in English?" he asked, reaching for her hand with his, which she limply held.

"Because I can't even think straight."

She let a long pause linger in the air before continuing.

"I booked a ticket on the train back to Paris first thing tomorrow. I'm flying home."

Théo's expression suddenly changed, snapping into a pained awareness. "Flying *home?* To DC?"

"Yes. I can't be here right now."

"I understand wanting to leave the chateau," he slipped down onto the floor across from her, "but why would you go home?"

"You can't be serious." She looked at him, unable to stop her tears from springing anew.

"Well, yes. . . aren't there some things left to do before guest bookings start?"

She felt almost offended at this invocation of her obsessive professionalism—as if he were leveraging it to keep her there, as if he knew about the remaining loose ends better than she did.

"Théo, I have to resign. I'm not going to suffer the humiliation of letting your father fire me, or asking me to leave."

He was becoming more desperate with each response. "He wouldn't ask you to leave. He loves you. He loves your work."

Lea stood up, angrily wiping the tears from under her eyes.

"I truly can't have another person tell me what your father is or isn't going to do with me."

He looked up at her from his seat on the floor, seeming more boyish than ever, having gotten himself into more trouble than he knew how to deal with. "My dad is just panicking right now. Things will settle down tomorrow."

Lea suddenly felt a great, overwhelming shame bubble up inside her, turning her stomach. There was a reason romances like this didn't work, but she had been naïve and reckless enough to completely ignore it, to pretend that theirs would be the exception, that she could be grown-up enough for the two of them, when she wasn't even grown-up enough for herself.

But his behavior tonight—declaring his love at the exact wrong moment, running across the room to attack his brother, casually insisting that everything would work itself out, despite the gravity of the situation—cast into stark relief the distance between them. The effortless way he moved through life, and specifically through his interactions with her, suddenly felt deadly unappealing. She was a grown woman who knew better, and he was a young, idealistic college student who was a very good person and an excellent lover with whom she had no business trying to get serious.

She cautiously started, knowing where she needed to end their conversation. "You do not understand how bad this is, and I don't blame you for not understanding." It was not lost on her that this was almost exactly how Stephanie had spoken to her when she broke the news of her divorce, and only now could Lea truly hold the weight of those words. "This is the worst possible thing that could have happened to me. This is my career, this is my family, my closest friendships. This is literally everything I have, everything I built in my life, going up in flames all at once." She was sobbing.

He stepped toward her to comfort her as she instinctively pulled back, so he offered his protest from several feet away. "I know this is a really difficult moment, but now we're out in the open. Now we can be together, like we wanted."

How stupid, Lea thought, *to have ever thought I could have this.*

"You think I care about having a boyfriend right now?" She could barely contain the venomous tone of her voice.

"Excuse me? What is that supposed to mean?" His tone had shifted, now more offended than sad.

"It means that I'm an actual adult, and I have to actually deal with this. My solution is not just punching Gabriel in the face and feeling like a hero, or declaring my love to the group like Cyrano de fucking Bergerac." She looked at him, considering for a moment before plunging forward in her reproach. "All you did was make this so much worse."

Théo sounded stunned, and now more viscerally angry, returned to his native tongue to admonish her. "Lea, I don't want to disrupt your worldview, but not everything is about you. I didn't punch Gabriel to help you, or to be a hero. I punched him because I couldn't take one more second of his bullshit after years of him ripping apart this family because he can't be happy with himself."

A familiar feeling—that Théo was right, and that Lea couldn't handle it—started pulling at her. So she fought it as best she could. "And because you're a twenty-four-year-old who has no sense of the consequences of any of this."

"Does it make you feel better to be cruel to me right now? Is that the solution to your problems?"

"I'm not being cruel. I'm being honest."

"No, you're not. You're trying to make me feel bad for having my own reactions. And I'm not going to apologize for not letting you stage-direct me."

"You're right. You're allowed to react however you want to. But you're going to head back to Boulogne and live in your father's house and continue working on your consequence-free internship. And I have to return to real life."

"That really does make you feel good, doesn't it?"

"What?"

"To pretend like my life is meaningless because I'm younger than you. You know I cared for my mother in hospice, right? You know I took care of my sister while my father was visiting my brother in rehab every weekend? You know I've spent the past five years running around picking up the pieces so my father can pretend everything is normal and happy? You think my life is consequence-free?"

Shit, she was attracted to him again. But now, in her attraction was a glimmer of pity: not for him, but for herself. Pity that she had never wanted something more, or could have it less. He wasn't going to convince her to stay, to meet up with him in Paris, or to do anything other than return to DC to lick her wounds. But she couldn't bear to go on hurting him like this.

As if he could sense her on the back foot, he moved toward her, and this time she didn't step back. But rather than approaching her, even in this incredibly heightened moment, he sensed that what was necessary for her to return to him was to keep his distance, to not bend to her need to control and manage the situation. He walked over to his desk and sat, calmly looking at her from across the room.

After several moments of him not speaking, she finally broke the silence herself.

"I meant everything I said to you."

"I know you did."

"But this is not something that's just going to magically work itself out in the morning."

"I never said it was. I said that my father wasn't going to fire you, and that things would be calmer in the morning.

Gabriel is going to realize what he did, and he's probably going to check himself into rehab again. I'd put money on it, actually." He checked his watch, back to his unflappable calm that infuriated and desperately excited her.

But the weight of the humiliation—and her need to regain control—was much stronger. "Théo, I can't just finish this job out like everything's normal. Stephanie and Maya hate me for this, and I can't think about trying to somehow maintain a long-distance relationship on top of that and a thousand other things. Stop making me feel like a terrible person for being honest about that."

"I'm not going to help you torpedo this relationship just because you think destroying us is some kind of penance."

Tears silently streaming down her face, she whispered, "It's not about penance."

"Then tell me why you're leaving me. I need you to tell me."

"Because," she replied, her quiet voice cracking with tears, "because I can't be with anyone. Because something is wrong with me. Because I was capable of doing that to my niece, who is more like a daughter to me, who is one of the only people I've had this close in my entire life." Her eyes darted to the corner of the ceiling, struggling to keep composure. "I promised to take her if anything ever happened to Stephanie, and I betrayed her in the worst way anyone could. This is like a stake through her fucking heart, Théo. *What is wrong with me?*"

His voice was soft with reassurance, and more than a little sadness. "Nothing more than whatever is wrong with me. We fell in love. Sometimes it happens under unideal circumstances."

She stifled a small, delirious laugh at the ridiculousness of his understatement before composing herself again. "It doesn't matter, anyway. You shouldn't be with me. You should be with a girl your own age, who can give you a future, and children–"

"Which I never said I wanted."

"Which you will eventually want. All French men do."

"First of all, not *all*, look at Uncle Nico. Second, not to split hairs, but we could have children."

"No, we couldn't, Théo."

"Why?" Suddenly they were in a tennis volley instead of a breakup conversation, and she had to get it back on track.

"Because I'm a million fucking years old. But forget the kid thing, how about just finding someone who doesn't start the relationship by destroying everyone she loves, just like my mother did over and over."

"You are not your mother."

"Really? Because that was pretty uncanny." Her laughter at her own words was manic and full of self-hatred. "The only thing that would have made it more on-the-nose would be if you were some musician about to go on tour for six months."

He was stoic, unmoving. "I'm not going to help you beat yourself up."

"Fine. I don't need you to. But I can't talk anymore."

"Then stop talking."

They looked at each other for a long while, silent.

Then, as if under a spell, she found herself walking over to him, suddenly so deep in need of him that she couldn't allow herself to remember anything that had happened beyond the walls of the room. She dropped to her knees in front of him and buried her head in his lap, crying softly.

He stroked her hair, whispering that it would be okay. And after a while, when her tears had stopped, he took her hands in his and walked her over to his bed, turning off the overhead lights as he went and leaving them lit only by a single, dim wall sconce. In the warm darkness, nothing mattered, and Lea could allow herself to be the person she knew she couldn't be in the light of day, that she would probably never be again.

And knowing it was almost certainly the last time, she allowed herself to be taken under by the gluttonous abandon of someone about to go on a strict diet in the morning. She pulled at him to bring his weight down on top of her; she kept her lips glued to his as she guided his hands and helped him rip away her already-negligible clothing. She kept raising her hips to meet him, to take in more of him, forcing herself to maximize and remember every minute detail as best she could. She felt like an animal, possessed by an unspeakable need, biting his neck and taking his fingers into her mouth to silence herself, to feel overtaken by him at every angle.

She helped him bring her to orgasm after orgasm, continuing their insatiable ravaging of each other long after the partygoers had gone, ignorant of the other family members talking in hushed tones in the hallway, almost certainly noticing that her room was empty or the noises indicating that Théo's wasn't. It didn't matter. She was already humiliated, she was already degraded, she had already lost everything that mattered. All she could do now was enjoy herself, ask him to give her everything she wanted, and then, once obliged, ask for more.

Somewhere in the late hours, when even the caterers had stopped cleaning up, she walked the two of them over to one of the enormous double-door windows and opened them, feeling the cool wind on her back as she leaned naked against the ornate railing, him kneeling between her legs, tears rolling down her cheeks as she brought her closed eyes up to the sky and opened them, wondering if this was the last time she'd ever feel this way. She knew that she would be gone in the morning, and that he would probably grow to hate her as she closed herself off, the way she had done a hundred times before. But for now, there was just this moment between them, and a rawness to the full experience of life that could only come from experiencing both sharp pain and extraordinary pleasure in such a short amount of time.

He arose from his knees after a time, coming up to lean himself against her, enveloping her with his skin and the subtle scent she'd first breathed the moment she stepped onto the property. He knew better than to ask what she was thinking, what she would do in the morning—most likely because he already knew the answer to both. He contented himself to kiss her more deeply than he ever had, to run his fingers through her hair, still damp with sweat despite the evening breeze. He brought his lips down to her ear the way he had on the dance floor that night at Apostrophe and said, simply, "I will always love you."

Despite herself, a soft moan escaped her, something within the depths of her body that longed to mourn for everything she was about to lose.

The train was to depart at 6:45, and Lea had arranged for the one taxi service she could get a hold of to pick her up at 6:15 sharp. After Théo had fallen asleep in her arms, sometime around three AM, Lea had slipped back into her own room and started the most rapid-fire version of her methodical, seamless packing routine. She had little time—barely enough to take a shower and put on a decent outfit—and knew if she were here when the chateau started to awaken, or god forbid when Théo came looking for her, that she may not have the strength to do things the way she needed to do them.

She slipped out the front door as silently as she could with all of her bags in tow, rushing across the driveway to help the driver pack the trunk and get on the road as quickly as possible, terrified that someone might come out and try to speak to her, or even acknowledge her existence. The chateau façade in the cool light of pre-dawn felt like even *it* was in mourning, and she had to turn away and squeeze her eyes closed as the car pulled off, unable to draw a proper breath until she was away from the property and on the main road, where it could no longer hurt her with its sad, beautiful stone.

Suppressing the tears that were fighting to escape, she pulled out her iPad to finish the email she would send to the entire chateau—the family, *her* family, Marie, Philippe, everyone —before they awoke, so that there would be no conversation amongst them without having seen it. She couldn't speak for herself in real time (even if they'd asked her to stay, she could never bear it), but she could at least be her own spokesperson from afar, and that's what she had to attempt to do.

To the Hôtel Château Victoire,

It is with deepest sadness that I must tender my resignation, as of this morning, August 19th. Along with this resignation from my day-to-day duties, I will also be abdicating my remaining fee to account for the few remaining items on my list of deliverables, as well as to offset any need to hire an interim consultant to oversee our final preparations.

I will be reaching out to Alain separately to ensure a smooth transition, but I am confident that Marie will be an excellent steward in welcoming the first wave of guests, and that Philippe will bring in all remaining renovations under budget, ahead of schedule, and with his impeccable level of quality.

As most of you know, I engaged in an inappropriate relationship with one of the members of the Lévesque family, and I'm sure those who aren't yet aware will be hearing about it in the coming days. While I deeply regret my behavior, and the pain and complication it has caused for my own family as well as the Lévesques, I must advocate for myself in saying that despite my recklessness, I never wished to compromise my work or these relationships I so value and care about. I hope that with time, everyone might learn to forgive me, and that in the interim, if nothing else, everyone will remember just how fondly I think of them.

Last night notwithstanding, this project has been the most fulfilling, exciting, and creatively invigorating of my career. I am immensely proud of what we have created together, and am humbled to have been charged with leading things as long as I have. I am also deeply

*grateful to have inadvertently brought together Alain and
Stephanie, two incredible people whose love is inspiring
and has brought joy to every day I've spent working here.*

*A good consultant's job is to know when her work is
essential, and when she is no longer needed. And though
my goodbye comes earlier than I might have hoped, and
under worse terms than I could have anticipated, I wish
nothing but the greatest success for everyone involved in
this incredible project. I will think of you all often, and
fondly.*

*Warmly,
Lea Mortimer*

By the time she finished typing out the French version
of her email, the taxi was drawing to a slow stop in front
of the train station. She wiped her eyes as best she could,
unable to stop the constant stream of tears the driver was too
embarrassed to ask about, and started unloading her bags from
the trunk, still early enough to grab a coffee.

24

FOUR MONTHS LATER

A sugary dusting of snow was beginning to fall outside the windows at Branca, where Lea was waiting alone, adjusting the festive holiday micro-bouquet on her table. Her leg nervously rapped against her chair, heightened by the one cappuccino she'd downed before ordering the decaf before her, all without having so much as touched the oversized bottle of sparkling water she'd ordered to go with it. She could still barely eat these days—had lost ten pounds since leaving the chateau—and had switched to a wardrobe of nearly all black, as it demanded the fewest number of brain cells when getting ready in the morning.

Stephanie and Maya were still not speaking to her, not answering her emails or texts, not giving her the faintest sign of life. Her only conversation with Alain had been a terse, clipped back-and-forth about the remaining tasks at the chateau she hadn't been able to complete, and even that mostly consisted of his new assistant Sandrine asking Lea to speak more slowly so that she could take proper notes. Even Théo, her wonderful, gorgeous Théo, had finally stopped reaching out to her after receiving what limited, cold responses she could manage to send in her state of total humiliation.

The self-loathing and remorse she felt were so great, so all-consuming, that to have a man be kind to her only heightened her self-loathing, as if she were taking advantage of his youth, because only naïveté could explain why he failed to understand how much of a mess she was.

She'd also removed all social media from her devices, as seeing the goings-on of these people, none of whom had the mercy to block her, was too painful to bear. She knew there would be ample photos of Stephanie and Alain, of the chateau opening, of Maya back at school, of Théo—probably with an age-appropriate girlfriend, more beautiful and free than Lea had ever been. And just imagining what was there, what might accost her as she mindlessly scrolled her feeds, made her navigate the internet like it was a game of Minesweeper. That meant carefully opening only the minimum windows necessary to not lose her apartment and to remain generally functional, nothing more.

She had summoned the strength to venture out only through complete desperation. With her support system all but gone, and about to leave for the holidays, she needed someone to talk to. Her brother would prefer to not hear about any messiness, her mother was predictably without a working phone plan, and her father would berate her about her reckless behavior. Her lesser friends, her other cousins, her work acquaintances, or, god forbid, her former clients: none of them had the context or the safety that would permit her to speak earnestly. Only after she caught herself thinking, almost casually, that she wished she could close her eyes and never open them again, did she finally accept that she needed to speak to someone. Dr. Miller would take an emergency session, but she also knew he wasn't who she most needed to talk to now.

From across the warmly white cafe with elegant, romantic wall sconces—just as Lea would have designed them, she often thought approvingly—David swung open the large glass door, pulling his knit scarf against himself to stave off the cold. Seeing her, he waved in a friendly, open way, and Lea immediately burst into tears.

One hour, two decaf cappuccinos, and a sheepish pivot to red wine later, Lea told him everything as he gently held her hand across the table. He was a married man, and she knew that under any other circumstance, this moment would seem highly inappropriate. But in this case, they both understood that there was nothing sexual or even vaguely romantic about this gesture. He was showing her love and compassion without expectation, because he was a good person, a truly *good person*—a thought that overwhelmed her anew each time she thought about it, increasing the steady river of tears that were already streaming down her cheeks. Normally she would be embarrassed by such a display, even from the corner table, but she was too past the point of humiliation to care about something so petty.

She told him about the chateau, about the work itself, about Marcus cheating—*"Guarantee you that wasn't the first time,"* David had taken a moment to note—about Maya falling for Théo at first sight. She told him about the parties and the dinners and the tennis matches and the days by the pool that felt like one long Hockney painting come to life. She told him about her relationship with Théo, about their life-changing sex (she was too delirious to be prudish about the details), about how she fell in love with him, about how it all came crashing down, about how Théo had told her that Gabriel was now in a treatment center for the second time and Uncle Nico was staying in France to help manage the family, as well as the hotel's launch.

She leaned into the unique lack of shame she'd always felt with David, even if she'd always believed it came from disrespect on her part, and purged herself of every thought she'd had about her summer like poison from a wound.

"Wow, Lee—" he started when she'd finished, brushing a hand through his surprisingly long, dense hair, the corners of his mouth turning up in a reluctant smile. "That's pretty fucking crazy." His voice caught a laugh on the word "crazy."

She let a small laugh out along with him, out of relief as much as agreement. "Yeah, it's insane."

"*Literally insane,*" he said, his laughter picking up steam.

She was suddenly unable to stop herself, doubling over along with him. "Someone needs to pay me for this story," she said, now crying tears of laughter.

"I knew there was a reason you loved those trips so much. You're out here having an episode of *Maury* at a French chateau."

The two of them laughed until their sides hurt, in the process bypassing the need for any explanation as to why she needed to speak to him or what his role was in this entire saga. He knew, and mercifully, he would give her what she was too timid to outright ask for.

"Well, Lee, I'm guessing you probably want me to tell you that you're a terrible person for all of this." He sipped his glass of Malbec, maintaining eye contact as she valiantly tried to wipe the accumulated mascara under her eyes.

"Why do you say that?"

"Because that's your favorite game. You render some horrible judgment about yourself, and you get angry with people until they finally agree with you."

"Have you been talking to Dr. Miller?"

"Hah, no, I don't have that kind of money. I have a kid."

"I know. He's beautiful."

"I know."

"And so is your wife."

"Yes, she is. And, I should say, very impressed with your work."

Lea blushed. "That's very kind."

"Everyone is." His eye contact never broke, willing her to accept the compliment.

"Well, thank you. But I don't know what good that does when I can't even keep around the few people who actually loved me."

"Stephanie is going to come around, I promise you. She knows how much you took care of her all those years with Marcus. She knows how much you helped with Maya."

"Maybe."

"This will pass. I know it will."

"How?"

"Well, I. . ." He hesitated, choosing his words carefully. "I want to be honest that when you reached out, I called Stephanie."

"You *what?*"

"Lea, you scared me. I thought you might have done something drastic, and I was really worried."

She was too desperate for intel to bother pushing back. "Well, and? What did she say?"

"I'm not going to betray her confidence"—his maturity was always something to behold—"But yes, she's really upset with you. I think she's really upset with herself, too, even if she didn't say it in those words."

"With the court summons stuff?"

"With all of it. She knows that she blew off a lot of responsibility this year, and I don't think she understood how much financial danger she was putting herself and Maya in by treating this divorce like an optional thing."

"I *told* her."

"I assumed you did. But she did the thing that Stephanie does sometimes—she hitched her wagon to someone and hoped for the best. She's lucky that Alain is a good guy. Hell, she's lucky that you bringing them along turned out as well as it did for her, given everything. It could have been a disaster."

"Yeah, I guess that's probably true."

"Anyway, I would just give it more time. Let's not forget that she's currently going through a messy divorce with a literal narcissist. It probably feels pretty good to be angrier at someone else than she is at herself."

"She *should* be angrier at me."

"I mean, maybe? I can tell you that your opinion means a lot to her, and she probably feels pretty damn embarrassed about how this all went down, and the side of her you saw. I don't think you realize how intimidating you are to other people."

Lea shot her eyes to the floor, unable to take in his words completely. "I've never gone this long without speaking to her, not since I was five years old. This feels different."

"It *is* different. But that doesn't mean it's forever."

She took in a long, deep breath, feeling a shred of clarity for the first time in months. "Why are you always so reasonable?"

"Hah! You should tell my wife that."

"I'm serious. You're being so nice, and so level-headed, and you don't owe me anything." She paused, looking down at the table. "And you were always this way. So nice to me, even when I wasn't nice to you."

"You didn't love me as much as I loved you. I went over that about a thousand times with my own therapist, when I had one. I was treating you nicely because I loved you, and that's what love looks like."

"And now? Why are you being so nice to me?"

"Because I still care about you, and I want you to be happy. I want you to be okay. Also, not to downplay my own gallantry here, but I'm listening to you tell a crazy story over a glass of wine, not buying you a home, Lea."

She laughed. "But do you regret it? Being with me?" She felt embarrassed at the gratuitousness of the question, but she couldn't help herself. "I wasted a lot of your time."

He gave her a deadpan, almost bored look. "Oh, come on."

"What?"

"You need me to do this?"

She broke into a coy smile.

"Of course I don't regret being with you. You opened me up to so many things I would have never otherwise

347

experienced—I probably wouldn't have been good enough for Cady if I hadn't been with you first. And it was *not* a waste of time: you're beautiful, you're intelligent, you're hardworking, you're incredibly talented, you're cultured, you're independent, and you're funny. Anybody would be lucky to spend a day with you, let alone six years. Does that answer your question?"

Her smile had broken into a full-on grin. "I guess so."

"And I wasn't what you wanted." The corners of her mouth fell. "I told myself for years that I was too short, or too boring, or too much of a 'nice guy.' But I eventually realized when I met Cady that it wasn't really any of those things. I just wasn't the guy you wanted."

"You make an incredible friend."

"Are you friend-zoning me six years after you dumped me?"

"Maybe?"

"Anyway, it sounds like this Théo guy loved you, too. He must have his reasons." Her heart leapt into her throat at the mention of his name.

"He did love me," she said, quietly.

"And it sounds like you love him way more than you ever loved me. I mean, I've never seen you this passionate about anything that wasn't a reclaimed credenza."

She laughed. "It sounds like I 'love him,' present tense?"

"Present tense."

"Yeah, I mean, I guess there's no point in lying. Yes, I do still love him. I'll probably love him for a very long time."

"Then why not give it a try? Or at least send the guy a text message, I'm starting to feel bad for him."

Her voice and expression became deadly serious; she was withdrawing into herself again. "Because he's a child. And our so-called relationship cost me everything. I'm not going down that road again."

He finished the last dregs of his wine before signaling for the check to the server. "First of all, I think it's a little extreme to say he 'cost you everything.' Stephanie is mad at you, yes, and you left a job early, but you already have a new client here and Stephanie *will* get over it. And why do you keep calling him a child?" He raised his eyebrow. "How old is he, really? You make it sound like I need to call the cops."

"He's twenty-four."

"Okay, and how old are you?"

"Thirty-six."

"And how old are Stephanie and Alain?"

"Stephanie is forty-four, and Alain. . . just turned fifty-eight."

He waved her away as she reached for her purse, sliding the dropped check over to himself. "So their age gap is even bigger than yours, and you didn't mention it once in two hours. You've never talked about what a pathetic old man Alain is, or how Stephanie is having to 'drag him around,' like you talk about Théo."

Lea took pains to hide the fact that this was, indeed, something she'd never once considered. "Well. . . it's different. They're both older, and parents with grown-ish kids."

"And the guy is older."

"Yeah, I mean. I'm sure that's part of it. We live in an extremely sexist society."

"There's the Lea I know! I say let's burn our bras and date the hot twenty-four-year-old!"

She laughed openly with him, feeling tears return to the corners of her eyes—how could she have ever felt anything but warmth for this man?

As he stood up to shrug his jacket back on, he leaned down and gave her a small kiss on the forehead. "Take care of yourself, Lee," he whispered. "You deserve to be happy, and you already have everything you need to get there. Just reach out and take it."

"Thank you," she said, looking up, tears in her eyes. "I mean it."

"So do I."

The wind that came through the doors when he left Branca chilled Lea to her bones. And though outwardly she was already preparing to forget or deny everything he told her, before she found the courage to stand up and face the rapidly-falling temperatures on her walk home, she headed to the App Store to reinstall Instagram.

Packing for Christmas in Denver was always a bit of a nightmare: gifts for her nieces and nephews, outfits her father would only grunt at disapprovingly rather than overtly criticize, board games to make conversation to ward off the many drawn-out silences she often shared with her sister-in-law. And given that her mother would be stopping by with her new boyfriend, a white man with dreadlocks named *Brahm*, the distractions had to be even more ample than usual. Lea was packing so as not to leave a second of space for her own internal monologue, or for anyone else's.

Her checklist was impeccable as always, despite her emotional state. She had also given special attention to work-related tasks, as she had her first meeting with a new client shortly after her return. She was tasked with converting a historic mansion on the outskirts of DC into a new boutique hotel—her first project in the States. And combined with the afternoon's conversation, just looking at the limited number of items remaining flooded Lea with serotonin. She was ahead of schedule, her happy place.

- *Pull weekender bag from cupboard above hall closet*
- *Set OOO email [REDIRECT TO HOTEL LANDING PAGE?]*
- *Set out plane outfit [BLUE MAJE PANTS, WHITE CASHMERE SWEATER, LONG CAMEL COAT, NEW BOOTS]*
- *Fill & set up watering bulbs*
- *Pack handbag*
- *Get keys to neighbors in case of emergency etc.*
- *Download new GBBO episodes for flight [URGENT]*

Weekender bag successfully retrieved from its storage nook and mostly filled with gifts and DC-centric food items, Lea opened her email to engage in the glorious ritual of setting her out-of-office message for the next twelve days (six for her family, six for solo skiing and hot springs). Before she could click over to the right tab, though, a name popped up that stopped her heart in its tracks.

She had a new email from Stephanie Bryce.

Bracing herself for the worst, Lea walked over to her couch and sat down, pulling up her legs underneath her, a box of tissues not far away in anticipation of more of the same brutal disappointment.

Lea,

I know it's been a while since we've spoken, and I want to start by saying I'm sorry for that. I read through all of your emails the other night after David called me (he made me promise that I would), and I have to admit that I cried a lot, both from your words and from the sadness they created in me, especially from where I'm sitting right now. Maya and I arrived at the chateau for Christmas a few days ago, and although I can't think of a more beautiful place to spend the holidays, it's also so full of nostalgia and memories that are inextricably linked to you. I'm sure you've heard that the hotel is already a success, but I want to tell you myself: you created something really special here. Your fingerprints are on everything, and the guests can't stop talking about how fun or chic everything is.

Speaking of which, my French is getting better, and so is Maya's. She was hesitant to come at first, but the alternative was spending the holidays with Marcus and Emilia, so. . . you do the math. Her grades are excellent, I'm happy to say, and she actually let me meet her new boyfriend for a lunch date (!!). Gabriel is back home and over 100 days sober, but he's still in Boulogne right now. He'll be coming here for the actual holidays, but his therapist says it's not good for him to be away from his home base this early on. The rest of the kids are here and doing well, helping out a lot with the hotel work. It's still pretty understaffed.

Now, onto a more unpleasant topic. . . my ongoing divorce. Things are finally going okay, and we're currently working on dividing assets and settling things like spousal support. My lawyers gave me a really stern talking to when I got back to Jersey, and it made me realize that I probably should have listened to you. It's a lot harder now than it would have been if I'd just dealt with it from the get-go, but now I get to spend lots of time in divorce court!! Fun, right? Well, at least on my end, I'm just doing everything I can to make this go quickly and painlessly. Apparently Emilia is pregnant, which. . . if that's true, all I can say to her is good luck!!

And honestly, I'm not really concerned about what I walk away with, which brings me to my next subject: Alain and I are engaged!!!

I know, I know. What's a forty-four-year-old divorced mom doing even having a wedding? But I want one, dammit! So the plan is to finish out this school year, then I'll be moving here full-time in the fall to teach at an American school in Paris while Alain splits his time between the chateau and Boulogne. It's all pretty overwhelming, but I can't say I'm not extremely excited. More to come on all that! These visa things are no joke. . . I have a new respect for you dealing with this every year. . .

But, onto the subject of you and me. I know that you handled it badly, but I also know that you didn't mean to hurt anyone, and honestly you've put up with enough of my mistakes and bad decisions over the years for me to forgive one of yours. I'm starting a new chapter of my life, and that means taking stock of the people who really matter, and you are one of them. (Yes, still!) And at the end of the day, you gave me the greatest gift of my life this past summer in meeting Alain. I still owe you so much for that one.

Well, anyway, I should probably get back to work (Marie is still such a drill sergeant, maybe even more so now that there are actual guests!). But I just wanted to wish you a Merry Christmas, and say that I love you. Maybe I can come down to DC over spring break? You definitely don't want to come to my craphole apartment in Edison. . .

Joyeux Noël, and give my love to the family! (What's your mom's boyfriend's name this time. . .?)

Stephanie

Lea's alarm went off, reminding her she had to leave for her flight in exactly one hour. She looked down to turn it off, unable to read her screen through her tears.

25

SEVEN MONTHS LATER

The rehearsal dinner and ceremony were to be held at the chateau itself, which had been closed for several days to accommodate the festivities. (This spoke highly to Alain's commitment, as it meant missing out on serious tourism dollars during the high season.) Lea was pleased to find everything as she had left it, the stones almost seeming to sigh with a friendly welcome as she walked through the empty lobby. The colors were brighter, the plants were lusher, and she wondered to herself if she had ever fully noticed just how lovely this space actually was. As the *Architectural Digest* profile had put it, this hotel was indeed the crown jewel of her work, airy and spacious and full of color and history.

She had run through a thousand scenarios with Dr. Miller in the weeks leading up to her trip, mapping out the possible commentary or rebukes or coldness she was likely to encounter. Each had its own plan, not just in terms of in-the-moment responses but also for how she would process it after the fact, and what it would mean on a greater level. He had reminded her that this was going to be one of the most important things she'd ever do: enter a space in which she was totally exposed and vulnerable to all experiences and emotions, and just the fact that she was doing it was cause for celebration. And it was true: she felt a distinct pride walking back into the chateau without shame, even if her reception wasn't ideal.

She'd also spent entire sessions poring over Théo's Instagram, where an alluring woman named Janice had been increasingly making appearances. They looked happy, and unaware, and sexy together. The phrasing he'd used in his stories was seared into her mind, even if she now knew better than to screenshot them for future torment: *"Back in Marseille, back to life."* He'd even written it in English, which felt inscrutable to Lea. Was he trying to speak to her, or to get back at her? Or was it just the ad copy-like English that French people loved to use on their social media posts? There were quick videos of her dancing in darkened clubs with other friends, tiki mugs clinking together, stylish shots of the Vespa she drove parked outside of cafe terraces. It was infuriatingly European, and intimidating enough to drive Lea out on a few dates herself, most of them with a perfectly nice man named Nicholas who was smart and funny, but who only made her ache for Théo more.

But she found that upon arriving, upon being thrust back into this space and into the orbit of the people she had missed so acutely, the anxieties about how she would navigate the situation began to melt away. Despite the tragic ending, this was the place where she had become a different person, allowed herself to love and be loved as she never had before, where all of the richness and vibrancy of life revealed itself to her. Even if Théo was with someone else now, to be here and tell him she was sorry, to say that she would always love him and leave again on the note she wanted, would be so much more satisfying than nothing at all.

As soon as she saw Stephanie enter the lobby, her entire body relaxed into a familiar openness. Dropping her bags, she practically ran to join her in a warm, extended embrace where they both rocked back-and-forth, saying how happy they were to see each other. As their hug continued, Marie emerged from the hotel restaurant where she was pointedly overseeing the caterers for that evening's rehearsal dinner. She was exactly as Lea would have wanted her, sturdy, sleeves rolled up, green drugstore reading glasses secure on her head, and already complaining about something that didn't arrive on time as she embraced her for a *bise*.

When Philippe came bounding down the stairs, full of his usual, wiry energy and paternal affection, Lea felt even more at ease. She wanted to cry, but willed herself to pull it together, at least until she could blame it on a few glasses of champagne later. (And certainly after the toast she was asked to give.)

Stephanie briefed Lea that Maya was at the florist (*"The kind of thing we never used to appreciate when you did it!"* she reassuringly joked), but would be back later, and that the three of them would be getting ready together. The rehearsal dinner and wedding itself would both be intimate and comprised the same group of around fifty: immediate family, the chateau crew, a few close people flown out from the States, Sofian and the A-list locals, and a handful of stragglers from Paris. Alain had stated in one of his recent emails to Lea that at his age, he had no need for some extravagant ceremony. He just wanted his family, his terroir, and his beloved.

When he came in from the garden and approached Lea, she couldn't help but give him a loving, pained look of nostalgia, which he quickly returned. As inexplicable as it was, he already felt like family to her. And, she dared to hope, maybe he felt the same way about her.

Pulling back from him and moving to grab her suitcase, she asked, "Where's—"

"Théo is picking up Gabriel," Marie quickly answered, instantly looking chastened.

Lea smiled at her. "I was actually going to say, where's my room? But thank you."

Alain laughed nervously before grabbing her bag. "You're actually in your old suite. I'll drop your bags there."

"You didn't have to do that," she said, following him up the stairs.

He turned around at her and winked slightly. "Of course I did."

The dinner felt heavily inspired by the tasting meal she'd had with Caroline, the first time Théo had touched her. The immense number of tapered candles were magical and intoxicating, and string lights crisscrossed through the trees, the chateau, the awning, and nearly everywhere in-between. Combined, it all felt like a million fireflies rising off of the gathered tables at once. And Lea felt as good as ever in her outfit, a ground-skimming, navy, silk dress with a deep V-neck and plenty of gold jewelry that felt like armor. Her hair was freshly cut, shorter than usual, and tightly waved. She felt like an ancient Greek goddess, and every time her eyes wandered over to Théo, she needed the confidence of one. He was mostly gravitating around his friends—and absent a plus-one—in his beige suit with white Italian shirt underneath, looking impossibly dashing.

Stephanie and Alain had eschewed formal seating charts—and Lea had to fight a brief, piercing thought that it was to avoid the awkwardness of assigning her to a table where she wasn't wanted—but it ended up not mattering at all. People were milling happily with their plates of buffet-style food and copious glasses of local wine. Lea's table was (usually) composed of Marie and her husband, Sofian and his wife, two of Stephanie's close friends from work, and Maya and her boyfriend, Jacob.

Luckily, and almost certainly buffered by the fact that Maya seemed incredibly happy, she and Lea had gotten the conversation they needed to have out of the way in Lea's suite, almost upon her arrival. She tearfully apologized to Maya, explaining how much she loved her and how she'd spent the last year feeling terrible about herself and wishing she could do everything differently. And Maya—with newly short hair that made her look exponentially more grown up than what was chronologically possible—gave her the grace of a soft landing.

"It was a crazy summer for everyone," was the euphemistic way she had phrased it, before bringing Lea into the deep hug both of them likely needed. "And everything worked out okay in the end." It was clear that neither of them wanted to speak of the embarrassing details, but Lea could feel the return of their old, familiar shorthand.

Back at their table, there was a jovial, slightly tipsy exercise in finding common linguistic ground, with Maya and her budding French serving as translator, much to the delight of Jacob, and newcomers pulling up a chair every now and then to join the conversation. Eventually, one of those newcomers was Gabriel, in a perfectly crisp pair of white trousers and a double-breasted, navy blazer, hair freshly cut but still persistently wavy. He looked even more fit than usual, likely from the running that'd replaced his other drugs of choice, according to Stephanie.

He clinked his seltzer with cranberry to Lea's champagne and asked if he could sit. She nodded, gently.

"Hi, Lea."

"Hi, Gabriel." She smiled, no longer afraid of him.

"I like your dress." It was so bizarre seeing him chastened like this, like a wild animal that had only recently been domesticated.

"Hey, thank you. I like your jacket."

"Thanks. . ." He stopped, looking around briefly before getting to the heart of the matter. "I would love it if we could have coffee tomorrow morning, maybe we can step aside at breakfast?"

"I would be happy to have coffee with you."

His eyes pierced hers, and she allowed herself for the first time to truly appreciate their deep blue, so much like his brother's, so much like the ones she ached with love for. "Thank you."

"It's no problem, really. I'm not angry," she said, putting a hand on his shoulder.

"You could be," he sadly replied, his eyes darting to the floor. "I did a lot of bad things last year."

"And you're nearly a year clean now," she said, making a point to wait until he met her eyes to continue. "And that is amazing."

"Yeah? I guess it is," he laughed, regaining a bit of his usual swagger. "It's also pretty boring."

"Well, you look amazing, I can say that."

"With any luck, I'll look like Uncle Nico in a few years."

"You'll need to get the man bun going again."

"It's funny, I–"

His words were absorbed into the tinking of a fork against a glass, Alain standing up at his table a few feet away. Marie looked over to Lea and said, "That's you!" probably a little louder than she intended. Lea smiled at Gabriel, who quietly walked back to his seat, before raising herself to stand.

She smoothed out the paper in her hand as the DJ drew the music to a quiet hum, the noises of the chateau at night— the crickets, the leaves rustling, the creek flowing—suddenly coming to the forefront. She knew better than to actually look at Théo, but she perceived him enough out of the corner of her eye to know that he was turned toward her. At the very least, he was listening. Clearing her throat, she turned to Stephanie and Alain, who were embracing at their table, looking like the very picture of love. She looked down at her papers, on which she'd written her toast in both English and French to make it accessible to all parties, and used the solidity of the ink to give her confidence as she spoke.

"Johnny Cash once said his definition of paradise was, 'This morning, with her, having coffee,' about his wife, June Carter Cash. And I was lucky enough to share so many morning coffees with these two, watching their love unfold and their hope be restored in each other. In those moments, the two of them together really *did* seem like paradise, like the greatest thing anyone could aspire to, and I'm grateful to have witnessed it all. I'm grateful to have inadvertently brought them together, and I'm grateful to be celebrating with them here today."

She looked up from her pages, trembling slightly, and deliberately met Théo's eyes. His gaze was one of utter tenderness, and her body shivered with the intensity of it, the exquisite love she felt for him and *knew* that he had felt for her, even if they couldn't be together. A delicate line of tears formed along her bottom lashes, but she soldiered on.

"I have known Stephanie my entire life. She is the closest thing I've ever had to a sister, and I am indebted to her for every good thing I've ever thought about myself. She has given me so much over the years, has always been the example of everything good and loving, so it feels almost cosmically imbalanced that she would be giving me something now, having already received so much.

"But I must confess that she is.

"In marrying Alain, she is giving me the greatest lesson I've ever learned: that life is long, that second chances are many, and that our stories are only over when we decide to stop writing them. They are both getting a new, shining chance at lifelong happiness today, under these stars, after the long and winding roads that brought them to each other.

"Alain and Stephanie, you deserve nothing but the greatest happiness, and I am impossibly lucky to be here sharing that happiness with you today."

She raised her glass, tears now falling freely from her eyes. Stephanie rose from her chair, fully sobbing, to grab Lea into a bear hug as the entire group burst into cheers. Out of the corner of her watery eye, Lea saw Théo smiling, looking on at them with an expression of deep approval and joy. Catching her eye, he nodded gently.

Later, in line for one of the many buffet stations, Lea found herself face-to-face with Nico for the first time since her arrival. There was a unique shorthand between them. He had seen her only once, but at the most embarrassing moment in her life. And besides that, he had obviously lived about ten lives before he found himself parked at the chateau to help his younger brother—he had done things far more recklessly than Lea ever had. She felt herself relax into his benevolent, charmingly disheveled presence.

"I think I was here first," he joked, elbowing her gently with the dinner plate in his hand.

"No way," she laughed, asserting her place in line.

"It's good to see you here, Lea."

"It's good to see you, too, Nico. I'm glad you stayed."

"Really?" He smiled knowingly. "You keeping tabs on the place?"

"Of course. Just because I leave a project doesn't mean it leaves me."

"Well said, well said." The line moved forward slightly, and they resettled themselves before he continued. "Alain probably never told you, but we have a lot in common. Or, I have a lot in common with Théo, I guess."

"How so?"

"Well, for many years, my girlfriend was much older than me. She was actually Alain's professor once, if you can believe it."

"Oh, my god." She couldn't help but laugh, bewildered at the frankness of this revelation.

"I know. She and I separated when I moved to Lisbon, which is where I got into so much trouble. Too much porto." He winked, gesturing down to his tattoo signaling twenty-one years clean. "But for a long time, she was the light in my life. For almost ten years."

"Why did you leave?" They filled their plates as they spoke, careful to keep their voices discreet.

"Because I got a job opportunity, and she couldn't leave her life in Paris. It just didn't work out."

"I'm sorry to hear that." She walked them both over to a random, mostly empty table.

"Oh, you know. Life goes on. I've done and seen many great things since then." He smiled, tucking into a forkful of couscous. "But I will never regret that time. She made me the man I am today, and I think I can say that I made her a better woman, too."

As he chewed, Lea stabbed at her lamb meatball, unsure how to proceed. "I'm sure you did."

"All of this to say, from the beginning, I have told Alain that your love with Théo is a gift to you both, no less valid or special than his love with Stephanie." He dipped a meatball in a generous helping of toum before continuing. "He thinks that by keeping everything under his control, he can prevent another tragedy, but all of the beautiful things in life happen when we let go of control."

She could feel herself flooding with emotion. "Well, thank you."

"I know my nephew, and the two of you are well-matched. I think your story would be wonderful, and I hope that the two of you may write it."

Her throat was too full of nascent tears to respond, and seeing this, he nodded. Grabbing his plate to head back into the party, he bumped her shoulder again while standing. "Enjoy the party, Lea."

The din of the reception grew overwhelming around her, and her appetite was completely gone, replaced by a weightless, out-of-body joy. She had to go find him.

Behind the spa, Théo's shirt was unbuttoned, his glass of wine dangling dangerously from his left hand. Lea was much more nervous, but willed herself to be open to any outcome—honesty was its own victory, in and of itself.

"How have you been?" she opened.

He burst into laughter, the way he had when she'd first asked him how his internship was going. His tone became jokingly formal, as if he were at a job interview. "I've been okay, Lea, how have you been?" He smiled down at her.

"I've been. . . okay."

"Yeah?"

"Yeah." She looked around at the trees, and they both silently sipped their drinks for a moment before she pushed on. "It's so great to be here again. This is a really spectacular place for a wedding."

"You made it that way."

"Heh, well, yeah. I guess I did." She drew a circle in the gravel with the toe of her sandal.

"Well, even if you don't want to give yourself proper credit, all of the magazines are."

"You mean *Architectural Digest?*"

"Well, I meant several, but yes, that one stands out."

"You're more up to date on my press clippings than I am."

"You don't want to know."

"Oh?" She cocked an eyebrow.

"I may have several copies on my bookshelf as we speak. Can't confirm or deny."

She felt her chest ache with gratitude and the words tumbled out of her mouth before she could stop them. "Where's Janice?"

He paused, shifting slightly on his feet. "Why do you know her name?"

"Please. Don't act like you don't know how I use the internet."

"I shudder to think of how far down the rabbit hole you've gone on her."

Lea smiled, slightly contentious.

"Well, I hate to disappoint you, but we're not together. We never really were."

Her heart soared, and she couldn't hide her pleasure. "Good."

He smiled. "By the way, I know you've been dating, too."

"How?"

"I see the restaurants you've been posting from. You don't just go to them for girls' night."

"I don't really have girls' nights."

"Well, you don't go to them to eat pasta alone at the bar. What was his name?"

"Nicholas." There was no reason to be coy.

"Like Uncle Nico? Ugh, what an awful mental image. Are you still seeing him?"

"Not really."

"Not really, hmm? Well, then, tell me about this Nicholas, who you may or may not still be dating."

"He works at the National Institute of Health—"

"Ooh, a smartypants."

"Mhmm." She smiled, sipping her wine. She could feel herself taking her usual imperious stance that turned them both on so much. "He was actually a Rhodes Scholar."

"Ahh." He mimed taking a shot to the heart. "Now you're just trying to hurt me."

"And he's very handsome."

"Brutal. Tall?"

"Not as tall as you."

"Phew."

"And. . . he's thirty years old."

"Hah!" He clinked his glass to hers. "So is Janice, if you can believe it."

"Really?" She was genuinely taken aback.

"Yeah," he laughed, looking out toward a car pulling into the driveway.

"So I guess it's an older woman thing with you, huh?"

"No." He smiled. "It turns out it's just a 'you' thing." He wiggled his eyebrows jokingly, cutting the seriousness of the statement.

Her heart jumped to her throat. "I know what you mean," was all she could manage.

"Well, you could have told me that earlier, because I have been out here pining like an idiot for a year straight. I could have saved a lot of tissues."

"Tissues for crying, or tissues for—"

"We don't need to get into all that now." She leaned forward into him in laughter as he pulled her waist into his, looking down at her more seriously. "I'm glad you came alone."

"Me, too. Théo, I'm so sorry I left you the way I did. I couldn't stay here, and I couldn't face everything that happened and still have space for you. I wouldn't have been a good partner at that time, even if you didn't deserve that."

He kissed her forehead. "The good news for you is that I've already yelled at you about a thousand times in my head, and you've said something along those lines, and I've already forgiven you. So we can just go ahead and skip to the forgiveness."

"You really forgive me?"

"Of course I do. I wasn't being realistic about the situation, even if you were being a bit of a bitch."

"*Bitch*?"

"Well, you know. Asshole."

They both laughed again, still looking at each other, letting the music from the party wrap around them.

"When do you go back to Boulogne?" she finally asked.

"I don't live in Boulogne anymore."

"Oh?"

"I have a terrible flat in the 18th, which you're free to come visit. You can help me with the wall sconce motif."

"You can't afford me."

"Let me see your rate card." He was leaning down closer to her.

"And actually, I'm renting an apartment in Paris, too— probably a less terrible one than yours."

"You are?"

"Yes." She paused. "I tried working in the States and it wasn't for me. I honestly just missed being in France."

"You missed being with me," he said, smugly.

"That's what you want to hear?"

He paused briefly before slipping down to her ear, whispering now.

"Yes. Tell me."

She closed her eyes, whispering back to him, allowing herself the freedom to say exactly what she felt, regardless of the risk. "I miss you so much, Théo. I miss you every second of every day."

She fell silent for a moment, letting the words linger in the air. His body had taken on that lustful heaviness again, barely able to stand upright.

A gentle, barely audible *"Don't stop"* was all he could manage.

The words poured from her, raw, full of truth.

"I couldn't touch Nicolas, I couldn't be with anyone else, I could barely even *look* at anyone else. I tried, but you are the only person I've ever wanted like this, and I'll never want anyone else again. You've ruined me."

He stood perfectly still, breathing her in, his hand pressed to her heartbeat. "Tell me you still love me."

Trembling, the words flowed more effortlessly than anything in her life ever had. "Oh, Théo, I still love you. I've never stopped loving you. I've never stopped loving you and I never will." She stopped only to take a breath, flooded with desire and catharsis, eyes squeezed closed. "I love you so much it hurts."

Suddenly, he pulled back from her, wearing that broad, casual, infuriating smile she'd seen so many times last summer.

"Well, that's exactly what I wanted to hear. Unfortunately I have to get back and do a humiliating dance performance with my father now, but I would like to take this moment to formally ask you out for dinner when we get back to Paris. I'll email you a list of restaurants I think you'd like."

"Are. . ." She could barely breathe, full of confusion and frustrated energy. "Are you serious right now?"

"Yes, absolutely. I want to continue this conversation with you somewhere that isn't my father's chateau, and now that I know you want it, too, I would like to schedule a proper date." His smile never faltered, and he sipped the last of his wine.

Seeing her looking at him in a pained, expectant way, he reassured her. "*And,* as much as I would love nothing more than to rip off that dress and take you right here on the gravel, I would *also* like to look at you from across a dinner table first, like we're not both fugitives on the run for once."

She laughed in spite of herself. It was true, it *would* be nice to actually go on a date with him. "Yes, of course, let's do that. You can email me some options, and I can do Monday or Thursday of next week."

"So many plans in Paris already?" he laughed, heading back toward the party. "You really haven't changed."

"Well, I'm sorry, I–"

"No. It's wonderful."

She smiled, flooded with that familiar warmth of total acceptance.

He was almost back around the far side of the spa when he stopped, turning on his heel to look at her, the warm glow of the party illuminating him from behind, casting him in gold.

"Oh, and Lea?"

"Yes?"

"I fucking love you, too."

Acknowledgments

Thank you:

First and most importantly to my darling husband, the one who makes everything possible, and everything worth doing.

And to my family, who gifted me with the secret superpower of believing I can do anything in life, and that I *always* owe it to myself to go for what I want.

To my exquisitely talented editors: Stephanie Georgopulos, my line editor, who makes me sound much better than I have any right to. And to Jane Doe, my developmental editor, who must remain nameless for now but whose impeccable taste is all over this book.

To my marketing partner Mackenzie Newcomb, the person whose partnership assured me that doing this independently wasn't just possible – it was the only right way to do it.

To my artist Elizabeth Lennie, the painter who so richly imagined the gorgeous scene on the cover.

To my designer and longtime collaborator Lauren Ver Hage, the only one whose visual taste I would trust with such an important project.

To my reader Jihane El Atifi, who helped me make the storytelling in this book even more accurate and nuanced.

To ST Gibson and Jennifer Martina, both of whom helped me bring publishing details to life in such important and thoughtful ways.

And to Rob Price at Gatekeeper, who was endlessly patient with all of my requests, and ensured that this was exactly the final product this story deserved.

About the Author

Chelsea Fagan is an author, avid home cook, and the CEO of The Financial Diet, the largest independent women's financial media company. She lives in Manhattan with her husband and dog, and can usually be found hosting a dinner party or riding her bike around the city with silly little groceries in the basket.

https://aperfectvintagebook.com
Instagram: @faganchelsea
TikTok: @faganchelsea
Twitter: @Chelsea_Fagan